THE BANK OF FEAR

Other Avon Books by
David Ignatius

AGENTS OF INNOCENCE
SIRO

DAVID IGNATIUS

THE BANK OF FEAR

AVON BOOKS ▰ NEW YORK

AVON BOOKS
A division of
The Hearst Corporation
1350 Avenue of the Americas
New York, New York 10019

Copyright © 1994 by David Ignatius
Published by arrangement with the author
Library of Congress Catalog Card Number: 93-44858
ISBN: 0-380-72280-1

Published in hardcover by William Morrow and Company, Inc.; for information address Permissions Department, William Morrow and Company, Inc., 1350 Avenue of the Americas, New York, New York 10019.

First Avon Books Printing: August 1995

AVON TRADEMARK REG. U.S. PAT. OFF. AND IN OTHER COUNTRIES, MARCA REGISTRADA, HECHO EN U.S.A.

Printed in the U.S.A.

RA   10   9   8   7   6   5   4   3   2   1

For Eve, Elisa, Alexandra and Sarah.
And for my brave Arab friends who are living
the struggle for human rights
and democracy.

Here is a people turning
their very faces to the hoofs.
Here is a land humiliated
like a coward's house.
                        Who shall
tender us a bird, just
a bird?
        Just a tree?
Who shall teach us
the alphabet of air?
                        We wait
at the crossroads.
                We watch the sand
submerge our beacons.
                        The sun
disintegrates within the wrinkles
of our hands.
                O my country . . .
Your skin is a lizard's.
                        Your perfume
is the stench of rubber scorched.
Your sunrise is a weeping bat.
You bring such holocausts
to birth.
                You give your breasts
to vermin.

—ADONIS (the pen name of ALI AHMED SAID)
    from "Remembering the First Century,"
    collected in *The Pages of Day and Night*,
    translated from the Arabic by Samuel Hazo;
    published 1994 by The Marlboro Press

Prologue

The Coyote Investment building was a gray concrete block at the west end of Knightsbridge, with small, beady-eyed windows that shielded the interior from view. There was a revolving door at the front that was always locked, forcing people to use the narrow door that passed by the security desk. The only color on the facade was a rust-red stain that trickled down from the ledges and downspouts, so that, at a quick glance, it looked almost as if blood were seeping out from inside the walls. It was the sort of place most Londoners wouldn't have entered unless they had some business there, and then only for the time required. Late one Saturday evening, a black Daimler limousine pulled up in front of this forbidding building. A gray-haired Arab gentleman in a tuxedo emerged from the backseat and took the elevator to his office on the fifth floor, where he began making phone calls. His name was Nasir Hammoud. He owned the building and a great deal else, besides. But on this particular evening in March, he had a problem. His first call was to his chief of security.

"There has been an accident," Mr. Hammoud informed the security man when he arrived twenty minutes later. "At my house in the country. A woman got hurt." He talked slowly, holding on to each word as if he could control its effect on the listener. He was not used to accidents. As he spoke, he brushed an invisible piece of lint off the silk lapel of his jacket.

1

The Arab gentleman's face was as carefully contrived as his evening dress. The features in themselves were unmemorable: square cheeks, a broad nose with a slight hook toward the bottom, a weak chin. But the face had an unnatural glow, at once rosy and pale, as if he had just come off an embalming table. The skin was too smooth, as in a retouched photo. The teeth had a shiny, sharpened look, and the fingernails were freshly manicured. There were traces of a recent scar on one cheek, but it had been repaired so artfully that in the evening light, it was almost invisible. The only feature that appeared untouched by the cosmetic arts were the eyes, which focused down to sharp black points. It was this combination—of effete, almost feminine, grooming and the raw savagery that shined out from his eyes—that gave Nasir Hammoud an air of calculated cruelty.

"Ya sidi," assented the chief of security. *Oh, sir.* He bowed ever so slightly.

"I have been here in London all day," Hammoud continued. "The chauffeur brought me to the office. I heard about this . . . accident on the telephone."

"Ya rayess!" said the chief of security. *Oh, my president!* He was an Iraqi-Armenian by the name of Sarkis, known to everyone but Mr. Hammoud as Professor Sarkis.

"I want you to do something for me, please," said Hammoud.

"Ya amir!" answered Sarkis, approaching the desk. *Oh, my prince!* The chief of security was an angular man, with sallow cheeks and a huge nose that overwhelmed the rest of his face and made him look like a Levantine version of a tropical bird. He leaned toward Mr. Hammoud. "Should I call a doctor?" he asked.

"No!" said Hammoud. "No doctor."

"Should I call an ambulance?"

"Phhh!" said Hammoud, gesturing with his hand as if he were brushing away another piece of lint.

"What would you like me to do, then, *sidi*?"

Hammoud walked to the safe behind him. He opened it and carefully counted out fifty thousand pounds from the cash drawer. When he was done, he put the money in a manila envelope, scribbled an address on it, and handed it to Sarkis.

"Tomorrow morning," he said, "I want you to go to this man and give the envelope to him. Him only. He is a police chief. Tell him the money is for a reward. For information about who killed the woman. Tell him I am very sorry about the news. Tell him I was in London all weekend."

Sarkis bowed and took the envelope. "She is dead, *sidi*?"

Hammoud didn't answer. He had already picked up the phone to make another call. He was an immensely controlled man who had momentarily lost that control, and he wanted to reestablish it as quickly as possible. A few moments later he turned on the computer screen on his desk to begin sending messages to his traders around the world about the positions he wanted them to take when the markets opened on Monday. Professor Sarkis let himself out the door and headed to Berkshire to tidy things up.

Even in the small world of Arab London, Nasir Hammoud was something of a mystery. It was whispered among the Iraqi exiles that when he was a young man in Baghdad, he had killed a man by pounding nails into his head. But that was a long time ago, and nobody remembered the details. Now Nasir Hammoud owned a steel mill in Spain, and an electronics factory in Lyons, and a real estate company in New York, and a construction company in Turin. He was rich—famously rich, with assets worth billions of dollars. But no one seemed to know much about him or where his money came from.

Rumor had it that Mr. Hammoud was friendly with the Ruler in Baghdad, and that this was the real source of his riches. But people always said that about wealthy Arabs. They imagined that money fell from the sky into the hands of the Ruler and then into the hands of his friends. That made them envious—these *jahal*, as Mr. Hammoud called them—the ignorant ones who wanted money without earning it. So they made up stories about successful people such as Mr. Hammoud. It was envy, no more than that, Mr. Hammoud told his friends. Pure envy.

Like so many wealthy men of the East, Mr. Hammoud had come to London with the idea of settling down. It was messy back home in Baghdad. The Time of the Wars had passed, but the leaders there were still wearing military uniforms and commissioning heroic poems about themselves and pounding nails into the heads of their enemies. Mr. Hammoud had had enough of that. So he had made his way west, via France and Belgium and Switzerland, and with each move his bank account had grown larger and his origins more obscure.

He was a neat, compact man who, as he grew older, had become neater and more fastidious. When he moved to London a few years before, one of the first things he had done was visit a tailor and order a half-dozen suits, each with a pinched waist and a break in the trousers, just so. In his new clothes, he looked like any other wealthy international businessman. London, Paris, Hong Kong, Berlin—what did it matter? With a good tan and a new suit, everyone looked the same.

Although he was rumored to own a dozen or more subsidiaries, Mr. Hammoud operated through his holding company, Coyote Investment. The name led the few people who had heard of it to assume that it was an American concern, headquartered perhaps in Houston or Denver. But it was actually registered in Europe, and its money, to the extent anyone knew its origins, appeared to be Iraqi. The Arabs politely call this sort of deliberate deception *taqqiyya*. For Mr. Hammoud, it had become a management principle.

The layout of Coyote Investment's offices on Knightsbridge reflected Mr. Hammoud's passion for secrecy. He had, in effect, divided the company into two parts: one for the public and one that was real. Leaving the elevators on the fifth floor, a visitor would see a brightly lit reception area on his right and a large sign that said COYOTE, with a picture of a wolf-like animal drawn next to the name. This was the company's public entrance, and through its double doors lay the offices of the vice presidents for investor relations, corporate communications and personnel. These executives were all British. Mr. Hammoud provided them with memberships in London clubs and Bentley sedans and paid them handsome salaries to represent him in the London financial world. They appeared to be powerful, but they were not. They were decoys.

The real power lay to the left of the elevator block, down a dimly lit passageway that led to the accounting department. It could be entered only by punching a special code into an electronic lock. This was the domain of the silent ones, the Iraqi ''trusted employees'' who made up the inner circle of the company. To visitors, the accounting department looked very modest indeed. The desks and file cabinets were simple gray metal, the drapes smelled of mildew and cigarette smoke, and the carpets were stained and threadbare. But it was here that the real business of Coyote Investment was done. The Arab employees embraced the corporate structure instinctively. In the East, it was understood that wealth and power were things to be hidden. What was visible usually was not real.

Mr. Hammoud's large corner office straddled the two sides of his company, and the office had two doors. The public door opened onto a spacious waiting room and a bonny, big-breasted British secretary. The private door opened onto an ill-lit warren of paper occupied by Professor Sarkis, who doubled as the chief of the accounting department. He was the only person, other than Mr. Hammoud, who had a full grasp of the company's operations. But it wasn't clear that even he knew all the secrets.

-I-

The Age of
Ignorance

1

amuel Hoffman knew he had made a mistake the moment the man entered his office. The visitor was a Filipino in his mid-twenties, with bad teeth jutting out in different directions like a mislaid picket fence and eyes that darted back and forth, avoiding contact. He had a rosary clutched in one hand and a worn photograph in the other. And he was crying. Not a loud wail, but the suppressed sniffling of someone who seemed to feel unworthy even of his own tears. A man at the Philippine embassy had told him to come, he stammered. He needed help, please. Hoffman wished he had never let him upstairs.

"Five minutes," said Hoffman, looking at his watch. "No more."

Hoffman retreated to the bedroom behind his office and returned with a lit cigarette. He was a solidly built man in his early thirties, not quite six feet, with a narrow face and dark, intense eyes, and he moved about the room with the restlessness of a zoo animal that needed a bigger cage. He was dressed that day in his usual uniform of a gray suit and an open-necked blue shirt. That was his only eccentricity—the fact that he always wore a suit and never wore a tie. He seemed, as a result, to be perpetually overdressed, or underdressed, but never in between. It was part of what made him seem unfinished, a work in progress.

Hoffman stubbed his cigarette in the ashtray after two puffs and looked at the handwritten card the Filipino had

9

given him when he arrived, with the words "Ramon
Pinta" in neat block letters. There was no address or
phone number. He wondered for a moment who at the
Philippine embassy had sent him, and then remembered
the businessman from Manila whose brother, a Roman
Catholic priest, had disappeared in Saudi Arabia. Hoffman
hadn't found the priest, but he had tried. And now this
little man with the handwritten card was sitting across the
desk, looking as if he were about to implode from fear.

"What can I do for you, Mr. Pinta?" asked Hoffman,
hoping the answer was "nothing."

"Please," said the Filipino, clearing his throat to give
himself courage. He leaned toward Hoffman and offered
him the picture he had been holding in his right hand.
He held it outstretched, imploringly, until his hand began
to shake.

Hoffman reluctantly took the photograph. It showed a
Philippine woman in her early twenties, with large, watch-
ful eyes, prominent cheekbones and neatly curled hair. She
was wearing a uniform—black dress with a white apron—
and looked like she might be a maid at a fancy West End
hotel. It was like a First Communion picture. Her mouth
was open slightly, expectantly. A small, gold crucifix hung
from her neck.

"My wife," the man said, pointing to the picture. He
was sniffling more loudly. Hoffman handed him a box of
Kleenex from atop his desk. The young man blew his nose
and placed the tissue up his sleeve for later use. He stared
at the floor for a moment, as if summoning strength for
what he was about to do, and then looked Hoffman in the
eye. He removed another photograph from his coat pocket
and handed it across the desk, facedown.

The room was still. The London traffic outside was a
hum, barely audible through the window. The cursor on
Hoffman's computer screen was blinking in perfect regu-
larity, one pulse per second, waiting for him to resume
the report he had been drafting for a client in New York.
The law books sat at attention on the edge of his shelves:
spines firm, pages crisp, ready for the next foray. It was

a world of plans and expectations, frozen momentarily in time, in the instant before it collided with another world, previously unseen. Hoffman looked at his watch again. How could he get rid of this damned Filipino?

Hoffman turned the picture over carefully. When he saw the lurid, flash-lit color, he winced. It was a police photograph, taken at a crime scene, and it showed a woman's body lying on the grass. She was naked, except for her brassiere. There were bruises on her face, and blood had crusted around her pubic hair and along her thigh. A pair of panties had been stuffed in her mouth. It appeared from the blue-brown hue of the body that she had been dead for some hours by the time the photograph had been taken. But the face was still recognizable. Hoffman shook his head. He wished, again and with greater conviction, that he hadn't let the Filipino come upstairs. Now he would have to say something.

"I'm sorry," he murmured, turning the photograph over to hide the woman's nakedness and pushing it back across the desk. The young man let it lie there, as he struggled with his emotions. The sniffles became louder, and in a moment his head was buried in his hands. The rosary beads fell to the floor. They were the wretched of the earth, the Filipinos, thought Hoffman. The doormats on whom the rich and powerful scraped the mud from their shoes.

"Get a grip on yourself," he said, handing Pinta the box of Kleenex again. That didn't work, so he walked over to the young man and put a hand on his shoulder. "Come on. I'm sorry about your wife. What do you want me to do?"

"Please, Mr. Hoffman," said the Filipino. He had put his palms together prayerfully. "I want to hire you."

"To do what?" asked Hoffman.

"To find the man who killed her."

Hoffman shook his head. He was a rationalist. He lived in a world of books and reports. He was not in the redemption business.

"I'm sorry," he said, "but I don't do that kind of work.

Whoever told you at the embassy that I work on homicides was mistaken. I'm a financial investigator. I investigate companies. Projects. Investors. Business. See?'' He pointed to his bookshelves, stacked with law books, commercial codes, investment guides. "I don't do murders.''

"But this will be easy for you to investigate, sir.'' A glint of revenge was shining in his sad eyes. "Because I know who did it.''

"You do?''

"Yes, sir, I do. He is an Arab businessman. My wife and I worked for him. She was the maid. I was the cook.''

Hoffman arched his eyebrows. "You have any proof?''

"Myself only, sir. I was there when they found her body. It was in a field near his house in the country. He said he was away that weekend, and his friends lied for him. But I know he was there, because I saw him. He wanted a woman. . . .'' He stopped, in shame and sadness, and then realized that he had forgotten the most important detail. "The name of this man is Nasir Hammoud.''

"I see,'' said Hoffman. He had heard the name before, but he couldn't remember where. He looked at his watch once again. A few more minutes and he would get rid of the poor man.

"He was always looking at my wife, sir,'' the Filipino continued, "but she was always ignoring him. I think he got angry.'' He turned away again.

Hoffman nodded. "What does this Nasir Hammoud do?'' he asked.

"He is a very big businessman, sir. From Iraq. He is richer than anyone, and he doesn't care what he does to other people. He has a company in London, which buys other companies. Perhaps you have heard of it?''

"What's it called?''

"Coyote Investment, sir.'' His eyes brightened as he sensed that Hoffman, despite himself, was becoming interested.

"Is that so?'' Hoffman remembered now where he had heard Hammoud's name. There had been a deal for a tire factory in Portugal a few months before. The factory had been sold for eighty million dollars, and the buyer turned out to be an Iraqi businessman nobody had ever heard of, named Hammoud. At the time, Hoffman had made a mental note that he should find out more about this new player in the Arab financial game, and then had forgotten about it.

"Yes, sir, Coyote Investment. And he has many other companies, everywhere. That's why he doesn't care what he does. He is too rich."

The young man's narrative was interrupted, suddenly, by the sound of a motorcycle roaring up North Audley Street, and a car honking its horn in protest. The noise burst the bubble that, for a moment, had enclosed the two men. Hoffman looked out the window. Across the street, two men in boxy suits were talking. One of them was looking up at Hoffman's building. They looked bored. Hoffman turned back to his visitor.

"This is all very interesting, Mr. Pinta. But like I said, I don't do murders. Tell the police. Let them investigate. That's their job."

"I told the police, sir," he said quietly, "and they have done nothing. I told them two weeks ago, and they do not even want to talk to me. They say that Mr. Hammoud is not a suspect in the murder of my wife, and they are looking for clues, but so far they do not have anything, and they are very sorry but what can they do? They don't care. He is a rich Arab, and I am a poor Filipino. So you see? That is why I have come to you."

"Don't be silly. The police will investigate. This is England. They have laws here."

"Not for people like Mr. Hammoud. Like I told you, sir, the police don't want to hear nothing about Mr. Hammoud. They keep telling me that he is very important person, and a friend of this one and that one, and if I have any more questions I should go to the Philippine embassy. I tell you, sir, they are afraid of him. So you must help me to find some information to give the police. Otherwise, there is no hope." He nodded toward the picture of his dead wife, still laying facedown atop the desk. "No hope."

Hoffman looked at him scrunched up in the big chair across the desk, trying to take up as little space as possible. He reminded Hoffman of a pet guinea pig he had owned when he was a boy, whose only survival skill had been to hide. It was impossible not to feel sorry for this young widower or to want to do something to help him.

"I'll tell you what," said Hoffman. "Let me see if I can find anything about Hammoud's business in one of my directories. It will only take a minute. But that's all I can do, I'm afraid. Then I have to get back to work. Would that help?"

"Oh, yes, sir," nodded the young man. "That would be very helpful, I think. If you find something bad about his business, then maybe the police will listen to me. Maybe so."

Hoffman went to his bookshelves and pulled down a fat volume that listed all the companies that were registered in Britain. He opened it to the Cs and hunted for Coyote, turning the pages back and forth several times. "That's odd," he said. "It's not listed." He returned to the shelves and took another, even fatter volume that included all companies that had offices in Britain, regardless of where they were officially based.

"Here it is," he said after a few moments. "Coyote Investment, Societe Anonyme. Registered in Geneva. Chairman and president, N. H. Hammoud. Four other directors, all with French names. Revenues, not available. Profits, not available. London office on Knightsbridge. Not a bad address for a company nobody has heard of. But it's not much to go on, I'm afraid."

"No?" The young man was still wide-eyed, expecting Hoffman to find some gem of knowledge among his investment guides and legal tomes that would crack the case.

"No," said Hoffman. "This man Hammoud obviously works hard at keeping his business secret. I heard he bought a factory in Portugal a few months ago, but I'm not even sure about that. Sorry. I wish I could tell you more."

"Nothing else in those books?"

Hoffman shook his head. He was disappointed himself.

Hammoud was the sort of person that interested him, an Arab businessman with lots of money and a fetish for privacy. Hoffman had built a modest busines penetrating the secrets of people like that. "Sorry," he said again.

"But maybe you could find out some more, if you investigate."

"Maybe. But you can't afford to hire me, Mr. Pinta. Honestly. I do my work for big companies, not for cooks. I'm expensive."

Ramon Pinta sat up in his chair and straightened his shoulders. He was offended by the reference to his profession. "Sir, whatever you cost, I will pay. They tell me at the embassy that you are the best man in London for this job, so I come here to hire you, and that is what I am going to do. Please."

Hoffman laughed. He had to admire the little man's persistence. "But they were wrong at the embassy, Mr. Pinta. As you can see, I'm useless. Try the police again."

"Please, sir." His palms were together again. Hoffman was afraid he would get down on his knees and beg if he didn't do something. He had wasted too much time already with this Filipino houseboy. The only way to get rid of him was to say yes.

"Look," said Hoffman. "I'll ask a few questions about Hammoud. See what I can find out. Okay?"

Ramon's mouth fell open as if he were about to sing for joy. "Yes, sir! Okay. How much money, please?"

"Nothing. It's free. Whatever I find out about Hammoud will be helpful for me, too, so let's forget about money. It's the least I can do for your wife."

"I want to pay, sir, like anyone else." His dignity was still offended.

"We'll talk about it later, all right? Now it's time for you to go, because I have other work to do." Hoffman rose from his chair. Ramon stared up worshipfully at his new friend and protector.

"We shake on it, then? No money. A handshake is enough, because this is England."

Hoffman nodded. He extended his hand and thought, as

he did so, that perhaps he should have taken some money. That way, Mr. Pinta would merely be another client. The young man shook Hoffman's hand solemnly. Now it was official.

"One more thing," said Hoffman. "Do you know anyone who works for Hammoud who might talk to me about how he does business? That would help. If I'm going to ask questions, I need someplace to start."

"Not really, sir," said Ramon. "The people who work for him are all Arabs, too. They would not help." He stopped and thought a moment. "Except maybe for one person."

"And who is that?"

"A woman who works at Coyote Investment. She was the only person who wrote to me after my wife died. I still have her letter. You want to see it?"

"Yes, please," said Hoffman.

Ramon removed a crumpled piece of notepaper from his wallet and handed it over. It was a simple, two-sentence letter of condolence, expressing sorrow at the death of his wife. The writer said that she could sympathize because she had lost both of her parents. The letter was signed "Lina Alwan." There was no return address. Hoffman wrote the name in a notebook and handed the letter back to Ramon.

"Thank you, sir," said the young man.

"Wait a minute. How can I reach you if I find out anything?"

"I do not have a phone, sir. Or an address. I am sorry."

"So how will we communicate?"

"I will call you, sir."

Hoffman just nodded, with no sense that this might be the last time he would ever see the little man with the bad teeth. "Give me a few days, okay? And I'm not promising anything. Understand?"

"Thank you, sir," repeated Ramon. He was still walking on air.

Enough! Hoffman put his hand on the little man's shoulder and steered him toward the door. As they walked past the window, Hoffman saw the two men in boxy suits still standing across the street. This time, they were both looking up at his building. "Who the hell are they?" muttered Hoffman to himself. Ramon Pinta's eyes followed Hoffman's down to the street.

"Oh, sir!" he said sharply, reaching for Hoffman's arm. "I know them." He pointed down below to the two men. His hand was trembling.

"Who are they?" Hoffman repeated, studying the two men through the tinted glass.

"They work for Mr. Hammoud."

"What are they doing here?" asked Hoffman. But he knew the answer.

"I think they are following me, sir."

Hoffman shook his head. "Shit," he said. Now he really would have to do something.

"I am frightened," whispered Pinta. The skin on his round, brown face was drawn tight, like the surface of a drum.

"Listen to me," said Hoffman. There was a subtle change in the tone of his voice, as if he had slipped into a different gear. "There's no need to worry. They can't see in through these windows, so they don't know you came to see me. There are a lot of other offices in this building. There's a dentist on the top floor, and a lawyer below him. If anybody asks, you went to see one of them. Understand?"

"Yes, please," said the Filipino.

"Okay." He put his hand on Pinta's shoulder. "Now do exactly what I say. Take the stairs down to the basement. Not the elevator, but the stairs. When you get to the bottom, there's a laundry room that's shared by this building and the next one. Go through the laundry room and up the stairs to the lobby of the next building. Understand? The front door will let you out on Brook Street. They won't even see you leave. All right?"

"Yes, sir." But he just stood there, terrified.

"Now go," said Hoffman, pushing him out the door. "Do what I said and you'll be fine. Call me in a few days. I'll do some checking on Hammoud. I promise. And if I find anything, I'll go to the police.''

Pinta nodded. There were tears in his eyes. He took a few steps and then stopped in the hallway, just outside Hoffman's door.

''Go!'' Hoffman repeated. ''Now!'' He closed the door and then opened it a crack to make sure that Pinta was following instructions. The little man disappeared down the stairwell.

Hoffman went back to the window and watched the two men, still staring dumbly at the red-brick building. They had the bland muscular look of bodyguards. Who the hell was Nasir Hammoud? he wondered. It wasn't simply that he had promised the Filipino; he really wanted to know. It was only when Hoffman returned to his chair that he noticed the picture of Pinta's wife lying facedown on the desk. Evidently it belonged to him now.

2

Sam Hoffman stood on the sidewalk across from Nasir Hammoud's headquarters the next morning. With his hands thrust in his pockets and his hair combed tight against his head, he looked like an off-duty cop. It was raining. He put on a pair of sunglasses and began walking toward the gray concrete office block. He had to wait a moment on the curb while a parade of black taxis whizzed by on their way to Mayfair; they looked like miniature spaceships, with cellular telephones and electronic meters and wordless cigarette advertisements along the side panels. Hoffman reached the building and pushed open the narrow door. A man in a uniform with moussed blond hair and large biceps was sitting just inside, guarding the elevators.

"Hold on, then," said the guard. "You have an appointment?" He looked like a reformed London street tough, the kind who stood on the terraces at Highbury and pissed on his neighbors rather than walk to the lavatory. Hoffman ignored him and scanned the directory on the far wall until he found what he was looking for. In small type, near the bottom of the list of tenants, were the words "Coyote Investment Ltd.—Fifth Floor."

The guard moved toward him and asked to see his identification, but Hoffman pretended he didn't hear. He strode into the open elevator, pushed "5" and waited for the doors to close. But they didn't, and in an instant the guard was standing next to him, with the slightest trace of a smirk on his face.

"Sorry, squire," he said. "You need a key. Or an appointment."

Hoffman thought a moment and decided, What the hell? "I'm here to see Miss Alwan," he said. "Is she in?"

"And who are you?"

"Mr. White. I have a message for her from a friend."

The guard repaired to his kiosk and phoned upstairs. When he returned, the smirk had become a sneer. "She never heard of you, mate," he said. "You've been rumbled."

Hoffman mumbled something about having the wrong address and retreated quickly toward the door before the guard had a chance to ask any more questions. So Hammoud really did have an office on Knightsbridge, and there really was someone named Lina Alwan who worked for him. He knew that much, at least.

Hoffman reclaimed his spot on the sidewalk and pondered what to do next. The rain was coming down harder now. He removed his sunglasses and put them back in his pocket. His father had once observed that a man should always wear sunglasses on surveillance, regardless of the weather. But Hoffman had concluded that on this issue, like so many others, his father was an unreliable guide. He turned away from the gray building and began walking along Knightsbridge, looking for an alleyway. He had one more gambit to try before leaving.

"Oh, Jesus," muttered Hoffman as he neared the corner. One of his clients, a garrulous Nigerian by the name of Onono, was walking toward him. Mr. Onono had once hired Hoffman to investigate a rival in Lagos who had been trying to steal his commissions on oil sales. He was dressed today in a blue cashmere overcoat and smoking a big cigar. Walking just behind him was his English bodyguard, carrying an umbrella. "Hello, there, old boy!" said Mr. Onono jauntily. Hoffman said nothing and stared at the pavement until the great man had passed. "Cheerio!" said the Nigerian, continuing on his way.

The truth about modern-day London, Hoffman suspected, was that it represented the revenge of the colonized. It was evident in the magisterial gait of Mr. Onono, in the condescending faces of the Asian businessmen who gazed out from the backseats of the limousines that cruised the West End, in the Arabic signs that graced the windows of the jewelry shops and art galleries in Mayfair. Even stately Harrods, which loomed over the neighborhood like a red-brick battleship of commerce, was owned by an Egyptian now. They were all in on the joke: the high-toned Pakistani grocers, the sweet-tongued Lebanese pastry sellers, the polysyllabic Indian video merchants. They all understood that the world's polarity had been reversed. Hoffman had begun to comprehend it the day he wandered into the Charles Jourdan boutique on Knightsbridge, reputedly the finest ladies' shoe store in the world, and encountered a Saudi grandmother dressed head to toe in black. She was trying unsuccessfully to communicate with the sales clerk, and Hoffman had offered to translate for her. "How much is this one?" she asked, holding up a black stiletto heel. "Two hundred pounds," answered Hoffman in Arabic. "Offer him one hundred," she said slyly. And Hoffman did. Fuck Charles Jourdan. The Arabs had the money, and they could do what they liked. The juice ran the other way now.

Everyone seemed to get it, in fact, except for poor Mr. Pinta, who had a dead wife and nobody to help him, other than Sam Hoffman.

Around the corner, Hoffman found what he was looking for. It was a small alleyway, just wide enough for a trash truck, that led to the rear entrance of the gray office block. Atop a loading dock at the bottom of the alley stood a large Dumpster. Hoffman walked quickly toward it. As he neared the Dumpster, he felt a pleasurable surge of fear. He hoisted himself up on the metal frame and gingerly stepped in, pulling the lid down behind him but leaving it open just enough to illuminate the debris.

The trash had been gathered into green plastic bags, each secured with a wire band. Hoffman opened the bag closest to him and pawed through the contents. He found cigarette butts, old newspapers and magazines, indecipherable phone messages and a few wadded-up balls of scrap paper bearing the logo "Swami to the Stars." He studied each item but found nothing he could connect to Coyote Investment. A second bag contained a similar agglomeration of trash, plus used tea bags and coffee filters. A third bag was full of computer printouts, which looked promising but turned out, on examination, to be the accounts receivable of a Finnish import-export firm located on the ninth floor. A fourth bag smelled of rotting melons, and a fifth was full of wet paper towels. But the sixth bag contained the jackpot Hoffman had been looking for.

Uncrumpling one of the pieces of paper near the top of the bag, Hoffman saw the name "Coyote," and below that the words "From the desk of N. H. Hammoud." It was a memo to the travel department, asking them to make arrangements for his cousin, Hussein, who would be arriving soon from Baghdad. It was signed "Hammoud," and below that the secretary had typed "Chairman of the Board." Hoffman smiled. So the owner of the mysterious Coyote Investment was indeed an Iraqi. That was something.

The rest of the bag was mostly trash. But near the bottom, in a smaller plastic bag, Hoffman found a treasure. He almost didn't open it, it had so little weight. But when he held the bag up to the light, he saw that it contained tiny strips of paper. It was a shredder bag! Hoffman formed his lips into a kiss against the plastic. That was enough for one afternoon. Clutching Hammoud's memo and the bag, he extricated himself from the Dumpster and retraced his steps down the alley, eager to escape before the janitor arrived with the next load.

Hoffman carried his discoveries across Hyde Park to his office on North Audley Street. His enthusiasm grew as he began assembling the shredded paper on the floor—laying out the strips one·by one and lining up the bits of type like a jigsaw puzzle. Matching them up proved easier than he had expected, and it occurred to him suddenly that it was *too* easy. Except for a few lines of type at one end, the strips were all blank.

After he had assembled several of them, Hoffman could see that they were all blank pieces of stationery. At the top of each was an identical letterhead that read, "Oscar Trading Co., S.A.," followed by a postal box number in Panama City, Panama. Below that were two phone numbers—one in Tunis, the other in Geneva. And then, nothing. He pieced together a sample sheet with Scotch tape and put it in a desk drawer. He was so disappointed that it didn't occur to him to wonder, until much later, why anyone would bother to shred blank pages of stationery.

3

Lina Alwan was one of the silent ones. Her office was a small room in the accounting department of Coyote Investment, down the hall from where they kept the computers. A lamp stood atop the gray metal desk, along with pictures of her parents in silver-plated frames, which she polished once a week. Otherwise, the office was as worn and spartan as those of the other "trusted employees" of Coyote Investment. She waited silently at her desk until six-thirty that evening, wondering if "Mr. White" would return. She had no idea who he was or why he had come calling, but she was intrigued by the very idea of a visitor. That had never happened before. People simply didn't visit the Iraqis who worked at Coyote Investment.

Professor Sarkis, the chief of the accounting department, stuck his head in the door at six-fifteen and asked why she was still at work. Though he was always addressed as "Professor," his only known teaching experience had been at a night school in Baghdad, where he had briefly taught accounting. In one ear he wore a hearing aid that never seemed to work adequately, so that he was forever thumping at it with the palm of his hand.

Lina mumbled something about getting an early start on the monthly audit. She could tell, from the look in his eyes, that Sarkis knew about the unauthorized visitor. As he hovered over her, his huge nose sniffing for trouble, Lina wished that he would just come out and ask—"Do you know anyone named Mr. White?''—so that she could answer, no, she had never heard of him and had no idea why he'd called. But Professor Sarkis didn't ask. He just looked at her dubiously and shook his head, which was a bad sign, because it meant that she was under suspicion.

Don't think about it, Lina told herself. That was her method for dealing with most of the peculiarities at Coyote Investment, and it was the same for most of her Arab friends. Keep your head down; cash your check; spend your money. That was how the silent ones lived. Lina had joined the accounting department three years before, initially as a bookkeeper and later as head of data processing, and she had learned to ask as few questions as possible. She had no idea where Nasir Hammoud's fortune came from and no interest in finding out. Like most of Hammoud's "trusted employees," she was frightened of him. She remained with Coyote Investment for the same reason as most of the other Iraqis: The pay was good, and she was too scared to leave.

A young Iraqi named Youssef stopped by after Professor Sarkis had left. He had recently joined the accounting department and, within a few weeks of his arrival, had developed a chronic infatuation for Lina. He sent her flowers and boxes of dates and Arabic love poems and stayed late at the office to ask her out to dinner. He was a pest. Tonight he was wearing a pungent cologne, which was a bad omen. He propped himself on Lina's desk and, with a look of perfect, unwarranted male confidence, informed her that he had made a reservation for that evening at Blake's, which he boasted was the most expensive restaurant in London.

"I'm busy," said Lina. She didn't even bother to look at him.

Youssef looked shaken. "You are busy every night?"

"Yes, every night." God, he was a pest. She could tell, by the look of him, that he was the sort of Arab man who pretended to be modern but would do everything in his power to turn his beloved into a pregnant house slave as soon as he got the chance. They were all like that, more

or less. That was why Lina would never marry. She locked
up the file cabinets, ignoring the despondent suitor who
was still parked on her desk.

Lina had learned to put up with this sort of moon-eyed
Arab nonsense long ago. She was attractive, with the kind
of face and figure that made people notice her even when
she was trying to stay out of the way. She had lustrous
black hair cut tight against her head, so that it bristled like
animal fur; it was matched by black eyebrows that looked
as if they had been drawn twice with a sharp crayon;
completing the face were high cheekbones and a prominent
nose. It was the face of a Muslim princess, and so, inevitably, Lina compensated by wearing the shortest skirts and
tightest sweaters the Occident had to offer. That was a
form of *taqqiyya*, too. But Lina could not escape the real-
ity that she was in both worlds at once; that she was at
once a woman of the East and the West, a creature of fate
and free will. That was another trait that was typical of
the silent ones. They did not know who they were.

Lina Alwan was an Iraqi exile, too, although from a different vintage than Mr. Hammoud. She was descended from
the old aristocracy, from the people who had once looked
with disdain on newly rich men like Hammoud but had
learned, in recent years, to make a grudging peace with
them. The family had left Baghdad in 1968, when the
Ruler came to power, fleeing first to Amman and later to
London. Her father had become in exile a sort of Arab
version of Ashley Wilkes: a gentle patrician who tried his
best to adjust to changed circumstances but had never entirely succeeded. His wife had died soon after the family
moved to England, and he had raised his only child to
be strong and independent—and fully a part of her new
surroundings—in a way that he could never be. Lina was
Daddy's girl, and all the intensity of Arab family life was
compressed into that one relationship.

Growing up, she had been all the things an only child

can be: petulant, manipulative, uncertain—a willful young girl who was indulged by her gentle, confused father. But there was a seriousness to her too, from the beginning. Her father had assumed, from the moment they had left Iraq, that she would eventually go to college and get a job. That was the way people did things in the West, and he was determined to be a modern and enlightened Arab, even if it killed him. It was fortunate that he had never lived to see Nasir Hammoud.

Lina was five years old when they left Baghdad, and what she chiefly remembered about the city were its smells, which were so much more varied than those of London: the musty odor of her grandfather's vast house in the Waziriyah district; the sweet smell on her fingers when she touched the bags of nutmeg and cardamom in the spice bazaar of the old souk; the aroma of grilled *masgouf* fish at the restaurant on Abu Nawas Street, along the Tigris River, where her father took the family on Thursday nights.

Lina also remembered the smell of fear. It was everywhere in the city that summer, after the Ruler's tanks seized the presidential palace, and the fine old families of Baghdad panicked and fled for their lives. Lina remembered the suitcases lined up in the hall, and the car racing along the desert road to Jordan before the border was closed, and the empty look of grief in her mother's eyes as they left Baghdad for the last time. The Ruler had already established his interrogation center in a Baghdad suburb. It was called the Qasr al-Nihayyah, the "Palace of the End." Within a few months, a new kind of code had developed among the exiles. When one of their friends or relatives was arrested, they would say, "*nayem jawah*"—"He is asleep, inside." By the time Lina was in her late teens, nearly every adult male Iraqi she knew had been "asleep," or killed.

Iraqis had become used to the smell of fear in the years since then, in the way that people living near a refuse dump can become used to the smell of garbage. It was the damp, acrid smell of something trapped deep in the body that was rotting from the inside out. You could feel it: a sudden tightness in the throat, an involuntary tremor in the neck, a palm that was always moist with perspiration. It was the hollow look of shame and surrender among the men who were arrested and tortured that first summer, and every summer thereafter. For them, and for their mothers and sisters and nieces, the fear was never far away.

Lina's introduction to Mr. Hammoud had come about in a typically grisly Iraqi way, and it was something she never discussed. Not long after her father had died, at the time she was completing her degree in computer science at London University, she had been visited by a man who worked at the Ministry of Foreign Trade in Baghdad. He claimed to be a friend of Lina's Aunt Soha, who worked at the same ministry, and to prove it he brought a letter from her. Lina read it with apprehension. Her father had always described Soha as a kind of family hostage, who had been given a job in government—forced to take a job, would be more accurate—after the rest of the family had fled the country.

At the end of the letter, after several paragraphs of too-cheery news about life in Baghdad, Soha had suggested that Lina should contact a businessman named Nasir Hammoud about a job when she graduated from university. Hammoud needed people with technical skills, she said, and it would be a patriotic thing to do. Even in her youth, Lina had understood the essence of that letter. Her aunt was frightened. If Lina didn't do what she asked, Soha would suffer for it. And so, like a generation of Iraqis, Lina did her duty, cashed her check, covered her eyes.

Because Lina was marked by this imprint of fear, she was quickly embraced by Mr. Hammoud as a "trusted employee." He assumed that anyone with roots in Baghdad would be afraid of him, do what he said, not ask questions. He never made explicit threats, but he never needed to. Everyone understood. That was the hidden web that held enterprises like Coyote Investment together and made them almost impenetrable to outsiders. The London exiles were bound to a place a thousand miles away, distant in time and space but immanent in the imagination, where a man was holding a hammer and nails over the head of someone beloved. The terror was inescapable. It held an entire nation hostage; they were all asleep together.

4

Sam Hoffman's phone rang the morning after his foray to the Dumpster. It was his father calling from Athens. The loud, careening voice suggested that, as was so often the case lately, Frank Hoffman was drunk. "Sammy," he shouted into the phone. "How the hell are you?"

Sam braced himself. This was a part of young adulthood that he had not anticipated, dealing with a father who was out of control. "Okay, Pop," he said. "How are you?"

"Fan-fucking-tastic, that's how I am. I just made five million bucks." He was almost screaming, so loudly that Sam had to hold the phone away from his ear. Hoffman senior had retired a few years before, and he now played at making money the way other retirees played at golf. The old man began recounting his latest triumph, which seemed to involve buying up Libyan letters of credit at a discount in Malta and selling them at an enormous profit in Rome. Or something like that. Sam tried to follow what he was saying, but when his father got to the part about the sea of money, he knew it was time to get off the phone.

"This whole world is floating on a sea of money, sonny boy," Frank Hoffman sputtered into the phone. "You can suck it up with a straw if you're not too stupid, or scared!" The *s* words were all coming out slurred.

"I'd love to hear about it another time, Pop. But I have to go. I'm just starting work on a new case."

"Oh, yeah? Big deal."

"Maybe you've heard of the company. It's run by an Iraqi."

"Stay away from the Iraqis, son. They're nuts. Always killing each other. Completely nuts."

"Okay, Pop. Whatever you say."

"Fuck the Iraqis, anyway. Don't get me started on the goddamn Iraqis. And don't give me that busy-busy crap. You always say that. Wake up and smell the coffee."

"I am awake, Pop. I really have to go."

"That sea of money is all around you, son. If you would open your fucking eyes. You just have to lean overboard and take a big gulp. Because it's out there. Billions of dollars, bubbling up out of the ground like water, and it doesn't stop. Ever! There's so much dough, the banks can't hold it. It just goes splashing over the walls and into that big old sea of money. And some of it is waiting for you. Listen to your old man, for once. Just find yourself a straw, and lean over the side, and suck it up. You get me?"

"Absolutely, Pop. Definitely."

"Right now, son. No bullshit. Today. You follow me?"

"I follow you, Pop. I'll get a straw today. I promise."

"No, you won't, you teetotaling little prick! You don't listen to me. You could be making a fortune if you weren't such a tight ass. You know that?"

"Sorry, Pop. I hate to be rude. But I have to go."

"You think I'm just an old drunk, don't you? Admit it. Don't lie to me, boy." He was getting maudlin now. In the next part, he would start talking about how nobody appreciated him at the CIA.

"I have to go, Pop. Really."

"Fuck you, son. You, you . . ." He searched for the word and then began sniffling. It sounded like he was weeping.

"Sorry, Pop. Gotta go. I have work to do."

There was a new bark of noise from the phone. Sam hung up. He knew from experience that his father would keep talking regardless of what he said. When he put the

phone down, Sam realized that his hand was shaking. He
was not so uninvolved in his father's world as he liked to
imagine. The old man could still overwhelm his defenses
with something as simple as a phone call.

Like many sons, Sam Hoffman had defined his life partly
in reaction to that of his father. If his father was a drunk,
he would be sober. If his father had been a CIA officer,
he would stay as far away from the agency as possible. If
his father was matter, he would be anti-matter. But in the
end, this very process of reaction had only tied him to his
father more.

Sam had grown up in Beirut, where his father had been
chief of the large and active CIA station during the late
1960s. He was an only child, which meant that he had
faced his father's gale-force personality alone. Frank's idea
of a good time was taking his ten-year-old son on a stroll
down Hamra Street, stopping at one of the gamier bars to
chat with the clientele and guffawing as his son watched,
wide-eyed, while the Egyptian strippers disrobed. Things
got worse after his father left the agency in the early
1970s, following a quarrel with headquarters. Frank had
started a security business in Saudi Arabia, but things had
gone badly with his Saudi partner, and his marriage, never
a happy one, had finally ruptured. After listening to one
tirade too many from Frank, Gladys Hoffman had packed
the bags. "You can take care of me now, little man," she
told Sam. They took the next flight out of Dhahran. From
that point, the father had begun a slow decline into irasci-
bility and dipsomania, and the son had tried, in various
ways, to escape the debris.

At first, his father's emotional decay had given Sam a
perverse pleasure. He had located an A.A. chapter in Athens and lectured his father about attending meetings and
sent him regular bundles of self-help books. He had even
urged his short, fat and famously inactive father to join a
health club. But none of it had worked. Drinking was a

lifestyle for CIA officers of his generation. Sam had decided, eventually, that the problem didn't interest him. The CIA old boys had turned their children—and the entire nation, for that matter—into codependents for forty years, but it was over. The Cold War was finished. The great binge had ended. Nobody drank anything harder than iced tea now, and Frank Hoffman would have to fend for himself. But, of course, it wasn't that easy for Sam to cut himself loose. Father and son were bound head and toe, and the harder they worked to free themselves, the tighter the knots became.

It was clear to everyone but Sam Hoffman that the career he had ultimately chosen—as a private financial investigator—was as close to that of a CIA officer as you could get without actually being one. What Sam provided his clients amounted to a kind of private intelligence service. He knew the details that were never included in the chamber of commerce handbooks. He knew which Saudi princes were clean and which ones were dirty; which ones would pay their bills and which ones always held back 10 percent. He knew which Lebanese middlemen would deliver and which ones would disappear to Brazil. He knew which Arab banks were real financial institutions and which ones were made of paper. He knew, in short, how to do business in the land of liars.

What made Sam especially useful to clients was the fact that, for all his suspicions about individual Arabs, he had a deep affection for the people and their culture. The fascination had begun when he was a boy in Beirut—in the embrace of his Moroccan nanny, in the long lunches with his father's friends in the Lebanese mountains, in the bonds and rivalries he formed with his Arab schoolmates—and it was an itch he could never quite scratch. He still loved the courtly manners of the Arabs, the intimacy of their friendships, the self-mocking laughter of their dinner conversation, even the intensity of their feuds. He kept up with Arab political gossip the way some people keep up with baseball statistics; he knew, without asking, who were the leading presidential candidates among Leba-

non's Maronite Christians, and what the Druze Muslim
leadership thought of them; he knew which Saudi prince
was buying which London newspaper, and why. He loved
the Arabs. That was part of Sam's problem. If he had
liked them less, he wouldn't have minded so much the
cruelty and corruption in which they had ensnared themselves. He would simply have gone along, and gotten
along. Instead, he had become a free-lance meddler, moti-
vated by a cynicism and idealism that were so tightly
intertwined they were inseparable.

Sam Hoffman had initially embarked on a more traditional career. He had joined a big New York bank after
graduating from college and gone to work in its private-
banking division. Because he spoke Arabic, and because
his father seemed to know every prince and bagman in
Araby, the bank had decided that young Hoffman should
cultivate clients in the Persian Gulf. It was fertile ground,
especially for the children of American foreign-service officers. One ambassador's daughter had set herself up in
Geneva as a private banker to the young women of Saudi
Arabia and Kuwait; she now managed hundreds of millions of dollars. Another well-heeled private banker in Geneva claimed to have just five accounts, each worth more
than five hundred million dollars. He carried a cellular
telephone everywhere he went—to the movies, to play
tennis, to dinner. The phone number was known only to
the five clients, but a call from any one of them and he
would be on his way to the airport.

Hoffman had tried this line of work for three years. He
had made a real effort: wearing suits with ties, opening
his mail regularly, even carrying a cellular phone. But one
problem had proved insurmountable: He loathed nearly all
the people whose money he managed. With few excep-
tions, they were corrupt and dishonest men whose chief
goal was to hide their wealth from those who quite prop-
erly wanted to take it away. The breaking point had come
when one of those clients, a young Saudi prince, had tried
to involve him in a deal that was so thoroughly and shame-
lessly corrupt that Sam winced to remember it. The worst

of it was that the Saudi had assumed, as a matter of course, that he would say yes.

But Sam Hoffman had said no. He had quit the bank and started his own financial consulting firm whose specialty, as it evolved, was to investigate the very people whose money he had previously been soliciting. It was a more comfortable fit. But even in this new job, Sam could not escape the people who were forever telling him that they had known his father in the old days in Beirut, and giving him a wink. They all seemed convinced that whatever ideals he professed, Sam knew how the world worked and would, in the end, do what was necessary.

5

Framed on the wall behind Sam Hoffman's desk was a quotation from Oscar Wilde: "The mystery of the world is the visible, not the invisible." It was a precept for life—to know what was knowable and not worry about the rest. It was also, for Hoffman, a sensible business plan. Begin by investigating the facts that were available—especially, in this modern age, the ones that were available electronically. That was the way he always started an investigation. And yet, for all his belief in the surface of things, there was something in Sam Hoffman that was pulling him down deeper, to where it was murkier and harder to discern visible from invisible, truth from falsehood. This week, the cement block tied to his waist was a Filipino cook named Ramon Pinta.

Hoffman sat down at his desk and scowled at the computer. An extension of the visible. He logged on to the network he used to search databases. He began with the United States, instructing the computer to search the names Coyote Investment, Hammoud, Nasir and Hammoud, N. H. in the abstracts of state corporate and partnership records. Eventually, the computer regurgitated two matches: N. H. Hammoud was listed as chairman of a Nevada corporation called NH Holdings, whose business was described simply as "investments." He was also listed as a partner in a New York real estate venture called 442 Madison Avenue Partnership, which owned an office building at that address and certain other properties, all unnamed. He tried NH Holdings and the partnership on other databases, but came up with nothing. They were dead ends.

"He's a slippery SOB," said Hoffman to the computer screen. He made himself a cup of coffee and turned to the real estate database, which listed tax-assessor records and recorder-of-deeds information from most states. He searched Coyote Investment and Hammoud—as owner, buyer or seller of property. That yielded a few more hits. A Nasir Hammoud owned a house in Aspen and a two-hundred-acre farm in Middleburg, Virginia. Two years before, an N. Hammoud had sold a two-acre estate in Santa Barbara to a company called Jidda Holdings. But so what? Any rich Arab had similar properties in the United States. A house here, a farm there. A place for a mistress or an aged mother or a wayward brother. U.S. real estate was like a security blanket for the wealthy classes of the East— a landscaped sanctuary if the natives back home ever got too restless.

Hoffman called up a database for filings under the Uniform Commercial Code, which summarized records of debtors and secured parties in business transactions. Nothing there. He tried another on-line service that listed federal- and state-tax liens and civil judgments, and again came up with nothing. As a final shot, he searched federal-district-court and bankruptcy-court records and, for good measure, New York State Supreme Court records and Los Angeles County municipal-court records. No match. Nothing. Hammoud hadn't left a trace.

Hoffman was peeved. The U.S. search was supposed to be the easy part. Databases were still primitive in most other parts of the world. He tried a British on-line service that listed ratepayers to the various boroughs of London; that yielded some scanty information about Coyote, including the fact that the company had a leasehold for the entire building on Knightsbridge rather than just the fifth floor. He then searched a Europe-wide corporate registry compiled in Brussels; it coughed up the same meager facts about Coyote's board of directors and Geneva registration he had found the day before in the printed directory. Hoffman was getting angry now. The only consolation for staring at a computer screen was the sudden spark that connected a name with a transaction, but there were no sparks here. Nasir Hammoud had disconnected any visible wiring. It was as if he had realized, long ago, that someone like Hoffman would come looking for him.

 Hoffman's eyes hurt. He put on his suit jacket and walked to his favorite Chinese restaurant in Soho. It was a dark, anonymous place where the food was good and the waiters made a point of ignoring the customers. That suited Hoffman on both counts. He ordered Szechuan spicy bean curd; the waiter brought a chicken dish instead, which was very tasty, and a beer, which Hoffman hadn't ordered but decided to drink anyway. A fortune cookie arrived with the bill. Hoffman opened it and read the message: "The secret of life is . . . I can't tell you. It's a secret."

There it was. The ineffable mystery of things. Closed. Unknowable.

After lunch, Hoffman paid a call on the police. There was a particular constable he knew in Kensington who, on occasion, was willing to share records of pending criminal investigations. The constable happened to be a passionate fan of the Arsenal Football Club, and Hoffman happened to have come up with a pair of season tickets. They were friends; they helped each other out. So he had no qualms, that afternoon, asking the constable if he could locate any information about a recent murder case in Berkshire involving a Filipino woman named Pinta. Hoffman said he would be particularly interested in whether an Arab gentleman by the name of Hammoud was a suspect in the case. The constable placed a call to a friend in the central records division and came back with a quick reply: The case was officially listed as "Unsolved" and had been put in the inactive file. The Pinta woman had been raped. The medical examiner concluded that she had died from injuries she received resisting her attacker. An investigation of an N. H. Hammoud had been opened the day of the murder but closed the following day for lack of evidence. Not only did Mr. Hammoud have an alibi, he had offered the police a generous sum as a reward, to help in the investigation.

Hoffman checked his messages when he returned to the office, expecting that the tiresome little man from the Philippines would have called to check on his progress. But there was no word from Ramon Pinta. It occurred to Hoffman that the cook might still be in the employ of Nasir Hammoud, who had probably taken his passport when he arrived in Britain, to make sure that he would stay put. That was worrying, but Hoffman didn't know what to do about it, so he did nothing. The Filipino would call eventually, and Hoffman would have to tell him that he had failed.

———

There was a stubbornness about Sam Hoffman—a kind of moral vanity that made him finish what he had started, regardless of its initial or intrinsic importance. A Filipino cook had walked into his office, and in trying to get rid of him, he had promised to help out. One thing led to another, and suddenly he was spending hours pursuing something that initially meant nothing. The promise was still real to Sam, no matter how nonsensical the mission. In this sense, there was something Eastern about him. He regarded life as a series of chance encounters, in which a person incurred responsibilities and obligations like links in a chain. If any single link was abandoned, the chain might break.

It was this stubbornness, and an abiding curiosity about Coyote Investment, that led Hoffman to try one more avenue. Like most investigators, he knew a few back doors that gave him access to information that wasn't publicly available. The most useful was something called the Office of Companies, which maintained voluminous records at a depot in the Welsh city of Cardiff. What made the office so valuable was that, if you happened to know someone there, you could occasionally get access to tax records gathered by the Inland Revenue.

Hoffman always made the journey to Cardiff himself, even though it took a full day out and back along the M4 motorway. He had cultivated a particular friend at the Office of Companies named Sally; she was a young Welsh file clerk to whom he had given, at various times, a gold watch, pearl earrings and other tokens of his esteem. She, in return, had demonstrated an uncanny ability to obtain documents from the British bureaucracy. Hoffman would tell her what he needed, and she would do the rest. He had called Sally the previous evening to say that he would be coming, and asked her to be waiting at ten-thirty outside the car park.

Sally was there at the appointed hour, as Hoffman knew she would be, wearing a tight skirt and looking like she might burst from her blouse. He gave her a kiss on the cheek and handed her a piece of paper with the name and address of Coyote Investment. "Are you staying?" she asked, meaning "For the night?" It pained Hoffman to say that he would be returning to London that afternoon.

Sally met him again at one-thirty at a French restaurant that was actually run by Greek Cypriots. She was carrying a thick file of documents, which she laid down regally on the table like a lioness presenting a new catch to her mate. Hoffman kissed her on the lips. When they had ordered a cocktail, he handed her a brightly wrapped box that contained a large zirconium ring he had purchased at a local jewelry store a few minutes before. It looked almost like a diamond. The Welsh girl went into the ladies' room to admire it in the mirror and returned with fresh lipstick and more perfume. For lunch, she ordered the most expensive item on the menu and talked animatedly about pop music and movie stars. Hoffman gazed at her dreamily and nodded at whatever she said and rubbed her thigh under the table with his leg. He didn't open the file of documents until he was back in his car.

When he had leafed through the pages, Hoffman wondered if he should have bought Sally a more expensive ring. She had delivered the complete Inland Revenue file on Coyote, which appeared to have been faxed to Cardiff an hour before lunch. The documents showed that Coyote had been paying British taxes for the past eight years, in progressively larger amounts, on income earned in the United Kingdom. The British material went on for pages and looked interesting enough. But what caught Hoffman's eye was an odd-looking document on the bottom of the stack. It was Coyote Investment's current annual report, as filed with the Registre du Commerce de Geneve and forwarded from there to the Inland Revenue. Delicious, tarty Sally had hit the jackpot.

The Coyote annual report was written in French. The first page listed the company's five directors; other than Hammoud, they all had addresses in Switzerland. Following the list of directors was a one-page letter from the chairman, discussing the previous year's results and plans for the future. It was all gibberish: high hopes, broad strategies, sound plans, no specifics. Then came the numbers: Coyote Investment's consolidated profit-and-loss account for the prior year and a consolidated balance sheet, both figured in Swiss francs. Hoffman checked the *Financial Times* when he got back to North Audley Street before converting the results to dollars with his calculator. He thought at first that he had made a mistake, and did the calculations a second time to be sure.

The numbers were astonishing. The unknown company with the silly name had made a profit the previous year of nearly $160 million, on revenues of $1.7 billion. Most amazing of all, it claimed total assets of $5.1 billion, made up primarily of investments in other companies. It seemed impossible, but if the numbers were accurate, the owner of Coyote Investment was one of the richest men in the world.

Hoffman continued turning the pages of the annual report. Among the notes to the accounts, he found a list of subsidiaries that stretched two pages. Coyote seemed to own companies in nearly every corner of the world. Finance, real estate, manufacturing. An aluminum smelter in Belgium, the new tire factory in Portugal, an aircraft-leasing venture in Canada. A pharmaceutical plant in Thailand. There was nothing, it seemed, that Hammoud was not willing to buy. A note to this note stated that in some instances, Coyote's ownership in the subsidiary companies was held by other, associated companies that were not, therein, named. That was an accountant's way of saying that Coyote's ownership was concealed by front companies. No wonder the search of U.S. databases had yielded so little.

Hoffman was puzzled by one item in the consolidated statement of changes in financial position. It showed, under sources of funds, that income from operations accounted for only a third of the total. The rest was from "other sources," which were not otherwise described. That seemed odd for such a large company; but then, everything about Coyote was odd.

Hoffman turned, at last, to the accountant's letter at the back of the report. The letter was from a Swiss firm, unconnected to any of the large international accounting giants. That in itself was a red flag, but the actual letter was more like a flashing red light. He read it several times, making sure he was translating it correctly from French, but there was no mistake:

> *During the year, the officers of the company regrettably lost certain accounting records during the relocation of some administrative functions. Thus we were unable to ascertain the nature of a number of receipts and payments. We are therefore unable to form an opinion on whether the financial statements give a true and fair view of the company's affairs at the end of the latest period, or of its profits and sources and application of funds for the year then ended. In all*

other respects, the company's records are in accordance with international accounting standards.

The letter made no sense. How could such a large company, with global resources and billions of dollars in assets, simply lose its accounting records? Given its reservations, why had the accounting firm not resigned the account altogether? And if, as the letter suggested, Coyote Investment was cooking its books, why had the Swiss authorities—and the British Inland Revenue, for that matter—done nothing about it? There was one other thing about Coyote Investment that puzzled Hoffman, the more he thought about it. It was evident that the company was controlled by its chairman, Nasir Hammoud. But there was nothing in the annual report—not one word—about who owned it.

A final item caught Hoffman's eye as he perused the documents that Sally had delivered. It was a brief accounting report, summarizing Coyote's leasehold on the building on Knightsbridge. It was signed by Hammoud's London accountant, a certain Marwan Darwish with offices in South Kensington. When Hoffman saw the name, he let out a sigh of pleasure. He knew Marwan Darwish! They had gotten to know each other when they represented rival companies during the long bidding war over a contract to install a new telephone system in Dubai. You could almost say that they were friends.

Hoffman called the Iraqi accountant at home that night, asked after his wife and family, said it had been too long and expressed the hope that they might see more of each other. Darwish responded, as Hoffman knew he would, by inviting him to come to the house. It happened that he was giving a party the next weekend for some of his Iraqi friends and clients, to celebrate his purchase of a new home. Sam would be welcome, most welcome. Hoffman mentioned that there was a woman he had met at a party not long ago whom he was particularly hoping to see again. Her name was Lina Alwan.

"Ya habibi!" said the Iraqi accountant. "She will be there."

As the day of Darwish's party approached, Hoffman waited to hear from his Filipino client. But there was no phone call or message, and it began to occur to Hoffman, by the night of the party, that he might not be hearing from Mr. Pinta again.

6

The Darwishes' party was held in early April at their new house in Hampstead. It was a large brick structure that had been done over by an expensive decorator. Every room conveyed the feel of new money: creamy white walls, oversized furniture covered in raw silk; Orientalist paintings hung in elaborate frames, each illuminated with its own brass light; exotic flowers arrayed on glass-topped tables; fine carpets from Qom and Ispahan. Padding about these lavish rooms were waiters carrying trays of food provided by the most expensive Lebanese caterer in London.

Marwan Darwish's wife, Salwa, was greeting guests at the door; she appeared to have been made over by an expensive decorator as well. She wore a low-cut beaded gown in a deep shade of green, with a diamond necklace draped across her bosom so that the pendant nestled in the round V between her breasts. She looked for all the world like an oversize, bejeweled version of the traditional Arab dish known as *koussa mahshi*, or stuffed squash. It was a gesture of the Iraqi nouveaux riches—dressing up your wife like a showgirl—at once a defiance of the Islamic conventions of the old world and a garish parody of the new.

The silent ones were all there—the young Arab businessmen, artists, clothes designers, lawyers, journalists. All shining with the patina of money. They filed in the door admiring the house and its many embellishments and chatting to themselves about the Darwishes' newfound wealth. After years of drudgery, Marwan had suddenly struck it rich! Nobody needed to ask where the money had come from. In the world of the Iraqi exiles, it was understood that sudden wealth could come from only one source. Darwish was friendly with "certain circles in Baghdad," remarked one guest. He was "well connected," said another. But they all took his wine and hors d'oeuvres happily enough, even the ones who privately detested the regime in Baghdad. As the Arab proverb said, When the monkey is king, dance before him.

Hoffman arrived early, determined not to miss his chance to meet Marwan Darwish's Iraqi friends. He was wearing his usual gray suit with no tie, although in deference to the occasion he had buttoned the top button of his shirt. His dark hair was combed straight back on his head, in the manner of a movie actor from the 1930s. He looked almost dashing. He took up a position in the parlor, facing the door, so that he could see each new arrival. If Nasir Hammoud showed up, Hoffman planned to introduce himself as a financial consultant, offer some tantalizing gossip about potential acquisition targets and propose that they meet for a private lunch. He wasn't sure what he would say to Lina Alwan.

Hoffman had been making small talk for nearly an hour when he saw a young woman in her late twenties enter the front door. She was dressed simply, in a short black dress, high heels and a strand of pearls. She introduced herself to the hostess and kissed the air next to each of Salwa Darwish's cheeks. Hoffman moved toward the young woman and was about to introduce himself when another Arab woman, shorter and bouncier than the first, called out "Lina!" and pushed past him to greet her friend.

"Ya Randa!" said Lina Alwan. She embraced her friend and then took a step back to look at her. "Quelle robe, habibti." It was a short cocktail sheath with no back and very little front.

"I know," said Randa Aziz, with a predatory smile. She was an Iraqi Christian girl who worked as a secretary in the accounting department. She was a "trusted employee," thanks to her uncle Elias, an arms dealer who lived in Paris and had been doing shady deals for years with the Ruler in Baghdad. Randa was a party girl. She was pert and pretty, and she liked to hang out with the richest and most corrupt of the Arab playboys who moved through London. She was always jetting off with them to places like Marbella and Cannes, to return with astounding stories of money and debauchery. Lina liked her enormously. She was one of the few employees of Coyote Investment who did not appear to be perpetually afraid.

"Did you see her?" whispered Randa, nodding back toward Salwa Darwish. "She put rouge on them, I swear."

"On what?" asked Lina, looking around the room. Her eyes settled for a moment on Hoffman and then moved on.

"On her boobies! Didn't you see? They were all rosy on the sides. She must think they're not big enough."

"Don't be ridiculous. Even Salwa wouldn't do that."

"How did Marwan get so rich all of a sudden?" asked Randa, taking a *kibbe* off a silver tray from a passing waiter. "I thought he was just an accountant."

"Friends in Baghdad," said Lina quietly. Another waiter strolled by, offering glasses of champagne. The bottle was on the tray so that everyone could see the label.

Hoffman moved toward the two women to introduce himself. Don't be cute, he told himself. She's probably heard every pick-up line from here to Basra.

"Hello, there," he said to Lina. "My name is Sam Hoffman. I don't think we've met." He extended his hand, easy and friendly, American style.

She was cool and correct. "My name is Lina," she said, shaking his hand. "This is my friend Randa." Hoffman greeted the other woman and then turned back to Lina, who looked almost regal in her close-cut black hair, black dress and white pearls. She was prettier than Hoffman had expected, which put him off his stride.

"You look a bit like that actress Anouk Aimée," he

said. "Did anybody ever tell you that?" He didn't want to sound like he was hitting on her, but he couldn't help it.

"No," she said, laughing. "What an appalling line! Have you used it before?"

"First time," said Hoffman. He was embarrassed, but only slightly. And it was true. She did look like Anouk Aimée.

"Well, now," said Randa, rolling her eyes. "I think I'll leave you two to get acquainted."

"Don't go," said Lina. But her friend had already pranced off toward a group of young Lebanese bankers in the parlor, who were laughing loudly about one of their college classmates who had become an Islamic fundamentalist.

Hoffman tried a gentler approach. "How do you know Marwan?" he ventured. "Are you a friend of the family?"

"I'm an Iraqi," she answered. "We all know each other."

"What do you do? At work, I mean." Hoffman was still fumbling a bit. She was so beautiful, she made him nervous.

"I work with computers in an accounting department."

"That sounds intimidating."

"Only to men who are insecure."

"Not me. I'm very secure. Where do you work?"

Lina paused. "A financial company."

Hoffman smiled. "Who owns it? Americans?"

"No." She looked uncomfortable and began fiddling with the string of pearls around her neck.

"Saudis, then?"

"No. It's owned by an Iraqi, if you must know."

"I see." Hoffman nodded. She obviously wasn't going to tell him anything she didn't have to. "Let me take a wild guess. You work for Coyote Investment. Am I right?"

Her eyes froze momentarily, as if the power had gone out. She looked up warily at him. "How did you know?"

"Because I know that Nasir Hammoud is one of Marwan's clients. So I thought you probably worked for Hammoud. Especially when you didn't want to talk about him. Is he coming, by the way?''

"I doubt it," said Lina coolly. "He's traveling." She had put the brakes on, hard. There was a long pause. Hoffman wondered whether to keep pushing and decided that he had no alternative.

"What's he like, then? Hammoud, I mean. I've heard so many stories about him.''

"You ask too many questions, Mr. Hoffman," she said. "It makes me uncomfortable." She turned and started to walk away.

Hoffman reached for her hand. "Hey, I'm sorry. I didn't mean to pry. Come back. I'll buy you a drink.'' He took a glass from a passing waiter and handed it to her. He really did sound sorry. Lina deliberated a moment and then took the glass. Whatever his faults, Hoffman looked more interesting than most of the other guests at the party.

"There's something you need to learn about Iraqis," she said quietly. "We really don't like to answer questions.''

"Got it," he said. "I won't make that mistake again.''

Hoffman escorted her to the garden. The night air was moist, and fragrant with the first budding flowers of spring. They talked about books for a while, then about movies, then about music. Hoffman asked if she had a boyfriend, and she paused before saying no, in a way that suggested she had one once but not anymore. When food was served, they went together through the buffet line and then sat down together in the library to eat. Hoffman was enjoying himself, talking loudly in the American way. He barely noticed the two Iraqi gentlemen who had settled on the couch nearby, smoking cigarettes and fingering their worry beads.

"What do you do, anyway?" asked Lina when it was her turn to pry.

"I'm a financial consultant.''

"What does that mean?''

"I work with companies that want to do business in the Arab world. I help explain things to them.''

"Such as what?"

"I tell them who to do deals with and who to stay away from."

"Is that why you're interested in Mr. Hammoud?"

Hoffman shrugged. "Sort of. But it's not why I'm interested in you."

"Are you a detective?"

"Something like that."

She lowered her voice to a whisper. "Do you work for the CIA?"

Hoffman laughed loudly. "Of course not. I loathe the CIA. I'm just a financial investigator. I find things out, and then I share the information with my clients. It's very harmless."

"I should probably stay away from you, just the same. You sound like trouble."

"Who, me? Who could I possibly be trouble for?"

"My employer. He doesn't like detectives. Even ones who call themselves consultants."

Hoffman gave her a wink. She was telling the truth about that, at least.

As they talked, a man in dark glasses had come in the front door and begun moving across the salon. He was accompanied by a young woman, who walked just ahead of him, extending her right arm. He looked to be in his late forties or early fifties, but his legs seemed frail. He carried himself slowly, as if he were dragging an invisible chain behind him. A few people murmured greetings to him, awkwardly, as if his very presence among them was a reproach. The other guests, who had been chattering away about the latest bits of gossip, suddenly fell silent. Salwa Darwish looked mortified. It took Hoffman a moment to realize that the man was blind.

Hoffman glanced back toward Lina and saw that a look of sadness had fallen across her face. "Who is he?" he asked, gesturing toward the blind man.

"His name is Nabil Jawad."

Hoffman searched his memory. "What does he do? What company is he with?"

"He's a poet," she answered. She was clipped, abrupt. She didn't want to talk about the new arrival.

"Remind me. What does he write? Is he famous?"

"To Iraqis, he is famous. He writes about our country. Or he used to. Now he doesn't write anymore. He has a foundation."

Hoffman continued to watch the pageant of this simple man, dressed all in black, making his way across the crowded salon. People pulled back as he approached, whether out of fear or pity, Hoffman couldn't tell.

"Who is the woman with him?" he pressed.

"His daughter. Don't ask so many questions. I told you, they make me uncomfortable."

"Okay," said Hoffman. But he kept his eyes fixed on the poet Jawad, who seemed to exert such a powerful hold on everyone. The blind man continued to make his way around the room on the arm of his daughter, but oddly, no one had yet moved to talk to him. Lina could see that Hoffman remained fascinated by the visitor.

"He is very brave," she said under her breath. "But he should not be here."

"Why not?"

"Because it is dangerous."

Hoffman nodded. "Let's go talk to him. No one else seems to want to."

She shook her head. They were silent for ten seconds, fifteen, twenty. Hoffman studied the blind man as he continued his way around the room. Still, nobody was talking to him. It was as if they were all afraid, or angry. The commotion of the bustling dinner party had been reduced to an embarrassed silence. Hoffman looked to her, imploringly, but again she shook her head.

Eventually, Marwan Darwish approached the blind visitor. The host looked ashen. All the earlier self-congratulation was drained from his face. He leaned toward Jawad and whispered something in his ear. The poet fixed him with a sightless gaze and then turned and walked slowly with his companion back across the room to the door. Then he was gone. Most of the guests had turned away while this ballet took place, but Hoffman had watched every moment of it.

"That was awful," he said when Jawad had gone and the buzz of conversation started up again. "People acted like he had the plague."

"Shhh," said Lina. If anything, she looked more nervous than before.

"But nobody would even talk to him. Why are they all so scared? This is England, for god's sake."

Lina put a finger to her lips. A heavyset Iraqi man was approaching the table where they were sitting. "Not now," she said. Her eyes were moist; but Hoffman failed to see it.

He leaned toward her and whispered in her ear. "Okay. But I want you to tell me later why everyone is so frightened."

Lina closed her eyes. A tear rolled down one cheek. "I have to leave," she said hurriedly and stood up. Hoffman finally saw that she was crying.

"Oh, Christ, I'm sorry." He handed her a handkerchief. She wiped her eyes and blew her nose. "Will you give me another chance?"

She shook her head. "I have to go."

"I'll give you a ride home if you're ready to leave."

She shook her head again. "No."

Hoffman looked wounded. She leaned toward him and spoke in a whisper. "I can't be seen leaving with you. It could get me in trouble. I'm sorry."

"Then I'll wait outside for you. I'll be in the white BMW, fifty yards down the street. I'll wait for half an hour."

"I have to go," she said again, pulling back. She shook his hand, stiffly, and turned and looked for her friend Randa.

———

Twenty-five minutes later Lina emerged from the front door, blowing an insincere kiss to Salwa Darwish. She found Hoffman right where he said he would be, sitting in his car. He was smoking a cigarette.

"Give me one," she said. "I'll tell you about Jawad now." She looked less frightened than before, but no less beautiful.

"That's okay. You don't have to. I'm sorry for being so nosey before."

"No, I want to, now that we're alone. Then maybe you'll understand why everyone was so scared. Nabil Jawad was our national poet. He wrote about the sailors of Basra, and about the *ma'aden*, the marsh people who live in the swamps, and about the Kurdish tribesmen from the mountains near Mosul. The whole country loved him. But then he got caught in the terror."

Hoffman nodded, but he realized that he didn't understand. "What happened to him?"

"He was arrested in Baghdad ten years ago, after he wrote some poems criticizing the regime. The poems were very subtle, but they made fun of the Ruler, and they found that unforgivable."

"How did he make fun of him?"

"Puns and word plays, that sort of thing. One example I remember was the word *jayyed*, which means 'good.' It's the Ruler's favorite word. He uses it sort of as punctuation, the way an English person would say 'very well.' So in one of his poems, Jawad had a stupid bumpkin from the countryside who was always saying *'jayyed.'* They didn't like that."

"What else? Do you remember any others?"

"In another poem, Jawad made a play on one of the party's favorite slogans. They're always chanting *'Umma Arabiya Wahida That Risalatin Khalida,'* which means 'United Arab Nation with an Eternal Message.' He changed *Umma* to *Rajiya*, so the slogan read 'United Arab Backwardness with a Legendary Message.' It was silly, but it made people laugh."

"And they arrested him for that?"

"Yes."

"What did they do to him?"

"They tortured him. That's what they do to everyone to make them confess."

"Confess to what?"

"To being agents of Israel or America or Britain. Whatever. But it was hard for Jawad. He was a poet. He didn't have anything to confess to."

"But they tortured him anyway."

"Yes. They don't need a reason."

Hoffman wasn't sure he wanted to ask the next question, but he had been drawn into Jawad's story from the moment he walked into the party. "I was wondering, how did Jawad lose his eyesight?"

Lina looked away. "I'm not sure you want to hear."

"Okay. No problem." There was a long pause. She looked at her cigarette, shook her head sadly and then tossed it out the window. Then she began again.

"The head of the secret police interrogated Jawad personally because he had dared to make fun of the Ruler and his party. He smoked cigarettes all through the questioning, one after another. When he was finished with each one, he would rub it out on a different part of Jawad's body. Arms, feet, buttocks, private parts. Everywhere."

Hoffman took a breath. He knew what was coming. Lina continued with her story, speaking evenly, staring out the window.

"After many hours of interrogation, Jawad still had not confessed. So the head of the secret police took his cigarette and extinguished it in Jawad's eye while the guards held him down."

Hoffman groaned. His hand moved instinctively toward his face.

"Then the man lit another cigarette and put it out in Jawad's other eye."

Hoffman shook his head. "Jesus!" he said. "What a country."

"Now you know. That's what they're like, the Ruler's men. That's why everyone was silent at the party. That's why you shouldn't ask too many questions."

"I'm sorry."

"That's okay. You're American. You don't think the way we do."

Hoffman sat for a long time and then turned on the BMW's engine. "Where do you want to go?" he asked.

"Take me home, please." She gave him an address in Notting Hill Gate. But Hoffman was still thinking about the Iraqi poet. He turned back to her.

"Why did they let Jawad live, after all that? Torturers usually kill their victims."

"They wanted an advertisement."

"What do you mean?"

"The Iraqi secret police like to show how cruel they can be. That's why they let Jawad come to England, so that he could frighten all the exiles here. They thought he would cower in an apartment somewhere. But they didn't realize how brave he is."

"Why did he come to the party tonight? He's obviously no friend of Darwish's."

"To show them that he isn't afraid."

"What will they do to him?"

"Kill him, eventually. They'll have to."

Hoffman waited a few moments and then put the car in gear and headed off down the hill. Silence filled the small compartment. Hoffman didn't break it. He had made enough mistakes for one evening. As they drove, he felt increasingly uneasy. When they reached Lina's flat, he turned to her.

"I wasn't completely honest with you tonight," he said. "I need to tell you something."

"Don't," she said, turning away. She knew what it was, or sensed it, and she didn't want to hear.

"I have to, so you'll understand. Do you know a Filipino man named Ramon Pinta? He works for Hammoud as a cook. He said he knew you."

She nodded. A look of pure terror had come over her face. The worst thing that could happen was happening to her.

"He came to see me last week about his wife. He thinks Hammoud was involved. I told him I'd help him. Now he's disappeared and I'm worried about him. He said the only person in Hammoud's operation who bothered to send him a letter of condolence was you. He thought you might be willing to help. So I tried to see you at the office. I used another name. Will you help?''

There was a long, ghastly silence and then Lina spoke, her voice a croaking sound, barely audible, the words squeezed by fear. ''I can't.''

Hoffman put his hand on her shoulder, but she pulled back.

''Are you sure?'' he asked.

''Yes.'' She was scanning the pavement outside now, checking to see who might be watching.

''Where is Pinta?'' asked Hoffman. ''Is he still working for Hammoud?''

She nodded almost imperceptibly.

''Can I see you again?''

''No,'' she said. ''It wouldn't be a good idea.''

Hoffman thought a moment, then reached into his pocket and removed a business card. ''Here's my address and phone number,'' he said. ''If you ever need anything, call me. Maybe I can help.''

He stared at her perfect face, frozen in distress. In her vulnerability, she was even more beautiful than before. Without quite knowing what he was doing, he leaned toward her and tried to kiss her. She pulled back sharply and put her hand on the doorknob.

''No,'' she said. She opened the car door and walked to her building. Hoffman waited to see if she would look back, but she didn't.

7

Lina Alwan rose early for work Monday morning, as if her diligence might erase the mistake she had made at the Darwishes' party. She had busied herself Sunday tidying her flat, to remove any hint of the disorder of real life. Stuffed animals from childhood were arrayed on the bed. On the dresser was a gallery of pictures of her family, including a photo of them all together on the beach at Aqaba a lifetime ago, building sand castles. In the living room, above the gas fire, was a large poster of the Ishtar Gate in Babylon, the yellow and green tiles painstakingly reconstructed by German archaeologists. She even had a picture of the Ruler, in a closet, in case one of Hammoud's men came calling.

Lina dressed quickly and took the subway two stops to Lancaster Gate, which was a short walk across Hyde Park from the office. It was a cool, clean morning—cloudless except for a few wispy trails way up in the jet stream—and the sun acted on Lina like a kind of disinfectant, bleaching away memory. In the dark of her purse she still had Hoffman's business card, and she paused at a rubbish bin just inside the park to toss it away. But it occurred to her that someone might be watching and come fish it out of the trash later, so she left it there in her wallet. It would be enough today that she looked trustworthy, clean, washed by the sun.

Lina walked down the meadow, past the bone-white

Henry Moore statue where the gay men gathered in the summertime and asked each other for cigarettes, and toward the bridge that crossed over The Serpentine. A flotilla of ducks was moored along the bank, waiting for someone to throw bread crumbs. Just across the water, Lina could see the statue of Peter Pan, pipe in hand, ready to lead the children of London off to never-never land. What a happy British fantasy. If an Iraqi had written the story, Peter Pan would have ended up working for Captain Hook.

A white Porsche was parked near the Serpentine Gallery—red leather seats, convertible top, a woman's gold lipstick case on the dash. Lina stopped to admire the car. This was one of her more active fantasies—the dream that she would save her money and someday buy a Porsche and drive off to Surrey or the Cotswolds, or some other never-never land, at one hundred miles an hour: dark glasses shielding her eyes, silk scarf trailing behind her in the wind; picking up a man along the way and, if she didn't like him, tossing him out the door. A woman in a Porsche had standing in the world. She was an object of desire, yes, but with the speed and power to escape. It was the spike heel of the road, a Porsche convertible, but it was so expensive. Lina knew that if she ever stopped working for Hammoud, she could forget about driving a Porsche anywhere. She would instead be thrown back in the tank with the other Arab girls, trying to be a *khosh binaya*, a "good girl" who could act like a virgin even if she wasn't and catch a husband. The thought was unbearable.

Lina was almost to Knightsbridge now. To her right she could see the chunky pedestal of the Albert Memorial, a stolid red-brick monument to the perfect Victorian husband. The statue reminded Lina of her own father. As he grew older and more listless in the years before he died, Mr. Alwan had spent entire days in Hyde Park, reading the Arabic newspapers and brooding about his various business reversals. That had been her father's one great failing—his inability to make money—and Lina suspected that it was a cause of her present difficulties. Mr. Alwan had been a wise and cultivated man, a man of the Arab enlightenment, who had sent his daughter to American schools in Baghdad and Amman and then to the University of London, who had savored every academic prize she won as if it were his own. But he had been slow to realize that his beloved age of enlightenment was collapsing all around him. In this new era, the most humble and backward of the Arabs—the Bedouins of the desert—would buy and sell the educated Arabs like so many camels. The Iraqis, once the most learned among the Islamic peoples, would be ruled by a clan of thugs and torturers. And the British and Americans, the missionaries of progress who had first lit the light, would prostrate themselves before both the Bedouins and the thugs.

Before he died, Lina's father had taken to calling it the *Asr al-Jahiliyya*, a new age of ignorance like the one that had existed in the Arabian peninsula before the arrival of the Prophet Mohammed. In such a world, the only thing Lina understood was that she needed money. Money, and silence, were the keys to survival in the new age of ignorance. Money meant independence, and a measure of security, even if it came from Nasir Hammoud. Silence meant survival. As Lina neared the gray concrete block on Knightsbridge, she thought again of her Porsche. Did she want a white one or a black one?

Lina took the elevator to the fifth floor and punched the code into the cipher lock, opening the thick door to the accounting department. It was just past eight, and the office was nearly empty. She went looking for the Egyptian coffee boy, and when she couldn't find him she made a cup for herself. Then she settled in behind her gray desk, logged on to the computer system and began her auditing routine.

The computer system at Coyote Investment embodied Mr. Hammoud's obsession with security. He had purchased it with the instinct of a businessman who knows that he needs modern tools to do his job, but that he must also limit access to them. In this, he was typical of the Iraqis, who alone among the Arabs had developed enough respect for technology to want to control it. The regime in Baghdad had a policy, for example, of confiscating all typewriters at the border. They saw even these simple machines as powerful tools of information, which had to be controlled by the regime rather than by its enemies. Mr. Hammoud applied the same rules at Coyote.

Lina's basic job as manager of the computer system was to spy on her fellow employees. Mr. Hammoud didn't describe it that way, of course, but that was the point. He and Professor Sarkis had installed a system that could operate as a vast tracking device. Any time an employee opened one of the files, he would leave a mark that could be monitored and tracked, and it was Lina's job to check these footprints in the snow each day to see where everyone had been.

She began by reviewing the previous workday's activity of each of the twenty-five people at Coyote who had login/password accounts. She had prepared user profiles for each of them. She knew what files they accessed regularly and the times of day and week they did their work. If she found any irregularity in these patterns—anyone requesting a file that wasn't directly related to his or her work, anyone reviewing a file after normal business hours—she was supposed to notify Professor Sarkis immediately. The only log-in accounts that were off limits to her review were those belonging to Mr. Hammoud and Professor Sarkis. "Never, never, never!" Professor Sarkis had lectured her when she became system manager. He warned that if she made any attempt to read Mr. Hammoud's personal files, she would leave a track of her own—which they could monitor.

That was the other eccentricity of the system. It was supposed to have two brains. Lina's job as system manager was to act as the lower brain, taking care of the ordinary functions—adding and deleting accounts, monitoring activity—the accounting equivalents of breathing and eating.

Like a trusty in a prison, Lina had been granted these powers on condition that she would do no more. Hammoud and Sarkis were the higher brain; they planned the transactions, moved the money. Like Lina, they had special powers to roam the system—searching other files and transacting business in any of the system's hundreds of accounts. But they insisted that their own files must never, ever be examined. It was the electronic equivalent of a one-way mirror, allowing Mr. Hammoud and his chief of security to be present everywhere, but invisible. Lina couldn't be sure, even now, that Professor Sarkis wasn't sitting at his terminal, watching her watching the other employees.

Helen Copaken would never have put up with it, Lina told herself. Helen had been her best friend in the computer-science department at the university, a woman so smart that she intimidated even the men in her classes. She and Lina still talked every few weeks, in rambling conversations that usually concluded with Helen's admonition to stop being so *nice*. If Helen had known about the system at Coyote, she would have denounced it as an outrage, a barbarism—a system manager who was forbidden to look at some of the files in the system!—and told Lina she shouldn't stand for it another minute. But what did Helen know? She wasn't an Iraqi. She had never been afraid.

Lina worked for nearly three hours that morning, scrolling through sign-on and sign-off times and checking them against the user profiles, but she found nothing unusual. It was almost lunchtime. She went looking for her friend Randa Aziz to see if she wanted to check out the new café on Beauchamp Place, but when she couldn't find her she decided to keep working. She wasn't that hungry, and Professor Sarkis would be pleased if he saw that she was working through the lunch hour.

So the good girl, the make-believe *khosh binaya*, pressed on. The next phase of her auditing routine was to review the company's cash-management system. The computer created a paper trail for each disbursement out

of the London corporate accounts and each payment into
it. Lina's job was to verify that nobody had tampered with
any of these records. The auditing routine involved what
was known as a "checksum" operation. The computer
gathered the parameters of every cash transaction—the
dollar amount of the payment, the numbers that identified
where it had originated and its destination, and the date
and time it was made—and summed them into a single,
unique number that represented, in effect, a wax seal. If
any variable was altered, the seal of the checksum number
would be broken. The computer regularly checked its own
checksums, but Nasir Hammoud didn't trust the computer
any more than he trusted his employees. So it was Lina's
job to double-check.

She tried not to look at the details of any of the cash-
management accounts. Just add up the numbers, Professor
Sarkis had said, and she tried to do that and no more. But
the transactions seemed so odd. They involved payments
to and from banks in the most unlikely places: the Netherlands Antilles, the Channel Islands, Liechtenstein, Panama.
There were no indications of what these transactions represented. Was Coyote seeking to acquire Panamanian real
estate, say, or a Dutch shipping company? Or were these
payments simply another form of deception, to shield
transactions that were actually taking place in Singapore
or São Paulo? Lina found no explanation in the electronic
records and, as Professor Sarkis liked to say, she had no
reason to know. So she did as she was told, skating on
the surface, trying to forget that she had any questions.

It was almost an accident, the way it happened. Lina
was finishing her review of the cash-management system
and summing the numbers to make sure they matched the
authorized list of disbursements that was circulated each
week to the accountants. When she compared the two to-
tals, she saw that there was an unusually large discrepancy,
totalling nearly twelve million dollars, between what the
cash-management records said had been paid out and what
had been authorized. Her only thought, at that moment,
was that she had made a mistake for which she could

be punished. She went quickly back through the cash-management records and saw that a payment for roughly that amount—$11,920,000—had been made that week by one of Coyote's trading subsidiaries to the account of a Panamanian company called Oscar Trading. The company was unknown to her.

Just add up the numbers. But what if they didn't add up? Once again, it was chiefly the fear that she might get in trouble that led her to search for the system's file on the Panamanian company. Who had it? she wondered. The Iraqi accountant who supervised accounts payable was so sloppy; maybe he had made a mistake. Using her power as computer manager, she made a system-wide request.

It was such a routine auditing move, she barely thought about it. But as the file came up on the screen, the air suddenly went out of her lungs. The directory specified: "HAMMOUD/PER." She had made a dreadful mistake. The document on the Panamanian company was in Mr. Hammoud's personal file. No one else was supposed to have access to it. She had breached the invisible wall, if only for a moment, and glimpsed the face of Nasir Hammoud. Worse, she had left behind an electronic footprint, which someone would inevitably see.

Lina's stomach hurt. She immediately closed the file and went on to other auditing business, but found after ten minutes that she couldn't concentrate. She was about to sign off and go to the ladies' room when the phone rang.

She knew before she picked it up that it was Professor Sarkis. He wanted to see her in his office right away. Lina said she would be there in five minutes, but he insisted that she come to his office immediately. No five minutes. Sarkis's voice was edgy and unpleasant, even by his standards. As Lina walked down the hall, she could feel the moisture gathering on her forehead and the tightness in her throat and the uncertain swaying of her legs.

Professor Sarkis's office was little more than a closet, adjoining the much larger office of Mr. Hammoud. His desk was cluttered with the annual reports of companies that Coyote Investment had acquired or was thinking of acquiring or had recently sold—all stacked high in wobbly piles: a chain of hotels in Asia, a property-development company in Miami, a credit-card-service bureau in Amman. The word was out on the street that Mr. Hammoud was a buyer, and more prospectuses were arriving every day. Atop the desk was a computer terminal; on the credenza behind were more tall stacks of paper, an Arabic accounting textbook, a bottle of Armenian brandy and a jar of aspirin.

Presiding over this jumble was Sarkis himself, the most trusted of the trusted employees. The Ruler, it was said, regarded the Christian Armenians of Iraq, such as Professor Sarkis, as especially vulnerable and therefore especially trustworthy. They had become the courtiers and financial advisers of the new Iraq, much as their ancestors had worked for the sultan in the old days of the Ottoman Empire. They served at the pleasure of the Ruler. Professor Sarkis's own father, a tailor, was said to have been so friendly with the Ruler that he had made uniforms for him in the early days. Professor Sarkis ostentatiously kept a large photograph on his desk of the Ruler as a young man in uniform, lest anyone forget.

Professor Sarkis's secretary pressed a buzzer as Lina approached. "Come in!" he called out through the closed door. As Lina entered, he rose halfway from his chair and leaned toward her. He looked angry. His face was red; the veins were visible along the slope of his great nose, and his lips were thin and pursed, as if he had been sucking on a lemon. The computer screen on his desk was aglow. He knew.

"Sit down, please," he said. He was very clipped and formal when he was upset. Lina took the seat across from his desk. She crossed her legs and reminded herself that she had done nothing wrong. As she sat there, clutching her purse, it occurred to her that Sam Hoffman's card was still in her wallet. She shifted her legs so that the bag swung away from the desk. The chief accountant was still glaring at her. Lina cleared her throat.

"Is something wrong, Professor Sarkis?" she asked. She didn't want to wait for it.

"What?" he asked, thumping his hearing aid with his hand.

"Is something wrong?" she said again.

"Yes," he said softly, eyeing her carefully up and down. "Mr. Hammoud will be very angry when he returns."

"Why? I've done nothing wrong. I'm only doing my job."

At Lina's protest of innocence, Professor Sarkis exploded.

"Liar!" he shouted, pounding his fist down on the table at the same time. "You are a liar!"

She waited for him to ask a question about her audit of the computer files, but he kept glowering at her, silently. "What have I done?" she pleaded again. This time it was almost a wail.

The Armenian wagged his finger and then pointed it at her like a gun. "You getting too smart for us here. Snooping around."

"I'm not snooping. I'm just doing what you told me."

"Oh, yes, lady, you are snooping. I told you never stick your nose in Mr. Hammoud's business. Never! But you do it anyway. How we gonna trust you now?"

"I'm sorry," she said quietly. "It won't happen again."

"What?" he asked, cupping his bad ear.

"It won't happen again," she repeated. "I'm sorry."

Sarkis snorted. "Why you been talking to that foreigner? Huh? That's what I want to know."

The tightness in Lina's throat returned, like a vise of fear compressing her windpipe. It was all she could do to force out the words, "What foreigner?"

"Etchmiadzin!" roared Professor Sarkis, taking the name of the Armenian holy city as an oath. He pounded the table again. "You know who I am talking about. The man you met at the Darwish party. The man you went home with. This man Hoffman. Do not play this game with me no more, lady!" He spat into the wastebin.

Lina's self-control was ebbing away. She felt exposed, as if her clothes were being torn away from her body. What frightened her was not that she had done anything wrong but that they had been watching her so carefully.

"Please," she said, a single tear coursing down her cheek. "I never met him before."

"Tootum kalogh!" he thundered, using an Armenian expression that means "melon head." He pounded the table again, shaking the mountains of paper on his desk. "You are a liar!"

"I never met him before," she repeated. "The first time was at the party."

"Liar!" He seemed almost to spit out the word. He was glaring at her with such intensity, it was as if his eyes had caught fire. "This same Hoffman came to see you at the office, when he called himself Mr. White. We got a photograph. So don't tell me no more lies. What you telling him? All our secrets! Huh?"

With this last assault, Lina's defenses collapsed entirely. She buried her head in her hands and began to cry. She felt utterly alone and vulnerable; it was almost a feeling of being physically violated. She had been prised open by Hoffman's charm and curiosity and then abandoned to the ravages of Professor Sarkis. The tears came from deep inside her.

"Eshek!" said Sarkis, dismissively. The word meant "donkey" in Armenian. He reached for the aspirin bottle, shook a half dozen into his hand and popped them in his mouth. "Sit up. Answer me! You must know something. Come on." He handed her a tissue, which, for Sarkis, was an act of vast generosity. She blew her nose.

"I'm so sorry, Professor Sarkis," she said, still trembling from her tears. "But I'm being honest. I didn't know Hoffman was Mr. White. I never met him before the party. I haven't told him anything about the company. He tried to pick me up, and I let him give me a ride home, but that's all."

"Achpar!" he said. The word meant "brother" in Armenian, but Sarkis used that as a curse, too. He leveled

his finger at Lina again. "You gonna see him again, this guy? Don't tell me no more lies."

"No, sir. Never. I told him I couldn't see him again when he dropped me at my flat. Honestly. I promise."

Sarkis rolled his eyes at the mention of honesty. "Did he give you anything, this guy? Phone number? Business card? Anything like that?"

Lina looked at him, feeling the terror inside her again. But her trembling had stopped. "No," she lied. "Nothing." Her voice was bolder in deceit than it had been when she was telling the truth. The purse hung at her side, dangling like a noose.

"Nothing?" Professor Sarkis studied her face, but it was hard to read her now that she had been crying and her eyes were red. Maybe she was lying, maybe she was telling the truth. But it didn't really matter. Sarkis knew that he had frightened her, and that was enough. He gave Lina an odious, thin-lipped smile.

"So what we gonna do with you now, after you been hanging around with these foreigners? You think you still a trusted employee now?"

Lina nodded, but she didn't answer. In that moment, she didn't know what scared her more—what they would do to her if she stayed at Coyote, or what they would do if she tried to leave.

Sarkis handed her another tissue and motioned for her to get up. "That's all. No more crying now, okay? Maybe you want to take the rest of the day off? Let yourself forget all these things. Not say anything to the other trusted employees. Not talk to nobody, please. I talk to Mr. Hammoud when he gets back to London and tell him you very sorry you make this big mistake, and we see what happens. Okay?"

"Yes," she mumbled. "Thank you."

"Okay. And no more snooping!" He walked her to the door. As Lina returned to her office to gather her things, she could hear Professor Sarkis shouting at his secretary.

8

The first thing Sam Hoffman did that Monday morning was call his friend Asad Barakat. Barakat was a Palestinian banker, but that description did not do him justice. He maintained what amounted to a private network throughout the Middle East, and he knew things that ordinary bankers did not know. Hoffman's father had made the introduction a few years ago, and Sam suspected that Barakat, like so many other fixtures of Arab London, had once been on the CIA payroll. He had become Sam Hoffman's most valuable tipster, and also his most expensive.

Hoffman knew that to get anything out of Barakat, he would need to offer him a modest gift. It was a custom, a ritual of Arab hospitality, like bringing flowers or a bottle of scotch when you went to someone's house for dinner. You never went calling empty-handed. Hoffman thought a few moments about what might make an appropriate offering and remembered a memo he had sent the previous week to a client in Texas. The Texan was trying to sell a refinery he owned in Galveston, and he had asked Hoffman's advice in evaluating the two bidders. The larger offer came from a Pakistani investor, but Hoffman had done some checking and discovered that this same Pakistani had owned a Karachi bank that had gone bankrupt a decade ago. Bad sign. So Hoffman had advised the Texan to take the smaller offer, from a consortium of Saudi investors that called itself Golden Sands. Hoffman reread

the cold, legalistic language of his memo, which repeated
the magic words "due diligence" four times. But the message was clear enough: The Pakistani was a loser, and the
Texan would be a fool to accept his offer. Hoffman had his
bait. He picked up the phone and dialed Barakat's number.

"Hello, *ustaaz* Asad," Hoffman said into the telephone,
addressing the banker in the way that a student might
address his professor. "What are you doing today?"

"Watching television," said Barakat. "And talking to
Geneva."

"What do they say in Geneva about the dollar?"

"*Ya habibi*, how do I know? They are all very nervous.
They don't say much."

"That's why they're so rich."

Barakat laughed gently, just once. Ha! His speech was
an amalgam of sweet Arab pleasantries and the crisp dic-
tion of a Western-educated banker. It was a pleasing combination, like honey dripped over a warm scone.

"How is your father?" asked Barakat, still making conversation. It was always a mistake to rush things with him.

"He's okay. Same as usual. I think he misses the
action."

"Maybe so. But don't count him out. Your father knows
more than he lets on."

"Yeah." Hoffman was getting impatient talking about
his father. "Listen," he said, "I'm sorry to bother you,
but do you have a minute?"

"Of course, my dear. Always. What can I do for you?"

"Not much, really. I'm calling mainly to pass on
something."

"And what is that?"

"I heard a rumor about that refinery deal in Galveston.
I don't think the Pakistani is going to make it."

"No?"

"No. I have a feeling it may go to the Saudis. They
have a good operation, and they're offering an attractive
price."

"The Saudis have a very good operation. My wife's
brother works there. He asked me to buy some shares."

"Is that right?" Hoffman tried to sound surprised. "It might be a good time to buy."

"Perhaps so," said Barakat. There was a pause, as they both registered the transaction.

"There was one other thing," said Hoffman.

"Oh, really?" Now it was Barakat's turn to feign surprise.

"I was wondering, how much do you know about Nasir Hammoud?"

"Quite a lot, of what can be known. The rest, nobody knows. This is a man with many secrets."

"Can you tell me about him?"

"Some. But not on the phone."

"Can I come see you?"

"Yes, of course. But I am busy. When do you want to come?"

"Now. In about twenty minutes."

"Psss. Right now?" Barakat obviously preferred otherwise, but he was, at least momentarily, in Hoffman's debt. "Make it half an hour," he said.

Barakat's bank, which he called BankArabia, had its headquarters just off Park Lane, a short walk from Hoffman's office. It was a modest building on the outside, much less imposing than the newer banks owned by Saudis and Qataris and Kuwaitis, who had settled on some of the most expensive real estate in London. Arab money had the same typology as any other kind. New money wanted to advertise its arrival. Old money wanted to demonstrate its permanence and solidity. Dirty money wanted to hide. Coyote Investment was definitely the last of these. BankArabia was somewhere in between.

Barakat was a large man, with a round face the size of a bowling ball. He liked to dress in the most modern Italian suits, and he had them made in overlarge sizes that draped his body like silk parachutes. He was looking at his watch when Hoffman arrived, which was a sign that he wasn't going to talk long, no matter how indebted he was to Hoffman.

"So what have you got on Nasir Hammoud?" asked Hoffman as soon as the door was closed. If he didn't have much time, he didn't want to waste it on pleasantries.

"Does your father know you have come to see me about this?"

"Yes," Sam lied. What difference did his father make?

Barakat arched his eyebrow and nodded at the same time, as if to say that he believed Sam, but would also check. "Very well," he said. "What do you want to know?"

"Everything you can tell me."

"Well, now," said Barakat. "The first thing I know is that he has been traveling."

"Is that so? Where has he gone?"

"The rumor mill says Baghdad."

Hoffman smiled. Barakat knew everything. "What does that mean?"

"It means that he needs to talk to someone. Or maybe that someone needs to talk to him. Or perhaps it means that his mother is sick, and he has gone to visit her. My dear Sam, how should I know what it means? We are talking about Iraq, and that is the land of no-one-knows."

"Right. No-one-knows. But what do you think?"

"I think something very strange is going on in Iraq. That's what I hear from anyone who knows anything. Something is happening in Baghdad. More than that I cannot say. Why don't you ask your father?"

"I tried. Let's forget my dad, and forget about what's going on in Baghdad and try something simple. Tell me about Coyote Investment."

"Why not?" answered the Palestinian. "I will tell you the basics. Because of my fondness for you, and your father."

Hoffman nodded and put his hand on his heart. Jesus, he thought. This is going to cost me.

"Coyote Investment is a holding company based here in London," began Barakat. "It owns many companies around the world. They have steel, aluminum, computers, chemicals. I can give you a list of these subsidiaries, but this is not the most important question.''

''Okay. What's the most important question?''

''The most important question is not what Coyote Investment owns. It is who owns Coyote Investment.''

''That's easy. Nasir Hammoud.''

''Not so easy as that, my dear Sam.''

''Then, who owns it?''

Barakat raised his index finger in the air and then tapped it against his nose. ''That's the question, isn't it? Who owns it?''

''Help me out. I need it.''

''Maybe. But in return, you must explain to me why you are so interested in this business.''

''I'm helping someone. A man who is very frightened of Hammoud and needs information about him.''

''Why is he frightened? Is Hammoud trying to take over his company?''

''Nothing like that. He's a nobody. Between us, he's a Filipino cook who thinks Hammoud killed his wife. I promised I would help him.''

''Ah, Robin Hood!'' he said, raising his finger again and tapping his nose once more. ''Okay. No problem, habibi. You Americans are always doing things like this. Helping little people. Fighting lost causes. It is what makes you so endearing. I am sorry for asking.''

''You were going to tell me who owns Coyote.''

''No, I wasn't. But now that I know this is a matter of charity, rather than business, I will tell you some things I have heard. It is gossip, you understand?''

''I understand. Shoot.''

''Coyote is very privately held, so the ownership is fuzzy. But there is a substantial body of opinion that Hammoud himself owns a relatively small share. Perhaps ten percent.''

''Then, who owns the rest?''

''Precisely. Wouldn't we all like to know that?''

''Come on, Asad. Who owns it?''

"My suspicion?"

"Yes, for chrissakes."

"The Ruler in Baghdad."

"For real?"

"Most real, my dear. I am told that the vast bulk of Coyote's shares are actually held by offshore companies that are owned beneficially by the Ruler's family. Not that you will ever prove it. But some people believe that this is the Ruler's nest egg."

"How much is it worth?"

"A minimum of five billion dollars. Maybe twice that. Maybe five times that. Who can say? Whatever the total, it is invested in the finest assets in Europe and America. And spinning off enough cash to help keep the old boy afloat in Baghdad indefinitely, despite the best efforts of the rest of the world to force him into early retirement."

"The profits go to the Ruler?"

"Presumably. If my information is correct, the profits are divided up each quarter, with Hammoud keeping his ten percent, or whatever it is, and the rest being distributed to the Ruler's front companies."

"Where would they be?"

"I don't know. Maybe Liechtenstein. Maybe Luxembourg. Maybe Panama. Probably Geneva. The Swiss are as secretive as the Panamanians but less of a nuisance to deal with. And they speak French in Geneva, rather than that absurd Spanish."

Hoffman tried to add up in his mind what Barakat had told him. "So Coyote is the Ruler's private bank, more or less, and Hammoud is his banker. And everything runs like clockwork."

"Yes. Unless someone gets greedy."

"What do you mean?"

"You know, my dear, with Arabs there are always rumors that someone is getting greedy."

"Sorry, Asad, but I'm not following you."

"I mean that if I have ten percent of something, it is a law of nature that I will decide that I deserve twenty percent. Or better still, fifty percent. And if I think no one is looking, I will be tempted to stick my hand into the jar to get it.''

"Has someone gotten greedy?''

"How should I know? Really, Sam. Don't be silly. We are talking about Iraq. No one knows anything about anything.'' Barakat was looking at his watch again. It was a sign that the interview was over.

"And suppose one of Hammoud's employees found out that he had his hand in the cookie jar? What would happen to that person?''

"*Haram,*'' said Barakat. It was an Arabic expression that meant, roughly, "what a shame.''

Hoffman wasn't sure what he meant. "Come again?''

"That person, I fear, would be dead.''

"Dead?''

"Yes. *Malheureusement.* Too bad. *Haram.*''

Hoffman was shaken by Barakat's bland pronouncement of a death sentence on anyone who pried into the affairs of Coyote Investment. He thought of Saturday evening and Lina and cigarette burns. Barakat was looking at his watch again.

"Please, Asad-bey. I need to know one more thing. Where did all this money come from in the first place? We're talking about billions of dollars. How did the Ruler get it out of the country without anyone knowing?''

"Last question, my dear.'' He wagged his finger to show that Hoffman was being naughty in taxing his hospitality. "There is a theory held by many people that the money comes from commissions the Ruler took on Iraqi oil. Five percent of all revenues were sent to a secret account somewhere. And that is where the money came from. That is what many people think. But I am not so sure.''

"Why not?''

"Because too many people have heard this story. It cannot be true. You cannot have a secret pile of money that everyone knows about. This is not the way the world works.''

"So where did the money come from, if not from commissions on oil?"

"I will tell you what I think. But only because I admire your father."

"Tell me."

"Ten years ago, the government of Iraq made a deal to buy fighters from France. It was a two-billion-dollar deal. A contract was signed. But Iraq was fighting a war against Iran at the time, and there was an arms embargo, and the fighters were never delivered."

"Right. I remember reading about that deal."

"But you see, Iraq may have paid for the fighters in full when the contract was signed. Do you follow me? And that money may actually have been paid into a numbered bank account in Switzerland, where it was supposed to remain until the fighters could be delivered."

"What happened when the war ended?"

"Poof! The money was gone. Or at least, that is what is believed by a certain school of thought. Two billion dollars, gone. And who do you suppose was the agent on the French fighter deal in question?"

"Nasir Hammoud?"

"The very same man." Barakat looked at his watch. All the talking had made him tired.

"Who else might know something about Coyote? Can you give me any suggestions?"

"That's enough questions, my inquisitive friend. You must go now."

"Please. Help me get started."

Barakat sighed. "There is a man in London who does a great deal of business with Hammoud. They are partners in a petrochemical deal, I think. He is a Saudi. But he will never talk to you." He stood up from his desk and began walking Hoffman toward the door.

"What's his name?"

"Stop it," said Barakat. "You're beginning to whine. It's unattractive."

Hoffman was standing in the hall now, outside Barakat's office. He knew that he was taxing even the most expansive norms of Arab hospitality, but he had no choice. He needed information. "What's his name?" Hoffman repeated.

"Prince Jalal bin Abdel-Rahman," said Barakat. He shook his head and sighed like a weary schoolmaster and closed the door.

Standing alone in the hallway, Hoffman felt a kind of vertigo, as if he were suddenly in a free fall, tumbling out of the present into the past. The name Barakat had mentioned was very familiar indeed. The same man had once been a client—almost a friend—until he had made a request that was so outrageous, and yet so ordinary, that it led Sam to conclude that he could not continue as a banker. Indeed, if there was one man who could be held responsible for Sam Hoffman's flight into his present career, it was Prince Jalal. There was no one on the planet he wanted less to see.

And the worst of it was that Barakat was wrong. Jalal would be eager to talk to Sam Hoffman, if only to prove a point.

9

A courier packet from London arrived that week in the Washington offices of Hatton, Marola & Dubin, Attorneys at Law. It was one of several dozen such packets to arrive that day, but this one received special handling. The putative recipient, Arthur T. Peabody, although identified as a partner at the firm, did not, in fact, exist. The name was a pseudonym used by the senior partner, Robert Z. Hatton, for sensitive communications; all mail addressed to the pseudonymous Mr. Peabody was immediately removed from the mailroom by the chief clerk, who had been with the firm since it was founded, and delivered to Mr. Hatton's office on the top floor of the building.

Hatton's office overlooked the sparse thatch of grass in the center of the downtown business district known as Farragut Square. The firm had chosen to stay in this venerable spot—at a time when most of the other legal giants had decided to move east, to the "new" Pennsylvania Avenue, or west, to the "new" West End—so that Hatton could remain near his beloved Athenian Club, where he liked to play squash. The only peculiarity about his office was that it was bereft of any personal adornment. There were no plaques or testimonials on the walls; no framed degrees or pictures of Hatton shaking hands with famous people; not even any pictures of his family. There was only the man himself, sitting behind a vast desk, surveying the human comedy of Washington through his window.

Hatton was on the phone when the courier packet arrived. He looked at it, noted the London address of the originator and put it aside until he was finished with the conversation. On the other end of the phone was a United States senator who believed, evidently with some justification, that he was about to be indicted. Hatton would have to listen to him for some minutes before delivering the pithy advice for which he had become famous: "Don't do anything." That was always Hatton's advice, and it was nearly always correct.

Robert Hatton had helped make his law firm one of the pillars of the Washington establishment. Like most of what endured in the nation's capital, it had its roots in the Democratic Party. The firm had been created in the 1960s by a group of young Kennedy-era lawyers who had decided that, with Camelot in ruins, it was time to get serious about making money. And that they had done. In the thirty-odd years since, the firm had prospered under Republican and Democratic administrations alike, and had broken through to a kind of permanent prosperity. It was hard now for most clients to remember what the senior partners had done before starting the firm, but they had all come from somewhere else. Seymour "Sy" Dubin had been assistant counsel of the House Ways and Means Committee. John Marola had been head of the corporate crime section in the Justice Department's criminal division. As for Hatton, even old friends seemed a bit hazy about what he had done before entering private practice—something overseas, it was said—which in itself was a kind of tip-off. When pressed by important clients, Hatton would say that he had worked long ago for the Culinary Institute of America and give them a wink. Either they understood or they didn't, but in either case, there was no point in explaining.

By the 1990s, Hatton, Marola & Dubin had grown to more than one hundred lawyers. Like most of the big law firms in town, it advertised itself as a full service operation that could handle whatever problems might arise for its major clients, so that they would have no need to go elsewhere for legal advice. The firm had a tax department, still presided over by Dubin; a criminal-defense practice, headed by Marola; and a litigation department, a real estate department, and a regulatory department. The firm's income had continued to grow over the years, and most people ascribed the firm's extraordinary success to the skill of its lawyers and the breadth of its client base. This explanation was believed by everyone except the management committee of the firm, which knew that it was a lie. The truth about Hatton, Marola & Dubin was that most of its activities—however worthy in their own right—were a cover for the real work of the firm, which was to service the needs of a handful of prominent and wealthy Arabs.

These Arab clients dealt exclusively with Hatton, and in many instances, he was the only person in the firm who knew the actual names of the people everyone was working so diligently to represent. Hatton parceled out the work himself and gathered it together when it was done. He had evolved a system a bit like that of the CIA, in which his personal clients were known in the firm only by pseudonyms. He chose simple Welsh or English names such as Smith or Jones, occasionally throwing in a Latin or Japanese name to confuse everyone further. But the system worked smoothly enough. A junior partner would be told to prepare a memo on, say, the U.S. tax consequences of purchasing one thousand acres of farmland in rural Virginia for a foreign client by the name of Hubert J. Smith. The memo would be written, and the firm would undertake the purchase, usually using one of the dozens of dummy corporations it controlled. The ultimate purchaser of the farmland probably lived somewhere like Jidda, but the junior partner would never know the difference. If anyone raised questions, Hatton would inevitably respond: Don't do anything. And the problems would eventually go away.

The senator on the other end of the phone finally acceded to Hatton's advice, allowing him to hang up the phone and get on with other business. He opened the courier pouch addressed to Arthur T. Peabody and removed the contents. It was a nine-page memorandum, which bore no markings as to who had prepared it or why. The title page was blank except for a brief summary of the contents, which had been typed all in capitals: "RECENT ACTIVITIES OF SAMUEL HOFFMAN." Hatton read the report once, quickly, and then a second time more carefully. When he had finished, he took the memorandum and walked to a door on the far side of his office. The door had been painted the same soothing beige as the rest of the office, so that it was barely visible. But it was made of reinforced steel, and it was double-locked. Hatton tapped a code into the lock and then took a large key from his pocket and turned the deadbolt lock. The door opened onto a small, windowless room about the size of a walk-in closet. This was Hatton's private-document room, where he stored all the sensitive materials of his unusual legal practice. He opened one of several safes in the room and placed the memorandum inside.

When he had locked up his document room again, Hatton visited his secretary to gather the morning's phone messages. Atop the stack was one marked "Urgent" from an old friend in London, a man who for many years had been a senior civil servant and was now in semi-retirement. Hatton placed the call immediately. He talked for more than twenty minutes—a long call for Hatton—and then, when he was finished, walked back to the steel door that guarded his document room and repeated the laborious process of gaining admission. Inside, he opened another safe and retrieved from it the name and telephone number of an attorney in Manila. The Philippine attorney was another old friend of Hatton's who, during the Marcos years, had served with that country's security service. He was one of the hundreds of such contacts that Hatton had developed over a lifetime of handling sensitive matters, and he took care to see that this man—and the many others like him—received whatever legal business or other help the firm of Hatton, Marola & Dubin could throw his way. It was an article of faith to Hatton that the whole of the world's endeavor could be condensed into the basic activities of making money and hiding money and, if the first two were successful, spending money.

Hatton placed the call to Manila himself. He apologized for waking his old friend in what was the middle of the night in the Philippines. Then, after only the briefest small talk to allow the other man to get his bearings, Hatton made his request. It was simple and direct and took no more than five minutes, after which Hatton thanked his Philippine friend and invited him to come stay at his weekend house when he was next in Washington.

The brief telephone call set in motion a chain of events that stretched around the world. It began the next morning in Manila, when the Philippine attorney called on one of his contacts in the ministry of foreign affairs and made a special request. The diplomat, in turn, arranged to send an urgent cable from his ministry to the embassy of the Philippines in London. The political officer in London who received the cable did as he was instructed and placed a call to the number of a financial consulting company in London. At the end of this chain was Sam Hoffman.

"Hoffman Associates," he said into the receiver. "How can I help you?" Sam had been answering his own phone ever since the West Indian woman who had worked as his secretary had quit to become a full-time cabaret singer.

"This is Counselor Costanza, from the Philippine Embassy," said the voice on the other end. "I'm sorry to disturb you, but I have been asked to give you a message."

The mention of the Philippines made Sam feel uneasy. He had become increasingly worried during the past week about the fate of his Filipino "client," and frustrated by his inability to make contact with him. "Who is the message from?" he asked.

"The message is from Mr. Ramon Pinta."

"Great!" exclaimed Sam. "I've been hoping to hear from him. How is he?"

The diplomat continued with his script. "You have been doing some work for him, I believe?"

"That's right. I've been trying to help him. His wife died, and he didn't seem to have anywhere else to turn. How is he? Is everything all right?"

"Yes. I am happy to say that Mr. Pinta returned home to the Philippines yesterday to be with his family."

"Oh," said Hoffman warily. "That's nice."

"Before he left, Mr. Pinta asked the embassy to please give you a message. That is why I am calling."

"Right. So what's the message?"

"He said to tell you that because he is returning home, he no longer wishes you to pursue the matter he discussed with you. He would like you to stop investigating, please. He said that you would know what that meant."

"I see," said Hoffman quietly. "Thank you for the call."

When he had hung up the phone, Hoffman pounded his desk so hard that it made his hand throb with pain. He knew exactly what the message meant. It meant that Ramon Pinta, the little man with the bad teeth, was dead.

-II-

The Evil Eye

10

The Anvil began to fill up at five-thirty, as the office blocks along Knightsbridge disgorged their daytime prisoners. Sam Hoffman took a seat by the window and gazed up at Hammoud's building across the street. In the late-afternoon light, the facade looked almost pink. He counted up five floors and scanned the windows. People were still at work in most of the offices, but the blinds were all drawn so it was impossible to see in. The large office at the corner of the building was dark. It was like a macabre piggy bank: stuffed with money, but closed to the world. Lina Alwan was inside. He wanted to get her out.

A young woman sat down next to Hoffman. She was wearing a short skirt and a bustier, and she had a baseball cap turned sideways on her head. Dangling from her ears were two condoms made up to look like earrings. She asked Hoffman for a light in an accent that was unmistakably American. Hoffman lit her cigarette and returned to staring out the window until she left. Her seat was taken a few minutes later by a young man from the north of England, to guess by his accent, who was dressed in a slick double-breasted suit and carrying a cellular telephone. He sat down with his beer in one hand and the phone in the other and began calling his mates back home in Wigan or Scunthorpe or wherever it was, boasting about how much money he was making in the big city. He was either a drug dealer or a securities trader, it was hard to tell. Eventually he noticed the American girl in the bustier, now propped against the bar, and drifted over to talk to her. Hoffman felt old. He disapproved.

Out on the street there was a moment of excitement as a police cruiser suddenly broke from its lane and raced down Knightsbridge toward Harrods, its siren wheezing like a double harmonica. Hoffman thought at first that it might be another bomb alert, but the siren noise gradually disappeared into the caverns of Belgravia.

A few minutes past six, the offices on the fifth floor of Lina's building started to go dark one by one, and a stream of people began flowing out of the building. Hoffman was afraid he would miss her, so he moved to the door of the pub. A motorcycle messenger was standing just outside, cradling his helmet in his hands, catching the last of the late-afternoon sun. He had blond hair, the color of straw, and looked like a motorized Viking. The messenger turned away when Hoffman caught his eye; he walked to his huge Honda and roared off.

Hoffman almost didn't see her, she slipped out the door so quickly and threaded so deftly into the crowd. It was only the tight black tuft of hair and the sharp profile that made her visible at all, bobbing along amid the stream of sallow pedestrians. He lost sight of her momentarily, then saw her float to the surface again at the corner, where she waited to cross the street. Hoffman thought it unwise to show himself yet—they were still so close to the office— so he followed thirty yards behind until they were inside the park and had crossed the arched bridge over the little grove of flowers and ferns known as The Dell. As Lina headed up the hill toward Marble Arch, Hoffman quickened his pace until he was almost even with her. She turned toward her pursuer, and when she saw that it was Hoffman, her eyes registered at once fear and relief.

"Hi, there," said Hoffman. "What a coincidence, running into you like this."

"Go away," she answered. Her eyes darted across the meadow to see who might be watching. They were alone except for a woman, sitting on a bench and listening to her Sony Walkman, and a Pakistani schoolboy kicking a soccer ball. Her gaze settled back on Hoffman. The eyes were flashing little darts of light now, more like anger than fear. "You mustn't do this. I can't talk to you." She turned abruptly and continued on her path toward Park Lane.

"Hey, wait a minute," said Hoffman, running to catch up with her. "I need to tell you something." He reached out for her arm, but she pulled it away.

"I can't," she said angrily. "It's not safe here. They may be watching."

Hoffman scanned the hillside. He gestured over the crest of the hill, toward a dark and deserted area where the park keeper had his cottage. "We'll be okay there," he said. "Just for a few minutes. We need to talk. Really."

Lina looked carefully in all directions. They seemed to be alone, but it was impossible to know. Hoffman reached for her arm again; this time she followed. They walked in silence toward the glen, both of them glancing back over their shoulders every few steps to make sure no one was following. As the brush grew thicker around them, Hoffman stopped and turned to her.

"I had to see you," he said. "To warn you about your boss, Hammoud. He's dangerous."

She stared at him, incredulous for a moment. "Is that what you had to tell me? That Mr. Hammoud is dangerous? That's very thoughtful of you." She shook her head.

"I'm serious," said Hoffman. "Do you remember the Filipino man who came to see me about his wife? He's disappeared. The embassy fed me a story about how he's gone home and doesn't need any more help, but it's a lie. I think Hammoud had him killed just because he came to talk to me. Now I'm worried they might come after you."

Linda's voice was like ice. "They already have. That's what you don't understand." She started walking again, toward a stand of trees and shrubs that formed a kind of natural enclosure.

Hoffman pursued her. "When?" he asked.

"After the Darwishes' party. The chief of security warned me about contact with foreigners. He seemed to know who you were."

"What did you tell him?"

"The truth. I said I never met you before the party and I had no intention of seeing you again. Now will you leave me alone?"

"I'm sorry," said Hoffman. "I didn't know. But we're safe here. I'm sure no one followed me. And it's nice to see you again." He tried to smile.

Lina didn't answer. The canopy of trees was tighter now as they went deeper into the enclosure, and there was a woodsy smell of wet moss underfoot. It had a familiar feel; she had a sudden recollection that it was in a forest glen like this that she had let a boy put his hand on her breast for the first time. Then he had slipped the other hand inside her panties, and she had run away.

"I have to go," she said.

Hoffman knew he should let her leave. He had delivered his warning, and every additional minute she stayed with him was risky. But there was something else he wanted. He leaned toward her, so that his lips were nearly touching her ear. "I need help," he said.

"With what?"

"To get enough information to go to the police about Hammoud. The man is dangerous. Unless somebody does something, he'll keep terrorizing people."

"It's not my problem," she said slowly. "All I did was drop Mr. Pinta a note about his wife. I was just being polite."

Hoffman looked at her, imploring her with his eyes as he had done the night of the party. They were coming to the edge of the wooded enclosure. On the path fifty yards ahead, a man was walking a dog. They didn't have much more time, and Hoffman knew that he wasn't just on a mission of mercy, he was working. He still had a client, even if he was dead, and he still wanted information.

"Who really owns Coyote?" he asked in a whisper. "Do you know?"

"Stop it," she said.

"Please. I need help. I promised Pinta I would do something, but I can't go to the police without more information. What's Hammoud doing in Iraq?"

"Stop it!" she repeated. She had stepped up her pace now so that it was almost a trot. With her clipped hair and her long legs, she looked like a show horse.

Hoffman threw out a last card. It was all he had. "What's Oscar Trading?"

Lina turned back and looked him dead in the eye. Her face was suddenly ashen. "I don't know," she said sharply. "Leave me alone."

They were leaving the wooded enclosure now and returning to the open meadow, on a path that cut diagonally toward Speaker's Corner. There were benches every few dozen yards, with a few hearty souls sitting alone in the dwindling light. Hoffman quickly surveyed them and then stopped as his eyes settled on one face, perhaps thirty yards away, staring dumbly at a newspaper. He had seen it before. The man wasn't carrying a helmet now, and he had put on a gray trench coat to cover his clothes. But it was the same straw-blond hair. The motorcycle messenger who had been sunning himself in front of The Anvil a half hour before had now surfaced on the other side of the park in a new set of clothes. Hoffman scanned the meadow, wondering what to do. Lina saw the tension in his face.

"What's wrong?" she asked.

"Nothing," said Hoffman. It wasn't even a good lie. He thought a moment, and then spoke to her in a whisper. "Now listen to me, Lina. Please do exactly what I say, and you'll be fine. Understand? First, I want you to slap me, hard. And then I want you to say to me, as loud as you can, that I should stop following you. And then run away. Got it?"

Her eyes showed that she understood, but her body was frozen by the realization that they had been followed.

"Do it, goddammit!" said Hoffman. "Now!"

She swung hard, startled by his voice. Her palm hit his cheek like a sudden crack of thunder.

"Stop following me!" she shouted. Her eyes were glinting. The rage was real. "You bastard! I told you I didn't want to see you again after the party, and I meant it. So fuck off!" She slapped him again, even harder, and then took off running across the meadow toward Park Lane.

Several people in the park looked up from their benches, including the motorcycle messenger. Hoffman watched Lina run away, feeling the sting on his cheek and cursing himself for his stupidity. At least he had given her an alibi.

11

Lina wandered in a daze after leaving Hoffman. She crossed Park Lane and walked south, then east into Mayfair, then south to Piccadilly. It was aimless motion, almost random, as if she were trying to escape not a person or a place but something inside her own body. She tried to think what she would tell Professor Sarkis, but her mind was pure anxiety, with no space left for thought. It was like hearing that she had a disease. A few hours before, she had been well; now, suddenly, she was ill. The only therapy was to keep moving. She boarded the subway at Green Park and rode it one stop to Victoria Station, where she submerged herself for a few minutes in the ebb tide of commuters. She knew Hammoud's men must be watching her, even there. They were like a light you couldn't extinguish because you didn't know where it was. She headed back to the Underground and took the Circle Line one stop to Sloane Square. She wasn't ready to go home yet, so she got off there and waited for another train.

Lina sat on the wooden bench in the dirty station, staring up at the posters of women discarding their clothes in their enthusiasm for tonic water and candy. A street musician was singing Bob Dylan songs off-key at the exit. A gypsy woman in rags was working her way down the benches, pleading for money in an unrecognizable language. It was a scene of spiritual devastation that matched her inner turmoil. Lina felt suddenly that she should say a prayer, but she wasn't sure she knew how. That was another of her problems. She was alienated from her own religion! She still baked cookies on the Eid al Fittir, and politely asked God to vouchsafe the good health of anyone who walked in the front door, but she couldn't pray. Her Islam was little more than a vague Arab Unitarianism—a sense of a hidden Allah somewhere out there, who was visible in sunsets and flowers and the birth of children but was unreachable in a crisis.

Another train was arriving in the station. The doors were opening, beckoning. Lina took a seat and closed her eyes against the dirt and commotion of the Circle Line. As the car swayed back and forth, she repeated to herself in Arabic a prayer she had heard her father say: "God is the light of the Heavens and the Earth. The likeness of his light is . . ." She tried to remember the rest, but it was gone. The only thing she could think of was the simplest prayer of all: *La ilaha illa-Llah. Mohammed rasul allah*— "There is no God but God, and Mohammed is His Prophet." It felt strange to pray. Her young Arab friends would be embarrassed for her. Prayer was for Iranians and crazy men with woolly beards. *"La ilaha illa-Llah. Mohammed rasul allah."* She said it over many times, the words as soothing as the sound of water passing over a stone. The train reached her stop at Notting Hill Gate; Lina stayed on one more stop to Bayswater and then walked back toward home.

Haram. It was like a game, all this praying and changing of trains and missing stops. She wasn't trying to fool Hammoud's men, who had already seen the worst and knew everything that was knowable. She was trying to fool the deeper cause of her misfortune, the universal but invisible force the Arabs called *Al Ain*, or the Evil Eye.

Whatever her confusion about God, Lina believed in the Evil Eye. It was a force of nature, omnipresent and utterly unpredictable. People spoke about the Evil Eye in vague terms, as if it were the personification of bad luck, or fate, but it was something more specific and menacing than that. The Evil Eye was the embodiment of the trait in human nature that wishes other people ill. It was envy; it was delight in the suffering of others; it was the thirst for revenge. The Evil Eye was like your worst enemy: It took from you what you prized the most. If you had beautiful legs, and the Evil Eye saw how much people admired them, then you would have a terrible accident and your legs would be broken and disfigured. If you loved to read books, the Evil Eye would conspire to make you blind; if you were born to be a musician, it would make you deaf. To keep away this insidious force, you had to trick it. That was the only hope. When a child was born to a neighbor, a simple Iraqi peasant woman would say, "How ugly the child is." This was meant to fool the Evil Eye, to make it think there was nothing to envy, and therefore nothing to destroy, so that it would leave the child alone.

But what if the Evil Eye was so intent on destroying you that it ignored all your tricks and changing trains? Then you had to take desperate measures. When Lina finally reached her flat on Lansdowne Walk, she went straight to her room and opened her jewelry box. Like every woman of the East, she had been told as a girl that there was a special way to protect yourself from the Evil Eye, and that was to wear turquoise, which was to *Al Ain* what a cross was to a vampire. *Feyrouz*, they called the stone in Arabic, and it was no accident that this was also the name taken by the Arab world's most beloved singer, who sang of ancestral villages and lost innocence and doomed love. Lina had laughed at the silly superstition often enough. But now she took a turquoise brooch from her jewelry box and pinned it to her silk blouse. And felt better for it.

━━

Lina turned on the television, thinking it might distract her, but it only made her feel more alone. All she could find were comedy shows, with the sound of hollow, pre-recorded laughter echoing in the background as the characters said unfunny things to each other. She opened a can of soup and then, realizing that she wasn't hungry, poured it down the drain. She dialed the number of her university friend Helen Copaken in Blackheath, but there was no answer. She paced the length of her small living room. The poster of the Ishtar Gate loomed on the wall like the entrance to a prison.

She wandered into her bedroom and retrieved from the closet a picture of her one serious boyfriend, which she looked at nowadays only when she was very upset. He was the man her father would have wanted her to marry, an Iraqi exile from an even more aristocratic family than her own, who had lost touch with his roots so completely that he could no longer read or write Arabic. He professed to be a rebel, and took Lina to reggae bars and parties where people snorted cocaine. For a year, he had pressed her to sleep with him. When Lina finally relented and passionately made love with him, in the hope that this prize might warm his cold heart, he had quickly lost interest. It turned out that he was like the other Arab men. He wanted to marry a virgin. She put the photograph back in the closet and lay on the bed for a while. Finally, after taking off her clothes and putting them back on again, she decided she had better call her friend Randa Aziz.

"Shaku maku," said Lina into the receiver, trying to sound cheerful. It was an Iraqi slang expression that meant, roughly, "what's going on?"

"What happened to you after work, *habibti*? I thought we were going to rendezvous on New Bond Street and go shopping."

Lina groaned. She had completely forgotten. "I'm sorry. I was busy. I lost track of the time." Her heart was suddenly racing again, and she had trouble getting the words out.

"Busy? With who?"

"Nobody. I don't want to talk about it."

"Ho-ho. Who is he?"

"Nothing. Forget it. He's bad news. And so am I."

"Hey, is everything okay? You sound a little strange."

"I'm all right. Just tired."

"Well, take care of yourself, girl."

"Listen, Randa, I was wondering: What are you doing tonight? Can I come over?"

"I guess so. Tony is here. We were about to have dinner."

"Of course. I forgot about Tony. We'll do it another time." Tony Hashem was Randa's wealthy new boyfriend. Lina tried to sound cheery, but the disappointment in her voice was obvious.

"Hold on. Tell you what. Why don't you come over in an hour, okay? I was going to read Tony's fortune after dinner. I'll do yours, too. We'll have a party."

"No, you're busy. You and Tony want to be together. Some other time."

"Come! I insist. I need an audience. And it sounds like you need company."

"I could use some, actually. I'm feeling a little strange."

"See you at ten," said Randa. "Bring us a bottle of wine and I'll be your friend forever."

———

Lina arrived promptly at Randa's flat in Chelsea, wine in hand, and rang the buzzer. It was misting outside, and she stood shivering for nearly thirty seconds before Randa finally opened the door, with a giggle. Standing behind her was Tony Hashem, smiling like the cat who just ate the canary. He was tall and dark, and too handsome for his own good. He looked as if he had, seconds before, zipped up his fly.

"Maybe I should come back," said Lina.

"No, no," answered Randa, adjusting her dress. "Come in. We were just doing the dishes. You know Tony, don't you?"

Lina nodded. Tony Hashem was the eldest son of an exiled Iraqi businessman who, like Marwan Darwish, had become rich in a hurry. Decent Iraqis rolled their eyes when they talked about such people. What saved young

Tony from being just another hoodlum was that he was utterly uninterested in politics. His ideology began and ended with the concept of having a good time. He was, in that sense, a perfect match for Randa.

Randa opened the wine and poured a glass for each of them. As she handed one to Lina, she noticed the turquoise brooch. *"Feyrouz!"* she said. "Are you in trouble?"

"No," said Lina quickly. "Not that I know of. I just thought it looked nice."

"Um-hum. Very nice." Randa nodded her head. She was unconvinced.

"I'm celebrating tonight," said Tony merrily, oblivious to anyone's concerns but his own.

"Why is that?"

"Because tomorrow is my thirtieth birthday, when I will no longer be a slave to the draft."

"Does that mean you can go home again?" asked Lina. Like most young Iraqi men in exile, Tony had stayed away from Baghdad for years to avoid serving in the army.

"Why not? Now they'll have to fight the next war without Tony Hashem. Just like the last one, and the one before that."

War had been a fact of nature in Iraq for more than a decade, like wind or rain. As in every war, the burden mostly had been borne by poor people, who couldn't afford to get out of the way. For these ordinary Iraqis, the decade of war had been misery compounded on misery. But for people like the Hashems and Darwishes and the Hammouds, it had been a decade of opportunity. The Ruler had survived all the wars. Even sanctions were an opportunity to make money, if one had the right contacts and could smuggle things across the border.

"Maybe there won't be another war," said Lina. "Maybe he has finally learned his lesson."

"Who? The Ruler?"

She nodded.

"Never!" said young Hashem, emboldened by the glass of wine in his hand. "The Ruler needs war like a baby needs milk."

"Tony!" said Randa, raising her hands. Iraqis didn't say things like that, even at home, even in London.

"Sorry." He kissed her on the cheek. "But the Ruler doesn't matter anymore. Not the way he did."

"How brave you are tonight," said Randa. "But what are you talking about?"

"The Ruler is ill," said Tony in a low voice. "That's what I heard from one of my father's friends the other night. He said that something is wrong in Baghdad, and my father said it's true. I heard them talking."

"What did they say?"

"That there must be a problem in Baghdad, because the Ruler's family is fighting. The brothers are angry at each other, and especially at their cousin Osman. It's like they're all getting ready for a punch-up when the old boy is gone. That's what my father said, anyway. I know he's worried, because he just moved some money to Switzerland, and he wouldn't do that unless something was really happening."

"That's nonsense," said Randa. "Don't you think, Lina?"

"I don't think anything." She frowned. Talking about the Ruler reminded her of the office.

Randa changed the subject. "I'll put the coffee on," she said. "How do you like it?"

"Medium sweet," called out Tony and Lina at the same time.

Randa went to the kitchen and put a brass pot on the stove. She let it boil once, then twice, then a third time, and then poured out the thick black coffee into three small cups. She arranged them on a tray with some sweet Arab pastries and carried it into the living room.

"Drink your coffee, darlings," she said. "Then I'll read your fortunes."

The three attacked their tiny cups, sucking the thick black foam off the top and letting it slide down their throats, leaving the heavier sludge on the bottom. Tony lit a cigarette for himself and for Randa and offered one to Lina.

"No thanks," said Lina. "I'm giving them up."

"Since when?" said Randa. "You really must be worried about something. The Evil Eye doesn't care if you smoke. Believe me. Have a cigarette. It will calm you down."

"All right," said Lina, taking a cigarette from the pack.

Tony was the first to finish his coffee, leaving a dark pool of grounds on the bottom. He turned the cup over on its saucer and waited for the grounds to dry into the pattern that, when read, would constitute his fortune.

"You, too," said Randa, nodding toward Lina.

"Not tonight," said Lina. "I'm not in the mood."

"Come on," said Randa. "You need some good news. I can tell. There are only good fortunes tonight. The Evil Eye is very far away." Prodded by her friend, Lina turned her cup over.

When Tony's cup had dried, Randa picked it up and held it to the light. She turned it slowly in her hand, looking all around the circumference, and then smiled at Tony. An ordinary mortal would have seen in the cup nothing but dried coffee encrusted in a random pattern. But in Randa's skilled hand, the cup contained the whole universe.

"I see a peacock," she said, pointing to an indistinct smudge. "A big peacock. That's very good. It means that you are a proud man, proud of yourself. Proud of your body." She gave him a wink, then continued.

"Then I see a fish. That's very good, too. It means good luck. See here, this little squiggle? That's the fish. So you are lucky, and good things are happening to you. And you feel proud, but not too proud.

"Then, I see wide, open spaces." She pointed to a part of the cup where none of the black lava had spread. "This is very good. Problems are far away from you. You are easygoing, you have no worries."

"I'm out of the army!" said Tony.

"Yes. Perhaps that's what it means."

"Excellent!"

"Now, after the wide, open spaces, I see a tower of

glory! This is very important.'' She pointed to the residue
of a long drip of coffee grounds that flowed to the lip of
the cup. ''See the tower of glory? This means that you
will have some big achievement soon. Maybe you will
make a lot of money. Yes, probably that. A lot of money.''

''*Ya salaam!*'' said Tony, smiling. ''Why not?''

''And then,'' she was beaming now, ''you won't believe
me, but this is what I see, right here in the cup. I see a
bride. What else could it be?'' She pointed to a last black
blob of dried coffee. ''Yes. It is a bride. See the veil and
the face. Here's the nose and the chin. See? Which means
that you will be married soon.''

''And who will it be? Is she beautiful?''

''Oh, yes,'' said Randa. ''Very beautiful. And very
sexy.''

Tony gave her a wet kiss on the lips. Lina wondered
whether the two of them might start up again on the couch,
but Randa disentangled herself and turned back toward her
friend. She still had work to do.

''Now your turn,'' she said, taking up Lina's cup. She
held it up to the light and frowned. She turned it 180
degrees, looked at it more carefully and then frowned
again. ''This must be my cup,'' she said.

''No, it's not,'' said Lina. ''It's mine. What's wrong?''

''Nothing. It's just strange, that's all.''

''Read it.''

''Maybe later. Let's have another glass of wine.''

''Read it!'' repeated Lina.

''Okay.'' She took a deep breath. ''First, do you see all
these spots?'' She pointed to a part of the cup that was
dotted with small round spots of dried coffee.

Lina nodded.

''They are eyes. This means that a lot of people are
watching you. There is a lot of envy. People are jealous
of what you have, and they want it.''

Lina touched the turquoise brooch for protection. *Al Ain*
seemed to be in the cup, too.

''Okay. So these people are watching you. I don't know
why. And then, there is a lot of confusion. See, here.''

She pointed to a crooked, uneven rim of coffee grounds that had dried in a kind of gray-black mist. "This means confusion. Things are swirling around, and you don't know what to do."

"What comes after that?"

"It's a funny shape. Here, look. Do you see it? I think it's a camel. Yes, it's a camel. See the four legs?"

"What does a camel mean?"

"It's good. It means that you will go on a trip outside the country. Yes, it's good."

Lina froze. "Could it be Iraq, the country that I'm going to?"

"It could be. I don't know. Probably not. Why would you go to Iraq? No. It's probably someplace nice. France. Or Tahiti."

"What comes next?"

"After that it's hard to read. There is a lot of black. It's all black, really. It's hard to see a pattern."

"Let me see," said Lina. She looked at the cup, where Randa was pointing, and saw a broad swath of dried coffee, dark and impenetrable. She shook her head. "I know what that means. Black means bad luck."

"Yes, sometimes. It can mean bad luck, and sadness. But it can also mean that the real pattern beneath is covered over. So don't worry about it. I don't think it means bad luck. It could be good."

"Stop trying to be nice. What comes after the black?"

"That's the strange thing, actually. After that, it's all white. I'm not sure I've ever seen a cup like this. So much black and then nothing." She held up the cup and showed Lina. After the dark swath of black, the cup was pure white nearly half the way around, as if no coffee had dripped on that side at all.

"Oh, God. What does it mean?"

"I don't know. But I think it's good. It's a long, long period of no problems after all this black. See? It's as if you break through the clouds into blue sky. That's what I think it probably means."

"Come on. Tell me the truth, Randa. What else could it mean?"

"I'm not sure. Different people read the cups different ways."

"What does it mean?" Lina's voice was almost a shout.

"Some people could read it some other way, but I don't believe it. Do you want me to say, anyway?"

"Yes."

"Okay. Sometimes, a long white space after so much black means that a person is in heaven. In paradise. Pure white."

"Dead."

"Yes, dead."

"Who is the person? Is it me?"

"Maybe you. Or someone you love. But I'm telling you, Lina, I don't think that's what the cup says. I think it means that after this hard time, when people are watching you, and everything is confused, you will be happy for a long, long time. Pure happiness."

"Don't worry, be happy!" said Tony Hashem mindlessly. He was bored. He wanted to get back to couch dancing with his girlfriend.

"Right. Be happy!" said Randa.

"Right," said Lina. "I have to go."

"I'll walk you to the door," said Randa, taking her friend's hand. Lina was walking slowly and unsteadily, a step at a time. Randa led her into the hall and then closed the door behind so Tony couldn't hear what she was saying.

"Now, listen to me," said Randa softly. "Forget this business with the coffee cup. It's superstitious nonsense. I don't know what's upsetting you, but I can tell you one thing: You're worrying too much about work. You've been looking awful the past few days. Do you know that? Awful. The rumor mill says Professor Sarkis was ragging you about something the other day. Is that right?"

Lina nodded.

"Well, Professor Sarkis can kiss my bum. How do you like that? He can kiss my bum."

Lina tried to laugh. It was little more than a loud exhale.

"Seriously, dearie, if you let Hammoud and the boys get to you, they'll drive you crazy. Completely bonkers. So don't take them too seriously. What's the worst they could do? Fire you, right? I mean, this isn't Baghdad, and they don't have any army, and the only thing they have going for them is that they scare everyone. I mean, you don't have any family back in Iraq, do you?"

"Yes," said Lina. "One person. My aunt."

"Oh. Sorry. You never told me. But believe me, they're not going to do anything to her. They have too many other things to worry about. So I say the hell with them. Let them play their little games, and definitely take their money, but don't let them get you down. Right?"

"I prayed today," said Lina.

"You *what*?" Like most of Lina's young Arab friends—Christian and Muslim alike—Randa was devoutly secular. To them, religion was the enemy of having a good time. It was for fanatics who chanted *"Maku wali illa Ali"*—"There is no governor except Ali"—and cut off people's hands for stealing.

"I prayed," repeated Lina.

Randa shook her head. Her friend was in worse shape than she had thought. "You want a Valium? I have some extra."

"No," said Lina. "I'm okay."

"Don't let them get you down," repeated Randa. "Remember, fear is all they've got. Now, get some sleep."

Lina nodded. Randa was right. But she wasn't sure the brave talk would fool the Evil Eye.

12

Sam Hoffman telephoned Prince Jalal bin Abdel-Rahman that night. It was a kind of penance for his mistake that afternoon with Lina, and his mistake before that with the Filipino cook, and so many mistakes he had made over the years in trying to prove that he was not the sort of selfish and irresponsible man that the Saudi prince had taken him to be. As luck had it, Jalal was in London that week, and of course he wanted to see Sam again after so many years, and why not that very night? For if there is one thing that Arab men are better at than starting a feud, it is ending one—embracing, forgiving and forgetting. As he put down the phone, Sam could almost feel the prick of Jalal's beard against his face as he kissed Sam on each cheek and welcomed him back to the tribe of reasonable men.

Prince Jalal lived in a grand Regency town house in Hyde Park Square. The prince's architect had left standing the cream-colored facade of the building—with its perfectly proportioned Doric columns and its window pediments in the neoclassical style of Robert Adam—and scooped out everything inside so that there was nothing left except the shell. Within this elegant and austere container, the prince had built himself a modern pleasure palace. It was the product of an imagination that had feasted on too many *Playboy* magazines when the prince was a student at Colorado State. The sub-basement contained an indoor swimming pool, with thick glass walls like an aquarium so that the prince could watch his guests cavorting in the water. On the floor above was a squash court and an exercise room and, next to them, a game room with pinball machines and video games and a change machine that dispensed American quarters without the need to put in an American dollar. The next two floors contained the normal attributes of a wealthy man's home: formal living and dining rooms, bedrooms, offices, pantries, salons. Above that was the defining feature of the house: a two-story pleasure dome that seemed to have been created entirely for sex. There were beds surrounded by mirrors, a Hollywood-style screening room with easy chairs and a sofabed; there was even a small room in which the prince had installed the remains of an automobile so that he could have the pleasure of mounting some of his younger women guests in the backseat of a car, just as he had at Colorado State.

Hoffman arrived just after ten, which he recalled was the hour when things began to get lively at Jalal's house. A British bodyguard answered the door and led him through the metal detector. He was the modern version of Jeeves, polite and deferential but capable of hitting a target between the eyes at a distance of fifty feet. It had become the fashion among Saudi princes to hire as their footmen and valets former N.C.O.s like these from the Special Air Services. The pay was adequate, and the SAS men got their pick of leftover food and women.

Jalal was waiting for Hoffman in his lair on the third floor. He looked just as Hoffman had remembered him: perfectly groomed and perfectly horrifying. His skin was a creamy brown, without a blemish or a wrinkle. The beard was like a Seurat painting, as if each hair had been painted in separately, each with its own particular shade. The eyes were wide and dreamy from so many years of pleasure and drug use, but the body was still trim and well toned from daily workouts in the gym. He was dressed in fine linen trousers, a silk shirt that, on a woman, would be called a blouse, and a cashmere jacket so perfectly cut that it fit like a second skin. Hoffman extended his hand, but Jalal gathered him in an embrace.

"My dear, my dear, my dear," said the prince, kissing Hoffman once, twice, a third time. He had that soft, silky way with other men that, among Gulf Arabs, was meant to convey not homosexual desire but good manners. It was, like a limp handshake, a sign of gentility.

"You're looking well, Jack," said Hoffman, using the name Jalal had picked up many years before, when he was a student in Boulder.

"Come with me," said the prince with a trace of a smile. "We're watching movies."

He led Hoffman into the screening room. Two girls, who looked no older than fifteen, were lying on the bed. One was blond, one brunet. Both were wearing only their bras and panties. Both looked very nervous.

Jalal nodded toward them. "They're from Romania, I think. Or Albania. I don't know. Where are you from, girls?" They smiled up at him dumbly. They didn't speak English, apparently. Sam was standing uncomfortably at the edge of the room. Jalal took his hand and pulled him inside.

"Come, my dear Sam. I want to show you my new movie. Then we can eat some food, and then we can teach these nice Romanian girls about sex. What do you say?"

"I came to see you, Jack. I want to talk."

"Of course, of course. We will talk. But not yet. Where are your manners? What would you like to drink? Arak? Whiskey? I have some very good cocaine. The best! What do you like, my dear? I'm drinking Polish vodka."

"A beer," said Sam.

The prince called out to one of his servants, who brought the drinks and took away the girls. Jalal settled into one of the easy chairs. He pressed a button somewhere, and the lights dimmed and the movie started. Sam awaited the show with a sense of dread. For years, Jalal's favorite hobby had been making movies that recorded extremes of human perversity and debauchery, particularly his own.

"You will love this one," said the prince. "It is about parachutes."

As he spoke, the screen was alight with footage of Jalal himself, skydiving. He was wearing a bright red jumpsuit and had a demonic look on his face, which was visible even beneath the helmet. He was waving to the camera with one hand. The credits were rolling now, repeating Jalal's name over and over—produced by, directed by, conceived by—while the camera followed his long descent to the ground.

"Let me explain what you're about to watch," said Jalal. "I invented a game that is a bit unusual. It's a kind of Russian roulette with parachutes, you see. I offer anyone one hundred thousand dollars if they will jump with me. But each of the divers must choose from six parachutes, with the knowledge that one of the six will not open. That is the fun, you see? They pick, and then I jump with them, and I get to watch."

Hoffman closed his eyes. This latest game was vintage Jalal. A few years before, in Saudi Arabia, he had organized a hunting party that featured a live man from Somalia as the prey, rather than a fox. That had been recorded on video, too. Hoffman had watched it during one of his last visits with Jalal, before the rupture. It was hard to describe the feeling Hoffman had then, and now, of being in the presence of a man who could buy anything. These princes of the desert routinely experienced everything that ordinary men dreamed of: the most beautiful women, the purest drugs, the most exquisite food. What was left, to tickle the senses? Only the pornography of pain. Every decadent society creates something similar. The Romans had their lion pits and gladiator contests. The medieval Europeans had their public dismemberments and hangings. The only modern innovation had been to capture this sort of thing on video so that it could be enjoyed later.

"Here we go," said Jalal. "Watch this!" The tape showed a frightened-looking man standing in the open cabin of a small plane, looking at six parcels arrayed on the floor.

"See, here, this fellow is named Bill, I think. See him picking the parachutes. He looks so nervous! He picks up one, then another, weighing them. What a silly boy! Of course they all weigh the same. See his face, so scared, but he wants the money, too, so he's going to play. Now he's trying on one of the parachutes. No, it doesn't feel right. Try another. This one feels good. Yes. Okay. Now I'm telling him it's time to go. That's my hand, waving. The door is open and we're walking to the edge. See the sky and the ground, way below. Look at his face. He's so scared! Can you see? Now we're about to jump. He's closing his eyes. Ha! He's praying. Now he jumps, and I'm following him with my camera. I'm catching up to him, and now we're even, so you can see his face. What was his name? Bill. I'm giving him the signal. Now watch. See him pull the cord. He's waiting for it. Where is it? He pulls the cord again. Where is it? Do you see the look on his face? Nothing is happening! He's terrified. See his little legs flapping in the air, like a bug! He's trying to run away. Here's a close look at his face. Do you see the mouth open? He's screaming, but nobody can hear him. And now he's grabbing for me. See the arms flailing. He can't bear to look down, the ground is coming up so fast. Do you see? He's so scared. So frightened."

The excitement in Jalal's voice suddenly peaked and then fell to a normal tone. "Ah, well. That's the end of the good part. Here, now, Bill feels a jerk and suddenly he's slowing. He can't believe it! The parachute is opening. He's alive! He isn't going to die after all. I've tricked him, you see. That is my game! All six parachutes are good. All of them! But they're all rigged with a time delay so that each person who plays my game will think that he has chosen the one chute that doesn't open. It's a clever idea, isn't it? Like safe sex. All the fun, but nobody gets hurt."

The screen went dark, and the lights came up. Hoffman rubbed his eyes.

"What do you think?" asked the prince, with a gesture toward the screen.

"Me?" Hoffman thought a moment. "I think you're out of your mind."

"You do?" The prince was smiling. Evidently he took it as a compliment. "My dear Sam, it is so good to see you again. You are so honest."

Sam was still trying to make sense of what he had just seen. "Did you pay Bill the money?"

"Of course," said Jalal. "What is money, for a show like this?"

Hoffman took a deep breath. What frightened him most about Jalal was how easy it was to fall back into the same fellowship they had known before. No wonder Jalal had been surprised that Sam—after watching his movies and ogling his women and sharing his drugs—had suddenly discovered scruples over a puny business deal. How rude that must have seemed. But the past is always forgiven when you are in the prince's tent. That was part of the princely demeanor, to be always fearless and nearly always forgiving. Jalal was looking at him now with a twinkle in his eye.

"Shall I call the girls? Or shall we eat? I have pheasants, I think. Or maybe they are quails."

"Neither. I need to talk. That's why I came."

"Very well," said Jalal, affecting to be bored but, of course, secretly curious about what had brought Sam back after so long an absence. "Perhaps something more to drink?"

As if summoned by an invisible buzzer, a servant entered the room with another bottle of beer for Sam and a tray of caviar and canapés. A second man, a Sudanese, judging by the ink-black color of his skin, arrived with a bottle of vodka for Jalal. He poured a few ounces into the prince's glass so that it was at the same even level as before—neither too much nor too little—and then retreated. Sam recalled that this same servant had accompanied Jalal when he and Sam had traveled once to the Riviera. Wherever they had gone, regardless of the waiters who were nominally employed in the restaurants and bars, he had served the prince his food and drink in this same way—personally delivering to his plate a few morsels to replace what the prince had eaten, pouring a few drops to replace what he had drunk—so that the royal plate and glass were always half full. After a while, this bizarre ritual had come to seem normal to Sam. Anything else would have been crude and impolite and unworthy of a prince.

"So, what do you want to talk about?" asked Jalal, after taking the smallest sip of his vodka.

"I need a favor," said Sam.

"Oh, good. And what is it?"

"I need some information about an Iraqi businessman named Nasir Hammoud."

"Tsk! Tsk! So this is mere business, eh? I was hoping it was something more delicate. That you had developed some unspeakable desire I could help you fulfill. Or that you had committed a dastardly crime and needed my help to find a hiding place. But it is nothing so interesting as that."

"Nope. Just business. Someone told me that you have some investments with this man Hammoud, so I figured that you must know a bit about him."

"I do, indeed. We are partners in a number of ventures. We are building factories in the desert. That sort of thing. And we share the same lawyers."

"I heard that you were partners on a petrochemical deal. Is that so?"

"Yes. Very good! That deal was supposed to be secret. You are such a clever man, my dear Sam. But why do you care about Nasir Hammoud? What can he have done to harm you?"

Hoffman knew it was useless trying to lie to Jalal. He would find out the truth quickly enough, anyway. "He harmed a client of mine, since you asked. A man who worked for him as a cook. I think he had him killed. That upset me. And I'm worried that he might try to hurt other people who work for him. The man is dangerous."

Jalal snorted regally, like a prize bull. "Of course Hammoud is dangerous! That is the management style of these

Iraqis. They have no manners, I am sorry to say. But there it is. And there is nothing you or I can do about it.''

"But I'd like to do something about it. Hammoud is a bully. He intimidates his employees, maybe has them killed. That's not allowed in London. Or at least, it shouldn't be.''

"My dear Sam, you really haven't changed. You are such a naïf. Of course it shouldn't be allowed. But it is. And there you are.''

"Look, Jack, I'm sorry to sound like a prude. But if I could get some information about Hammoud, I could go to the authorities, and they could put some heat on him.''

Jalal snorted again and drained his glass of vodka, which was very unprincely and brought the Sudanese servant padding into the room like Hop-Sing to restore the glass to its genteel mean. "Sam, Sam, Sam," said the prince. "I must explain something to you.''

"Yes. I'm listening.''

"All this talk about Nasir Hammoud is quite beside the point. Really. The issue is not Hammoud. Take my word for it.''

"What's the issue, then?''

"Others. Friends. Don't you understand who is involved?''

"No. Tell me. Who's behind him? The ruler of Iraq?''

Jalal laughed at Sam's innocence. "Yes, of course. But it is more than that, my dear Sam. With this one, you have bitten off a good deal more than you realize.''

"Who else is involved with Hammoud?''

Jalal laughed again. This was becoming another of his games. "Oh, I think you would find a number of other princes of the House of Saud who have invested with this same gentleman. Quite a few. And there are others, in other places.''

"Who else?''

"You might ask certain friends of the king of Jordan.''

"No! Is that so?''

Jalal smiled. "You might ask certain friends of the king of Morocco.''

"What would they say if I asked them?"

Jalal roared. "They wouldn't say a damn thing, of course! And they would take you out and have you shot for even asking the question. But my dear Sam, you are such a lovable fool that even now you do not understand what I am telling you. Because all of these people I have mentioned—these kings and princes, to say nothing of a little worm like Nasir Hammoud—are nothing without the aid of their friends and protectors in the West. And that, my dear Sam, is why you are wasting your time with this silly campaign against this Iraqi chap. Nothing will come of it. The man has friends. So give it up."

"But he's dangerous."

"Give it up. Relax. Enjoy life. I tried to tell you that a few years ago, but you wouldn't listen."

Sam winced at the memory. Five years before, in what had seemed like another lifetime, Jalal had proposed to him a simple business arrangement. Routine, he said. Private banking.

He would pay Sam the sum of five hundred thousand dollars per year if Sam would agree to be the nominal owner of assets worth many times that. The deal was simple. Sam would open in his own name the accounts in the Cayman Islands into which the funds would be deposited, and then turn over the bank books and all other records to Jalal, along with a power of attorney giving Jalal absolute control over the money. It was so easy. All Sam had to agree to do was lie, to claim that he owned certain funds that he did not, in fact, own. But Sam had wanted more information. He had asked why Jalal needed to hide so much money, and how had it been obtained in the first place, and had anybody committed a crime in obtaining it. He wanted to know whether the money came from drug dealing or gunrunning or any of the other activities at which Jalal played to augment his income. But the prince had simply put a finger to his lips, as if to say: Friends don't ask questions. Sam had hemmed and hawed for a few moments and finally—to his own surprise and the much greater astonishment of the prince—had said no. He couldn't do it. It wouldn't be right. In that case, said Jalal, perhaps he should look for another banker. Whereupon Sam had accused his client of trying to bribe him. Which, while technically true, had seemed to the Saudi prince to be a gross breach of manners. And so the friendship had ruptured. Sam had left Jalal's office that day with the conviction that he never, ever wanted to depend on such a man again. And yet, here he was, back again, asking for a favor.

Jalal studied Sam's face. He seemed almost to be reading his mind. "My offer still stands, by the way, anytime you are ready to come down off your high horse. I always need help in opening new accounts."

"No, thanks," said Sam. "Not my line of work."

"Pity. You were such a good banker before you went into this absurd investigation business, or whatever it is."

"Listen, Jack, I really ought to be going. It's late."

"No, it's not. The night is young. The fun is just beginning. Let me call the Romanian girls. I am told they are the last virgins in Bucharest." He clapped his hands and called out in Arabic to the Sudanese servant. The servant entered the salon a few moments later leading the two girls by velvet cords that had been tied around their necks. Each had been dressed in a schoolgirl costume, with a white shirt, navy-blue skirt and knee socks. On a command from the servant, each girl lifted her skirt to reveal her nakedness.

"Are you sure you won't stay, my dear Sam?" asked Jalal.

Sam didn't answer. He looked away from the two poor girls toward the prince and mumbled his thanks: It was late; he really must go. He was in no position to be censorious. He had asked the prince for help and received as much as the prince could offer. It was enough to go away quietly. The prince momentarily left his two Romanian beauties, wrapping their velvet leashes around the doorknob, and walked Sam downstairs to the front entrance.

13

When Lina arrived at work the next morning, she was summoned to Mr. Hammoud's office. It was a rare event. In three years of working for Coyote, she had never been inside his office. She was escorted down the long corridor by Hammoud's British secretary, who seemed to sense how nervous Lina was and kept up a stream of chatter. The old man had returned from Baghdad the previous day, she explained, and had spent the evening at home talking very late with Professor Sarkis. When he came to work that morning, his first request had been to see Miss Alwan. His first request! And now, here they were. The secretary smiled helpfully and punched in the code for Mr. Hammoud's door. As it swung open, the first thing Lina saw was a large portrait of the Ruler, caught in that cruel, blank stare favored by the court photographers. Below the portrait, sitting behind a huge oak desk, was the chairman of Coyote Investment.

Mr. Hammoud rose from the desk when Lina entered the room and then, stiffly, sat down again. He had the tight, compact body of a fighting dog—a boxer or a Rottweiler—but the edges had been softened by his personal masseur and hairstylist and manicurist and valet. The silver-gray hair was perfectly combed. And he wore his clothes as neatly as they had been laid out for him that morning: a dark blue business suit accompanied by a shirt of just the right shade of light blue; massive gold cuff

links; a red paisley tie and a matching red paisley handkerchief in the pocket. The precision of his dress was
intimidating, but it also made him look somewhat uncomfortable, as if he secretly wanted to rip the whole
ensemble to shreds.

"Mabruk!" he said gruffly when she had taken her seat.
"You have been promoted."

"Excuse me?" said Lina. She thought she must have
heard him wrong.

"You will have a new job. Director of advertising. I
will give you a raise of one hundred pounds a week. This
is to show you that we take care of our trusted employees
if they are loyal." He said it all in such a stern monotone
that it sounded more like a funeral announcement than a
promotion, but Lina tried to appear grateful.

"Thank you," she said. "When do I start?"

"Immediately. Today. Someone is moving your things
right now, out of the accounting department to the new
office."

"Thank you," said Lina again. She was beginning to
feel uneasy. They were moving her from the private side
of the company to the public side. What did that mean?
She tried to remember Randa's advice the night before,
about not letting them intimidate her, but it was all a
blur now.

"You are pleased?" Hammoud seemed to want an assurance that she would be locked tightly in this new
compartment.

"Certainly, sir. What will I be doing in the new job?"

"Advertising." He tried to smile.

"But we don't do much advertising, sir. In fact, I don't
think we do any."

"That is why we need a trusted employee. If we do it,
it is not a problem. We can get anybody. But since we
don't do it, we must be careful. We need someone we
can trust."

"I see," said Lina. She didn't ask for any further explanation. It was patently absurd.

"You will like the job."

Lina nodded. It sounded like an order. There was a pause in the conversation. She wondered whether it would be permissible to ask why she had been transferred. Hammoud had stopped trying to smile and looked slightly more relaxed, and that, in turn, emboldened Lina. She cleared her throat and spoke up.

"Why are you moving me from accounting? Did I do something wrong?"

"No. There is not any problem." He instantly looked uncomfortable again.

"Professor Sarkis seemed to be upset that I talked with an American man at a party. But I tried to explain that I didn't know him, and when the American tried to talk to me yesterday in the park I hit him. So I hope you aren't angry with me about that."

Hammoud raised his hand, as if to cut off the discussion. He didn't like talking about security matters, even with the person involved.

"I'm sorry if I did something wrong."

He raised his hand higher and clenched his fist, lowering it only when it was clear that she had stopped speaking. His face was flushed. The scar on his cheek, usually barely visible, had become a bright red welt. He fixed her with his intense, black eyes.

"Do not leave this company," he said slowly, driving home the words like a metal spike. "That would be a mistake."

Lina's body tensed. It was a threat, unmistakably. Her mind shifted into that idling gear that a generation of Iraqis had used to survive. "I like working here," she said. "You have always been very kind to me."

He nodded. The moment passed, and he seemed to relax again, now that he had threatened her. But he wasn't finished yet.

"*Habibti,*" he said, using the Arabic word that means "my dear girl."

"Yes, *sidi?*"

"Have you ever wondered where my money comes from?"

She froze again. "No, sir."

"Come now, it is a natural question. I think many people must wonder. When I make a deal with someone in the West, it is the first thing they ask me. How did I make so much money? Where does it come from? You must have wondered that, too."

"No, actually, I haven't." She changed position on the leather chair, which made an awkward, squeaky noise.

"I tell people the truth. I explain that I am a good businessman, and I am very lucky. I tell them how I began in Baghdad with nothing but my clever mind, and how I looked for opportunities. When I saw something I liked, I bought it. You understand?"

"Yes. Of course."

"That is how I bought my first company in Belgium. I had some money from a deal, and the company was cheap, so I jumped like a cat. And the Belgian franc went up, and suddenly I was rich. So I bought another company, and that did well, so I bought real estate. And then the real estate market doubled, and doubled again. And so I became very rich. That is not so mysterious."

"No. It's not mysterious."

"But sometimes people spread terrible lies about me. Maybe you have heard them. They say that I hide money for the Ruler. That I am his secret banker. Some others say I steal money from the Ruler. Imagine that! These are terrible lies told by ignorant people. And by Jews."

"By Jews?" She shifted uneasily.

"Yes, Jews. And do you know what I do to these liars?"

Lina shook her head. "No."

"I cut out their tongues!"

Lina swallowed. Was it a joke? She felt her own tongue, dry as a stone, pressed against the roof of her mouth.

"Have you ever heard the story of the journalist Salim Hourani? No? I will tell you. He wrote the most terrible things about the Ruler in his magazine. One day they found him by the side of the road in Beirut, on the way to the airport. I think his fingers had all been cut off, the ones he used to type his stories. And his tongue had been cut out. Or that is what they tell me. How would I know?" He waved his hand dismissively.

Lina's fingers had clenched into brittle claws as she listened, and there was a tremor in her neck, so that her head was shaking slightly. Hammoud saw her fear and smiled. It was working.

"But this is England," he said slyly. "If a businessman tries to spread rumors, I get my lawyers to stop him. If they try to use their politicians, I use my politicians, and mine are stronger. All these things are a part of doing busines. You understand me?"

"Yes, sir."

"But inside these walls it is not a business. It is a family. And the one thing I will never allow is for a member of my family to be disloyal. That would be like the betrayal of a son or a daughter. Do you understand?"

"Yes," said Lina. Beads of perspiration were forming on her forehead and in the palms of her hands.

"This I cannot accept. Ever."

"No, sir." It was a struggle to keep her composure, but she was determined not to give way to her fear, which would only give Hammoud more power over her.

"One more thing," he said, in a voice that was even colder than before. "I have some news for you from Baghdad."

"What is it?" asked Lina. But there was something in his tone that told her the answer before he said it. She saw in her mind an image of an Arab spinster in her late fifties, with gray hair and careworn eyes, who had clung to her books from Paris and her letters from London—and to the idea of civilized life they represented—through all the years of horror.

"It is sad news, I am afraid," Hammoud continued. "About your Aunt Soha. I must inform you that she is dead." He waited for Lina to start crying, but she sat there silently, taking it in. Her pupils had focused to tiny dots that were staring so intensely at Hammoud, they might have burned a hole in him.

"What was the cause of death?" Lina asked. There was a quiet in her voice, of grief and something else.

"Cause of death unknown." He said it with almost a smirk.

"Was there a funeral?"

"No. The body was held for disposal at the ministry of the interior, I believe."

"Why was it there?"

"Because your Aunt Soha was under investigation. It seems there was a security problem." He let the phrase die in the air, signifying everything but saying nothing. Again, he waited for her tears, but her eyes remained dry.

"Why?"

"She disobeyed the rules. She tried to write letters outside the country without permission." He removed a small packet of letters from his coat pocket and waved them in the air before Lina. "They were all to you, I think."

Lina recognized Soha's perfect handwriting on the envelope. "May I have them, please?" she asked.

"No," he said coldly. He took a gold cigarette lighter from his pocket, lit the flame and touched it to the packet of letters. As they caught fire, a perverse look of pleasure came over his face, as if this opportunity for cruelty was like a sweet chocolate in his mouth. He dropped the burning letters into an ashtray on his desk. In a few moments, they were gone.

Lina bowed her head, which Hammoud took to be a gesture of submission.

"So, we understand each other," he said. He stood up from behind the desk and gestured toward the door. The executioner had finished. The interview was over. The sentence for treason had been announced, in advance. He buzzed for the British secretary to escort the visitor out. As Hammoud shook Lina's hand, he had a look of perfect confidence on his face, as if he were certain that this news of her aunt's death would be the final blow to Lina's independence and the guarantee of her loyalty.

But in this, Nasir Hammoud had miscalculated. What he had done was to make Lina angry. Soha had been her sole remaining relative in Baghdad, and her presence there had been a kind of emotional blackmail. Lina had known that if she were disloyal, her aunt would suffer for it. Now that the worst had actually happened and her aunt was dead, it felt like a kind of release. The chain of fear and obligation that had bound Lina to Hammoud was broken. She felt something else as she departed Hammoud's office. It was the simplest and perhaps purest emotion a human being can feel when someone they love has been injured. What she felt was the desire for revenge.

Hammoud's secretary led Lina out by the public door, down the corridor where the British employees of Coyote Investment had their offices, to a small room with a tiny window. Atop the desk someone had placed Lina's purse, a few personal belongings from her old office, a London telephone directory and a new stapler and tape dispenser. Several of her new British officemates stopped by to introduce themselves. They didn't seem to have a clue about the real workings of the place. On the other side of the building, however, the mood was more somber. It was the same tight silence as back in Baghdad, when the *moukhabarat* came and took someone away in the middle of the night. Nobody asked questions; nobody breathed. But the Arabs who understood the inner workings of the company knew that something important had happened. Mr. Hammoud never made changes unless he had a problem.

Late in the morning, Randa Aziz ventured over to Lina's new office to say hello. "Nice," said Randa, surveying Lina's new digs. "It even has a window. Now you can scream for help."

"Shhh," said Lina. "I'm in enough trouble already."

"What happened? Why did they transfer you? Is this what you were upset about last night?" Randa wasn't one to beat around the bush.

"I thought something was coming, but I didn't know

what. Mr. Hammoud told me my new job is a promotion, but it doesn't feel like one."

"Did he give you a raise?"

"Yes."

"Then it's a promotion. Never forget, working here is about money! Only money. How much more is he paying you?"

"One hundred a week."

"*Ma'aqoula?* What's up? You must have done something really terrible if they need to pay you so much!"

"Shhh! I didn't do anything terrible. And don't talk so loud."

"Take me to lunch. Now that you're so rich, we can go to that tearoom at the Carlton Tower Hotel—La Chinoiserie—and watch the Arab girls shopping for husbands. It's priceless. All those fat girls in tight dresses. You have to see it."

"Not today. I'm not in the mood. I need to think."

"About what?"

"I don't know yet. That's why I have to think."

Randa looked puzzled. Thinking wasn't her strong suit. "Okay. Whatever you say. But I'm going to La Chinoiserie." She gave Lina a wink and looked at her watch. "Gotta run."

———

Later that day, Lina tried signing on to the computer. Her new office didn't have a terminal, but she found one in an empty office at the far end of the hall. Lina sat down at the machine and typed in her user name and password, but she was unable to log in. Her account seemed to have been purged. She then tried signing on as system manager but couldn't do that either. The old password had been changed. That worried her more than the change of office. It was a more decisive change of status. She suspected that she could still get into the system if she had to. But the reasons for her sudden electronic exile mystified her.

Why was Hammoud so frightened? What was he afraid she might discover? What did he think she already knew?

She paid a call on Youssef, the amorous young Iraqi who had been appointed that morning to take her place supervising the data processing group. She figured he would be an easy mark. As she entered the accounting department, her old officemates pretended to be busy or looked at the floor. Apparently she was out of bounds. Lina stuck her head in Youssef's door and said hello. Instead of the over-eager boy she had remembered, she found the young Iraqi cringing at the sight of her.

"I seem to have lost my access to the computer," she said sweetly. "It must be some mistake. I thought maybe you could help."

Youssef shook his head. He looked scared. "I am very sorry," he said. "Orders from Professor Sarkis."

"Did he say why?"

"No." Youssef was looking at his watch. He wanted her to leave.

"It's just that I have some personal files in the system. Addresses and telephone numbers, things like that. I thought maybe you could help me."

Youssef shook his head again, violently. "You will have to see Professor Sarkis. I do not have the authority."

"It will only take a few minutes. You can sit next to me."

"Talk to Professor Sarkis. I am sorry."

Lina nodded. "Right. Then I guess I should go see Professor Sarkis. Is he in?"

"No." The young Iraqi shook his head. He seemed increasingly uncomfortable talking with Lina.

"Where is he?"

"He left London today. He will be back in a few days."

Lina's heart sank. "Where did he go?" she asked. But she knew the answer before the young Iraqi said the word.

"Baghdad."

Lina nodded. Baghdad was where they took people for interrogation. Maybe they suspected that Professor Sarkis was in league with Lina. That would serve him right. She looked at Youssef, so skittish with fear that he could barely sit up straight, and it occurred to her that this was the way she must have looked, most of the time, when she had the same job. How frightened was he? she wondered. She leaned toward his desk.

"Listen, Youssef, you know how you're always talking about having dinner?"

He nodded.

"Well, I don't have any plans tonight, and I was thinking that maybe it would be a good night to go out. I can explain how the system works, teach you things. How does that sound?"

He looked stricken. "I am sorry. It is not possible for me. I am busy."

"Okay. Maybe tomorrow night."

"No. Impossible. I am busy then, too. Very busy." He was backing his chair away from her as if to avoid contamination. He really was pathetic. The amorous toad of a few days before had been transformed into a castrated toad, cringing and cowering at the thought that his masters might see him talking with one of the untouchables. In disgust, she turned and began to walk away from his office, and then stopped.

"You know, Youssef, you really are an asshole."

Lina wasn't quite sure why she said it, but the moment the words were out of her mouth, she felt a sense of relief. She said it again to herself. *Asshole.*

As she made her way past the elevator bank that separated the private side of Coyote from the public side, Lina wondered what to do next. She needed someone to talk to. An ally, perhaps. In her fright, she had long ago discarded Sam Hoffman's business card, but when she reached her office, she opened the telephone book and searched for his name. The directory listed an address on North Audley Street, just below Oxford Street on the edge of Mayfair. She thought of calling ahead to ask if she might stop by, but decided that she didn't trust the telephone. She looked at her reflection in the window. She was dressed in her usual short skirt and tight sweater. She wished now that she had worn something more businesslike.

14

The sign on the door said HOFFMAN ASSOCIATES. Lina knocked softly at first, without getting any response, then pressed the buzzer. Through the door she could hear the sound of a woman's voice. She had a West Indian accent and was singing "I love it when you call me names." Lina listened carefully to make sure it was a recording and then knocked again, harder. She felt skittish and not quite sure where she was heading, like a caged bird taking its first free flight.

"Nobody's home," called out a voice from inside.

Maybe I should come back tomorrow, thought Lina. He's probably with somebody. But when she thought about returning to work without having talked with Hoffman, she felt a clutch in her stomach. "Please open the door," she called through the mail slot. "It's important."

"Hold on," grumbled the voice. The door opened a crack, and Hoffman stuck his head out. He was dressed in sweatpants, a T-shirt, and a baseball cap that said "Havana" on the crest. He looked sleepy-eyed and bemused, as if he had been awakened from a nap. His hair, usually slicked back tight against his head, was tousled. He looked like a spring that had come unsprung. When he recognized Lina, a look of surprise and embarrassment came over his face.

"What are you doing here?" he said. "I thought it was the cleaning lady."

"Can I come in?" She was almost glowing with anticipation—fresh lipstick, red cheeks, nervous smile. Visiting Hoffman was an event for her, a sort of coming-out party.

Hoffman pulled back the door a few more inches, allowing her to slip in through the opening. He was fully awake now, but no less confused by her presence. He took off his cap and scratched his head.

"Seriously, Lina," he said. "What are you doing here? Isn't this dangerous for you?"

"I was careful. I changed subway trains twice, and then I took a taxi."

"That's nice," said Hoffman. He was still wondering what could have transpired during the past twenty-four hours that would have overcome her earlier fears. She would either explain it, or she wouldn't. "Have a seat," he said, leading her to one of the two couches that framed the far end of the room. They both sat down, then he rose again to turn off the stereo, which was still booming out "I love it when you call me names." The silence seemed very loud.

"Can I get you anything?" he asked, settling onto the couch again. "I'm sorry the place is a mess. My secretary is away. She quit, actually, a few weeks ago." In his confusion, Hoffman was babbling.

"I know I've come at a bad time," said Lina, "but I had to see you. I should have called ahead."

"Hell, no! I'm just surprised. After what happened in the park yesterday, I figured you wouldn't want to get near me again. What happened? I mean, you know, what's up?"

Lina didn't answer at first. She adjusted her skirt, wishing again that she had worn a longer one. "I should explain why I'm here. This isn't a social call, Mr. Hoffman."

She sounded so formal, Hoffman had to suppress a smile. "It's not? That's too bad. What is it, then?"

"It's business."

"Great. What kind of business?" He tugged at the ankles of his sweatpants, which had risen up to mid-calf, exposing two hairy legs.

"I've given a lot of thought to what you said about Mr. Hammoud being a menace to everyone, and I decided that you were right. And I want to help you do something about it, if I can."

She was talking in a rush, and her face was flushed with excitement. As she spoke, Hoffman watched her lips form the words. Perhaps it was the fact that he had just awakened from a nap, but he couldn't stop looking at her. She had finished her little speech now, and was waiting for Hoffman to say something.

"You want to help?" he asked, still gazing at her.

"Yes, I do. I would like to help you gather enough information about Mr. Hammoud to take to the police, so they'll do something about him."

"But he's dangerous, like you said."

"Of course he is. That's the point, isn't it? He can't be allowed to continue."

"Right. But you don't have to be the one to pull the trigger. To be honest, it makes me nervous just having you here. Someone might be watching."

"But I want to help you, Mr. Hoffman. That's what I'm saying. You're not making me do this. I want to."

"It's out of the question, unless you stop calling me Mr. Hoffman. My name is Sam. Now, maybe you should start by explaining what happened in the last twenty-four hours that made you decide to come see me."

"Yes, good." She took a deep breath. "What happened is that Mr. Hammoud tried very hard to frighten me this morning, and it backfired. It made me angry. And I realized that I was tired of cowering all the time. And I wanted to take a stand. So I came to see you."

Hoffman closed his eyes a moment, pondering what she had just said, and realized that he still didn't understand. "Let's try again. What did Hammoud say this morning, exactly, to try to frighten you?"

"It was a series of things. First he said he was promoting me to a new job, but what he was really doing was moving me out of the accounting department so I wouldn't have access to sensitive information. Then he warned me that I shouldn't leave the company and told a story about someone who wrote nasty things about Iraq and was killed in a horrible way, and how he would destroy his enemies here in London. And that disloyalty by someone like me—an Iraqi—would be unforgivable. And then he told me that my aunt in Baghdad had been killed by the security service for writing letters to me."

"And that was when you got angry?"

"Yes. But it's been building for a while. I can't go on running. I've got to do something."

"Why don't you just quit?" It seemed to Hoffman like the obvious thing to do. If she wanted to get out, she should get out.

"Because it would be too risky, at least right now. You saw what he did to Mr. Pinta. If you can get the police to do something about Hammoud, then I'll quit. Otherwise, I think he would come after me."

"Why? I mean, why should he care if a computer person quits? He can hire another."

"Because . . ." she began, and then she faltered. Her voice was suddenly as thin and dry as a desert wind. "Because I know too much."

Hoffman closed his eyes. He reached into his T-shirt pocket for a cigarette, but they were all gone. He opened his eyes again and looked at her. "How much do you know? I'm not sure you ever told me exactly what you do at Coyote Investment."

Lina glanced at the ceiling overhead, as if she were looking for hidden listening devices. "Is it safe to talk here?"

"Safe here as anywhere."

"Okay. I was manager of the computer system. Until today. I audited all the records of the accounting department."

"You had access to everything?" He patted his pocket again for a cigarette.

"Yes and no. I had system-wide powers, but I was ordered never to look at Mr. Hammoud's personal files under any circumstances. They think I disobeyed the order and went snooping. That's why they're so angry.''

"Were you snooping?"

"No. I only looked at Mr. Hammoud's files once, and that was by accident. But I've seen enough over the past three years to understand what the business was about."

"So, what's the business about?"

"Hiding money. It flowed in through one pipe, which I could never see. It would get invested in various investments and partnerships that were supposed to look legitimate. Then it would flow out again through other pipes that I usually couldn't see. But sometimes, I couldn't help noticing a few names."

"Like, for example?"

"Like Oscar Trading. The company you asked me about yesterday. I saw that name in the accounting records. It's based in Panama, I think. Coyote sent twelve million dollars to that company's accounts a few days ago. I found the transfer when I was doing my audit. Mr. Hammoud controls the file personally. The chief of security saw me looking for it."

Hoffman nodded. No wonder she was scared.

He got up from the couch and walked to his desk. From the drawer he removed a sheet of paper that had been pieced together with adhesive tape and brought it to Lina. "I found this in the trash behind your building. It's a piece of stationery that had been shredded. Is this the same name you saw in the computer files?"

Lina studied the Oscar Trading letterhead for a moment. "Same name," she said. "Why were you looking in Mr. Hammoud's trash?"

"The same reason you were looking in his computer files. I don't like him."

"So we agree. He's vile, and we should stop him, now. What do you want me to do?"

"Hold on," said Hoffman, raising his hand. She was so eager now, she was almost impetuous. It occurred to Hoffman that the real reason he was talking with her now, encouraging her to risk her life, had less to do with Ham-

moud than with the fact that he wanted to sleep with her.
As he was deliberating this moral dilemma, the telephone rang.

"Who the hell is that?" he said. The phone continued
to ring, but he stayed seated on the couch, waiting for the
answering machine to kick in. The caller, as instructed,
left a message after the sound of the beep. He had a
smooth-sounding voice, like someone who made his living
talking on the telephone.

*"This is Martin Hilton calling. I would like to stop by
tomorrow morning to see Mr. Samuel Hoffman, to inquire
about retaining his services. I am calling at the suggestion
of a friend of his father. I propose that we meet at eleven.
If this is impossible, Mr. Hoffman can reach me at 71-
966-4037. Thank you."*

Lina was unsettled by the voice. "Who's that?" she
asked.

Hoffman shrugged. He didn't know anyone named Martin Hilton.

"What did he mean about your father? What does he
do?"

"He's retired," said Hoffman. "Now, where were
we?"

"I was offering to help, and you were dragging your
feet, I think."

Hoffman looked at her on the couch. He glanced at her
legs, descending so gracefully from the tiny skirt, and then
looked away. He was feeling guilty again. "I'm not dragging my feet," he said. "I'm just trying to be careful.
And I've got other clients to worry about, like this guy
Hilton who just called, whoever he is. This is not a charita-
ble institution I'm running."

"Then I'll hire you." Her eyes were burning. She had
never imagined that if she offered to help, Hoffman
might refuse.

"I'm expensive."

Her cheeks were flushed and her sharp black eyebrows
were pointed down like little sabers. "You should be
ashamed of yourself, backing away now after working so

hard to gain my confidence. I had expected better from you, frankly.''

Hoffman rolled his eyes. She was right, and she was also wrong. "Now, listen to me," he said, speaking in the firm tone he used with clients. "I'm going to give you some advice. It's the kind I usually charge people a lot of money for, but I'm going to give it to you for free.''

"Wonderful.'' Her eyes brightened.

"My advice is: Sleep on it.''

"That's it?''

"Yes. People make mistakes when they're excited. Wait a few days and see if you're still ready to go after Hammoud.''

"You're no help at all," she muttered. "Don't tell me you're afraid of him, too.''

"I'm not afraid of him, for chrissakes!'' Hoffman had forgotten this special gift of Arab women, their ability to taunt men into doing what they wanted. It was an appalling trick, but it usually worked, especially when the men in question wanted to sleep with them. "Excuse me a minute,'' he said.

He walked to the bedroom and retrieved a new pack of cigarettes, lit one, took a puff and slowly exhaled and then stubbed it out. Lina was waiting for him when he returned, poised on the edge of the couch.

"Let's go to the police, Sam,'' she said. "Now.''

"Fine. With what?''

"You can give them the Oscar Trading letter. And you can tell them about the twelve-million-dollar payment.''

"But that doesn't prove anything. There's nothing illegal about paying money to dummy companies. People do it every day. What would we tell the police next?''

She gave him another withering look of reproach. She was a woman in distress, coming to him in her moment of need, and he was lecturing her about details. "You're a man,'' she said archly. "You should know what to do.''

Hoffman smiled and shook his head. She didn't get it. "Lina, listen to me. To get anywhere with the police, we'll need evidence that Hammoud has committed a crime. Evidence that he's hiding money or cheating on taxes, or something. Otherwise they'll just tell us to piss off. And the only person who can get that evidence is you. I'm sorry, but that's the truth.''

Lina thought a long moment. She hadn't considered the practical problems of gathering information. ''How would I do it? Get the evidence, I mean.''

''You'd have to get it out of the computer system.''

''But I don't have access to the system anymore. They took away my system-manager account. There's no way for me to get in. Unless I could find a trapdoor.''

''What's a trapdoor?''

''A way to bypass security. There's usually some way for technicians to get at all the files, in case the system crashes or people forget their passwords. I was always too scared to look for one at Coyote.''

She was gesturing with her hands as she described the trapdoor. As she talked, Hoffman looked at her slender fingers. The only way he would see her again, he knew, was if he agreed to work with her. ''So what do you think?'' he asked. ''Can you crack the system?''

''I think so,'' she said. ''If I can figure out a way to get in without getting caught.''

Hoffman nodded. He walked to the window. A line of black taxis was moving slowly up North Audley Street. He studied them, trying to think of what else to say. Lina rose from the couch and joined him by the window. She touched his arm and held it. It was the gentlest and least sexual contact possible between two bodies, but it subtly changed the tone of their interaction.

''And you'll help me, Sam, if I do it?''

Hoffman nodded. He couldn't very well refuse to help her just because he found her attractive. ''Yes,'' he said gently. ''Of course I'll help you.''

The tension and impetuosity had drained from her face. All that showed now was a simple look of relief, as if she had just managed to transfer a large parcel from her arms into someone else's. She touched his cheek. ''Thank you,'' she said.

Feeling her hand on his face, Hoffman wanted to take her in his arms and walk the short distance to the bedroom. But she was a client now, sort of. He tried to think of what to say. "Be careful," he whispered.

But she just smiled. This wasn't a day for being careful. "I have to leave now," she said. As she headed out the door, she blew Hoffman a kiss. Which made him think, for a moment, that he knew where they were heading, and that it all made sense.

15

Martin Hilton arrived promptly at Hoffman Associates the next morning for his appointment. Sam had forgotten about it. When the doorbell rang, he had his feet up on the desk and was watching the rerun of a darts tournament on television. There was something soothing about televised darts. There was so little action: Two fat men, tossing little objects a few feet across the room. The biggest commotion was when the announcer shouted out the score. Hoffman reluctantly turned off the television and went to the door.

Hilton had dark features and wavy well-combed hair, and he shook Sam Hoffman's hand as if it were a strength test. Hoffman found him hard to place; he would have looked swarthy if he hadn't been wearing such an expensive suit, and he spoke with an almost accentless American English, so bland that it sounded like it had been recorded over something that was there before. His manners were vaguely Continental—more careful and controlled than those of the typical American expatriate. And he had an odd way of walking, like a bodybuilder, flexing his way across the room as if he could feel the sinews stretch and tighten with each step. Hoffman sensed, before he said a word, that the visit of this well-spoken young man must have something to do with Nasir Hammoud. Everything Hoffman touched these days seemed to become attached to that particular thornbush.

"I want to hire you, Mr. Hoffman," said the visitor. His card was no more helpful than Hoffman's. It described him as an import-export broker.

"I'm expensive," said Hoffman. It was his standard defense.

"That's not a problem. I'm rich."

"Lucky fellow. I never cared much about money, myself."

"What is your retainer, Mr. Hoffman?"

Sam put his hand up in the air as if he were stopping traffic. "Hold on! We can talk about money later. First you had better tell me what you're after."

"It involves a banking matter."

"Oh, yeah?"

"Yes. A banking matter. I am interested in information about an Arab financier."

Hoffman couldn't stop himself from smiling. "Let me guess. He's an Iraqi gentleman."

"Correct."

"By the name of Hammoud."

"Yes." Hilton raised his eyebrow slightly, as if perturbed by Hoffman's indelicacy in saying the name out loud.

"And what makes you think I know anything about him?"

"Intuition. And professional training."

"What profession is that?" Hoffman looked at the card. "It says here, 'broker.' "

"Yes. But you know very well what I do."

"No, I don't. Who do you work for?"

"Let us say I work with friends of your father."

"That could mean the CIA. Then again it could mean Dunkin Donuts. Sorry, you'll have to be a little more specific."

"You will forgive me, but I cannot be specific." He seemed offended at the thought that his bona fides would be questioned.

"Okay. Let's stipulate for the purpose of this conversation that you work for the CIA, but you don't want to say so."

"Stipulate whatever you like, Mr. Hoffman. This is a business proposition. I believe you have information about the Iraqi gentleman and his money. And I am offering to pay you for it."

"Hold on. Do you want Hammoud's money? Or just information?"

"Information only. I am in the information business. Not the money business."

"That sounds boring."

"Money gets spent. Information lasts forever."

"Yeah, yeah. I used to hear that sort of crap from my dad. Spare me. Why do you think I know anything about Hammoud? I'm just a business consultant. I don't work for anybody and I don't know anything."

"But you have friends who know things."

Hoffman narrowed his eyes. "Big deal. So does any other investigator in London. Why don't you call one of them?"

Hilton seemed pained at having to explain. "I am told you have friends at Coyote Investment."

Hoffman's face was blank. He wanted to protect Lina, if he could. "Don't be so sure," he said.

"Where you get your information is your business, Mr. Hoffman. I am prepared to buy it from you. That is my proposition."

"So how much is it worth to you, this information I don't have?"

"A lot. I told you. I am rich."

"My retainer is one million dollars, in advance."

"That's outrageous."

"Maybe. But so is barging in here with a phony business card and a lot of mumbo jumbo, trying to hire me to steal information and violate British banking laws. I don't do business that way. And I don't like spies."

"Don't be angry, Mr. Hoffman. I just meant that one million dollars is a lot of money. It is entirely possible that we could pay you that sum for the information that I have described. But I'll have to see about it.''

"See whatever you like. For the record, if you're wearing some spy tape recorder under your fancy spy suit, I refuse to have anything to do with this illegal activity. I will make that clear in a memorandum of this conversation for my attorney.''

"Stop talking about attorneys, Mr. Hoffman. I came here to do business. Not engage in litigation.''

"My number is on my card. Call if you get work.''

Hoffman led him to the door. When he opened it, he saw that a second man was waiting outside in the hall, covering the door for the inquisitive Mr. Hilton. This second man was also dark, with curly hair and the wide, rolling walk of a circus roustabout.

"Take your boyfriend out for a drink,'' said Hoffman to the man in the hall. "He seems a little tense.''

———

When his visitor had departed, Hoffman did something unusual. He called his father in Athens to ask his advice. It was early afternoon there, and Frank Hoffman sounded like he had a hangover. Sam was worried that he might get the sea-of-money lecture again. But his father seemed to have forgotten the earlier conversation. The hurricane was now a spent force.

"Hi, Pop,'' said Sam.

"Who is this?'' It was a silly question since he had only one child, but Frank Hoffman didn't like to be rushed.

"It's Sam. How are you doing today?''

"I feel like shit. Too much ouzo last night with a gynecologist from Qatar. He had the most amazing stories about the private lives of the esteemed guardians of the two holy mosques. How about you?''

"Not bad, Pop. Can't complain. Lots of business.''

"Don't talk so loud. My head hurts.''

"Sorry,'' whispered Sam.

"That's better. Now, what prompts this call from out

of the ether? Not filial devotion, I trust. You must want something."

"I need some advice, actually, Pop."

"How touching. That's what daddies are for. Paying bills and giving advice. What can I do for you?"

"Does the name Hilton mean anything to you?"

"Sure. He runs a hotel chain. Stayed in 'em lots of times. Next question."

"Give me a break, Pop. I don't mean that one. His name is Martin Hilton. Is that a work name you recognize?"

"I dunno. What's he look like?"

"Medium build. Thirty-five years old. Dark. Nice manners but his suit didn't quite hang right, if you know what I mean. He reminded me of some of your old colleagues, except smoother."

"What did he want?"

"Information. But he wanted it real bad. He kept insinuating that he worked for you-know-who, without quite saying so. And he seemed to have a lot of money to throw around."

"Anything else?"

"Not that I should say on the phone."

"Phone security! Very impressive. Are the Ay-rabs involved?"

"Yes. Definitely. What do you think? Does Hilton work for the Culinary Institute of America?"

"No way. If they wanted something from you, they'd just come out and ask you for it. Or have me do it, although they should know by now that I would tell them to go fuck themselves."

"Save the tirade, Pop. It's lost on me. Who do you think Hilton works for, if he doesn't work for the outfit?"

"Fuck you too, son. How the hell should I know?"

"Come on. You know everything."

"True, but why should I tell you?"

"Because you love me. And I'm your son."

"Okay, if you cut the father-son crap. My guess is that Hilton probably works for the Southern Company."

"He's from Dixie?" It was a code that old Beirut hands

used to refer to the Israelis, the unmentionables from down south. Sam had been hearing his father mutter about Dixie and the Southern Company since he was a boy.

"Definitely Dixie. It's their m.o. Razzamatazz. False flag. Flash some bucks. Bad tradecraft. Half-baked mumbo jumbo. It's gotta be them."

Sam nodded to himself. Despite his father's peevishness, it made sense. "What did they do to you, anyway, to piss you off so much?"

"Plenty. But that's beside the point. I'm pissed off at everybody. What did this Hilton guy ask you about, anyway?"

"It involves a certain Arab country whose name begins with the letter *I*. And it involves money."

"Oh, shit." There was a long silence. Sam finally broke it.

"What is it, Pop? Something wrong?"

"Nothing, Junior. But I'm going to give you some advice. Which is what you asked for, so shut up."

"Yes, sir."

"Be careful. The Arab world is a mess right now, even by local standards. And be especially careful with those goofball Iraqis. Some kind of big mudfight is happening in Baghdad. Don't ask me what, because I don't know. But I hear on the drum that something's going down."

"What's happening in Baghdad?"

"I just told you I don't know, goddammit! Jeeesus Christ! Nobody listens to me. Just take my advice, son. This is not the time to be playing games with Iraqis. Or with people named Hilton."

"I don't follow you. What are you talking about?"

Frank Hoffman sighed. "You're right. You don't follow me and you never will, so don't try. Just do what I say, and don't give me any shit. All right?"

Sam had the feeling it was time to get off the phone. It sounded like Vesuvius was about to erupt again. "I gotta go, Pop. Anything I can do for you? I owe you one."

"Tell Gladys to stop bugging me for money. I've given her too much already."

"Your lawyer can do that. What else are you up to?"

"A lot of big fucking shit."

"What does that mean?"

"Wouldn't you like to know?"

"Not particularly. But I'm glad you're feeling better. You sounded a little ragged the other day, with all that sea-of-money stuff."

"Son, you are an ingrate. And a fool. If you listened to me, you would be rich."

"I do listen to you. I love you. You're my dad."

"Give me a break, son. Number one, you don't have a fucking clue what I'm talking about. And number two, if you loved me, you would come see me more often, and have a drink with me, and listen to my advice. You should be nice to me. Maybe you'll need my help for real some day."

"I doubt it, Pop. But I'll keep it in mind."

"Suit yourself, jerk-off."

"Good-bye, Pop. Thanks." Sam Hoffman hung up the phone and rubbed his head. He felt like he had a contact hangover.

16

Nasir Hammoud left London again suddenly, a day
after his meeting with Lina. Nobody knew, at first,
that he had gone. People went about their business in the
gray building on Knightsbridge the next morning without
asking questions. The news reached Lina in its raw form,
as gossip. She was sitting alone in her new office, pretending like the other public employees to be busy, when
her friend Randa appeared at the door. She had a sly look
in her eyes, which foretold a secret she couldn't bear keeping to herself any longer. She entered Lina's office and
closed the door stealthily behind her.

"Guess what I just heard from Yasmine Dalloul, the
Palestinian girl who works in the travel agency across
the street?"

"I haven't a clue," answered Lina.

"Our very own fearless leader recently purchased a
ticket to travel to an exotic place."

"Mr. Hammoud?"

"Um-hum. And guess where our wise and noble master
has gone?"

"I don't know. Paris."

"Very good. But that's easy. Where did he go next?"

"I have no idea."

"Tunis. He went to Tunis. And where did he go after
that? That's the zinger. Where is he today, at this very
minute?"

"Tell me. I can't guess."

"Baghdad. Can you believe it? He's gone back to Baghdad. What do you think of that? He must be in hot water with you-know-who!" Randa lowered her voice. "Serves him right." She was almost chortling, in her pleasure at finding out the boss's itinerary.

"Baghdad?" Lina whispered. She put a hand to her forehead and rubbed her temple. Her head was suddenly pounding. She was relieved, in a way, that Hammoud was gone, since it would give her more time to think about how to get into the computer system. But she was also worried. Things were moving too fast.

"Yes. Isn't that delicious? And Yasmine says he isn't the only one going home. In the last two days, all kinds of people have been making reservations to fly to Baghdad, and just as many have been trying to leave. The planes are all full, both ways. Something is going on, I'm telling you."

"What on earth?" Lina was still puzzled, trying to make sense of this latest event against the background of the past few days. "What does your friend Tony Hashem think?"

"He just said it's 'boogie time.' I'm not sure what that means. I don't think he knows. He said he would talk to his dad."

"Well, keep me posted," said Lina. "I don't hear much gossip on this side of the building."

"I'm working on it. But nobody on my side seems to know anything, either. It's creepy, not knowing what's going on. Spooky. Everybody's just waiting."

And so they waited. A hush seemed to fall over Coyote Investment, in the way that birds and insects fall quiet before a thunderstorm. All the Arab employees seemed to know that something was happening, but nobody knew what it was. The pace of work slowed. People sat by the phones, waiting for them to ring, and asked each other in quiet tones if they had heard anything new. Nobody seemed to want to leave the office for lunch, and they stayed later than usual at night. They lingered like prisoners waiting for the warden to return.

———

Hoffman was restless. He had been waiting to hear from Lina about whether she wanted to press ahead—and he was getting nervous, pacing in that cage of an office. He called her at home and left a message on her answering machine and then repaired to his favorite derelict Chinese restaurant in Soho. When he returned home at eight-thirty, he called Lina again, but she was still out. This time, he did not leave a message at the beep. Hoffman was bored and beginning to feel sorry for himself. What was this restlessness? His college classmates had all, by now, settled into their careers and gotten married and begun having babies. Yet Sam was still floating in the stream of life, clinging to the driftwood of possibility.

The hell with Lina, he decided. He called an out-of-work actress he knew, by the name of Antonia, and asked if she was busy. She proposed that they go dancing at a new club that had just opened in an abandoned warehouse in Lambeth, south of the Thames. Hoffman agreed. He liked Antonia; she was recreational.

Antonia was waiting for him at her flat in Chelsea just after eleven, looking like a cartoon in a men's magazine: hair so blond it could only have come out of a bottle, breasts too big for the rest of her body. She was wearing spiky black heels and a black spandex dress, and she growled a little animal noise when he opened the door. Hoffman wondered if he had made a mistake. Crossing the Thames, he found himself thinking of Lina and the way her hand had grazed his cheek as she said good-bye.

The club looked like the old black-and-white newsreel footage of London during the Blitz. It was in a maze of derelict buildings in South London, in an area most Londoners never visited unless they were poor or lost. A trash fire was burning in a metal barrel at the entrance. Around it stood five burly black men from the West Indies, rubbing their hands against the late-April evening chill. They wore identical combat jackets and had walkie-talkies clipped to their belts, all squawking with static at the same time. They seemed to be bouncers. Hoffman walked past the biggest of them, avoiding eye contact. "Hold on, mon!" said the bouncer. "No drooogs, no gooons." He frisked Hoffman quickly, lingering along the inseam. "What about me?" asked Antonia. She looked disappointed when they waved her through without a hand frisk.

Inside, the club was a wall of noise, less music than pure percussion. "Industrial," shouted Antonia. Hoffman wasn't sure whether she meant the music or the building. The interior was swathed with linen sheets that had been ripped, discolored, marked with graffiti or otherwise disfigured. They added to the picture of bombed-out ruin and decay. Along the walls were lumpy couches that appeared to have come from secondhand furniture stores; they were draped with bodies of people who had passed out from drugs or booze or become immobile from the music. Over this human battlefield hung a low cloud of cigarette smoke.

Antonia was already on the floor dancing. She didn't need a partner, evidently. Hoffman leaned against the wall and bummed a cigarette from a pimply faced boy in a leather-sleeved warm-up jacket that said "Akron North" on the back. He watched Antonia's breasts bounce up and down in tempo with the beat. She returned to him after twenty minutes, wet with sweat. Her nipples were visible through the fabric of her dress. She caught him staring at her.

"Do you think my breasts are too big?" she asked. Her accent had a trace left of somewhere in the north. Sunderland or Hartlepool.

"No," answered Hoffman. He offered her a drag on his cigarette.

"My agent says they are. He says I'll never make it as an actress unless I have them fixed."

"He's out of his mind."

"Otherwise, he says I'll only get trampy parts. Not serious parts. He says women with small breasts look more serious. Do you think that's true?''

"No. It's absurd.''

"They make it hard to dance.'' She thrust her shoulders back and jiggled. "See?''

"Stop it,'' said Hoffman. He looked at his watch. If Lina wasn't home by now, it was time to get worried. "I have to make a phone call.''

She leaned toward him and closed her eyes. "Do you want to tie me up later?''

"No. I don't think so.''

"Why not?'' She looked offended. "Do you want me to tie you up?''

"Listen, I really have to make a phone call. I'll be back in a minute.''

Antonia pouted. She turned on her heels and walked back onto the dance floor, into a crowd of bodies.

Hoffman eventually found a phone and called Lina's home. This time she answered. It was twelve-fifteen. "It's Sam,'' he shouted into the phone. "I'm sorry to wake you up.''

"What?'' She could barely hear him over the noise of the music.

"I said, I'm sorry to wake you up.''

"I'm not asleep!'' she shouted. Her voice was almost giddy. Hoffman mistook it for fear.

"Are you okay? I was worried about you.''

"Yes, of course! I'm on top of the palm tree.''

"You're on top of what?''

"The palm tree. It's an Iraqi expression. *Fawq al nakhal*. It means I'm incredibly happy. Where are you? It sounds awfully noisy.''

"At a club on the South Bank. I tried to reach you earlier, but you were out. Did you get my message?''

"Yes. I called you back. I wanted to make sure you had heard.''

Hoffman still didn't get it. "Where were you tonight, anyway? I got anxious.''

"I was out celebrating, of course. With Randa.''

"Celebrating what?"

"My God! Haven't you heard the news?"

"What news? What are you talking about?"

"He's dead!"

"I can't hear you."

"The Ruler! He's dead! They announced it three hours ago on Baghdad Radio!"

"The Ruler is dead? Jesus! No wonder you're on top of the palm tree. That's incredible!" He was shouting over the sound of the music.

"Yes! Isn't it wonderful?" She sounded almost dizzy in her happiness and relief. "Isn't it just the best news you've ever heard?"

"Fabulous," shouted Hoffman. The percussion of the music was coming at him in waves that made the walls vibrate and the floorboards shake. He looked for Antonia and finally saw her across the room, swaying to the music with her bottom pressed against the crotch of one of the bouncers. He was relieved. She wouldn't need a ride home after all.

"Listen," he shouted. "We should celebrate!"

"What?"

"Celebrate. You and me."

"When?"

"Right now. I'll come over to your place."

"Sure. Why not? It doesn't matter now if anyone sees us together. Randa is here with me. We're calling every Iraqi we know. I even called Nabil Jawad, the poet, and asked him to come over. We can't stop talking about it! We're going to celebrate for a month!"

"Great! I'll be there as soon as I can," shouted Hoffman over the music. "I'm on top of the palm tree, too."

"It's over, Sam," she said, her voice bubbling like a glass of champagne. "It's over."

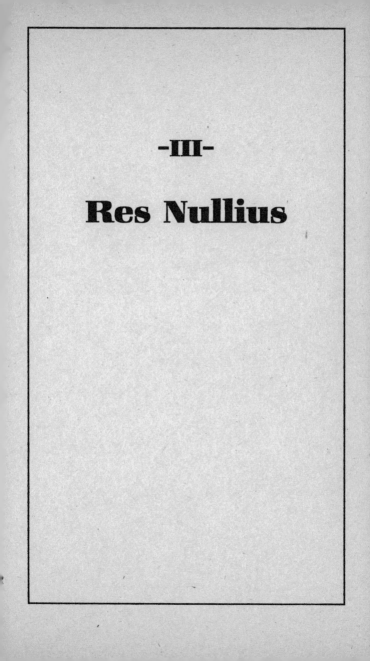

-III-

Res Nullius

17

And so he was gone. The news was announced just after ten, Baghdad time. The radio went silent for fifteen minutes, then returned with a mullah reading from the Koran; then it briefly went silent again and returned finally with the sound of martial music and the announcement that the Ruler was dead. No cause of death was given, and no details, but everyone seemed to know, instantly, that he was really gone. There was gunfire in the streets of Mosul and Basra; in the Kurdish towns of Irbīl and Süleymaniye; in the Shiite holy cities of Karbalā and Najaf; even in the city center of Baghdad. People rushed out into the streets as they heard the gunfire, and in the same instant they heard the news. It was a moment when the door of history seemed to be swinging wide open, and nobody imagined that it could ever swing shut again.

There was a full moon over the Tigris that night, illuminating the city like a paper lantern at a summer party. The bridges across the river, which had been bombed and repaired so many times during the years of war, looked like ghostly skeletons in the half light. The minarets of the great mosque of Musa al-Kadhim, encrusted with gold leaf, sparkled like a treasure box. Even the tawdry statues that had been erected by the Ruler over the years to celebrate his victories and mask his defeats had a noble look, like artifacts of an age that, whatever its defects, was passing into history.

The lights were still on in the concrete bunkers that housed the various ministries of state, but the buildings had emptied as people poured out into the streets. Within an hour after the first bulletin, the word began to spread that the Ruler had been shot—assassinated—by an unknown gunman who had managed to penetrate his private compound, which was usually accessible only to family members and bodyguards. Every street corner had a different version. The assassin was a Muslim fanatic; he was the Ruler's half-brother; he was a Circassian bodyguard; he was an Israeli agent; he was a Jordanian agent.

The first reaction of many Iraqis was to weep, even among those who had despised and feared the Ruler while he lived. It was as if the tent pole that held up the sky had suddenly fallen in. There was a sense of vertigo; people didn't know where they were, outside the world of illusion the Ruler had created. He had been the four points of the Iraqi compass. For a generation, his face had been on the front page of every morning's newspaper; it had been on television every night, in an endless cinema of lies that recorded his every whisper and movement; it had been displayed reverently on the walls of every home, shop, school and office in the nation. The Ruler had been as omnipresent and inescapable as the sun and the moon, and now he was gone.

The second reaction was rage. The massive portrait of the Ruler in his military uniform that dominated the main square of Baghdad was the first to go. A crowd gathered before midnight, as the news spread and the mental shackles began to fall away. The first brave soul dared to throw a rock at the huge portrait, four stories tall. It bounced harmlessly off the billboard, near the Ruler's mustache, and the crowd suddenly became silent. He lived! He was invulnerable! The fear returned, momentarily, and the crowd drew back. But then another man, apparently braver than the others, burst from this cringing pack and, with a shout, hurled a bottle filled with gasoline toward the Ruler's portrait. It hit near the epaulet of his uniform and burst into flame. Another gasoline bomb floated over the crowd, bursting against the Ruler's chin, and then another and another, until the Ruler's portrait was burning in a dozen places and the whole of the square was lit up like a Roman candle. *"Hajiz al-Khawf inkiser,"* they said to each other. *The barrier of fear is broken.* The crowd moved forward again, surging with the anger of caged animals that suddenly, in their moment of liberation, bare their teeth in rage. They rushed toward the Ruler's portrait, seething and chanting like one organism, battering the wooden braces that held up the massive painting and chopping at its foundation with axes and shovels and picks, tearing it out by its roots. A large truck suddenly careened into the square and headed for the huge billboard, striking it head-on like a battering ram, and again, and again, until finally the billboard crashed in a flaming pyre at the center of the square.

This fiery desecration of the Ruler's image only intensified the crowd's fury. They surged on to the next square, where stood another massive portrait of the Ruler, this time dressed as an Arab horseman. Again the gasoline bombs sailed over the crowd, igniting the Ruler's facade. And again a truck battered the flaming billboard until it crumpled to the ground. By dawn, not one of the Ruler's portraits, which had been as numerous in the city as traffic lights, was still standing.

No one thought to ask, in that first night of rage, where the gasoline bombs had come from. Or who had fired those shots in the streets as the news had spread. Or how the huge trucks seemed to arrive just when they did, to complete the destruction. Those were questions that rational people might have asked. But on that incendiary night, with the past in flames before them, few Iraqis bothered to ask questions. Where were the cadres of the secret police, which on every other night had held an invisible dagger at the nation's throat? Or the armies of informers and provocateurs? Iraq had four intelligence services, each controlled by a rival member of the Ruler's family, each spying on the others even as it spied on the Iraqi people. Where were they that night? What hidden levers were they

pulling? Who was issuing the orders to stay in the barracks
or march in the streets? In the delirium, it didn't seem to
matter. The Ruler was gone.

━━

Sitting on a rickety bench in Zawra Park early the next
morning was a middle-aged Arab man whose face was
pitted with acne scars. He was wearing sunglasses that
wrapped around his eyes like a windshield, and had a
leather cap pulled down over his forehead. Only a very
knowledgeable student of Iraqi court life would have recognized him as the late Ruler's cousin, Osman Bazzaz.
He sat on the bench, staring up occasionally at the glass-
enclosed restaurant known as the Baghdad Tower, which
rose above the park like a gaudy Christmas tree ornament.
He was pretending to be reading a newspaper, but it was
obvious that he was waiting for someone. The park was
nearly empty at that hour. All of Baghdad seemed to be
sleeping off the previous night's activities.

After ten minutes or so, a gray-haired man approached
the same rickety bench. He was carrying a leather briefcase. This one looked, from a distance, like a European
businessman; his clothes were neatly pressed and his shoes
gave off a shine, even in the dusty streets of Baghdad.
But on closer look, this second man had the sharp eyes
and dark features of an Iraqi. The perfect order of his
dress was marred by a fresh bandage wrapped around one
hand. As he approached the bench, he didn't embrace the
first man, or even shake his hand. He just sat down next
to him, placing the leather case between them. They con-
versed in Arabic, the way two strangers might. *As-salaam
alaykum. Alaykum as-salaam!*—the exchange of peace.
One might have thought at first that they didn't know each
other, but the conversation quickly became more animated.
They talked in a kind of code, as if they were discussing
a construction project.

"*Al-mashrooa al-mushtarak khalas,*" said the gray-
haired businessman. *The joint venture is finished.*

"Al-hamdu lillah," said Osman Bazzaz. *Thank God.*

"And you are safe?" asked the businessman. He was cradling his bandaged hand, as if his wound was recent, and still painful.

"Al-hamdu lillah," said Osman again. And what, he wondered, had been heard from *al-zaboon, the customer*?

"Nothing," said the businessman. He would talk later to *al-shirkah, the company.* Everything would be as he had promised.

Osman looked at the leather case between them. Was it perhaps a gift? *"Al-hadeeyah?"*

"Ya akhee!" Yes, *my brother.* The businessman with the shiny shoes patted his briefcase.

And what about the rest of the money? Osman Bazzaz wondered. What would happen to it?

"Moo mushkilah!" No problem. The details were being worked out in London. The matter could be discussed later in Geneva, *ala infiraad. In private.*

"Ya habibi." Yes, *my dear.* And now there was a kiss on each cheek. The businessman rose from the bench, straightening his trousers so they broke, just so, and walked away, leaving the late Ruler's cousin Osman sitting on the bench with his arms around the leather case, which contained his present. After a few moments, he rose from the rickety bench in Zawra Park and disappeared once more into the city of concrete and dust.

18

Lina's friends began to arrive at her apartment in Notting Hill Gate soon after she talked with Sam. Randa Aziz was already there, helping her make phone calls. Then came Farida Hamdoon, who was at film school at London University, and then Kenize Tuaima, who managed a dress shop in Camden Town, and her rich Saudi boyfriend. And then they all arrived at once: Burham Saadi and his wife, Majd, and Nadhmi Makloul and his cousin Antissar, and Nemir and Inam and Wahdat and Saad. Someone made Iraqi tea, and someone else brought an almond cake from the Lebanese bakery on Brompton Road, and another brought a case of champagne that had been liberated from the supplies of Marwan Darwish, whose fancy friends could do him no good now. Nobody wanted to sleep that night. Lina sat with them on the floor, dialing the numbers of their friends and shouting the news into the phone.

They circled the globe with telephone calls. Farida called the dormitory at the University of Indiana, where two of her Iraqi friends were studying medicine; Lina called a merchant bank in New York where one of her ex-boyfriends worked as a loan officer; Kenize called her sister, who worked in a boutique on Rodeo Drive. And as it got later, they called farther around the globe, to Lina's cousin in Hong Kong and Farida's boyfriend's brother in Tokyo and Randa's uncle in Bangkok. It was a family party line, and every conversation was the same: *Have you heard the news? Isn't it wonderful? Can you believe it? Fawq al nakhal.* They were all on top of the palm tree!

Sam Hoffman arrived a little past one and waded into the crowd of Iraqis on the living room floor. He was wearing a leather jacket and T-shirt and looked enormously pleased to have escaped from the club across the river. Lina gave him a kiss and handed him a glass of champagne. Sam settled down on the floor. He proposed a toast to "the new Iraq," and everyone clinked their glasses. Someone passed him a brass pipe filled with Lebanese hashish and he took a long drag.

"Mish battal," said Randa, nodding toward Hoffman as she and Lina stood together in the kitchen preparing another tray of stuffed grape leaves. "Not bad at all. But what's he doing here tonight? Are you sure he's not a cop?"

"Of course he's not," said Lina dreamily. "He's my *amir ala faras abayad. My prince on a white horse.* He's going to rescue me. Except now I don't need to be rescued anymore."

Randa whispered into her friend's ear, "How is he in bed? Is he, you know . . ." She made a gesture with her hands.

"Randa! I haven't slept with him!"

"Is he queer, then?"

"You're sick. You really are. He's just a nice, polite American boy, which is a relief. I'm tired of Arab men."

"You're drunk," said Randa, patting her friend on the bottom. "That's what you are."

As the evening gathered force, Lina brought out the tapes her father had made of an Iraqi folk singer named Nazem al-Ghazali. He had died in 1960, before the Ruler had begun trying to destroy the Iraqi national memory, and he was every Iraqi's link to the past. He sang simple folk ballads, some of them two hundred years old, with the accompaniment of a flute, called a *nay*, the guitarlike *oud*, and the drumbeat of the *darbaki*. His music was a kind of Iraqi blues. He would begin by reciting poetry and then break into a song that told of his troubles in love and life. Lina's

favorite song was "Samara min Qawmi Aissa," which trans-
lated as "Dark One from the Tribe of Jesus." It was about
the love of a Muslim man for a Christian girl.

Lina sang out the words with Al-Ghazali, looking not
so shyly at Sam. "Oh, beautiful one, from the tribe of
Jesus, I present my love to you. What is more important,
love or religion?" The song continued with a round of
coy questions and flirtatious answers: "Show me how
pretty your eyes are. My eyes are the eyes of a deer. How
tall are you? I am as tall and slender as a basil plant."
Sam tried to join in, singing in broken, gravelly Arabic.
The Iraqi exiles, gathered on the floor, chimed in, too.
Most of them remembered "Dark One from the Tribe of
Jesus" from childhood. And they all stood up and clapped
and drank more champagne when Al-Ghazali sang "On
Top of the Palm Trees."

Nabil Jawad knocked on the door at two. The poet was
dressed in his usual black, and he looked funereal amid
all the merrymakers. He declined Lina's offer of champagne and asked for a glass of water. With his eyes
shrouded twice over, by blindness and dark glasses, it was
impossible to know what he was thinking. He apologized
to Lina for coming so late. He had been working on an
essay about Arab democracy, hoping that the BBC or the
Voice of America might broadcast it that night on their
Arabic services, but they had refused. Lina sat down beside him on the couch, took his hand in hers and told
him she was honored to have him in her house. "Isn't it
wonderful?" she said. "You must feel so happy tonight."

Jawad shook his head. "Not yet," he said. "Who
knows what will come next?"

Lina tried to withdraw her hand, but Jawad held it
tighter and thanked her again for inviting him. He had
known her family before, he said, back in Baghdad. And
he had attended her father's funeral in London. What was
she doing now? Lina explained, with some embarrassment,
that she worked for Nasir Hammoud, but that she had
been thinking of leaving. Jawad clasped both of his hands
around hers, as if to protect them.

"You are very brave to have invited me here," he said.

"No, I'm not. I should have done it long ago, but I was too scared. Now it's easy. It's over."

"It is not over yet, *habibti*, and you are very brave." He stroked her hand and then held it tight again. "You know, Lina, it is the women who will save Iraq. I have given up on the men. They have all been corrupted. The women are the only strong ones left."

Lina was going to ask him to explain, but Sam had come over and sat down on the other side of Jawad. He was eager to meet the Iraqi poet who had cast such a spell at the Darwishes', and began asking him questions about his life and works, to which Jawad gave halting but honest answers. As the two men talked, Lina reflected on what Jawad had just said. It was certainly true that men were weak. That was a demonstrable fact in Arab London, where even the richest and most successful men seemed to have the morals of pimps. And perhaps it was also true that women were the strong ones. But what Jawad said about women saving Iraq was silly. Iraq had already been saved! The Ruler was dead.

The other Iraqis were gathering around Jawad now, asking him to recite some of his poems. He apologized to them, his hand on his heart. He would love to share his poems, especially tonight, but he had made a vow that he would not read his work in public again until he was back in his homeland. And that was still impossible. There was a groan of disappointment from the room and appeals for him to read a verse or two, so Jawad finally agreed to recite—not his own poem, but one written nearly a thousand years before by the poet Ibn Zaydun, who had been raised in Córdoba but lived most of his life away from his home city. It was a poem about exile, Jawad said. He recited it in flowing Arabic, which rose from his frail body like water from a desert spring.

"God has sent showers upon the abandoned dwelling places of those we loved. He has woven upon them a flower like a star. . . . How happy they were, those days that have passed, days of pleasure, when we lived with those who had black, flowing hair and white shoulders. . . . Now say to Destiny whose favors have vanished—favors I have lamented as the nights have passed—how faintly its breeze has touched me in my evening. But for him who walks in the night the stars still shine: Greetings to you, Córdoba, with love and longing.''

The Iraqis were all in tears when he had finished. They begged him to recite more, but it was too late, Jawad said, and he had too much work to do the next morning at his foundation. So they let him go and made promises to send him money that they knew they wouldn't keep. Lina walked him to the door. As she said good-bye, there were still tears in her eyes, but the poet could not see them.

When Jawad had left, the Iraqis went back to singing and opened more bottles of champagne and talked about the future. Someone toasted ''the boy King,'' King Faisal, who had been killed in the 1958 revolution that preceded the Ruler's rise to power. Someone else toasted the new parliament, whenever it might be convened, and another toasted the new constitution, whatever it might say. They all knew everything, and no one knew anything. Because even as the dawn broke, it was still Iraq.

19

It took official Washington only a few hours to digest the news of the Ruler's death. By the late-news specials at eleven-thirty, the networks had managed to assemble panels of experts who agreed that his assassination had been inevitable all along, and that it was amazing he had lasted as long as he had. The most likely culprits seemed to be Muslim extremists, who had somehow infiltrated the presidential guard. One group of Iraqi exiles, based in Paris, was in fact already claiming responsibility, and the Iranian government had issued a brief statement that, while denying any role in the killing, invited the opposite conclusion. Israeli officials, too, were issuing terse "no comment" statements about a possible Israeli role in the deed. That was the Middle East for you. It was a good thing to be thought capable of killing a head of state, even if you had nothing to do with it. Better to be feared than ignored.

The last place in Washington where anyone might have expected to see the lights burning late that night was the law firm of Hatton, Marola & Dubin. But when he heard the news around five that afternoon, Robert Hatton excused himself from a meeting with his partners to discuss the hiring of new associates and repaired to his office on the top floor, where he remained until nearly midnight. Hatton set up shop in the armored closet that contained his most sensitive files. He brought in a chair and a small table and then locked the steel door so that he could work undisturbed. He spent hours reviewing the legal papers for a series of five corporations he had helped create some years before. They were of the type known as dummy corporations, or front companies, in that their nominal ownership gave no hint as to who really controlled them. Two were registered in the Bahamas and three more were registered in Panama. Hatton reviewed the articles of incorporation for each, and the legal opinions he had obtained years before from local counsel in Nassau and Panama City about the procedures for distribution of assets in the event of a change in status. Then he turned to other documents that charted a small archipelago of partnerships, nominee accounts and investment companies that were part of the invisible network of funds he helped to administer.

It was a precept in the legal business that everyone— no matter how wretched—deserved to be represented by a lawyer. Hatton had more reason to question that rule than most attorneys over the years, but he accepted it as an essential fact of life. Peel away the veneer of any legal practice and it was about fixing problems for people who had money. If people did everything openly and legally, after all, why would they need lawyers? A lawyer was a fixer. But the point was, he actually had to fix things. If a company was incorporated in Grand Cayman Island, it was essential to know precisely what legal requirements would be imposed by the local authorities. If funds were to be transferred among accounts, it was necessary that each step in the transaction be completed precisely as the local rules required. As in auto mechanics, the soul of legal work was in the detail. When the job was done, the machine had to operate smoothly, noiselessly, cleanly.

Hatton broke at nine for dinner at the Athenian Club, a few blocks away. He was a tall, angular man, and he made his way down the street with a sort of aristocratic disdain, oblivious to the homeless men camped out in the park who were badgering him for change. When he reached the sanctuary of his club, he was welcomed by the maître d'—a distinguished old Palestinian gentleman who wore a tuxedo, even to breakfast—who showed him to his usual table by the window in the back. Hatton was a man who believed in routine. He ordered his usual vodka martini and posed his usual question to the maître d' about what he should eat.

"The grilled fish is very good tonight, sir." It was always the same answer, for the maître d' knew that Mr. Hatton always liked to eat grilled fish.

"And how is the melon today?" That was the one thing in Hatton's life that was not predictable. Melons were so difficult.

"The honeydew is not too sweet, but the Crenshaw is very good."

How did they always know, at the Athenian Club, whether the melons were good? They must cut a slice of each one to check. "I'll have the Crenshaw, then," said Hatton.

From where he sat, Hatton could just see the gray bulk of the Old Executive Office Building, its facade the color of an elephant's skin. He had been inside it many times over the years, to chat with members of the National Security Council staff about matters of state that intersected with his legal practice. That was one form of self-justification available to Hatton but not to most other lawyers. *Raison d'état.* A block away on G Street was the downtown office of the intelligence community, located in what was surely the most nondescript building in Washington. Hatton tried to avoid that building, for obvious reasons, and that was easy enough. When they needed anything, they came to him.

When he had finished his fish and his melon, Hatton returned to the steel vault in his office and assured himself, a final time, that all the documents were in order. Then he drafted three cables to be sent the next morning. The first was to the man who many years before had been designated as trustee for certain accounts maintained by a *banque privée* in Geneva. He reconfirmed to the trustee that the power of attorney he had received when the accounts were opened was still operative and that he thus exercised control of the accounts. The second cable was addressed to the private banker in Geneva who maintained these accounts, alerting him to expect a visit soon from the trustee and affirming the existing arrangements for managing the funds. The third and final cable was to the London office of Nasir Hammoud, confirming that all necessary arrangements had been made, as previously discussed.

Hatton wrote out the text of each message on legal paper and put it in an envelope, which he locked in his secretary's desk drawer. He left her a note requesting that the three messages be sent by encrypted electronic mail the next morning. As he was leaving the office a few minutes before midnight, Hatton saw that the Old Executive Office Building was dark. The bureaucrats, as usual, were behind the curve.

20

Professor Sarkis returned first from Baghdad, arriving back in London the day after the Ruler had been shot. The Coyote Investment offices had been closed for mourning, on orders of one of the British vice presidents, who thought it would be the appropriate thing, under the circumstances. The order was immediately countermanded by Professor Sarkis, who had his secretary call each of the Iraqi employees early that morning. It would be a normal workday at Coyote Investment, she said brusquely. All Iraqi employees were expected to report to work. Professor Sarkis would be addressing the Iraqi staff at ten-thirty in Mr. Hammoud's office. To Lina's surprise, she was on the call list.

The "trusted employees" gathered silently in Mr. Hammoud's office. The festive mood of the day before was gone. The portrait of the Ruler above Mr. Hammoud's desk was still there; now it was draped in black. Professor Sarkis entered the room from his adjoining office and stood before the group. He looked like he had spent a month in hell since leaving London. His thin face had become puffy, and he was walking with a limp. Dark glasses shrouded his once sly eyes.

Accompanying him on either side were two Iraqi men Lina had never seen before. They had the cold eyes and bad skin of young men who had grown up in military camps. Everything about them said "secret police." The suits that were too new; the scarred faces that weren't used to a regular morning shave; the cocked-gun tightness of their hands and legs as they stood next to Professor Sarkis, rocking on the balls of their feet. Looking at them, Lina wasn't sure whether the two young Iraqi thugs were Professor Sarkis's minions or his masters.

"This is a sad day," began Professor Sarkis, nodding up toward the black-draped portrait above the desk. "Our beloved Ruler is gone, and I know that the hearts of all Arab patriots are heavy. But we will do our duty, as Iraqis and as employees of this company. We will continue with our work. Does everyone understand?"

There were nods around the room. The appalling Youssef, who seemed to be the new stooge, spoke up and said, *"Nam, sidi"*—Yes, sir—and several of the other young men murmured the same thing.

"Mr. Hammoud, he cannot be with us today," continued Professor Sarkis, looking at the two young thugs for reassurance. "Mr. Hammoud may be away for some time. But I been instructed by certain responsible authorities in Baghdad to tell you that nothing will change at Coyote Investment. The business must keep going. Our enemies will be watching and waiting. But the Ruler's spirit will win. So, loyal employees, you will be rewarded; disloyal employees, you will be punished. Any questions?"

Of course, there were no questions.

Lina retreated to her office, wary of talking to anyone. It was a day to lie low, until the meaning of what she had just witnessed became clear. But Randa, as usual, could not wait. She appeared in Lina's doorway at eleven-fifteen. There were dark circles under her eyes from thirty-six hours of continuous partying.

"Shaku?" she said. "What was that all about?"

"I don't know," said Lina.

"Where's Hammoud? When is he coming back?"

"I don't know," she repeated.

"Who were those two creepy guys with Sarkis? They looked like busboys at Fakreddine. Those two, wow! *Tula tula al-nakhla, wa aqla aql al-sakhra!"* It was a derisive

Iraqi expression that meant "As tall as a palm tree, but with the brains of a goat."

"That's enough, Randa!" said Lina sharply. "Don't ask any more questions and don't make any more nasty remarks. They're dangerous." Her friend retreated toward the door, her eyes downcast. When Lina saw the reaction, she felt ashamed of herself. The Ruler hadn't been dead two days, but the fear and dissembling were starting again. "I'm sorry," she said. "It's just weird, that's all."

"What's going on, Lina?" whispered Randa. "Is this a coup?"

"Honestly, I don't know. Let's talk about it tomorrow. Maybe we'll know by then."

———

Just before five, as Lina was preparing to leave, she was summoned to meet with Professor Sarkis. He received her in Mr. Hammoud's office, sitting behind the big desk. The two Iraqi thugs were standing motionless on either side of him, like the two sides of a metal vise. The Ruler's portrait, still draped in black, loomed over all of them. Professor Sarkis was coughing as Lina entered the room. He looked infirm. Lina wondered what they had done to him in Baghdad.

"Sit down," said Professor Sarkis abruptly. This wasn't going to be a friendly chat, evidently.

Lina sat. She looked to Professor Sarkis for some hint of why he had summoned her, but all she saw was the dull glint of his dark glasses.

"We gonna have a new management team here at Coyote Investment," he began. The business jargon sounded absurd, like a Harvard Business School lecture in a torture chamber, but he continued. "Certain members of the Ruler's family have asked me to conduct a reorganization. These two gentlemen are my"—he searched for a word— "consultants. They been asking me who, other than myself and Mr. Hammoud, is familiar with the company. I told them that one of these persons is yourself, Miss Alwan."

He paused and removed his dark glasses. His right eye had been beaten so badly that it was nearly shut. The surrounding skin was a pus color, with shades of yellow and blue.

"I been considering whether to make you part of our new management structure here. But I got a problem. These gentlemen think it's not so smart to give anyone such as yourself more responsibilities at the company without further training. Reeducation, you might say."

"Where, Professor Sarkis?"

"Baghdad." He smiled for the first time that day, and Lina could see that several of his teeth were missing. She felt a grip of fear tighten around her stomach and squeeze her up and down like a toothpaste tube. She looked at the two young Iraqis and imagined them sitting on either side of her in an Iraqi Airways jet.

"Please, Professor Sarkis. I have always been a trustworthy employee. You have no reason to be concerned about me now."

The Armenian ignored her. "We can stop playing games, please. Do you know who these two men are? This is Mr. Hammadi on my right and Mr. Alani on my left. They are members of the Amn Al Khass, the special security force in Baghdad. You know what that is?"

"No, sir."

"The Ruler, he established the Amn Al Khass as a special part of the secret police to protect himself and his family. I was a guest of these gentlemen when I was in Baghdad." His voice fluttered momentarily when he said the word *guest*. That anodyne description was apparently too much for even an accomplished liar such as Professor Sarkis.

"They was worried about security problems here at the company, you see. So when I was in Baghdad, these gentlemen asked me many questions, all of which I tried to answer honestly. They asked me how we do business and where our money goes. They asked me why some of it seemed to be missing. They even asked me about Mr. Hammoud. And I answered them. You could say I was painfully honest." He leaned toward Lina. "Some of the questions they asked me was about you."

Lina looked toward the two secret policemen and then back at Professor Sarkis. "What did they want to know?"

"Whether you know the secrets of our business."

She swallowed. Her stomach was tightening again. "What did you tell them?"

"I said this Lina Alwan, she probably knows more about Coyote Investment than anyone at the company, other than me and Mr. Hammoud. They asked if you knew about the *real* business of the company—you know—and I said I didn't know. They asked if you had seen Mr. Hammoud's personal files, and I said maybe so. Yes, probably so. They asked if you were loyal, and I said I have some doubts. But, my little *eshek*, now we know the real traitor was Hammoud, so I'm ready to forgive you. But these men, they still gotta be worried. They wonder how much you know. They think it must be so much. Too much."

She avoided looking at the two secret policemen. "It isn't true, Professor Sarkis. I don't know anything that you didn't tell me. I've never seen any secret files. I don't know anything at all." She looked imploringly at the two Iraqis, still standing there like cocked pistols. "Please believe me."

"Belief? What is belief? These gentlemen are not interested in believing anything. They want to know."

"But how can I convince them?"

"By being loyal. Only by being loyal."

"Yes, sir. I have always been loyal to the firm."

Professor Sarkis cocked his head. His nostrils seemed to flare, like those of an animal that was about to pounce. "Then why you go and invite Nabil Jawad to your house two nights ago, if you are so loyal? Huh? *Achpar!* This man is an enemy of Iraq."

Lina blinked. How did they know that Jawad had visited her? Were they watching her flat? Had they tapped her phone? Or had one of her friends, one of the people sitting on the floor singing and toasting, informed on her?

Mr. Alani, one of the two security men looming over Sarkis, had taken a knife from his pocket and was using it to clean his nails. His hands were massive, and the knuckles were knotted like the trunk of a tree. He saw her watching in fear as he played with the knife; he gave her the slightest trace of a smile, no more than a crinkle around his eyes.

"So why you invite Jawad, if you are a loyal employee?"

"I did not know Jawad was an enemy of Iraq," she lied. "Someone else wanted to invite him."

Professor Sarkis removed his dark glasses again. He took a handkerchief from his pocket and wiped away some pus that had dripped from the eye that was swollen shut. "Be careful, Miss Lina," he said. "These men are serious."

Lina nodded.

"We gonna have to see whether you can be trusted. I'd let them take you to Baghdad right now, if I didn't need help with the computers. This idiot Youssef doesn't understand the system, and you got to help him. So you move back to the accounting department, please, where I can keep an eye on you."

"Does that mean I have my old job again, as head of data processing?"

"No. Just temporary. On loan. Until we decide whether you need more, you know, training." Sarkis sat back in his chair, a signal that the meeting was over.

Lina lingered a moment more. She was thinking of what Hoffman had said about quitting. If ever there was a time to leave, this was it. "Professor Sarkis, please. If you no longer have confidence in me, perhaps it would be best if I left the company."

The Armenian pointed a thin finger toward her. "Out of the question! You gonna stay, and you gonna be loyal. I gave you friendly warning. If you don't listen to me, you will deal with these two gentlemen and their friends back in Baghdad. That's all I got to say." He gave a little wave, as if he were shooing away a fly.

Lina walked unsteadily out of the room. She was afraid to go visit Hoffman, afraid even to go home. She went looking for Randa, who had already left the office, and eventually reached her at her apartment in Chelsea. She proposed that they have dinner together at an Indian restaurant, and Randa, to her relief, said yes.

"I shouldn't tell you this," said Randa as she ladled the *dal* onto Lina's plate. "But they asked me to spy on you at the office."

Lina stopped just as a spoonful of *raita* was about to reach her mouth. "Who did?"

"Professor Sarkis and his new boyfriends did, this afternoon. That's why I left the office early. I felt weird about it."

"What did you tell them?"

"I told them I would do it, of course. What do you think I am, crazy? I told them I would keep a careful eye on you and make sure you weren't doing anything nasty. So don't do anything they wouldn't like. Or if you do, don't let me see it."

"Randa! I can't believe you would spy on me. That's terrible."

Randa tried to look contrite. "I know. It's just that I was scared. And they offered me more money. Anyway, I won't do it very long."

"Why not?"

"Because I don't think Sarkis is going to last."

"Why do you say that? He sounded pretty tough today. And I think he's got some of the Ruler's family behind him."

"Because he's a jerk. And those two pimply guys he brought with him are pathetic, even by Baghdad standards."

Lina wasn't sure why, but she found the conversation with Randa reassuring. Professor Sarkis would fail because he was a jerk and because his security men had bad complexions. Randa would agree to spy on her best friend and

would also tell her that she was doing it. That was the
way of the world. On her way home in the taxicab, Lina
felt her sense of balance returning. The Ruler was dead.
No second-rate sadists were going to reclaim his mantle
of terror.

The reign of Professor Sarkis proved to be short-lived,
indeed. That night, on orders from the Home Secretary,
the police secured the premises of Coyote Investment.
When Lina arrived at work the next morning, two uni-
formed British policemen were standing guard at the elevator bank on the fifth floor. They nodded politely, and one
of them actually tipped his hat. The two Iraqi thugs, Hammadi and Alani, were gone. Lina wondered whether she
should go to her old office, on the private side, or her new
one, on the public side, and settled on the latter.

Just before ten, Mr. Hammoud's British secretary summoned Lina and told her that there was a meeting of all
Iraqi employees in Mr. Hammoud's office, immediately.
Out in the hall, Lina saw a line of Iraqi employees walking
like zombies toward the corner of the building. They
seemed almost in a daze, like concentration-camp prisoners shuffling off toward the cattle cars. Lina was one of
the last to join the line. On her way, she noticed that the
two bobbies who had been guarding the elevators had
disappeared.

Outside the heavy door to Mr. Hammoud's office, Lina
was stopped by a smooth young security man in a brown
Armani suit. He was checking identification. When he read
Lina's badge, he called over a colleague and began con-
versing with him in Arabic. Lina couldn't hear much of
what they were saying, but it sounded from their accents
as if they were Palestinians. After a brief discussion, they
let her pass. She was one of the last to enter the office,
so it took her a moment to see past the clutch of people
in front of her.

Standing imperiously behind his desk was Nasir Hammoud. His skin had the same plastic glow as before, but his eyes were full of rage and triumph, like those of a boxer who has just knocked his opponent to the canvas. Lina looked for Professor Sarkis in the crowd but couldn't find him. The pimply Iraqi secret policemen seemed to have disappeared, too, but there was a contingent of young men gathered around Mr. Hammoud's desk, including the two Palestinians who had been at the door. Several of them seemed to be holding automatic weapons under their coats, and one was speaking into a walkie-talkie microphone in his sleeve. Lina noticed one more thing: The old portrait of the Ruler above the desk, which had been draped in black just a day before, was gone.

When everyone had entered the room, the door closed and Mr. Hammoud began to speak. "So, my friends. Did you miss me?"

"Yes," went up a chorus around the room. Everyone shouted it, even Lina. The whole room seemed to shake with this false enthusiasm, welcoming the returning leader. Someone even began chanting in Arabic, "With blood, with tears, we salute you, O Nasir," which was like what they used to chant for the Ruler. Hammoud cut them off. He seemed to have lost his taste for such vulgar spectacles.

"It's good that you missed me. Because I missed you!" He raised his right hand in the air, in what might have been a Nazi salute. Lina could see, even from her place in the back of the room, that there was something wrong with his hand. The index finger was gone. A fat white bandage was wrapped around the stump.

"Now, my friends, we are back to business. The traitor is gone." He wagged what used to be his index finger at the crowd. "The liar. The unbeliever! The Armenian! He will not be with us any longer. He has been imprisoned by the authorities of Great Britain—yes!—for trying to take what did not belong to him. I myself swore out the warrant for his arrest last night when I returned from Baghdad.

"So what is going on in our beloved homeland? I know you are wondering, so I will explain. Everything is calm.

The Ruler has passed on, God grant him peace. Popular forces have control of the government. Certain renegade members of the Ruler's family attempted to take control after his death, the very ones who sent the dog Sarkis to steal the assets of Coyote Investment. But this conspiracy has been defeated. Even the Americans have recognized the new government in Baghdad. Thanks be to God.''

There was another murmur of approval, until the Palestinian security men glowered, and the crowd became silent again.

"And now, I have good news. For every loyal employee, there will be a bonus at the end of the month. The smallest of these bonuses will be five hundred pounds!'' There was a shout of gratitude from the group, like the groveling sound—not quite words—that beggars make when someone tosses them some coins. "Do not thank me! We have all suffered through these days of sadness and confusion.'' He gestured toward them with his hands outstretched, the way the pope does when greeting the faithful. The stump of his index finger was all anyone could see.

"So let us get back to work, my dear friends. Let us work hard to protect the wealth of Coyote Investment— which we created and which is ours—from any who would try to steal it. And to anyone who thinks of dealing with the dogs and traitors who pretend to speak for the family of our dear Ruler, I have a warning: The wrath of the Ruler will be like a gentle slap, compared to what I will do.''

When Hammoud was done, a few of the most egregious opportunists gathered around his desk to kiss him on the hand and profess their undying loyalty. Several of them, Lina noticed, were among those who had cheered loudest the day before for Professor Sarkis. Watching the jackals gather around Hammoud, Lina realized that she actually felt sorry for Professor Sarkis. He was a puppet; the strings had been cut, and he had crumpled.

She saw Randa amid the knot of people heading for the door and walked back to the accounting department with her. "What happened to Youssef?" asked Lina. "I didn't see him in the meeting."

Randa dragged a finger across her throat. *"Khatiya ath-wal."* It was an Iraqi expression that meant "poor fool."

"Haram," said Lina. *Too bad.*

Randa took her aside as they neared Lina's new office. She was wearing new red nail polish and an even shorter skirt than usual.

"Hammoud wants you back on the private side," she said under her breath. "Starting tomorrow."

"How do you know?"

"Because that cute new security man Hassan told me so a few minutes ago. He asked me to tell you. He said that Mr. Hammoud wants to make sure you're back in the family."

"Did he ask you to spy on me, too?"

"Uh-huh," said Randa, nodding her head up and down like Mr. Ed, the talking horse. "He certainly did."

"And you said yes?"

"Of course! We've been through that before. Don't give me a hard time. Come back soon. Ciao!" She blew an air kiss next to Lina's cheek and scampered off down the hall.

21

Hoffman was eating lunch that afternoon at his favorite Chinese restaurant, with its comforting, surly waiters, when a question occurred to him for which he had no ready answer. Now that the ruler of Iraq was dead, who owned Coyote Investment? He had put the whole subject of Nasir Hammoud out of his mind after the Ruler was shot, but the question nagged him, even after he had finished his wonton soup and his spicy bean curd and his lo mein. He wandered around Soho after lunch, past the punk-rock pubs and the dimly lit strip clubs and dirty bookstores. Usually, this landscape struck him as an urban pastoral. But this afternoon, the sex-show touts and the drunks barfing in the alleyways didn't seem so quaint, and there was still that question bothering him. Hoffman worried that he was getting old. He decided it was time to go home when he saw a short, fat man stumbling out of a pub and was convinced, for a moment, that it was his father.

When he got back to his office, Hoffman called Asad Barakat, who was the only person he knew—other than Prince Jalal—who was likely to have an answer. Barakat's secretary said he was busy and wouldn't put the call through, so Hoffman figured—*screw him!*—he would just go unannounced. The afternoon had turned dark and rainy, but Hoffman walked the few blocks to BankArabia.

Barakat was in fact busy, meeting with a group of visitors from Amman, so Hoffman had to sit in the waiting room. He perused the Sotheby's real estate catalog on the coffee table, wondering who could possibly buy all the houses priced at three million and four million dollars. They couldn't all be Arabs. Eventually Barakat emerged, shaking hands with his Jordanian friends, walking them to the door, walking them to the elevator, looking as if he might walk them all the way back to their hotels. That was part of Arab hospitality, not letting go of guests, but Barakat returned finally, shaking his head.

"They are idiots," he said, pointing to the elevator. "I don't understand how they got so rich."

Barakat shook his head again and walked back to his office. Hoffman followed, without being invited. Barakat pursed his large lips. "I do not wish to be rude, Sam, but what do you want? I have work to do."

"Coyote Investment," said Hoffman. "I need to ask you just one more question."

Barakat narrowed his eyes. "What is it?"

"Now that the Ruler is dead and Hammoud is gone, who owns Coyote?"

Barakat placed his hands together atop his large stomach, so that he looked like Humpty Dumpty. He couldn't resist answering. "Hammoud hasn't gone anywhere," he said. "He returned from Baghdad last night. They tell me he is in surprisingly good shape, except for a missing finger."

"What happened to his finger?"

"The Ruler's brother cut it off with one of those little power saws that carpenters use. It was an Iraqi touch."

Hoffman winced. He let himself think, for a moment, what they would do to Lina if they ever caught her, and then pushed the thought out of his mind. "Why did they cut off his finger? What were they after?"

"Money, of course. But Hammoud's friends rescued him before they could cut off anything else. It seems that there is a war of succession going on, and Hammoud's side is winning."

"What's the war about?"

"Money, my dear boy," repeated Barakat, as if he were

lecturing a child. It was late. He was impatient. "One of the prizes is control of Coyote Investment, if that's any answer to your question."

"Sort of. But who owns it now, this minute? That's what I want to know." Hoffman scratched his head.

"A complicated matter. Several other people called me this afternoon to ask me the same thing." Barakat frowned.

"What did you tell them?"

"I told them it was a complicated matter." He frowned again and turned away from Hoffman and pretended to study some papers on his desk. He clearly wanted Sam to go away. His manner was chillier than Sam had remembered. It was a breach of Arab manners to ask why, but Sam decided to do so anyway.

"Is something wrong, Asad? You seem upset."

Barakat gazed at him, his wide face carrying a look of reproach. "I am not upset, I am angry. You were not honest with me the other day when you said your father knew that you were coming to see me about Hammoud. That was a lie, as I discovered later from your father."

"I'm sorry, Asad. I wasn't trying to be dishonest."

Barakat had the righteous look of a man who knows that he has been wronged, and thus has power over his adversary. "Trust is the foundation of relationships in the East, my dear Sam. When it is gone, there is nothing left."

"Does that mean you won't talk to me?"

"It means that I must be careful. But I will try to answer your question about Coyote, only because it is important that you not make any more mistakes. The truth is that now that the Ruler is dead, his money is not really owned by anyone."

Sam nodded. Play dumb, he told himself. Get him talking. "So who can claim it, if no one owns it?"

"That too is another complicated question, from a legal point of view. The money belongs to the person who can establish title to it. If the original owner is dead, his heirs or other claimants can try to establish title, assuming they know where to look. And if no one can establish claim, then the bank holding it—in this case a Swiss bank, I believe—simply keeps the money.''

"Surely that's illegal, Asad. Even in Switzerland.''

"Not at all, my dear. There is a term in law for this sort of thing. It is called *res nullius*—'a thing that belongs to no one.' My lawyer friends tell me that the principle is well established. If I find treasure on my land that is not the property of the Crown, I can keep it. It is a settled matter of law.''

"So the money just stays in the bank?''

"Of course. How do you think the Swiss banks got so rich? *Res nullius.* The world's corrupt kings and presidents have been shoveling money into Swiss banks for generations—into secret accounts that are entirely unknown, except to themselves and the managing director of the bank. Being mortal, these kings and presidents have a habit of dying. And eventually, the banks take the spoils.''

"And the bankers never talk?''

"Of course not. My dear Sam, you do not seem to understand what a bank is. A bank is not walls and vaults and steel doors. A bank is trust. An untrustworthy bank cannot protect your money, no matter how thick its walls. A trustworthy bank will always protect your money, even if it has no walls at all.''

Hoffman shook his head like a student who didn't understand the great professor. "Asad, I'm not following you. You are speaking in riddles.''

"Very well,'' nodded Barakat gravely. "I will try to explain, but you must listen. The most secure way to hold money is not to hold it at all. If I put it in a bank, it can be traced to me. But if someone else puts it in the bank for me, that is a different matter. It doesn't belong to me anymore. The address is not my address. So if I want to hide a billion dollars, my dear Sam, the best thing I can do is to give it to you. It cannot be traced to me ever again. But if I trust you, I know that it is still mine, forever.''

Sam closed his eyes as Barakat spoke. What he was describing was, in essence, the same transaction that Jalal had proposed to him five years before. Sam wondered, for an awful moment, whether the money that Jalal had asked him to hide might actually have belonged to the Ruler. "And that's what the Ruler thought he had with Hammoud?"

"Precisely. He thought he could trust Hammoud, so he made him his banker and gave him control of his money."

"What about the Ruler's family? They're his heirs. Why can't they go to Geneva and try to claim his accounts?"

"I'm sure they will try, but they'll never find the money. These accounts were secret, after all. That was the whole point. The family wouldn't know where to look, unless Hammoud told them. And I doubt very much he would do that. If he had been prepared to do so, he would still have ten fingers."

"The family could look at the Ruler's checkbook."

"Evidently you do not understand Swiss banks. There are no checkbooks. There is no paperwork at all. Most numbered Swiss accounts are 'hold mail' accounts. The bank retains all statements in its files. The customer has to visit in person to review the account."

Hoffman smiled. "The Swiss are paranoid."

"Perhaps, but in this case they have a point. With something important, like money, a secret is not a secret if it is known by more than two people. Beyond two people and it becomes public knowledge. So the Swiss bankers make sure there is no mail, no record. No trace. They are a tidy people. They want the identity of a numbered account to be known to just two people: the depositor and his banker. Perhaps, in some cases, there might be a third person, an intermediary who will act on behalf of the depositor. That was certainly the case with the Ruler, who to my knowledge never set foot in Switzerland. I am confident that he chose some very unlikely person to represent his interests. More than confident, I know it. And I suspect that person is probably in discussions with Hammoud at this moment."

He smiled. It was almost a wink. "But the point is, my dear Sam, that it would be a mistake for anyone to try to interfere in such a delicate process. A very dangerous mistake. People who have worked so hard to keep things secret will not tolerate an invasion of their privacy. Do you understand me?''

Hoffman's head was spinning. He felt like he had been breathing pure oxygen. The point of Barakat's lecture seemed to be that he should stay out of Hammoud's way, but he wasn't sure why the Palestinian banker was making it in such an odd, roundabout fashion. He decided to ask a last, stupid question. ''What will happen to the money, then, Asad-bey?''

''Hammoud will take it, of course. He has the advantage of actually knowing where it is, or was. I'm sure the money will move somewhere else soon.''

''Why move it? Why not let it sit there?''

''Because we are talking about Iraq. Trust is in short supply. When it comes to money, no Iraqi can dare trust anyone for very long. Why do you think the Ruler was killed?''

''Money.''

''Yes, of course. Everything is always about money in the Arab world, no matter what anyone tells you. If a businessman gets a contract, it is because he has bribed the leader. If a terrorist takes up residence, it is because he has paid the leader, or the leader has paid him. If someone shoots a head of state, it is because a very large amount of money has changed hands. Do you see where I am leading, my dear Sam?''

He paused. With his round head and florid skin, he looked like the man in the moon. Sam sat motionless, still not sure how much Barakat knew, waiting for him to continue.

''What I am trying to tell you is this: It would be unwise to pick a fight with Nasir Hammoud unless you are very well armed. And it would be especially unwise for a young Iraqi woman to pick a fight with him that she cannot win. You understand? This man Hammoud has a long memory.''

Sam felt his heart beating. Barakat had taken a toothpick from his drawer and was poking at his teeth with it. He seemed to know about Lina, but Sam wanted to make sure. "What about this Iraqi woman, Asad-bey? Why is Hammoud so afraid of her?"

"Because she knows where the money is. Or at least, that is what Hammoud believes. I told you before, this is all about money."

"What if she doesn't know as much as he thinks?"

"Then she is helpless. *Haram.* Too bad."

Sam felt the words like a knife puncturing his too-soft skin. He closed his eyes and saw in them the image of Lina, limp and lifeless. Now that Barakat had delivered his message, he no longer seemed interested. The banker sat back in his chair, picked up a file from off his desk and began reading it. A chill settled over the room. The interview was over.

"Asad, please. You have frightened me. I need help."

"I have given you too much help already," said Barakat. He looked at his watch. "It's too late."

"Please. Someone's life is in danger."

Barakat shook his head in dismay.

"My dear Sam, you are a fool. Of course someone's life is in danger. Hundreds of lives are in danger. Thousands. You do not seem to understand how sensitive these matters are. You came to me some days ago, asking the most outrageous questions, and I tried to be helpful out of respect for your father. But you misled me. I have tried to tell you today how slippery is this slope you have been climbing. But you do not seem to understand, and I have said enough. So, please, leave me. You are giving me a headache."

22

Hoffman sat in his BMW with the lights out, across the street from Lina's flat on Lansdowne Walk. The afternoon rain had become a veil of mist. He watched as people came and went from the houses along the street, but nobody else seemed to be staking out the place. He had been waiting nearly two hours when he saw a woman turn the corner. She was carrying an umbrella that hid her face, but the walk was Lina's. Hoffman hopped out of the car and ran across the street. He took her hand.

"Let's go for a ride. We need to talk."

She followed him silently to the car and, when she was seated, removed her raincoat. The rain had soaked through to the skin. Hoffman headed a few blocks west and then turned into the narrow lanes of Holland Park, to see if anyone was following, and then returned to the main road. The streets were shiny with drops that looked, in the car's headlights, like little bits of silver.

"We have a problem," said Hoffman. "Hammoud is back."

"I know," said Lina. "He held a meeting at the office today to welcome himself back. He looked very chipper, like he had just won the lottery."

"He's still gunning for you, Lina."

"What do you mean?"

"I mean he's worried about you. He thinks you've figured out where his money is. He thinks you know all his secrets.''

"How do you know? Who told you that?"

"A banker friend of mine who knows a lot about Hammoud's business. He warned me that you should be careful, because Hammoud thinks you already know everything, and he's coming after you."

"Shit," she said.

Hoffman was surprised. He had never heard her swear before. "Fuck," he answered back.

She laughed. She had never heard him swear before, either. But the laughter quickly gave way to silence. "So what should I do?" she asked.

Hoffman thought a moment. The situation was no better, and no worse, than a few days before. But the stakes were higher. "Maybe you need an insurance policy," he said.

"Thanks. Perhaps you would like to be the beneficiary."

"That's not what I meant. Maybe you need to have what Hammoud thinks you've already got, so you can go to the police or even make a deal with him. It's your only leverage. The only other option is to run away."

"How far could I get?" she asked. But she wasn't serious. She didn't know where to flee and, more important, she didn't want to. "I'm tired of running," she said. "And he would come after me anyway, if he thinks I know all his secrets."

Hoffman nodded. It was true. She was in so deep now that there wasn't an easy exit. The BMW slowed as they reached the Shepherd's Bush roundabout. Hoffman headed north toward Wormwood Scrubs prison, the destination he had fancied for Nasir Hammoud.

"So how can I get some insurance?" asked Lina, gazing out at the dark mass of the prison.

"You need the computer files," he said. "Either that or . . ." He paused to think of another possibility.

"Or what?"

"Or you give up," said Hoffman.

Hoffman offered to take her to dinner or bring her back to his flat for a nightcap, but there wasn't much conviction in his voice. He knew it wasn't that kind of night. Lina kissed him on the cheek when he dropped her back at Lansdowne Walk and quickly went upstairs. She sat in her dark apartment for more than an hour, thinking about how to crack the computer system at Coyote. Before, as system manager, she had a "root" account that, in theory, gave her access to everything. Even then they had been able to monitor her activity, to make sure that she wasn't looking at Hammoud's files. Now she had no account at all, no way into Hammoud's secrets.

The system was meant to be invulnerable. And yet it was an article of faith among computer professionals that there was no such thing as an invulnerable system. There was always a trapdoor. Lina tried to remember who had first passed on that nugget of wisdom and remembered that it was her friend Helen Copaken. And then it was obvious to Lina what she should do: She should call Helen.

Helen Copaken was a computer guru. She had received the highest grades in the computer science program at the university, and when Lina had joined Coyote Investment after graduation, Helen had stayed on to do her doctorate in electrical engineering. Helen worked mostly at home, and in this isolation she cultivated what she liked to call her geekiness. Her idea of fun was roaming the Internet bulletin boards and "flaming" people she didn't like. She and Lina talked every few weeks, mostly about men. But if anyone would know how to break into a computer system, it would be Helen.

Lina put on her raincoat and rubber boots and walked to the pay telephone in the Pakistani grocery store around the corner. Except for Mr. Ahmad, the owner, it was empty. Lina cupped her hand around the receiver when her friend answered, and spoke in a whisper.

"Hello, Helen? This is Lina Alwan. I hope I'm not waking you up."

"Of course not. The night is young. It's only three in the afternoon in Menlo Park. What's new? How ya doin?"

"So-so. Do you have a minute? I need some advice about a computer problem." Lina looked down the aisle to the cash register. Mr. Ahmad was reading a magazine. He seemed oblivious. "It's sort of sensitive. If I tell you, you have to protect me. Will you promise?"

"Yeah, sure. All that stuff. What's up? It must be juicy."

Lina explained her problem in the most general terms. Something had come up at work, and she needed to get access to someone's personal files in the computer system. He was away and she didn't have his password. She needed help.

"I thought you were system manager. You should be able to access whatever files you want."

"Yes. But they changed my password. By mistake."

"Hmmm," said Helen. "I gather you can't get a new one."

"Correct. That is a non-option. But I need to get these files right away. And I need to do it sort of discreetly."

"Well, screw them. You're system manager, right? You can look at everything! The question is how to do it without raising eyebrows. Hmmm. Do you back up regularly?"

"What do you mean?"

"I mean, do you make a regular backup of the files, for security?"

"Definitely. We have a program that runs every Friday. It copies all the files onto one of those fat tapes."

"They're called Exabyte tapes, darling. What do you do with them?"

"I put them on a shelf, above the mainframe."

"Well, that may be the place to start. Get the backup tapes."

"Why? Nobody ever uses them."

"Precisely the point. They have the same goodies as the on-line system, but people overlook them. Plus, you can take them somewhere else, outside the office, to work on them. So that's where I would start. For sure."

"But how do I get into the files once I've got the backup tapes? I'm going to need some kind of trapdoor."

"Yes, you are, you naughty girl. I assume you have a UNIX system."

"Yes."

"Okay, then, this should work. The machine you use to run the tapes will have to be a few years old. Three or four years, at least. Got that? When you find one, you should log on as *tech*. Remember, *tech*. And your password will be *nician*. Cute, no? And don't tell *anyone* you did it, because this is *mucho secreto*. The techies hard-wired this account into the old UNIX machines so that they could get in if the users screwed everything up. It's an *s-u* account, so you can look at anything. And then, orgasm!"

"What does *s-u* stand for?"

" 'Superuser,' dummy. A root account. I can't believe you don't know this stuff. You're lucky I'm so smart."

"Lucky me. So how do I get to this guy's files once I'm inside? Explain that."

"If you just want a list of them, type *tar tv*. Tar stands for 'tape archive,' *tv* stands for 'table of contents, verbosely.' I know that sounds weird, but trust me. *Tar tv*. That will list everything in his personal directory."

"But I don't just want a list. I want the files. How do I get them?"

"Simple, for clever girls like you and me. Type *tar xv*. In this case, the *xv* stands for 'extract, verbosely.' Then a space, then a slash, then *user* and another slash, then the name of this poor clown whose files you're grabbing, then another slash, then an asterisk, which means you want all his files. Got that? It's *tar*, space, *xv*, space, slash, *user*, slash, name, slash, star. Presto. It's easy. Really. Now, what else can get screwed up?"

Lina looked at the phone and shook her head. "Everything. I don't mean to sound dumb, but I can't make any mistakes. Walk me through it."

"Step one: Get the backup tape. Step two: Find an old machine with a drive that will read the tape. Step three:

Log in through the trapdoor and do your *tar* routine. Step four: Read whatever you want, you naughty girl. Step five: Make copies of the files that pique your interest. Step six: Put the tape back where you found it, ve-ry carefully, and no one will be the wiser. Step seven: If you have made a mistake in any of the above, kiss your ass good-bye. Is that clear?''

"Almost. Where do I find a machine?"

"Using the machine in your office is absolutely out of the question? You couldn't come back late at night, when no one is around?"

"That would not be prudent."

"This is heavy stuff, I take it."

"Very heavy stuff. I wouldn't ask you for help, otherwise."

"What the hell. There's a UNIX host at school that will read your stuff. It's five years old, and I happen to *know* it has a trapdoor. When do you need it?"

"Tomorrow. Lunchtime."

"Go for it. It's in the CompSci Department on Gower Street, room 413. Remember where that is? Nobody will be there tomorrow except Shirley, the secretary. Everybody else is at a conference. I'll call Shirley and tell her you'll be using it. She won't mind. She's totally out of it."

"Will you be there?"

"Nope. I'm at the conference, too. You're on your own. But don't worry. It will be easy. And if you get caught, just say you're sorry. That always works for me."

Lina walked back in the rain, rehearsing in her mind all the steps Helen had described. It sounded almost easy, but that was the problem with people like Helen. They had, as she would put it, a different operating system.

The night seemed to last a year. Lina tried to sleep without success, turning back and forth in bed and glancing every half hour or so at the digital clock with its maddeningly precise chronology of her sleeplessness: 12:56. 1:48. 2:17. 2:34. 3:09. Finally she got up and took a sleeping pill, which left her feeling groggy the next morning. Which was, in its way, a blessing.

23

The Palestinian security man who had been wearing the brown Armani suit stopped by Lina's office early the next morning. He was wearing an olive-green Armani suit today, which hung on his trim frame as if he were a store mannequin. He looked sharp, angular, razor-cut. "Got a minute?" he asked. He was smiling, but Lina was still flustered. She had arrived at work only a few minutes before, and was already pondering whether it was safe to go after the backup tapes and what would be the best time to do it. And already, the security man was paying a visit.

"Can I sit down?" he asked. In addition to being "cute," as Randa had observed, he was polite and spoke English with an American accent. Lina pointed to a chair, and he sat down and crossed his legs. Lina noticed that he was wearing brown suede shoes that looked like they had come from Fratelli Rossetti in New York. He was an unlikely security man.

"I thought we might have a chat," he said. "Since I'm new here and you've been with the company for—what, three years?"

"Fine," said Lina. "Let's talk."

"Can I take off my coat? I'd feel more comfortable that way." He removed the coat and carefully hung it on the back of his chair. It really was Armani. He was quite a change from the garlic breath and grunts and groans of the two previous security men, Hammadi and Alani. Lina looked for a handle.

187

"Where did you learn to speak American English?" she asked.

"University of California at Santa Barbara," he said. "But now I spend most of my time in Tunis. Or I did, until Mr. Hammoud hired me. My name is Hassan, but my friends in California called me Haas."

"Okay, Haas. What's on your mind?"

He ignored the question, but he still had that friendly, easy smile on his face. "I gather you were having a few problems before. With Professor Sarkis."

Lina noted the mention of Sarkis rather than Hammoud. "Yes. That's right. But I hope I'm not in any trouble. As I said many times to Mr. Hammoud and Professor Sarkis, I have always tried to be a loyal employee."

"No. I don't think there's anything serious. Sarkis is history now, and I think Mr. Hammoud would like to turn over a new leaf." He turned his own hand over slowly, with the controlled movements of a man who was used to curling fifty-pound weights. His wrists were like fat crowbars, just visible under the starched cuffs of his shirt.

"He would?"

"Oh, yes. I think so. In fact, I'm sure he would. Mr. Hammoud isn't such a bad guy, you know. He just works too hard. Stressed out."

Lina nodded. *Stressed out.* She was still trying to take the measure of the well-dressed young man sitting across from her. His voice had the smooth, narcotic quality of an expensive cough syrup. What was frightening about him was his very blandness and the hint of suppressed violence that lay beneath the clothes and the manners.

"We'd like to see how you do at your old job," he said. "Back here in the accounting department. Just like before. How does that sound?"

"Fine," said Lina. "Thank you." He was creepier, with his mellow psychobabble, than the old cast of thugs.

"Well, listen. I know you've got a lot of work to do, and I really just wanted to stop by and introduce myself. We're glad to have you back at work. If you need anything, just ask me."

He picked his expensive suit jacket off the chair and shook her hand with a grip that had so little flesh and so much muscle it felt robotic. Lina watched him go, his crepe soles padding across the floor, and tried to decide whether he was for real. When she was seated at her desk again, alone, it occurred to her that it didn't matter. Whether or not he was serious about Hammoud turning over a new leaf, her choice was the same. She still needed "insurance." She looked at her watch. The time to make her run was the lunch hour. She had three hours to kill.

———

As twelve-thirty approached, the accounting department began to empty out. Lina watched as the "trusted employees" headed for the elevators. The computer room, across the hall from her, was vacant. She had been watching all morning, and no one had entered. Lina peered out her door and down the corridor. There was nobody in sight. She walked quickly across the corridor to the computer room and opened the door a crack. Empty. She entered the room and locked the door from the inside. It was cool and quiet. The computer hardware was arrayed against the wall, like a row of small refrigerators. There were no flashing lights and dials and random beeps. Just dumb metal boxes. Quickly, Lina told herself. Find the backup tapes and get out.

She couldn't find them at first. The shelves, which had been orderly only a few days ago, were now strewn with packets of sugar and plastic spoons. Someone had left a girlie magazine open on the top. Youssef was pathetic, really. She eventually found the most recent tape and put it in her purse. She grabbed a blank tape, in case she needed to make a copy, and shoved that in her purse, too.

She thought of taking the system manual, too—a large, loose-bound notebook—but decided it was too bulky. Never mind. She would have to puzzle things out herself. It was time to go. She tiptoed to the door and listened for footsteps but heard nothing. She opened the door a few inches, looked both ways and then slipped back out into the hall. Don't look back, she told herself. Quick steps and she was almost home. She closed her eyes when she opened the door to her little office, half-expecting to find Mr. Hammoud there, but it was empty.

Aywa! Yes, perhaps she had tricked the Evil Eye last night, tossing and turning in bed. Or maybe the Evil Eye had died with the Ruler. She retrieved her coat from the closet and peered back out into the hall. It was still empty. Where was everybody? She walked quickly to the elevator bank, praying that none of the security men would be there waiting, but all she saw was a British secretary from the other side, who had her nose in a book. It was working. The Evil Eye could see how much she had suffered the past few weeks, and it wasn't jealous anymore.

The university was in Bloomsbury, a half hour away by subway. Lina went directly to the Underground and took the Piccadilly line to Russell Square. It was drizzly and overcast, the sort of day when the cold of London seemed to hang on the body like a damp second skin. Lina headed for the campus where she had spent three years in happy scholastic oblivion. The pigeons in Russell Square looked as if they hadn't changed places since she left. Their necks were burrowed tight against their feathers in an effort to keep warm.

Lina went directly to the computer science faculty and took the elevator to the fourth floor. There was an old pensioner at the door in his blue uniform, supposedly guarding the place. But when Lina smiled at him, he just tipped his hat and smiled back. Shirley, the departmental secretary, was waiting in her office, just as Helen had said. She was reading *The Sun*. She remembered Lina from before, or pretended to. Lina apologized for disturbing her on a day when everyone else was away. "Not to worry," she said, and went back to reading her tabloid. It was a relief to be back in the sloppy embrace of the British.

Lina's biggest problem was the clock. She needed to

find the part of the tape that had the restricted files, copy it and get back to the office. She found a drive and loaded the tape. With a whir, the big computer began digesting the information. It took nearly forty minutes, far longer than Lina had expected. But eventually, the package was up and running, mimicking the system at Coyote. She looked at her watch. It was already past two.

She sat down to the computer terminal. A prompt asked for a user name. Lina typed in *tech*, as Helen had instructed. The machine recognized the account name and asked for a password. Lina typed in *nician*. The next line appeared with a new prompt character, #, and Lina realized she was inside. She typed *whoami*, just to make sure, and the machine echoed back *tech*. The trapdoor had worked!

Now Lina needed to find Hammoud's files, make copies and get out. She was trying to remember Helen's instructions, when she heard footsteps in the hall outside. She froze, afraid that the *pop-pop-pop* of the keyboard might be audible through the door. The footsteps slowed as they neared the door. That was odd. Helen had said the place would be deserted. In her sudden anxiety, Lina wondered if one of Hammoud's thugs might have followed her to Russell Square. She was a fool! She should have looked harder for surveillance. Lina quickly logged off the machine. Still, the footsteps hadn't moved from the door, and Lina thought she could hear someone breathing. She rose from the terminal and walked quietly to the door. Better to do anything than sit and cower. She closed her eyes and pulled open the door.

"Hallo, luv," said Shirley. She didn't seem the least bit embarrassed at being discovered. "I was just wondering how you were getting on? Would you like a cup of tea?"

"No, thanks," said Lina. "I'm fine."

Shirley lowered her voice confidentially. "They'll be coming back soon from the conference. Thought you'd like to know."

Lina nodded. "I'll be leaving soon, I promise."

"Ta," said Shirley, puttering back down the hall to her office. When Lina closed the door this time, she turned the bolt and locked it.

Lina returned to her work. She signed on again as *tech* and then typed carefully, as Helen had instructed: *tar tv / user/hammoud/**, requesting a directory of all of Hammoud's personal files. The screen dissolved and instantly re-formed, and the first of his secret files began marching up the screen. *Mazbout!* She had done it! The directory included twenty-three items; they all looked suspicious. She knew which one she wanted first. She typed *more oscartrading*. In an instant, the forbidden file was shining out at her from a thousand pixels. It was like seeing the dark side of the moon. The file was a simple, one-page document that read as follows:

OSCAR TRADING, S.A.
EDUARDO LARSEN, PRESIDENT
OMAR SANCHEZ, TREASURER
JULIO CASTILLO, SECRETARY
   CO ARSEN Y CASTILLO, ABOGADOS
   AVENIDA MEXICO Y CALLE 17 ESTE
   PANAMA 1, REPUBLICA DE PANAMA
   TEL: 507-25-6088
   BANK ACCOUNT NO. 38.50813,
BANQUE DES AMIS. 18 HENDRIKS PL., CURAÇAO,
NETHERLANDS ANTILLES.
   TUNIS OFFICE: OSCAR D. FABIOLO.
TEL: 216-1-718-075.
   EMERGENCY ONLY: R. Z. HATTON,
1700 J STREET, N.W., WASHINGTON, DC 20036,
USA. TEL: 1-202-555-9237.

There was no time to puzzle over what the document meant. Next to the system stood a laser printer. She typed *pr*; a few moments later she heard the high-pitched hiss of the rollers warming up to print. It was two-twenty. They would begin to wonder where she was soon. She would never have time to print out copies of all twenty-two remaining files. She decided to print out a few more highlights and save the rest for another time, when she had her own copy. She studied the directory. The file called "accounts" sounded interesting. She typed in the command *more accounts*, and up popped the requested document. It was simply a list of five companies and their addresses, followed by what appeared to be bank account numbers:

LINCOLN TRADING, LTD. RAWSON SQUARE, PO BOX J-3026, NASSAU, BAHAMAS. OBS # N4 808.537-0

GARFIELD INVESTMENT, LTD. RAWSON SQUARE, PO BOX J-3026, NASSAU, BAHAMAS. OBS # N4 808.537-1

WILSON TRANSPORT, INC. APARTADO 623, PANAMA CITY, PANAMA. OBS # B2 218.411-0

ADAMS INVESTMENT, INC. APARTADO 623, PANAMA CITY, PANAMA. OBS # B2 218.411-1

BUCHANAN TRADING, INC. APARTADO 623, PANAMA CITY, PANAMA. OBS # B2 218.411-2

As she stared at the list, it occurred to Lina that somebody had a sense of humor. The shell companies that masked the real ownership of Coyote Investment were all named after American presidents. What was OBS? It must be Organisation de Banques Suisses. Professor Sarkis had told her once, long ago when he still trusted her, never to ask any questions about Organisation de Banques Suisses.

She issued the print command and scrolled to the second and final page of the accounts file. It was a cash-management spreadsheet. The same five companies were listed again. But this time, next to each was a record of the movement of funds, in and out, during the quarter. The accounting summed to a bottom-line figure for each account, which was marked "Net Disbursements—1 January to 31 March." This number was the same for all five accounts: $21,128,056. She wondered how much Hammoud had skimmed before crediting those amounts.

She typed *pr* once more. It was nearing two-thirty. She knew she was pressing her luck, but she wanted to get as much information as she could before leaving. She returned to the directory once more and saw the file name "emergency." What was that? She typed in the command *more emergency*, and a moment later the document appeared on the screen. This was the briefest of all. It said, in its entirety,

M. 11, RUE DES BANQUES. NO. Z 068621.
CODE: 0526.

Lina studied the brief two lines of type and wondered what they meant. What on earth was the code? There wasn't time to bother with it now. She typed the print command. Back in the directory, she found the file name "banks" and typed *pr* again. This proved to be a list, with addresses and what appeared to be telephone numbers. Or perhaps they were bank account numbers.

1) OBELISK BANK. GRAYSON HOUSE, CORNER VERNON AND CHARLOTTE STREETS, NASSAU, BAHAMAS. 34.01.98.
2) BANQUE METROPOLE. 460 BOULEVARD RENÉ-LEVASQUE, SUITE 180, MONTREAL, CANADA. O-4877.
3) CRÉDIT OTTOMAN. 28, RUE DE PENTHIÈVRE, PARIS, FRANCE. LM5-R16.
4) ORDWAY BANK. 28 FORT STREET, GRAND CAYMAN, BRITISH WEST INDIES 6203-
5) BANQUE DES AMIS. 18 HENDRIKS PL., CURAÇAO, NETHERLANDS ANTILLES. 72.45813.
6) BANCOBRAGA. CALLE 51 ESTE, MARBELLA, PANAMA. 50876J.
7) NEW WORLD BANK. 79 MIGNOT PLATEAU, ST. PETER PORT, GUERNSEY, CHANNEL ISLANDS. D11870.6.
8) TARIQBANK. 48 KING FAISAL ROAD, MANAMA, BAHRAIN. TL 8078.

Lina typed *pr* once more. It was past two-thirty. She had to leave now. Absolutely, positively. She had managed to copy only four of the twenty-three restricted files, but there was no time left to do the rest. She retrieved her meager harvest from the printer: five pieces of paper. She folded them carefully and put them in the inside pocket of her jacket.

The tape. She still hadn't copied it. *Khalas!* Hoffman would be disappointed if she didn't find some way to copy Hammoud's files. She saw a manila envelope on a desk beside the terminal. On impulse, she took it and wrote on the outside: "Helen Copaken/Personal." She put the tape inside, along with a hastily scribbled note: "Helen: Please make a copy of 'user/hammoud/*' and take it home with you. Don't ask. xxx/ooo. L." She closed the flap as tightly as she could. On her way out, she handed the envelope to Shirley, with the brief admonition, "Helen asked me to leave this with you. She said it was important."

Shirley beamed. She liked to be helpful.

———

Lina took a taxi back to the office. The traffic was light, and she made it to Knightsbridge just after three o'clock. She was less nervous returning than she had been leaving. She didn't have the backup tape with her anymore, just the blank one she had brought to make a copy. When she reached the fifth floor, she punched the code into the cipher lock and entered the accounting department. The place seemed deadly still, as if someone had flipped a switch. "Hello," she called out in the direction of Randa's office. There was nobody there, or anywhere. She walked quickly back to her office. She was startled when she opened the door.

Sitting atop her desk was the slick security man in the fancy suit. Hassan closed the door. He wasn't smiling anymore. Lina's mouth felt dry and her fingertips were numb.

"Yumma!" she said under her breath. It was an Iraqi expression that meant, simply, "Mommy!"

24

"**W**here is the tape?" demanded Hassan. He had taken Lina by the wrist when she entered the small room and was squeezing it like a stick of kindling wood. His face had lost the controlled California look of a few hours before and was now drawn in a harsher, Mediterranean shade. Lina's mouth was open—emitting a sound that was at once a moan and a wail of fear—as he tightened his grip on her wrist. He had rolled up the sleeves of his fine cotton shirt, and his bare forearms looked as thick and hard as steel pipes. "Where is the tape?" he repeated.

"What tape?" she said, dizzy and grasping for air.

It was the wrong answer. Hassan pulled her toward him with his right hand, and with the left slapped her hard across the face. She crumpled toward the floor and was jerked back up again, still held at the wrist like a marionette. Hassan pushed her against the wall. A trickle of blood was flowing from her nose. He took one of his broad forearms and placed it across her throat, pressing her tight against the wall, and then brought his knee up between her legs so that she was pinned like a bug, at the crotch and the neck. "Where is the tape?" he repeated. "We know you took it. Where is it?"

"Purse," she gagged. "It's in my purse."

"Good girl," said Hassan. He released his knee and forearm and then pulled her by the wrist over to the desk where her purse lay. He turned it over and dumped out the contents. The blank tape clattered onto the desk. It said "SONY" in bright letters. The Palestinian picked it up and examined it, eagerly at first and then angrily. It was still wrapped in cellophane, unopened. He threw it against the wall, shattering it inside the wrapper.

"Not this tape, bitch!" He grabbed her by the nape of the neck and drove her head onto the desk top. "This is the wrong one." He pulled her up and slammed her head down again. "Where is the fucking tape?"

Lina gasped for breath. The last blow had cut her forehead, so that blood was running into her eye. She heard the voice of the Palestinian security man standing over her, repeating the same question. "Where is the tape?" The pain in her head was so intense it was impossible to think. If she didn't answer, he would hit her again. She knew that eventually, to stop the pain, she would confess, and he would find the computer printouts in her pocket, and she would be destroyed.

"Where is the tape?" he screamed again.

"I don't know," she cried. But she knew she was running out of time. His fingers were gripped so tight around her neck, it felt like the bones might break.

"Where did you take it, you dumb bitch?" He was sputtering with rage, tightening his grip with every word. "You gave it to your friend Randa, didn't you?"

"What?" wheezed Lina. She heard the words, but she couldn't think.

"The tape is at Randa's, isn't it?" he shouted again.

"Yes," she heard herself answer. It didn't matter what she said. As soon as they went looking for it, they would know she was lying. But at least it would buy her some time.

"It's at Randa's. I hid the tape at Randa's."

Hassan pulled her head up off the desk, tugging on her short black hair, and pushed her back against the wall. He placed his hand over her mouth and squeezed so hard the cheekbones seemed almost to crack. "If you're lying, you're dead," he said. "Now, where does Randa live?"

He took Lina out by the backstairs. A Jaguar sedan and a
driver were waiting in the alley, next to the Dumpster.
Hassan had been joined by a second Palestinian security
man, who he called Abu Raad. Each of them held Lina
by one elbow and shoved her toward the car. "Don't say
a fucking word," growled Hassan. He had pulled a
switchblade from his pocket and pointed the long, thin
blade at her back. They pushed her into the backseat between them and closed the doors of the big car. Hassan
yanked at her skirt, pulling it up toward her thighs; at the
same time he knocked her knees apart with the other hand.
He pressed the blade of his knife against her crotch so
that she couldn't move without hurting herself.
   "Do something about her forehead," he said. "It looks
bad. Somebody might see."
   The driver handed back a box of tissues, and Abu Raad
roughly dabbed at the blood that had clotted above her
eye and below her nose.
   "Okay. Tell him how to get to Randa's, and don't fuck
around." He pressed the blade harder, for emphasis.
   Lina gave him an address on Beltran Road in Chelsea.
It was where Randa actually lived. She had no idea what
she would do when they got to the flat, but she knew she
would have a better chance there than back at the office.
They headed south down Sloane Street, passing a policeman on the way. Lina thought of screaming, but the knife
pressed deeper against her flesh. "Don't get smart," said
Hassan. They cruised by Hans Place, Cadogan Square,
Eaton Place—some of the most expensive real estate in
the Western world, the fruit of vineyards that had been
tended thousands of miles away in the outposts of empire
and were now owned by Saudis, Lebanese, Canadians. The
car turned west onto King's Road, heading for Chelsea.
   "You are a very bad girl," said Hassan, relaxing his
grip on the knife slightly as the car sped along. He had
recovered a bit of his California bonhomie. "You know,
I don't think I have ever seen Mr. Hammoud so angry as

when I told him the tapes were missing this afternoon. He was really *mad*. Why did you think you could get away with that? Didn't you know we were watching you?''

"No," said Lina. All that was left of her voice was a hoarse whisper.

"You really are in deep shit, sweetie," continued Hassan in his snarky American accent. "You know that? I hate to think what they're going to do to you in Baghdad. They'll have to find out what you're really scared of. Are you claustrophobic? I hear they like to bury people underground in coffins. They give you a little straw for air and leave you there for a few days, a week, maybe forever. Or snakes? You like them? They're going to have a lot of fun with you in Baghdad. You're perfect."

He smiled that bland Santa Barbara smile, as if he were selling a juice machine or a Vegematic on television.

"And your cunt friend, Randa, too. What a bitch! She told us she would help keep an eye on you, and then she two-timed us. Mr. Hammoud is not going to be happy with her. Not at all."

"She doesn't know," said Lina. "I didn't tell her anything about the tape."

"Yeah, right. Give me a break."

They were in Chelsea now, driving past the industrial landscape of the gasworks and almost to the area where Randa had her apartment. "Where the fuck is it?" demanded Hassan impatiently. "Come on!"

"Turn left," she said, directing them toward Wandsworth Bridge Road. "And then right, onto Beltran."

"Which house is it?"

"That one." Lina pointed to the third house on the right. "Second floor."

The car pulled to the curb. Hassan removed the switchblade from between her legs. "Get out," he said. "And don't even think about pulling anything, because my friend Abu Raad has a gun and he is not a nice person." The other Palestinian removed a nine-millimeter pistol from his shoulder holster so that she could see the silver glint of the barrel. "Slowly now," said Hassan. "Careful."

Lina emerged from the car. She still wasn't sure what
she would do. The short street appeared to be empty of
passersby. Hassan took her by the wrist and pushed her
across the street. He had put the knife in the small of her
back, just above her buttocks. Lina scanned up and down
Beltran Road as they crossed the street, praying that she
would see someone. She had nearly given up when she
saw a figure in a dark coat emerging from the doorway
two houses down. He was carrying a large bag over his
shoulder. A postman. Hassan yanked her up on the curb
behind him. He was studying Randa's flat, wondering how
to get in. He hadn't seen the man in the dark coat.

This is it, Lina told herself. You either do something
now, or you die.

The scream took all the force of her will, but it suddenly
burst forth like the sound of a whistle—high-pitched and
scored with the terror that was in her throat and lungs and belly.
Hassan's head whirled toward the postman, and in the same
move, he jabbed the knife toward her. But Lina spun away in
that same moment, screaming as she tumbled toward the street.

"Stop!" shouted the mailman. He was loping toward
them in what seemed like slow motion, a big, gentle-look-
ing man in his mid-forties with his hand up in the air.
Hassan looked at him, then toward Lina, who was on her
feet and scrambling away, still screaming to wake the
dead. The Palestinian was frozen momentarily, wondering
which way to move. But his colleague, Abu Raad, had
made up his mind. He leveled his pistol toward the postman and pulled the trigger. The postman went down. The
gunshots echoed down the narrow street, and there were
screams from several windows.

"Shit!" said Hassan.

Lina was running hard now, back toward Wandsworth
Bridge Road. The driver had stepped from the Jaguar and
made a move to catch her, but he was too fat and slow, and
she was still screaming and running with the adrenaline rush
of someone who, a few moments before, had taken herself
for dead. People were coming from the main street now,
roused by the commotion, and several were approaching the

two Palestinians. Abu Raad took aim at Lina and fired once, but she was low to the ground and he missed. The sound of the gunshot sent the pedestrians diving for cover, but Lina kept running and, before Abu Raad could fire again, she had turned the corner and was gone.

"Fuck!" said Hassan. "Get in the car!" he shouted to Abu Raad. "Now."

The Palestinian fired once more into the air, and then ran with Hassan to the Jaguar. "Should I follow her?" asked the driver.

"Forget the girl," said Hassan. "Get out of here."

They were caught a few minutes later at a police road-block in Wandsworth. The headlines in the final edition of the *Evening Standard* said PLO GUNMEN NABBED IN TERROR RAID. There was no mention in the article of Coyote Investment or Nasir Hammoud. But the police were said to be searching for a third suspect, an Arab woman who had assisted the gunmen and fled on foot.

Lina caught the first bus she saw on Wandsworth Bridge Road. The wound on her bottom was superficial, and the bleeding had already stopped, but she was trembling like a sparrow. She kept patting her pocket to make sure the computer printouts were still there. A woman sitting nearby on the bus tried to comfort her, but she said she was all right, really, and the woman let her be. She checked in her purse to make sure she still had her wallet, and counted out her money. It was enough for a taxi. She wanted to take a shower and change clothes, and then worry about how to stay alive.

She got off the bus in Fulham and hailed a black taxi. "Notting Hill Gate," she told the driver. "Lansdowne Walk." But as the cab turned off Holland Park Avenue toward her flat, she saw a man perched atop a motorcycle, waiting. He was parked directly opposite her building.

"Shit," said Lina, slouching down low in the seat.

"Sorry, miss?" said the driver.

"Keep going," she said quickly. "Don't stop."

He turned around and eyed her suspiciously, but he kept his feet on the gas. "Where to, then, eh?"

"North Audley Street," said Lina.

The driver headed back east along Bayswater Road and turned onto Hoffman's street, just past Marble Arch. But as they neared his entry, Lina saw another dark figure, sitting in a panel truck with his eyes on Hoffman's door. The driver was slowing, getting ready to stop. Lina crouched down low in the seat and hid her face with her hand.

"Keep going, please, driver. Don't stop here. I'm sorry. Wrong address."

The driver looked back at her as if she were mad. "Where to this time?"

"Anywhere," she said. "Buckingham Palace. I want to do some sight-seeing."

He shook his head but continued on as commanded. Lina didn't mind that he kept glancing at her in the rearview mirror. Under the circumstances, it was almost reassuring.

——

Lina called Hoffman a few minutes later from a pay telephone on Birdcage Walk, just past Buckingham Palace. Her voice was shaky. He asked immediately if she was all right.

"No," she said. "I'm not all right. Two of Hammoud's men just tried to kill me. I was lucky to get away. But I got the evidence we talked about. It looks pretty good, if I can figure it out."

"Jesus! How did you get away?"

"I ran. I'm still running."

"Have you called the police?"

"No. But I have a feeling they may be looking for me soon. One of Hammoud's boys shot a mailman."

"Where are you? I'll come get you right now."

She paused to think a moment. She needed him and she didn't need him. He could help her, and he could hurt her. "I may do better on my own right now, Sam. They have you staked out. If you try to meet me, they'll follow you."

"What are you talking about."

"I saw a man on Audley Street a few minutes ago. I was coming to see you, but when I saw the man camped out on your doorstep, it seemed like a bad idea."

Hoffman looked out the window and studied the man in the blue truck. "You're right," he said. "What are you going to do?"

"I'm going to ground. Isn't that what you spies say?"

"I'm not a spy, dammit. I hate spies. I've spent my life trying to get away from spies."

"Good-bye, Sam. I'll call as soon as I can, from somewhere."

"Wait a minute. Can't we set up a meeting, in a park or someplace? I can shake my tail."

"See. You *are* a spy."

"No, I'm not. I'm your friend. I care about you. And you're my client."

The beeps had begun to sound, signaling that it was time to insert more coins in the phone box. "That's sweet," said Lina. "But I have to go now. I'm out of money."

Hoffman began to speak again, imploring her, but the phone went dead.

Lina knew her next destination. She hailed one of the cabs whizzing toward the Embankment. "Take me to Blackheath," she told the driver. "Anywhere near Greenwich Park would be fine."

"That's a long way, miss," said the driver dubiously. A twenty-pound cab ride to no particular address. Lina closed her eyes and sat back in the deep leather seat. When they arrived in Blackheath thirty minutes later, she paid the fare and walked a few hundred yards to a small, terraced house on Westgrove Lane. She stopped along the way, crossed the street and doubled back once to make sure no one was following her. After a final, furtive look, she rang the doorbell.

25

"**Y**ou look like shit!" said Helen Copaken when she opened the door. "What happened to you?" She was dressed in black jeans and a white T-shirt without a bra, and her long frizzy hair was piled atop her head with a wooden barrette. Helen lived in a time warp, somewhere between late bohemian and early punk. Her looks and dress were part of the protective cover of a woman who had always been smarter than anyone around her, including the men who dominated her field. She was just shy of being beautiful, and she seemed to like it that way. Years ago, when they were at university together, she had adopted Lina as a kind of Seeing Eye dog to the real world.

"Hi," said Lina faintly. "Can I come in?"

Helen pulled her in the door and gave her a kiss on the cheek, then stepped back. "Seriously, girl. You look strung out. What the hell have you been up to? Is everything okay?"

"No, everything's not okay. I'm in trouble."

Helen took a closer look at Lina's face. "What happened to your forehead? And your nose? Did somebody beat you up?"

Lina nodded. She was close to tears suddenly, after so many hours of being brave. "People at my office tried to kill me," she said.

Helen didn't get it. She thought Lina was making a

joke. "I'm not surprised, after that stunt with the tapes. People at my office want to kill me, too, by the way. The department chairman was not amused."

"Did you make a copy?"

"Yup! Got it right here. Want to tell me what this is about?"

"Not now. Maybe later. But I really mean it, Helen. People at my office want to kill me."

"Do they want to kill you or just maim you?"

"I'm serious, dammit. Two guys kidnapped me from the office this afternoon after I got back from the university. They wanted to take me to Baghdad, but I ran away. And then they shot a mailman. It will probably be in the newspapers tomorrow." Tears began trickling from her eyes.

"Baby!" said Helen, wrapping her arms around Lina, finally realizing that Lina meant exactly what she had said. She let her cry for a while, and then brought her a cup of hot tea, and a first-aid kit to dress her wounds, and a plate of sweet biscuits and a bowl of ice cream. It was only after she had ministered to her friend that Helen asked the question.

"Why would anyone want to kill you?"

Lina paused a moment before answering. "Do you really want to know? Because it's dangerous, and you have to promise not to tell anyone."

"I really want to know. And I won't tell a soul."

"They want to kill me because they think I know where the ruler of Iraq kept his money."

"Awesome! Is that what you were looking for in those files?"

"Yes. Unfortunately, they found out I took the tape."

"Awesome!" she repeated. "So the problem is, how are we going to get you out of this mess?" She was very businesslike now, having decided to take over the management of her friend's problems. "How long will it take for this whole thing to blow over?"

"I don't know. A year or two. It's hard to say, but I

think it's going to take a while. There's quite a lot of money involved."

"How much?"

"A few billion, probably."

"Dollars or pounds?"

"Dollars. But what's the difference?" Lina explained, as best she could, the details of what had transpired over the past week, and what she had discovered during her excursion into Nasir Hammoud's computer files, and the various Arab secret policemen who had been pursuing her since she first stumbled across evidence of the secret accounts. She mentioned everyone except Sam Hoffman, who was one secret she wanted to keep.

"So what are you going to do?" asked Helen when her friend had finished her narrative.

"Run away somewhere, I guess. I can't go home. I obviously don't want to go to Baghdad. Maybe I'll leave the country."

"Where will you go, sweetie?"

"I don't know. Anywhere but the Middle East. The money is in Switzerland, or at least that's what it looks like from the files I saw. Maybe I could go there and keep it company. What do you think I should do?"

"Run away. You certainly can't sit still. If you do, they'll get you. And then you're dead, which is an undesirable outcome."

"Maybe I could stay here," said Lina, surveying the comfy disarray of Helen's house. "This would be perfect, for a few days at least."

"Feel free. I would love to have you. But they'll find you here."

"How? I don't think I was followed."

"They don't have to follow you to figure out you're staying with me. They'll find you. How many times have you called me from the office in the last month?"

"I don't know. Once. Maybe twice."

"So they'll see my number in your phone records and trace the address. And then they'll be here. That's why you can't sit still. You have to keep moving."

"God, this is horrible."

"But it's cool, too. Sort of like Lara in *Doctor Zhivago*."

Lina shook her head. "Don't make any more jokes or I'll start crying again. I mean it. I feel like a cat who has been chased up a tree by a pack of dogs. How do I get out of this?"

"Do you want me to be honest?"

"Of course. You would be anyway, so what's the difference?"

"The truth is, you don't have any good options. They're all bad. So you need to think about creating some new ones."

"Maybe I should give up. Go to the police and tell them the truth, and hope the thugs don't come after me again."

"No way. Nothing is as unbelievable as the truth. And the police can't protect you from these creeps. Face it. If you stay here, Hammoud's men will eventually catch you and then torture you to find out what you know. They're probably all deviants. Sexually dysfunctional with women unless they tie them up. They'll take you to a cave in Yemen and tie you naked to a stake and smear you with honey and let ants eat you. And then, when they realize that you really don't know anything, they'll have to shoot you to cover up their crimes."

"Stop it, Helen. This isn't one of your weirdo bulletin boards. This is real. They really do things like that in Baghdad."

"I am serious. Not about Yemen but about getting some new options. You need leverage."

Lina considered what Helen was saying and realized that she was right. All her options were bad. She couldn't go home, she couldn't hide out at Helen's for very long and she couldn't give herself up. There was no escape from the top end of the tunnel, through which she had entered. Her only choice was to go deeper, in the hope of finding an opening on the other side. She needed leverage, as Helen had said. Maybe Hammoud's files would give her some, if she could understand them.

"By the way," said Helen. "There was something on the net last night about a woman in distress that was vaguely similar to your predicament. You want to hear?"

"Will it cheer me up?"

"I'm not sure. It was on the bondage board. The routing is 'alt.sex.bondage,' if you're interested."

"Not especially. They don't have 'alt.sex.normal,' I suppose?"

"You're right, they don't have that. But they have everything else: 'alt.sex.masturbation,' 'alt.sex.bestiality.' They even have something called 'alt.sex.sound.' People record themselves having sex. They make the most amazing sounds. Really."

"You wouldn't be talking like this if you knew how frightened I've been today."

"Oooh! Harder! Pleeease!"

"Helen!"

"Oh, *God*! Pleeeease. Harder! Oooooh. Oooooooohhhh."

Lina smiled. Falling into Helen's world of electronic fantasy was at least a kind of escape from her own troubles. "So? What did it say? The one that was similar to my predicament."

"It was from a woman who called herself Sandra. She was describing a scene she had gotten into with a man she had met from the net. Actually, she hadn't met him before. They had exchanged messages on a board called 'alt.sex.wizards.'"

"What are *wizards*?"

"People who know everything. In this case, they give expert advice on sex. They claim to know what they're talking about, although I have a feeling they're really just horny undergraduates who read about it in magazines."

"So what happened with the woman and the wizard?"

"He posted a message about sex and trust. He said the whole point about sex is to put yourself in someone's arms and trust them, even when they have the capacity to hurt you. For some reason, Sandra liked the sound of that, so she arranged to meet this guy."

"What happened?"

"They met in a park. She never even saw him. He came up behind her and before she could say anything, he put a blindfold around her head and took her to his car. Then he drove her to a motel. She didn't resist. She put herself totally in his hands. That was what she thought she wanted. But then it got weird."

"How weird?"

"Very weird. He wanted her to do a lot of totally disgusting things. He was bad news. Like the two guys from the office who want to smear you with honey."

"I'm so glad you told me this. What happened to Sandra?"

"Fortunately, she didn't get hurt. She screamed and ran away. The guy was pissed. He thought he was doing what she wanted. Anyway, she posted a message to the board—anonymously, of course—explaining what had happened and warning other women to stay away from this particular wizard. She got him in trouble, big time. Notified the system administrator that there was a wacko on the net. The administrator gave his name to the police. The jerk is electronic history."

"What does this have to do with me, anyway?"

"Not much, now that we talk about it. But the point is, the woman was involved in a major unpleasant situation, and she turned the tables by taking the offensive. Which is what you should do."

"Right. But I'm not dealing with weekend sadists from Internet, I'm dealing with the real thing. What am I going to do about it?"

"I'm working on a plan. I need to have another cup of tea first. And you need some rest. Go upstairs and take a bath. And then have a nap. I'll wake you in an hour or two."

Lina obeyed. For the moment, she was content to let Helen entirely take over the management of her life. She took a long bath and then fell asleep, and stayed asleep until nearly ten o'clock the next morning. While her visitor was resting, Helen signed on to Internet. She posted a message on a bulletin board used by the net's computer-security wizards, asking her fellow geeks for advice about the security of banking systems. Within a few hours, she had received several thousand words of electronic advice from around the world. It was a global network of Lilliputians, ready to help make trouble for Gulliver.

26

Helen awakened Lina the next morning and showed her the newspapers. The most complete account was in *The Times*. It named Lina as the mystery woman and provided a detailed description of her. It also quoted "knowledgeable police sources" saying that the Arab woman—Miss Alwan—had been working with two Palestinian terrorists from Tunis to steal the confidential files of a major London investment company where she worked. The company in question was offering a substantial reward for information about Miss Alwan's whereabouts. Lina shook her head ruefully. She had to credit Hammoud. He was smarter than she had realized.

"You have a problem, sweetie," said Helen, pointing to the newspaper. "You could use a new identity." The best Helen could do was provide Lina with a different hair color and a different wardrobe. The sleek Arab princess emerged from Helen's room an hour later as a peroxide blonde wearing granny glasses, a long skirt, a peasant blouse and a backpack. She looked almost Nordic.

Helen made breakfast. The two women ate in Helen's back garden, which was thick with vines and buds and blossoms and matched the disordered style of its owner. The morning sun occasionally shone through the clouds, lighting up the garden like a moving searchlight, so that every plant seemed to glisten in the sun and then fade back to a darker green. Enjoying this momentary escape from her troubles, Lina asked what her friend was working on.

Helen explained that she was designing a new computer game. It was called Feminist Alien Invaders. The working concept was that a new race of women had arrived on Earth from outer space. They were identical in every respect to the human variety, except that the game player could establish certain behavioral parameters, such as ambition and libido. The object of the game was to see whether the feminist alien invaders would take over the planet or be destroyed.

"The thing is," said Helen, "when ambition goes up, libido goes up, too. Successful feminist aliens want to have sex all the time. But they get too busy. And when they have less sex, they become less creative and less successful. That's the trick, see? To get the right combination."

Helen was explaining a further point of strategy when the phone rang. Neither woman moved, and there was suddenly no sound anywhere, except for the phone. One, two, three rings. Even the birds and the insects in the great outdoors seemed to quiet down.

"I guess you should answer it," said Lina. She followed Helen into the house. The world was intruding on their fanciful garden.

"Hello," said Helen. "Yes, this is Miss Copaken. Who's calling? . . . Do I know you? . . . What do you want?"

Helen shook her head grimly, then put her finger to her head as if it was a gun. "Who? Spell her name again. A-L-W-A-N. Yes, I know her. But I haven't seen her in a while. . . . No, I don't know where she is. . . . Yes, I would mind if you stopped by. I'm going out. . . . Good-bye."

Helen hung up the phone. "Oh, Jesus," she said.

Lina had collapsed on the couch. Her head was cradled in her hands and she was rocking gently back and forth, the way a mother rocks a baby. "Who was it?" she asked, without looking up. She already knew.

"A man from your office. He had an accent. They're looking for you. He said it was important."

"They know I'm here, don't they?"

"They'll probably guess it. I don't think I was very convincing."

"What should I do?"

"Move. Right now. They may be here soon. You've got to go. Pronto. We'll take my car. Come on." She reached out her hand to the couch, to pull Lina up.

"Where are we going?" Lina was still limp.

"To the airport. I figured out a plan for you last night. I was going to tell you in the garden, but I can explain it on the way to Heathrow. Come on, girl. Rise and shine!"

Lina rose slowly from the couch and gathered her few belongings. Helen was already a blur. She retrieved an overnight bag from upstairs, filled it with things she thought Lina could use and brought it down to her. In her study, she found a new laptop computer and loaded it—along with extra disks, applications software, modem cables, a portable printer and a power converter—into a carrying bag. She grabbed a handful of chocolate chip cookies in the kitchen and put them in a plastic bag. "Let's *go!*" she said.

Helen's car was an old Volvo sedan, so ancient that it still had rounded fenders. She loaded the bags in the backseat and put Lina in the front, pushing and prodding until her friend had fastened her seat belt, and they were on their way. "Eat your hearts out, you dickheads," she called out the window as she pulled away from the house.

"So what's the plan?" asked Lina as they turned onto Blackheath Road. "Where are you sending me?"

"Switzerland," said Helen, her breasts bouncing up and down under the T-shirt as the car weaved in and out of traffic. "You have to go there. That's where the money is. That's where you'll get your leverage."

"You're daft, Helen. That's where the crooks are. If they find me there, they'll really kill me."

"*Au contraire.* They'll kill you no matter where they find you. The reason to go to Switzerland is because that's the best place to break into the bank's computer net and find the money."

"But I don't want to break into the net."

"Oh, yes, you do. I told you. That's your best shot. Your only shot, really. And maybe the Swiss will help you. They would probably like to know that their banks have been laundering money for the world's leading despot. Listen to me, Lina. This is serious. I've done a little checking with some computer friends, and I think it will work."

They crossed the Deptford Bridge, clanking over the ancient structure and into a knot of traffic on the other side. Helen rolled down the window and called out to a cabbie, asking the quickest way to Heathrow. He rattled off a stream of directions. Helen grabbed a pen, looked for a piece of paper and, finding none, wrote the directions on her wrist.

"Okay," said Lina when they were on their way again. "How am I going to break into the bank network once I get to Switzerland, assuming that I go?"

"You start with whatever you know. Like the name of the bank where the money is kept. Do you know that?"

"Yes, I think so. It's Organisation de Banques Suisses, in Geneva."

"Okay. There you are. Now listen to me, because what I'm going to tell you could be worth several billion big ones. You listening, girl?"

"Yes, I'm listening."

"This is easy, if you do it right. The first thing you do when you get to Geneva is to get a brochure from this bank. Anything that has telephone numbers on it. And start calling numbers until you find a modem line. They all make that same weird buzz, even in Switzerland. Then play around with the communications software until you're hooked up with the mainframe in the bank. You may have to try different parity settings and reset the baud rate a couple of times, but eventually you'll get a log-in connection."

"You forget one thing, Helen. I don't have a computer."

"Yes, you do. I packed one of mine. It's a new 486 laptop with a built-in modem. It does everything."

"Okay. What next? Assuming I make this silly trip. Which I'm not going to do."

"Next you find a log-in name. Play around until you get a hit. Since it's Switzerland, I would stay away from Smith or Jones, Try Larouche or DeGaulle."

"Or Hammoud."

"Right. Try that. Eventually you'll find one that works. Now, when the computer registers the name, it will probably disconnect you. The reason it's doing that is for security. It wants to call you back, to make sure you're who you say you are. So you'll want to set the modem software parameters so that it doesn't respond to the hang-up signal by disconnecting. You want to stay on the line. You copying all this?"

"Yes." Lina looked out the window at the cars heading the other way toward Blackheath. She wondered which of them was carrying Hammoud's men.

"Do you think you can make the software modification?" pressed Helen. "Otherwise I can do it for you when we get to the airport. No problem."

"Don't patronize me, Helen. Just because I wear a bra and I'm not obsessed with computers doesn't mean I'm stupid."

"Ouch. Flame me!"

"Sorry."

"That's okay. People are trying to kill you. You're a little tense. No problem. So, as I was saying, to make the bank computer think it's doing the call-back procedure, you're going to have to record a dial tone and send it down the line at exactly the right moment. That will make the computer think you've disconnected, even though you're still on the line. Then, the bank computer will send out some dialing tones, trying to connect with Pierre or Jacques or whoever you're logged on as. But you've never really disconnected, see? So eventually, that magic word is going to pop up on the screen: *password*."

"And then I'm finished. How am I possibly going to get the right password?"

"Not easy. But not impossible. I gave you a disk that has sixty thousand of the most common passwords, and you could keep trying them until you got it. But that would be a pain. And you might get caught. The way to do it is actually fairly obvious, to a weird and geeky but extremely sexy person such as myself."

Lina laughed. "Tell stupid, ugly me how to do it."

"You call the number whose dial tone was generated by the bank computer when it thought it was calling back Mr. Big to verify the transaction. That will probably be a PC somewhere, at his home or on his desk. So you call the number and log on to his system. It probably won't have a password. Once you're in, look around. Check out his files."

"What am I looking for?"

"Anything that has the password for the main system. Old datacom files will sometimes have it. Or it may be in its own file. Try asking for a file called Password. People really are that stupid. It may take you a while, but you'll get it."

"Suppose the password is encrypted. Then what?"

"If the password is in the dictionary, you can break it by brute force. I have a DES decryption algorithm and a five-hundred-thousand-word dictionary on a diskette. But the point is, the password probably won't be encrypted. The secret truth about the Swiss is that they're sloppy."

"How do you know?"

"I had a Swiss boyfriend once, when I was at boarding school. He was sloppy."

"Not statistically significant."

"That's true. He wasn't."

"Okay. Let's assume I have the password. Then what do I do?"

"Now you're ready to play. You dial up the bank with your modem, you answer Mr. Whoozis at the prompt, you send the dial tone, you let the bank computer pretend to call Mr. Whoozis back on his machine, you type in the password at the prompt and you're inside. Then you browse. It will take a while to figure out the software applications the bank is using. And you'll have to get access to the datafiles to find what you really want. But you'll figure it out when you get to Geneva.''

"I'm not going to Geneva."

"Oh, yes, you are. The only way out of this is to run faster. Do you want me to tell you again about being tied to a stake in Yemen?''

"Stop it!" said Lina sharply. "Don't joke any more about torture. It's not funny."

They drove in silence for a while. Helen was making good time now that she was out of the maze of traffic along the South Bank and onto larger arteries. She looked at her friend, gazing out the window, her fists gripped into tight balls. "I'm sorry," said Helen quietly.

"That's okay. These things just aren't a joke for me, that's all."

———

They reached Heathrow a little before one. Helen looked for Swissair on the list of airlines and steered toward the terminal. "They must have lots of flights to Geneva. Take the next one. You have a British passport, right? So just flash it on the way out. The place will be crawling with people looking for Lina Alwan, but they all think she's an overdressed Arab and not a geeky-looking gal like you. So have fun. And don't be nervous."

Helen stopped at the curb, as near as she could get to the Swissair check-in. She took the gear from the backseat and handed it to Lina. "Here's the laptop. Modem is built in. In the bag is an extra battery pack and some diskettes with the fancy software, and a printer and cables. And an adapter, for those goofy outlets over there. I put some dresses and sweaters and stuff in the overnight bag."

Lina took the two bags and slung one over each shoulder. Helen took her wallet from her purse. "Here's my American Express card," she said. "You might as well pretend to be me. Stay at a good hotel. Spend my money. When I sell Feminist Alien Invaders, I'm going to be so rich it won't matter. And if you're going to die, you might as well enjoy it. You have your passport?'' Lina nodded. She had a foreigner's habit of always carrying her travel documents.

''Do you have any cash?''

''Some.'' Lina counted the bills in her wallet.

''Here's one hundred pounds,'' said Helen. ''It's all I've got. Here's my telephone credit card. And here's my cash card. The PIN code is zero-seven-two-one. Get some more cash at the airport. Buy some clothes and a toothbrush when you get to Geneva.''

''I'll pay you back.''

''Sure. Now go, before it's too late. Call me when you get there. From a pay phone.''

''I'm scared, Helen.''

''Get a grip on yourself, girl. This is the big time!''

27

Lina disappeared. There was no word of her, no hint of her fate, no sign that she even existed except for the footsteps of the many people who had been pursuing her. Hoffman sat guiltily in his office that morning, reading the newspapers and wondering whether, if he had been smarter, he could have seen what was coming. He was visited at midmorning by an officer from Scotland Yard. He was dressed in a policeman's idea of casual clothes—tweed jacket, tie slightly loosened, the top button of his shirt undone. He identified himself as Mr. Williams. After making the usual policeman's apologies about how sorry he was for the interruption, he asked if Sam knew a Miss Alwan. Sam said immediately that he did; they were friends. He made it a practice not to tell lies that could be easily disproven.

"And do you know where she is now, I wonder, sir?" asked the inspector.

"No, I don't," said Hoffman. "Do you?"

"That's police business. But the fact is, she's gone missing. She left her office rather suddenly yesterday, and she isn't at home. She seems to have flown the coop."

"So I gather from the newspapers. Where do you think she's gone? I'd like to find her myself."

"Would you really, now, sir? And why might that be?" Williams had a British policeman's technique of asking gentle but insinuating questions. None of the blustery

American cop-talk for the Brits. They actually caught criminals.

"Because I think someone is after her," said Hoffman.

"Well, that is most certainly true. Someone *is* after her."

Hoffman narrowed his eyes and leaned toward the British policeman. "Who?"

"We are, sir. Special Branch. I have a warrant for Miss Alwan's arrest."

"Arrest? You're kidding. What's the charge?"

"Theft of property. Misappropriation of funds. Conspiracy to murder a postman. The list is quite lengthy, actually."

"Those charges are ridiculous. Who's making them?"

"Her employer. A chap there named Hammoud notified us last night."

Sam protested that the charges were nonsense, that Lina was no thief and that if she had fled, it was because she was frightened of what Hammoud might do to her. As he talked, Sam noticed, Inspector Williams had taken out a small notebook and begun jotting down notes. "And why would she be frightened of him, sir?" the policeman asked sweetly.

"Because he's a killer."

Inspector Williams didn't write that down. He looked over the top of his glasses at Sam. "That's a rather serious charge, sir. I'm afraid you will need some evidence to support that one."

"Look. Let me explain this. Hammoud is after Miss Alwan because he thinks she knows where a lot of money is."

"Well, that's just my point, sir. I agree, that is why Mr. Hammoud is upset. He says Miss Alwan took some confidential files that were not, strictly speaking, her property."

"But they're wrong. She doesn't know anything. She's just frightened. People are chasing her. She thinks someone is trying to kill her. That's why she has run away. Do you have any idea how much money is involved here?"

"How much would that be, I wonder?" His pen was poised. Hoffman realized he had blundered. He was on his way to being named as an accomplice in whatever ludicrous case they were preparing against Lina.

"I don't know. A lot."

Sam tried to be more careful after that. The policeman wanted to know when Sam had last talked to Lina, and he said it had been the previous afternoon, around two. He had tried to set up a meeting with her, Sam said, but she had refused. He had no idea where she was now, and if Scotland Yard found out, he hoped they would call him. Inspector Williams tried to ask more questions about the nature of his dealings with Lina, but Sam refused to say any more until he had talked to a lawyer. At that point, the inspector closed his little leather book. He handed Hoffman a card. Hoffman showed him to the door.

———

Hoffman felt even gloomier after the policeman's visit. From the moment the Filipino cook had arrived at his door until now, his encounter with Nasir Hammoud had been a disaster. He pulled from his desk drawer the one piece of hard evidence he had managed to accumulate—a blank piece of letterhead stationery—and realized that he didn't even understand what that meant. He hadn't bothered even to call the Tunis contact number for Oscar Trading. He had been sleepwalking. As a kind of penance, he picked up the telephone and dialed the number listed on the stationery: 216-1-718-075. It rang three times before an American voice answered with a soft, southern twang.

"Hello. Can I help you?"

"Who is this?" asked Hoffman.

"Can I help you?" repeated the voice. It was a man, probably about Hoffman's age. There was an expectancy in his voice, as if he was waiting for Hoffman to give the right answer.

"What is this number?" asked Hoffman. "Who have I reached?"

The line went dead. The man in Tunis had hung up. Hoffman tried again, immediately, but the line was busy, and it stayed busy for most of the next hour. When Hoffman got through again, it was the same pantomime.

"Hello," said the southern voice. "Can I help you?"

"I'm calling about Oscar Trading," Hoffman said this time.

"One moment," said the voice, putting the call on hold. There was a pause that seemed to last sixty seconds. As Hoffman waited, it occurred to him that someone might be trying to trace the call. Eventually the man came back on the line.

"I'm sorry," he said. "I can't help you with that. There is no Oscar Trading here."

"What number is this?" asked Hoffman.

The line went dead. When Hoffman tried it again a few minutes later, a Tunisian operator came on and said the number was disconnected.

As Hoffman turned this strange encounter over in his mind, he had a distant memory of something from his childhood. There was a number that his father left by the phone at home in Beirut, to be used only in case of emergencies. One day, as a boy in Beirut, Sam Hoffman had dialed the number. A smooth, assured man's voice had answered it in the same way: "Hello. Can I help you?" And then, when young Sam Hoffman failed to give the right answer, he had hung up.

━━━

Hoffman decided that afternoon that he needed reinforcements. He was playing in the big leagues of deceit without understanding the nature of the game. After considering the problem for a few minutes, he placed a call to a Palestinian acquaintance in Paris named Ali Mattar, who was, quite simply, the most accomplished liar he had ever met.

Ali Mattar had grown up in a refugee camp near Tyre in South Lebanon. Like a Levantine Oliver Twist, he had managed to charm and cajole his way out of the camps and into a life of semi-respectability by providing information to the half-dozen intelligence services that had at one time or another owned a piece of him. At one magical moment during the early 1980s, he had simultaneously been providing intelligence to Syria, Israel, the PLO and Iran. He got away with it because it was assumed that he was really working, all the while, for the United States. And he was, sort of.

But in truth, Ali always worked for himself. That essential selfishness had been his protection. As a young man, he had come to Beirut and gotten a job as a driver at the American Embassy. He had quit after a few years and opened a travel agency, knowing in his heart that the friendly Americans sending him business must be intelligence officers (although he later insisted he had never suspected anything of the sort). Ali knew what he was doing. He was on the move. The United States in those days was the main ticket out.

Ali was recruited, if you can call it that, in the late 1960s and sent out to penetrate the Palestinian underground. Which he did admirably, although it was probably also the fact that he was recruited by the Palestinians to penetrate the CIA. Who can say where his real loyalties lay in the secret chamber of the heart, other than with himself? Now Ali lived comfortably in Paris at the gray margins of the intelligence world, trading in the odd bits of information that came his way. Sam Hoffman had been an eager buyer of information about Arab business deals. The thing he liked about Ali Mattar was that he actually knew things. He didn't make them up. It was an embarrassment to Sam that the introduction to Ali Mattar, as with so many of his other sources, had come through his father.

"I need some help, Ali," Hoffman ventured when he reached Mattar in Paris that afternoon. He hated talking business on an international phone line, but under the circumstances, he had no choice. "A few days' work. Handsome retainer. All expenses paid."

"What's the topic, *habibi*?"

"Iraq."

"*W'Allah!* My God, Sam. I cannot believe the Ruler is dead after so many years. What a shock it was to me. My God! So, what do you want to know?"

"About his money."

"A hot topic, my friend. I think everybody is asking about this today. You are the third person who calls me. Very hot topic. How much you pay me? Ha, ha!" The laugh meant it would be expensive.

"Two thousand a day. Plus expenses. I need good stuff, good enough to take to the police."

"I am sorry. I cannot do it, even for you, Sam. This is charity. Other people, you know who, they pay five times that for what I know. Ten times, maybe."

"Okay. Three thousand a day. That's all I can afford. But it's not bad for a few hours' work."

"I get an offer of five thousand just one hour ago from the man with the cut on his nose, you know who I mean. What can I do? I got to live. You are putting me in a very hard place, my friend."

Hoffman sighed. He liked Ali, but he hated bargaining. "Four thousand, plus expenses."

"My dear. No more talking about money. If you like what Ali finds out, you will pay for it. I know you, Sam."

"Four thousand," repeated Hoffman. He didn't want to leave it ambiguous.

"As you like, my friend. So what you want to know?"

"I told you. About the Ruler's money. And who killed him, and why. I'm particularly interested in anything you can find out about Nasir Hammoud."

"Ahaa! You got the right guy, maybe. How much you know about Hammoud?"

"I know he was in Baghdad right before the Ruler died. And I know that a lot of people think he's sitting on top of the Ruler's money."

"*Mish maouul!* This is tricky business, Sam. Four thousand a day is not enough. But okay. We make deal."

"That's right. We made a deal."

"I hope you are not hiring Ali to find out where this

money is. Because I don't know. And if I do know, I will not be telling you, even for ten thousand dollars a day. I will be getting the money myself.''

"No. I don't want the money. I want to know who's after it.''

"Everybody is after it, my dear.''

"From Baghdad, I mean.''

"Who is your client, *habibi*? Maybe that makes it easier for me to get answers.''

"I can't tell you. Except that I'm not working for any government. It's a personal matter.''

"I am at your service. Maybe I ask you how much this client is paying you.''

"That's easy. Nothing. Zero. *Sifr.*''

"So. You must be very rich now, Mr. Sam. You taking work for nothing.''

"Stop it. No more talk about money. It's giving me a stomachache.''

"Okay. Where you want me to go? How about Tunis?''

"Why Tunis?''

"Because I got friends there who tell me things. And nobody tell nobody nothing now in Baghdad, believe me. When you want me to léave?''

"Right now. This afternoon. First flight out.''

"But I have businesses here. I cannot just leave. This cost you extra, maybe.''

"Cut the bullshit,'' said Hoffman. "Just get there. And one more thing. I want you to check out a Tunis phone number: 718-075. It's disconnected now, but I want to know who it belonged to.''

"Hold on. I write this down. 718-075, yes?''

"Yes. When you know something useful, come to London right away. Don't tell me on the telephone.''

"Okay. I probably have to fly first-class. Just so you know. *Mas salameh.*''

"*Salaam aleykum,*'' said Hoffman, cradling the phone. Talking to Ali Mattar was exhausting, in addition to being expensive. But he couldn't think of any other way to find out what was really going on.

The police found Randa Aziz's body that night by the side of a road in Kent, on the way to Dover. She was behind the wheel of a rented car. They had made it look like a car accident. The car had hit a tree and the gas tank had exploded. The flesh was too charred for anyone to see what they had done to her body before they had killed her. The newspapers suggested that she was part of the same ''terror gang'' that had been trying to steal money from the London investment concern, and that she had lost control of her car while trying to escape on the Channel ferry. The usual ''reliable sources'' said the police were stepping up their search for the other Arab woman, still missing, who was believed to be the leader of the terrorist group.

-IV-

The Palace
of the End

28

A woman with short blond hair made her way carefully across the Geneva airport terminal. She wore a shapeless peasant dress and carried a bag over each shoulder. She walked hesitantly—glancing behind her, then peering ahead—as if she weren't quite sure where she was going. When the man at passport control asked her why she looked so different from her picture—blond hair instead of black—she laughed nervously and said she had needed a change. The passport officer rolled his eyes as if he already knew the story. This was a city that assumed the worst about everyone. It had grown rich hiding money for Frenchmen who were cheating on their taxes, and later opened its arms, and bank vaults, to Africans and Asians, Arabs and Jews. An entire world of people with things to hide. And what was one more? A young woman with striking dark features that didn't quite match her hair.

The passport officer waved Lina Alwan through. She didn't move at first. She was looking at the floor, averting her eyes from him, so she didn't see the shrug and the wave of the hand. It was only when a German man behind pushed her forward that she realized she was free to enter the country. She had another nervous moment at customs, when they asked to look at her computer. But all they wanted was for her to turn it on. Computers were not a problem, so long as they didn't explode. A sense of elation began to bubble up inside Lina, like fizz in a bottle, and when she cleared customs and emerged into the main concourse of the airport, she wanted to celebrate. She noticed a woman's boutique and stopped to buy herself a new dress, as tight and clingy as a piece of Saran wrap. It was wildly overpriced, but that didn't seem to matter. She paid for it with Helen's credit card.

Lina checked into the Beau Rivage, a grand old hotel on Quai du Mont-Blanc. It was the only hotel in Geneva she knew by name. Her father had always stayed there, back when he still had enough money to travel to Switzerland. They gave her an absurdly large room on the fourth floor, with a balcony overlooking the Jet d'Eau. The bathroom alone seemed the length of a bowling alley: It was a long white hall, lined with dazzling white towels and a massive sink, tub and bidet, leading to a separate room containing the water closet. Lina felt happily out of place. The hotel management must have assumed that only a very rich woman would be traveling alone.

It was late afternoon. Lina sat on her balcony for nearly an hour, watching the Jet d'Eau and thinking how lucky she was to be alive. She was hypnotized by the towering plume of water, rising hundreds of feet in the air above the placid surface of Lake Geneva and cascading down in a vaporous shower. She felt, at once, like the upward jet and the falling mist. She had burst through the surface of her life and broken free, but to what end? Helen's brave words about finding the money had almost seemed to make sense back in London. But now that Lina was in Switzerland, they were just so much mist, evaporating into the air. She still had her documents from Hammoud's restricted files, with their names and bank account numbers. But when she tried to think what to do with them, her mind was a blank. She wanted to call Hoffman and ask his advice, and she especially wanted to call Randa, about whom she was already feeling uneasy. But she knew it would be folly to call either, so she sat on her balcony a while longer, watching the plume of water catching the last rays of the afternoon sun.

Lina eventually took a bath and changed into her new dress and then went downstairs to the atrium bar. It was cocktail time, and the room was filled with international businessmen. Lina was shown to a table in the corner, away from the hubbub. She asked for a Swiss newspaper and a glass of mineral water. The view out the window revealed the blue-black water of Lake Geneva and the fuzzy outlines of the Alps, barely visible in the moonlight. She looked around the room. The guests all seemed very mannerly and polite, even the Arabs. Switzerland seemed to have that calming effect on people.

After a few minutes of reading and sipping her mineral water, Lina noticed that a man was staring at her. He was as thin as a piece of string, but expensively dressed in an Hermès tie and gold cufflinks. He was perhaps fifty years old, obviously eager for company, and he appeared also to be slightly tipsy. At first Lina averted her eyes and scanned the movie guide of *La Suisse*, as if she were waiting for someone and didn't want to be bothered. But after a moment's reflection, she realized that she wasn't waiting for anyone or anything, and that in fact she needed to make friends in Geneva, in a hurry. She looked up and returned his gaze, catching him full in the eye. He smiled, gave her a little wink and, when she smiled back, picked up his scotch and soda and jauntily strode over.

"Hello, there," said the string bean. He sounded American. *"Ou peut-être je dois dire: bonsoir!"* He seemed to speak fluent French, too. *"Aw, kayf taqool hello bilar-abee?"* His Arabic wasn't bad, either. Evidently Lina's blond hair wasn't such a good disguise.

"You seem to speak a lot of languages," she said.

"My name is Frederick Behr in every language. What's yours?"

"Helen," said Lina.

"You look like you need a friend."

"Everybody needs a friend in a strange city. Do you live here?" If he answered no, Lina planned to pay her bill and leave. Another tourist was useless to her. If he answered yes, she wasn't sure what she would do.

"Yes, indeed, I am part of the local flora. Or maybe I'm fauna. I can't remember which is which." He polished off his scotch and summoned the waiter to order another. "How about you?" he asked, pointing to Lina's glass. She ordered a glass of Lillet, on the rocks.

It didn't take Lina long to get the basic details out of him. Frederick Behr ("Call me Fred!") was an American from Boston who ran the Geneva office of an accounting firm. He wasn't a banker himself, but his clients included some of the larger Swiss banks. His wife had left him a year ago, and his idea of a good time was hanging around in hotel bars trying to pick up pretty women. Inevitably, Fred Behr wanted to know about her, too. Lina hadn't had much time to concoct an identity for herself, so she said the first thing that fell into her mind, making up the story as she went along.

"I'm in Geneva to sort out the affairs of my father," she said. "He passed away several months ago."

"I'm sorry," said Fred. "Did he live here?"

"No. He was Iraqi. But I think he kept some of this money here. Quite a lot, as a matter of fact, but in a secret account. And now he's dead, and my mother and I want to find the money. And I need help." She looked at him coyly. At the very least, she reasoned, she would get a brief introduction to the world of Swiss banks.

"Hmmm," said Fred, studying his highball glass. "Do you know where he kept it? I hope it wasn't in one of those private banks."

"No. I don't think so."

"That's good. Those little *banques privées* are too small, if you ask me. They stick out! You can't hide something in a small bank. It's too conspicuous. A big wire transfer and everybody says, 'Hey! What's old Freddie doing moving around a hundred million dollars?' It doesn't work. You can only hide money in a big bank. It gets lost in a crowd, just like people do. So what bank did he use, then?"

"We think it was Organisation de Banques Suisses."

"Then you're in luck, my dear. That should be easy."

"What should I do?"

"Just go to the OBS branch manager your father dealt with and tell him you've come about the money. If you know the number of the account and can show him proof that you're next of kin, he'll open it up for you. *Zut!*"

"But that's our problem. Mummy and I don't know what branch Daddy used, and we don't know which bank manager handled the account. We just know the account numbers. What should we do? It's driving my poor mother crazy."

"Touching problem," said Fred. He polished off his second scotch as he pondered the matter, and then ordered one more. "How much do you know about Swiss banks?"

"Nothing. Less than nothing. That's why I'm here. To find out."

"Well, maybe Uncle Fred can give you a few helpful hints. Would you like that?"

Lina nodded. "Yes, please."

"The first thing you have to understand about Swiss banking is that it's very big, and it's very secret. It's like an underground river that flows through the middle of the country. You can't see it, but it controls everything, and it's absolutely enormous. There is over one trillion dollars in secret Swiss accounts. Did you know that? And the amazing thing is, most of that money is stolen. Not to offend the memory of your father, but most people who put their money in Swiss banks do so because the money is hot."

"That's all very interesting," said Lina, steering him back toward her particular problem. "But who should I go see at Organisation de Banques Suisses?"

"I am prepared to tell you. But only if you let me buy you dinner at my club."

Lina protested just enough and then agreed. His club turned out to be a place called The Gargoyle, across Lake Geneva from the hotel. Guarding the door was a tall,

tough-looking blond woman. She recognized Fred through
the peephole and let him in the door.

They walked downstairs to a large and opulently decorated chamber. On one side was a small restaurant; on the
other was a vast bar and discotheque. The disco was arranged as a series of pits, each with its own circular couch
decorated in fabric the pattern of leopard skin. Lina
scanned the room. Most of the men appeared to be Arabs.
They were dark, well groomed, dressed in expensive suits
and shoes. Each table appeared to have its own chieftain,
surrounded by his own retinue of aides, brothers, cousins
and bodyguards. And women, of course. They were the
other striking thing about the bar. Nearly all of them were
blond Europeans—arrayed like so much smooth-varnished,
tight-pegged furniture in an IKEA showroom.

"Helluva place," said Fred. He smiled and waved at
several of the other guests and then led Lina away from
the disco toward the restaurant. They hadn't been seated
long when Lina started up again.

"So how do they work?" she asked. "The big banks
like OBS, I mean. How do they operate?"

"You are tireless, my dear. You sound like a newspaper reporter."

"I'm just interested in what you have to say, Fred."

"Hmmmm." He smiled. "The big banks are factories,
my inquisitive darling. That's the truth. Only one or two
people at the top really know who the money belongs to.
The underlings who manage the accounts are just pushing
paper. And they're terribly overworked. One account manager will handle as many as two hundred accounts."

"Does he know who the money belongs to?"

"Nope. It's an assembly line. Plan A: ten percent gold,
twenty percent German deutsche-mark bonds, forty percent
Swiss-franc bonds, thirty percent European real estate.
Plan B: same as above, but substitute American bonds for
German and Swiss. I mean, really! Here you have the
most expensive bankers in the world giving your account
less attention than you'd get from your local credit union.

Yet the fees are huge. *Huge.* And do you know why? Because what they're selling is *secrecy.*''

There was a commotion over by the bar. A particularly rich Arab gentleman had arrived, encased in a double-breasted suit buttoned tight across his bulky midsection. His face was unshaven, but his fingers were neatly manicured. He was accompanied by three spandex blondes, who trailed along behind him like helium balloons.

"Three!" said Fred, hitting his forehead with the palm of his hand. He was quite drunk by now. "Why just three?"

"*Al Arab jarabe,*" said Lina.

"That's a new one on me. What does that mean?"

" 'The Arabs are leprosy.' "

Fred laughed and leaned toward her. "You know why they come to Geneva? To get in shape! There's a clinic near here that specializes in treating impotence. The doctor shoots you in the you-know-what with a hypodermic needle and you stay hard for hours. Or so they tell me. Never had that problem myself."

"Fred!"

"Sorry."

"I thought we were going to talk about Swiss banks."

"Right. Just so. Swiss banks."

"Tell me about the depositors. How do they contact the bank, anyway? Do they usually come in person?"

He looked at her curiously. She really was determined to talk about banking.

"Some do," he said slowly, still cocking his eye. The drunker he got, the more suspicious he was becoming. "They'll pay a visit here every two or three years to check how things are. They'll go in and see one of the top men, who will give them a summary of the account and how it's being invested. They'll check the safe deposit box together. Maybe they'll go have lunch in the bank's private dining room. Then the client flies home to Zaire or Abu Dhabi a happy man, dreaming about his money."

"But some depositors don't come in person?"

"Correct. Some money is so hot the client doesn't want

to get near Switzerland. Or can't. So he'll designate an agent—someone who is authorized to deal with the bank on his behalf. And that guy will make the regular fly-by. Which was your dad?''

"Excuse me?''

"Your father,'' said Fred with a wink. "Would he have come himself or would he have sent someone?''

"Oh, I think he would have sent someone.'' Lina had the feeling that Fred was catching on to her ruse, but she was determined to press ahead anyway. She thought about the documents she had printed out from Hammoud's restricted files. Maybe Fred could help her with those.

"Listen, Fred,'' she said. "This will probably sound like a really dumb question. But have you ever heard of a bank known as 'M' that has an office on the Rue des Banques?''

Fred shook his head. "Not sure about that one. But it's definitely one of the private banks. They do that initial thing. It's supposed to seem more discreet.''

"How can I find out about this bank 'M'?''

"What's it worth to you?'' Fred winked again. "And don't give me any more bullshit about your father.''

Lina pulled back in her chair. "What do you mean?''

"I mean I don't believe that yarn you told me about looking for your father's money. An Arab girl doesn't come alone to Geneva to look for Daddy's missing fortune. Sorry. It doesn't wash.''

A look of desperation came over Lina's face. She was alone. Poor, chivalrous, lecherous Fred was all she had. She looked at him tenderly, helplessly.

"I'm in trouble, Fred. I need help.''

He squinted his eyes, as if trying to focus better. "Are you a crook?''

"No. Do I look like a crook?''

He looked her over carefully and shook his head. The answer was no. "What kind of trouble are you in?''

"It involves money.''

"Obviously, but whose? Yours or somebody else's?''

"Someone else's. He thinks I'm trying to steal it, but

I'm not. I'm just trying to find out where it is so I can protect myself.''

"Who does the money belong to?''

"Nobody. It used to belong to someone very powerful, but now he's dead.''

Fred shook his head. "How do I know this isn't a bunch of hooey?''

Lina took his hand and squeezed it. "Look at me. Look at my eyes. Do I look frightened?''

"Yes,'' he said.

"The truth is, I'm scared to death. You have to help me. You're all I've got.''

"What do you want from me?''

"I need to know who to talk to at OBS about some numbered accounts. And I need to know how to reach this private bank 'M,' or whatever it is. It could save my life. I know that must sound stupid and melodramatic, but it's true.''

"I like you,'' said Fred, dreamily. "You're nice, even if you are an appalling liar.''

"Thank you. But I'm not lying. Not about being in danger.''

"Yes, yes. Whatever. The man to see at OBS is Pierre Marchand. He's the managing director in charge of operations in Geneva. He's a funny little Swiss man. Very secretive, even by local standards. He supervises all the big Arab accounts. He never talks to anybody, but if you mention my name, he'll talk to you. Call his office tomorrow. The private bank is almost certainly Crédit Mercier. It's run by a man named Maurice Mercier, and when he says *private*, he means it. Believe it or not, the number is unlisted.''

"What about Marchand? Could we try him at home tonight? I need to get started as soon as I can.''

"Look, this is Switzerland. You can't go calling people in the midlde of the night. It's not done.''

"Rubbish! People are after me. My life is in danger. Have you got any money? I'm going to get Marchand's number from the operator and call him.''

"To tell him what?"

"I don't know. I'll figure that out when I get his number."

"You're out of your mind," said Fred. But he was smiling. He handed her five Swiss francs and pointed her in the direction of the phone booth.

Getting Marchand's number was easy. He lived just north of the city, on the Route de La-Capite. As she prepared to dial, Lina pondered what to say. Perhaps it was the wine she had been drinking, or the liberating experience of dropping into a new place, or the simple requirement of taking risks if she was to survive. But for whatever reason, an outlandish thought fell into Lina's head: If her ultimate goal was to get into the OBS computer, why not go directly after what she needed—which was Marchand's password—rather than waste time with Helen's complicated scheme of changing baud rates and searching through data files? But how? It seemed a safe bet that Marchand, like most executives, didn't understand computers, which would make things easier. And it might help, too, that it was nighttime and he was likely to be at home. And it would help most of all if she could find a way to appeal to his sense of responsibility, even as she was getting him to do something wildly irresponsible. A sober woman could never have solved this riddle. But as she cradled the phone, Lina evolved in her mind a ruse that was so absurdly simple that, late at night, if Marchand had had a glass of wine as well, it might actually work. And if it didn't work, well, then, she would try something else the next day.

"Excuse me, Monsieur Marchand," she said when he answered the phone, speaking in her best schoolgirl French. "This is Dominique, the new assistant systems manager at the bank. I am sorry to bother you at this hour, but we have a problem and they told me to call you."

"Do I know you?" asked Marchand. He sounded stiff

and formal, but there was a faraway tone in his voice that suggested he was sleepy, and perhaps a little drunk.

"No, sir. I'm new. I was transferred a month ago from London. I work in the computer room. I'm the only one working tonight."

"Have you called Zanetti? He's in charge."

Lina's response was instantaneous. "Yes, sir. Of course. He's the one who told me to call you."

Marchand's voice immediately relaxed. The chain of command had been established. "Ah! Very well. What is the problem, Dominique?"

"I regret that the system has crashed and we have lost some of our files." Gently, she told herself. Not too fast.

"Is it serious? Do I need to come in?"

"No, not very serious. We are trying to reconstruct the files tonight so we can work on the system overnight and get it ready for business tomorrow."

"Good." He sounded relieved. He didn't have to come in. "What do you need from me?"

"We are trying to reconstruct the passwords first, and we need to know"—*gently, now, make it sound logical*—"how many letters were in yours."

"What did Zanetti say?"

"He said to call you."

"Ah! I see. Very well. So let me think, it was—one, two, three, four, five, six—six letters. Is that what you need?"

"Yes, sir. There is one more thing. We have the last three letters, encrypted, but I'm afraid the system has garbled the first three. That's the problem."

"Do you need them?"

"Yes, please." Easy. Polite. Careful.

Marchand cleared his throat. "I cannot give you the password, Dominique. You know that." He was thinking about security, even late at night.

"No, sir. Of course. That is forbidden."

"Very well. So then, the first three letters are *s,e,c.* Will that help?"

"Yes, sir. Everything should be working again tomorrow. Thank you very much. I am sorry again for the inconvenience."

"Not at all. Tell Zanetti I was glad to help." And he was indeed glad to help a new employee late at night, and confident that he had done nothing inappropriate. What harm could three letters do, after all? The passwords were encrypted. The system was secure. Zanetti told him so every day.

"Good night," she said sweetly.

Lina returned to the table five minutes later, wearing fresh lipstick and a big smile. She looked like she had just won the lottery. Fred greeted her with a flourish and held the chair for her to be seated. He seemed to enjoy acting chivalrous in a place that was otherwise so disreputable.

"So? Did you get everything you needed from old Marchand?" he asked.

"No," said Lina, still smiling. "He wasn't in." She took a long sip of her drink.

"Come, now. You look awfully pleased with yourself, I must say."

"That's because I'm so happy to be here with you, Fred."

Fred laughed. "You are such an amazing liar! I don't know what's going on. But you must be a very clever girl."

"I *am* a clever girl. And I'm ravenous. I haven't eaten all day. Call the waiter."

━━

Lina was scanning the menu when she saw him, in the corner of her eye. An Arab man descending the stairs. She barely noticed him at first. There were so many other Arabs in the restaurant already that she had let down her guard. It was only as he moved into the dining room and began scanning the tables that Lina paid attention. He was dark, with tight, curly hair and hooded eyes. She froze, for a moment, and then pulled the menu toward her like a shield. It was a face she had seen several days before, standing among a group of Palestinian bodyguards in front of Nasir Hammoud's desk in London. They had discovered, somehow, that she was in Geneva. The Palestinian hadn't seen her yet. He was across the room now, talking with some friends. But if Lina stayed where she was, he was sure to spot her eventually as he made his way across the room. She leaned toward Fred and whispered in his ear.

"I'm terribly sorry, Fred, but I have to go right now. I'm not feeling well." She stood up quickly from the table and headed for the exit.

"Wait, for goodness's sake!" he cried out. "You can't leave now!" Every eye in the dining room turned, including those of Hammoud's security man. In the awkward silence that followed Fred's shout, Lina ran up the stairs toward the front door. Fred rushed after her. The Palestinian followed a few moments later.

Fred caught up with Lina just outside the door. She had removed her high heels and was running down the sidewalk in her stocking feet.

"What's wrong?" he wheezed. "Where are you going?"

Lina continued to run, forcing Fred to try to keep pace. The street was nearly deserted; there was a yellowish wash on the pavement from the streetlights overhead. Lina turned left into an alleyway, calling for Fred to follow. It wasn't until they were halfway down the alley that Lina saw it was a dead end. At the bottom was a brick wall and, on the other side, a bank of apartment buildings. Lina looked back toward the street. The Palestinian security man was turning the corner. It was too late to go back.

Lina raced toward the wall, calling for Fred to hurry. When she reached it, she turned to him and grabbed his hand. He was trembling from the excitement and the booze. The Palestinian was twenty yards away. She hiked up her skirt and tossed the high heels over the wall.

"Fred! Give me a boost. Now."

Fred formed a stirrup with his hands and hoisted her till she could grasp the top of the brick ledge. He watched as she swung one leg over the top, then the other. And then she was gone. As Lina scrambled toward the shelter of the apartment complex, she could hear Fred's tipsy voice from the other side of the wall. "Just a moment, my good sir. You needn't go any further. I can explain everything."

29

Lina moved out of the Beau Rivage early the next morning to look for something more discreet. She was standing at the front desk paying her bill when she noticed a young man in a fancy linen suit sitting in the lobby, staring at her. He didn't look Iraqi, so she didn't pay him much attention at first. But as she was walking toward the door to catch a taxi, the man approached and introduced himself. He had curly hair and a wiry athlete's body. The man gave her an eager handshake, too friendly for a stranger at eight in the morning. It was only when he mentioned the name of a mutual acquaintance that she suddenly paid attention.

"I'm a friend of Sam Hoffman's," he said. "I thought you might need some help."

"With what?" she asked warily.

"Hammoud," he said. He reached to help her carry the shoulder bag that contained the portable computer.

Lina pulled away, instantly mistrustful. She knew that Sam wouldn't send someone else to protect her.

"I don't need any help," she said, fending him off and calling to the doorman that she wanted a taxi. The man followed her to the door, where he handed her a business card. It gave his name as Martin Hilton. The name rang a distant bell, but she couldn't place it. On the back, he had written the number of his hotel and the words "Be careful."

As she entered the taxi, Lina looked over her shoulder to see if anyone was following her. The street was empty, except for a few trucks making early morning deliveries and a jogger heading toward the lakeside park known as The Pearl of the Lake. She tried to remember what people did in the movies when they wanted to get rid of surveillance. Cary Grant had once gone to a big building, wandered around and left by a different exit. "Take me to a department store," she told the driver. He deposited her at a large building on the Rue du Rhône, on the southern shore of Lake Geneva. She entered the store, took an escalator up, then down, stopped at the book department to buy herself a French dictionary and then exited by a different door onto a side street, where she caught another taxi.

The driver was a portly Swiss man. She asked him to suggest a quiet, inexpensive place to stay. He dropped her at a small pension in the southwestern suburbs of the city, near the freight yards. It was a simple house, neatly built, with two guest rooms, run by a Swiss woman named Jaccard. Lina explained to the woman that she was a student from London visiting Geneva to do some research. Her only requirement, she told Madame Jaccard, was a direct international phone line in her room. She used a computer to do her research, she explained, and she might need to communicate by telephone with a big computer somewhere. She would use her telephone credit card to pay for her calls, Lina promised. The Swiss woman agreed. There was a phone in the guest room and she could use it however she liked, as long as she paid her bill. She seemed dazzled by the idea of computers talking on the telephone. So complicated. And a woman!

As Lina unpacked her meager belongings, she thought again of calling Sam to ask him about the appearance of the mysterious Mr. Hilton, but decided against it. Calling London would be insecure, and more important, it would waste time.

Lina knew she had to move quickly. At some point, Pierre Marchand would call his friend Zanetti in the data-processing department and ask whether the computer problem had been fixed. Zanetti would respond, "What problem?" and Marchand would realize he had been tricked. In the ensuing panic, they would immediately change Marchand's password. So she had to move quickly. She plugged in Helen's laptop computer and gave herself a quick tutorial in how to use the system. After twenty minutes, she felt confident enough to begin her assault on the OBS computer.

First, Lina had to complete the simple riddle of Marchand's password. The clue was a six-letter word beginning with *s,e,c.* She opened the French dictionary she had purchased at the department store and turned to *S.* The first word she saw was *sec,* but that was just three letters. Then came *sécant,* a six-letter word that meant "cutting." That was possible, in theory, but it struck Lina as an unlikely password for Marchand. People like to be deceptive when choosing passwords, but not radically so. She continued her search. *Sécession, séchage, sécher,* "to dry." That was six letters, but again, it didn't make sense as a password. The next word, however, seemed like a good possibility. It was *second,* as in "junior, inferior." Maybe Marchand's father had the same name; maybe he had an inferiority complex. Lina wrote the word down on a pad and then resumed her hunt. *Sécot, secouement, secourable, secourir, secousse.* And then she saw it, jumping off the page of the dictionary.

Secret, as in "secret, private, hidden, reserved, reticent, discreet." The word had six letters, and it screamed to be a password. Lina looked through the rest, to be sure. *Secrétaire, sécrétement, sécréter, sectaire, secte, secteur, section, séculaire, secundo, sécurité.* That was it for *s,e,c.* It had to be *secret.*

Lina reckoned that she had broken the password, but she still needed the number of the OBS data-communications line before she could walk in the bank's electronic front door. She took the Geneva phone book from beside the bed and found the main number for OBS: 391-6000. Below that were listed a series of departmental extensions: 6100 for administration; 6200 for commercial banking;

6300 for private banking; 6400 for merchant banking; 6500 for trading and sales; 6600 for retail banking. Lina suspected, looking at this list, that the bank's computer operations must fall under "administration," which had the extensions between 6100 and 6200. She began dialing. It took fifteen minutes and nearly forty calls before she got lucky with "391-6138" and heard the high-pitched electronic sound that meant she had a computer on the line.

Lina was almost ready. She reviewed in her mind Helen's step-by-step instructions from the previous day. Then she removed from her purse the document named "Accounts," which she had copied a few days before from Hammoud's files. It contained the numbers of the five OBS accounts: N4 808.537-0, N4 808.537-1, B2 218.411-0, B2 218.411-1, B2 218.411-2. If Lina's assumptions were correct, those simple numbers were the address where several billion dollars lived.

Here we go, she told herself. She called up the telecommunications program and typed in the dialing command. The machine beeped out the numbers: 3-9-1-6-1-3-8. There was a pause, then a ring, then a high-pitched noise, then a scratchy electronic sound. On her screen, she saw the words "Dial complete," then "Ringing" and then "Connect." Then the prompt "Enter username" appeared, requesting her to sign on. That was a good omen. The OBS interface was in English.

She typed in *marchand* and waited for the system to request his password. But to her surprise, the words "Login incorrect" appeared on the screen, followed by a repetition of the command "Enter username." What was wrong? Had they already discovered Lina's ruse of the night before and removed Marchand from the system altogether? Calm down, she told herself. There was a much simpler possibility, which was that more than one Marchand worked at the bank.

She tried to sign on again, this time typing *marchandp*, adding his first initial. But again there was no connection, and the prompt "Enter username" appeared once more.

Now she was worried. Three unsuccessful attempts to log in usually terminated the session and triggered an electronic message to the system manager that someone might be trying to break in. Lina had one more chance. This time she typed *pmarchand*, with the initial first instead of last. Presto! It worked.

Lina readied herself for what would come next. Helen had warned that there would be an automatic disconnect so the computer could call back and verify that the call was from an authorized number. But the disconnect never happened. Evidently there was no automatic callback procedure. Maybe the Swiss really were as sloppy as Helen had said. Now came the final hurdle. The screen displayed the prompt "Enter password." Lina typed in *secret*, the word she had deduced must be Marchand's password. The screen dissolved and re-formed, displaying the OBS logo and a short menu of options. *Yes!* The bank hadn't yet changed his password. She was inside.

The menu on the screen offered her four choices: "Banking," "Trading," "Markets" and "Personnel." Lina selected the first option. The screen re-formed, with a new prompt asking whether she wanted information on retail, corporate, merchant or private banking. Lina chose the last entry. A final prompt asked Lina whether she wanted information on regular or numbered accounts—*r* or *n*—and Lina typed *n*.

A new prompt glowed back at her. "Enter account number." She was almost there. Lina sat back in her wicker chair and looked out the window of her small room. A few Swiss were making their way up and down the street, locked in their own bubbles of time and space. The bankers were in their counting houses. The money was in its vaults, sleeping. The cuckoos were obediently behind the doors of the cuckoo clocks. Lina was the only free electron in the ordered universe of Geneva. She turned back to her computer, so deft in its electronic mimicry of "pmarchand," and looked again at her list of the account numbers. Next to the prompt, she typed the number of the first of the two Nassau accounts: "N4 808.537-0."

The OBS computer digested her request, and the screen went blank for a moment. Lina wondered if perhaps she had hit a special security screen that restricted access to sensitive accounts. But soon enough the screen re-formed, offering Lina two choices, "Status" and "Balance." She chose the latter, with a sense of anticipation, wondering if the next number she would see on the screen would be in the hundreds of millions or billions. She was entirely unprepared for what actually emerged before her: "Balance—N4 808.537-0: SF 10,000."

That can't be right, Lina thought. It amounted to little more than five thousand dollars—chicken feed!—the minimum balance that was probably required to keep such an account open. She must have made a mistake, although she couldn't think what it was. She checked the account number again with the printout, to make sure it was right, and rehearsed her steps. Don't get frazzled, she told herself. Try the next one. She went through the same procedure for the second Nassau account, this time typing in "N4 808.537-1" at the prompt. The answer glowed back at her.

"Balance—N4 808.537-1: SF 10,000."

Lina shook her head. This was bizarre! She tried the third account, hoping for a different result. It was the first of the three opened by dummy companies registered in Panama. Maybe all the money had been transferred to the Panamanian accounts. She typed in the numbers slowly, with one finger, to make sure she didn't make a mistake: B2 218.411-0. This time, surely, the answer would come back in the billions. But the screen displayed the same story.

"Balance—B2 218.411-0: SF 10,000."

Another empty piggy bank. Lina continued with the exercise twice more, to make sure that the money hadn't all sloshed into one compartment. But the answer was the same in each case. The numbered accounts into which Coyote Investment had poured its profits now held a paltry ten thousand Swiss francs each. For all practical purposes, they were empty. The Ruler's vast nest egg, hidden away to support his family for generations, was gone.

Lina rubbed her eyes. She felt, for a brief moment, like crying. She had worked so hard, and risked so much, to open this door. And now she found there was nothing inside.

There was only one other door in Geneva left for her to try, but Lina didn't know how to knock on it. She lay down on the bed of her little room and considered the problem. After a few minutes' reflection, she called the concierge at the Beau Rivage, who had been helpful to her the day before. She was terribly sorry to bother him, she said, but she had lost the number of her private bank, Crédit Mercier, on the Rue des Banques. Did the concierge happen to have it? And of course he did. Lina dialed the number the concierge had given her and listened to it ring. The chance of reaching Mercier was slim, but she had few alternatives. When a Swiss woman answered, Lina asked if Mr. Maurice Mercier was in.

"On the part of whom?" The Swiss woman's voice was as stiff and sharp as a porcupine quill.

"My name is Salwa Bazzaz," said Lina, taking the name of the Ruler's family as her own.

The secretary put her on hold for what seemed a very long time and then returned. "Monsieur Mercier would like to know why you are calling."

"I wish to inquire about the accounts of my uncle," said Lina as grandly as she could. "I have just arrived in Geneva, and I would like to see Mr. Mercier as soon as possible."

There was another long pause while the secretary consulted with her boss. A Swiss banker needed to be careful. And yet, it was occasionally possible to be too careful and insult a potential client. The secretary came back on the line, sounding more congenial now, radiating a bit of the warmth conferred by the billions of dollars that had settled over the years upon the firm of Crédit Mercier.

"Monsieur Mercier can see you tomorrow morning at ten," she said.

———

Lina celebrated by taking a walk in the early afternoon. It was dangerous to leave her burrow, but it was a sunny spring day and she hated the feeling of being imprisoned by her own fear. She bought a dowdy hat and a green overcoat in a shop that was open near the station. She thought, as she studied herself in the mirror, that she looked almost Swiss. She continued on her walk, staying in the shadows whenever she could, keeping her head down, but she was drawn toward Lake Geneva as if by a magnet.

The lake looked from the southern end like a long, watery jewel set in the deep fissure of the Alps. The spring sun was glinting off the surface, while the Jet d'Eau spewed its misty plume overhead. This was the part of town to stay away from, but the Jardin Anglais along the southern rim of the lake was crowded with people out for an afternoon stroll, and she imagined that she would be invisible in the eddy of pedestrians along the quay.

Lina stopped to watch a flock of small sailboats darting across the water on their gull-white wings. The wind was picking up speed, and one of the boats, running before the wind, seemed almost to lift up out of the water, so that it was racing toward her across the surface of the lake as if it were on skates. The boat suddenly jibed away as the wind shifted direction, darting off toward the Mont Blanc bridge. It was then, as Lina's eyes moved toward the bridge, that she saw a figure standing near the stone facade, his hands thrust in the pockets of his overcoat. What frightened Lina was that the man was looking directly at her.

She began walking north, away from the bridge. She stopped after one hundred yards at a small park beside the lake, found a bench and looked back. The man in the overcoat was still behind her. There was a brazenness in his manner that she found unnerving. He was closer now, and she recognized the wavy hair and the sharp features and the muscular walk. It was the same man who had approached her in the lobby of the Beau Rivage, claiming to be a friend of Sam Hoffman. He had given her a card with his name, Martin Hilton, and the message "Be careful." And now he was following her too.

Don't panic and run, Lina told herself. Teach him a lesson. She saw a Swiss policeman standing in a kiosk near the lake, thirty yards away, and walked directly toward him. When Martin Hilton saw where she was heading, he halted suddenly. Lina called out to the policeman.

"That man is following me," she said in French, pointing toward the man in the overcoat. "He tried to expose himself to me."

The policeman trotted off toward the man, gesturing in the air and ordering him to stop. Hilton sprinted away, scrambling across the street and into the maze of the shopping district. The policeman turned back toward Lina, a look of sturdy satisfaction on his face, to offer her a few words of assurance. But she had vanished. During the policeman's brief pursuit, she had scampered off in another direction, drawing the cloak of anonymity back around her.

30

Sam Hoffman wasn't good at doing nothing. He sat in his office making useless phone calls until he couldn't bear it any longer, then went out to the gym or the Chinese restaurant to work off his rage, and then came back to the office to make more useless phone calls. The day after Lina disappeared, Hoffman had been convinced she would call him again if she was still alive. By the following day, he began to wonder if she was dead. He went to Scotland Yard a day later on one of his restless outings, to urge the police again to investigate Hammoud. But they wanted only to ask more questions about Lina Alwan's alleged criminal activities. Hoffman refused to cooperate and virtually invited the police to arrest him as a co-conspirator, if they had any evidence. Whereupon they asked him to leave.

Ali Mattar returned from Tunis that night. Hoffman hadn't been expecting him for another day or two, and was surprised to find the Palestinian operative looming at his front door. *"Ahlan, ahlan!"* said Hoffman, greeting his colleague. He was delighted just to see a friendly face. His chief occupation for the past few hours had been rolling pieces of Scotch tape between his thumb and forefinger.

"I need a drink," said Ali, easing his large frame down on the couch. He was the sort of man who made even a big room seem too small: tall and burly, with long curly hair and a droopy mustache. To Hoffman, he looked more like a burned-out hippie musician than an intelligence peddler, but that was part of Ali's charm. Hoffman poured him a large whiskey.

"So what did you find out?" he asked.

"Too much monkey business, Sam! I got whole story right here." He tapped his head. "I had to come back right away to give you this big news."

"So tell me. I'm all ears."

Ali looked disappointed. "What is the rush? Don't you want to talk first? Have a drink. Ask me about my family, talk about old times. You know, Arab style."

"Nope. Business first. Then we can talk about old times as much as you want."

"You are not so mellow today, *habibi*."

"Give me a break, Ali. I'm going nuts. I need some information."

"Okay, okay. I find out too much. You not going to believe it. Big conspiracy. Too big! Everybody going crazy in Tunis. You may want to pay me double for such good informations."

"Cut the crap about money. I mean it."

"Okay. Here is my scoops. You remember the Palestine Liberation Front, the nasty group in PLO that gets all the money from Baghdad? The man who runs it is big pal with ruler in Baghdad. They go hunting together, maybe. You remember that one?"

"No."

"Okay, never mind. So his deputy is my old friend Ayad, who owes me so many favors. You know I save his life once? He was hiding out in Beirut, after Syrians try to kill him, and I come see him every day and play trictrac. And these Syrians try to kill him again because they afraid of him so much. But I find out and tell Ayad to run away to the camps in Tyre, where I grew up, and my mother hides him so nobody know. And he never forget. So later, when I am arrested by Fatah and they accuse me of being CIA man, Ayad save me. He come to prison and order them to release me, and he is such a big

man, how can they say no? They all afraid of Iraq. So
here I am, thanks to Ayad. What you think about that?"

"Fascinating. I'd love to hear the whole story some
other time."

"Okay. So Ayad tells me everything that is going on.
Just so you know what I am going to tell you is number-
one, excellent, very expensive informations. Straight
from Baghdad."

"Got it. So get to the point. What the hell did you
find out?"

"Okay. Here goes. The man who killed the Ruler is
named Osman. He is the Ruler's cousin, I think. He lives
in Europe somewhere and looks out for the family money.
But he don't like the Ruler's brothers. Osman says they
too greedy. Last few months they got big family fight. Big
bullshit. My God, Sam! What do we do with these crazy
Arabs? And then few days ago, pow!"

"Osman pulls the trigger?"

"For sure. Only someone in family can get close to the
Ruler, you see? So they use Osman. And who do you
think is working with Osman for so many years?"

"Tell me."

"You know, Sam; yes, you do."

Sam thought a moment. Ali was right. He did know.
"Nasir Hammoud?"

"For sure, Hammoud. My friend Ayad tells me they
been working together for years, on money things. They
make too many deals. You remember those fighter planes
the Ruler try to buy from France, long time ago? Osman
was in that deal with Hammoud. How you like that monkey business, huh?"

"I like it."

"I got more. Who do you think backing Osman and
Hammoud, when they go after the Ruler like this, big
time?"

"No more guessing games. I'm going to cut your
retainer."

"Please, you hurt me too much, but I tell you anyway.
The ones backing Osman and Hammoud are my friends

in Tunis, that's who. The Palestinians. They provide all the muscle for this Osman gang. Fatah been buying people in Ruler's palace for years. A million for this one, a million for that one. Pretty soon, they eat away Ruler's security like rats eat away cheese. He got nothing left! And then, pow!''

"Good stuff, Ali. But who's behind the Palestinians?''

"The Saudis, I think. Must be them. They pay for everything, right?''

"The Saudis?''

"For sure. They friends with Hammoud too, big time. They all eating from the same bowl, you know what I mean?''

"I know what you mean.'' Hoffman thought of his friend Prince Jalal, sitting in his pleasure palace in Hyde Park Square, and how he had snorted when Sam had asked him who was protecting Hammoud. "Who else was involved in the operation besides the Palestinians and the Saudis?''

Ali stared out the window for a moment and then looked back earnestly at Hoffman. "The Americans, maybe.''

"Say what?''

"A lot of Americans in Tunis, *habibi*. Some friendly faces.'' His eyes were twinkling, but Sam was shaking his head.

"You're just guessing, aren't you?''

The Palestinian fixer shrugged his shoulders. "Questions like this one, my friend, the answers always are guesses. But you want to know, I find out. This information costs more because it is so dangerous, but I get it for you. No problem.''

"I'll think about it. What happened to Osman after he shot the Ruler?''

"*Haram.* Too bad for him. He thinks he got everybody in the palace paid off, but Ruler's brothers catch him the day after he pulls trigger. Nasty job, too.''

"What did they do to him?''

"They cut off his balls and stuff them in his mouth,

while he still alive, too. But he dead now. They was pretty angry at him.''

"Apparently so. What about Hammoud?''

"They get to Hammoud first, and cut him up. Finger, only. But he got rescued. Some of his Palestinian friends show up. Lucky boy! Then they go after Osman.''

"I heard about Hammoud's finger, but not the part about stuffing Osman's balls in his mouth. That's a new one.''

"See! I told you these is good informations. Worth every penny.''

"What else did you find out?''

"Okay. So the reason Ruler and his brothers were fighting with Osman was money. Hammoud and Osman been stealing plenty from the family for long time now! The Ruler trust them to hide money outside Iraq, and now he find out they been taking little bites on the side. Maybe not so little bites.''

"How much did they steal?''

"Maybe a billion. Maybe more.''

"A billion dollars?''

"Yeah. Maybe more. And all you pay Ali is four thousand a day. *W'allah!* My God, Sam.''

"Stop it. Who's in charge now in Baghdad?''

"*Moukhabarat*, same as always. This bunch get their paychecks from Riyadh, maybe.''

"And what about the Ruler's family? Now that they've whacked Osman, is that the end of it?''

"No way! Never the end for the Iraqis. Always somebody else to kill.''

"So who are they after?''

"Everybody. They don't trust nobody now, after Hammoud screw them. They don't trust Hammoud's people. They do everything to get hands on this crazy money.''

"Who are they leaning on?''

"You want all the details? Even my friend Ayad had trouble remembering all the names.''

"Yes, please. As many details as you can remember.''

"Okay. First they putting squeeze on Hammoud's com-

pany in London. Called Wolf or something. They bring
this Armenian guy back to Baghdad and beat the crap out
of him until he tells them everything. He was supposed to
be their man, keeping eye on Hammoud, but it looks like
he fucked up pretty good. So they make him remember
how glad he is to still have all his arms and legs, and
then they send him back to London to take care of the
family money.''

"Right. So what happened next?"

"Then Hammoud comes back to London with some of
these Palestinians. Ayad's boys, maybe. British let them
in. I don't know why. These British must like Hammoud
too much."

"What did Hammoud do when he got back?"

"He takes over this Wolf again."

"Coyote. It's called Coyote Investment."

"You too smart, Sam. Maybe you work for Ali some
day. Then we make some real money."

"Never. Go on. You were telling me what Hammoud
did when he got back."

"Right. Hammoud takes over this Cougar again. First
night he's back in town, he sends his new Palestinian
bodyguards to the home of this Armenian. *Poof*. No more
Armenian. Then they go after some Iraqi girl and, you
know . . ." He flipped his hand as if to say, "who cares?"

"Hold it!" said Hoffman. "Slow down. What girl?"

"I don't know. Laura, maybe. Or Lucy. I don't know.
Some kind of *L* name. Ayad wasn't sure what it was. She
works at this Cougar place for Mr. Hammoud."

"Why did they go after her?"

"Because they think she knows where the money is.
All the secrets. She steal them out of computer when Hammoud and the Armenian not looking. They think maybe
she working for the Israelis."

"The Israelis? Why do they think that?"

"Because she got some boyfriend who works for the
Israelis."

Hoffman tried not to look too interested. "Who was
that?"

"Ayad didn't say. You want me to ask?"

"No. Definitely not. What did they do with the Iraqi girl?"

"Nothing. They don't got her. They try to grab her, but she slip away."

"They don't have her?" Hoffman repeated, his heart quickening a beat.

"Nope. Don't have her."

"So where is she now?"

"I don't know. But if they catch her, she is in trouble, big time. For sure."

"How do you know?"

"Because they serious about this money. They figure that's all there is. Ruler is dead. No more Cold War. No more free ride with CIA or KGB. Not even wars with Israel no more. Only thing now is money. Same thing for Ruler's brothers. They gotta have this money, too. Everybody gotta have it."

"Jesus!" said Hoffman.

"What's wrong? You not like informations? These topgrade. Nobody else knows this but me. And you."

"No. The information is fabulous. I'm just scared what these whackos might do."

"Not Ali's problem. Sorry. End of story. Except for one more thing you ask me about."

"The phone number."

"Yes. Phone number. But it's not very interesting. Maybe you make a mistake with number. I ask Ayad, who ask his friend in Tunisian *moukhabarat*, who ask his friend in Tunisian PTT. But I think maybe it was a mistake. Big nothing."

"What was the number?"

"Just some extension in U.S. embassy in Tunis. One they never use too much. Not working no more. Sorry. Give me another number, and I can try again."

The U.S. embassy. Hoffman rubbed his eyes. He was tired and struggling to see clearly the pattern that was being stitched before him. "No, Ali. That's okay. It must have been a wrong number. Thanks for trying."

"So what you want me to do now, Sam, huh?"

Hoffman thought about it a long minute. It was as if Lina had become caught in a spider web that looped back against itself several times. The web was everywhere, but the spider was invisible. The only thing Hoffman could think to do was to try, somehow, to scare it off. He walked to the office safe and counted out a thick stack of money, then returned to his investigator.

"Here's ten thousand dollars for the two days. It's more than we talked about, but it's worth it. I'll give you another ten thousand if you can do something else for me."

"Okay. So what is it? No guns. I am strictly informations man."

"No guns. I want you to go back to Tunis and give a message to your friend Ayad, and have him give it to the people running the show in Baghdad."

"Okay. No problem. What is message, please?"

"Tell them that if they do anything to harm this Iraqi woman, they will be picking a major fight with the CIA. You got that? They should stay away from her, or they are in big trouble."

"She work for agency, then, this Iraqi girl? Not for Israelis?"

"She is just a low-level nobody. It doesn't matter who she works for. And she doesn't know anything about the money."

"Who should I say message is from?"

"Just say Hoffman. Don't say my first name. Just say Hoffman."

"So! Your father is giving you this message? *W'Allah!* Strange stuff! But okay. They all know your father. He tried to recruit half of them in Beirut."

"Just do what I say, Ali. Okay? Tell your friends that nobody should fuck around with this girl. Not the Iraqis, not the Palestinians, not the Saudis, not anybody. If they hurt her, they're in more trouble than they know. Tell them Hoffman says so. Got it?"

"Hader ya rayess!" He gave a smart salute. "When do you want me to go? Tomorrow, maybe?"

"Tonight. There's a late flight. You'll just make it if you leave now."

"Tonight is not so convenient, *habibi*. I was thinking of big date with old girlfriend, if I can remember number of escort service. Tonight is not so good."

"It's gotta be tonight." Hoffman went to the safe and returned with another thousand dollars. "Here's for expenses," he said. "There are lots of nice girls in Tunis."

31

The Rue des Banques sat astride the old business district of Geneva like a heavy gold bar. The canton's venerable banking houses lined both sides of the street, occupying somber buildings that epitomized Genevan discretion and respectability. There were no neon signs or corporate billboards reaching out to lure customers, or indeed any advertising at all, for the banks of that district preferred not to do business with the public. Most of them were *banques privées*. On their doors were simple brass plates with the name of the bank: Hentsch. Lombard-Odier. The great names of Swiss banking. For some of the private banks, even that was too public a form of advertisement. Their doors carried only the street number, or nothing at all. For these establishments did not exist in the normal universe of banking. They were the black holes of finance, sucking money into their invisible doors.

Lina made her way down the Rue des Banques, looking for number eleven. The morning sky was as gray as the architecture, so that the whole of the street seemed to be in shadow. Lina had trouble seeing the numbers through her veil. She had purchased it that morning, along with a demure business suit and a head scarf, to enhance her role as a woman of the East who had just lost her beloved uncle. But the lace made it hard to see. Up the avenue she could make out a few men in topcoats, who appeared to be bankers entering their counting houses. They had a

cautious, furtive look, even on their own grand avenue of
commerce. She continued up the street, looking for her
address. She passed number seven; the plaque read LEBON.
At number nine, it was C & CIE. Next to it, looking if
anything somewhat grayer than its neighbors, was an austere entrance with a heavy brass knocker on the door and
a plaque that simply said M.

Lina stood at the door rehearsing her lines a final time.
She had prepared carefully for her role and now, as the
curtain was about to draw open, she felt almost cocky.
She raised the brass knocker, feeling its weight in the palm
of her hand, and let it fall. The door opened instantly.
A well-dressed young woman, who seemed to have been
standing there awaiting Lina's arrival, asked her name and
then gestured for her to follow. They walked left down a
narrow cream-colored corridor, then to the right past three
small doors. The Swiss woman stopped at the last of them,
opened it and nodded for Lina to enter the small conference room. Then she closed the door, leaving Lina alone.
Scarcely a word had been exchanged.

The conference room was simple and cozy. A comfortable, well-padded chair for the client stood on one side of
a lacquered table; the banker's straight-backed wooden
chair stood on the other. Beyond the table was a window
that opened onto a small courtyard, no wider than the
conference room itself. A small brick wall enclosed the
courtyard on three sides, preventing anyone from seeing
into the room.

Lina gazed out at this secret garden. It was evidently
part of the mystique of Crédit Mercier. The building had
been designed like a maze to protect the privacy of the
bank's clients. Each visitor could be certain, as he sat in
his personal conference room, that no other visitor would
see him. The oil minister of Sharjah would never know
that he shared the same bank as the finance minister of
Peru. The chief of staff of the Kenyan army would never
have to see the face of the speaker of the Russian parliament. They were brothers in secret. Lina sat down in the

easy chair and waited, anonymously, for the arrival of the only man who saw all the faces.

After five minutes, there was the slightest rap at the door. Before Lina could answer, a compact man entered the room. He had graying hair, a finely trimmed gray mustache and a gray three-piece suit. The only hint of color came from his eyes, which were an odd tint of blue and seemed to sparkle unpredictably above the bland sobriety of his face and figure. He closed the door behind him before extending his hand and introducing himself. "Mercier," he said with the slightest bow. No first name, no title. He had the delicate manners of someone who had spent a lifetime handling dirty money without ever soiling his own hands.

Lina lifted her veil halfway and murmured, "Salwa Bazzaz." Then she let it fall back over her face. Mercier gestured for her to be seated, extending his arm toward her chair in the same way that a maître d'hôtel in a fine restaurant might. The technique was to seem better bred than his guests, yet entirely at their service.

"Now, Miss Bazzaz," he said. "How can I help you?"

Lina spoke in English overlaid with an Iraqi accent, like the one she had when she was a child in England. "I have come to inquire about the accounts of my uncle. God grant him peace."

The banker's face was solicitous, and empty. "A great tragedy, Miss Bazzaz. My sympathies. But may I ask, why have you come to me?"

"Because my uncle was a client of your bank."

The banker folded his hands in his lap. He closed his eyes, so that he was a portrait entirely in gray: gray suit, gray hair, gray manner. "I must apologize to you, Miss Bazzaz," he said. "I do not wish to be rude, but it is a policy of this bank that we do not discuss our banking relationships with anyone other than the client himself."

"But the client is dead, monsieur. And the money belongs to his family. And they have sent me to make inquiries."

"I understand, Miss Bazzaz. But I am afraid that does not change the bank's policies."

Lina sniffed in indignation. She had prepared for this. "If you do not talk with me, I will go to the United Nations. Or to CNN. My uncle liked CNN very much. I will tell them about the Swiss banker who has stolen my uncle's money."

"I see," said the banker. He adjusted his position in the chair ever so slightly as he contemplated the prospect of television cameras on the Rue des Banques. "I wonder, Miss Bazzaz, do you have any identification?" He asked it so gently, so politely, it sounded almost like an apology. But Lina was prepared. She had deliberately left all her identification behind, in case he should ask to see it.

"My passport is at the hotel," she said. "But I have other identification. It is better for you, I think."

"Well, then, perhaps you could show it to me."

"I have the numbers of my uncle's bank accounts in Geneva. My family said I should give them to you."

"Yes, indeed. That would be very helpful."

Lina reached in her purse for the "Accounts" document and, after lifting her veil, read the numbers on the first page. "First, at Organisation de Banques Suisses. My uncle had five accounts there, where he kept the profits from his London holdings. The numbers are N4 808.537-0, N4 808.537-1, B2 218.411-0, B2 218.411-1 and B2 218.411-2. Shall I read them to you again?"

"No, thank you," said Mercier. He had removed a handheld computer from the inside pocket of his coat and punched in numbers as she spoke. Now he studied the display. "Um-hum," he said.

"But when I contacted Organisation de Banques Suisses yesterday to inquire about these accounts, I was told that they were empty. All the money had been transferred somewhere else. I wonder who has done this, if my uncle is dead."

"I can't help you there, I'm afraid." Mercier sat primly in his chair, but the eyes were darting back and forth like an azure beacon.

"So I thought perhaps the money had been transferred here. Because my uncle had his account with you, and the family said it was a very special account, to be used in emergencies. Now can we discuss it?"

"I'm truly sorry, Miss Bazzaz. But as I told you before, we have our rules. And I'm afraid I can't comment on a deceased client's affairs, except under the most unusual circumstances."

She looked at him coyly, ready now to spring her last surprise. "Would it help if I gave you the number of my uncle's account at this bank?"

"Well, yes, actually," said Mercier, adjusting his tie. "That would help a bit, in terms of our rules. If you have the number, why don't you give it to me." He took up the computer again.

Lina searched in her purse for the "Emergency" file, and then held it close to her face. "The number is Z 068621."

Mercier punched in the numbers, waited a moment and then gently nodded his head. "Well, now," he said. "That is most interesting." The blue eyes sparkled with surprise. The number was exactly right.

"What is interesting, monsieur?"

"That you have this particular number, Miss Bazzaz."

"Why not? This is my uncle's account," repeated Lina, a tremor of anger in her voice.

"Yes. But this was a very private account, you see. A most unusual account."

"Not now. It belongs to the family now."

"Perhaps so, Miss Bazzaz. But I must ask you for one additional piece of identification. The PIN number, please."

"The what?" Lina had no idea what he was talking about.

"The PIN number. We require them for all of our most sensitive accounts, as an extra security precaution. If you don't have it, I am afraid I cannot discuss this matter with you further."

"The PIN number?" she said again.

"Yes, yes. In French, we call it *le code personnel*, or just the *code*."

Suddenly it was staring up at her from the brief, two-line "Emergency" file. "Code: 0526." She cleared her throat. "Of course I have the PIN number, monsieur. Of course. It is zero-five-two-six."

Mercier tapped the numbers into his computer. He closed his eyes and then opened them, wide as the world. His thin lips puckered slightly, and Lina thought she could hear the faintest sound of a whistle. Just one breath, but audible. "Now, Miss Bazzaz, with my sincere apology, I must tell you that I have a problem."

"Why? Should I repeat the number?"

"No. The number is precisely correct. That is my problem."

"What do you mean? You ask for two forms of identification, and I have given them to you. What more do you want?" Her voice was straining with what sounded like genuine emotion. Mercier handed her a silk handkerchief, which she dabbed against her eyes.

"Let me try to explain," said Mercier. "Your uncle, as you say, did maintain an account with this bank. A rather large account, as you may have imagined. But the terms of this account were very unusual. Because of the need for discretion, and the impossibility of your uncle visiting the bank in person, a trustee was appointed many years ago. A *fiduciaire*. And I am forbidden to dispose of this account in any way without authorization from him."

"This is all nonsense. What are you talking about?"

"I mean that we did not conduct business with your uncle directly, but through an intermediary. The beneficial holder of the account was not the signatory, if you follow me. Which makes things rather complicated now."

"Why? What is so complicated?"

"It is complicated because I am receiving conflicting instructions about the disposition of the account."

"What is the problem? I am sorry, but I still do not understand."

"My dear Miss Bazzaz, within the past twenty-four

hours, I have spoken with another person who claims to represent the heirs and beneficiaries of this account. *That* is the problem.''

"Who?"

"A business associate of your uncle. I must keep his name confidential, I'm afraid.''

"He is an impostor," said Lina.

"I think not. He presents the same evidence to establish his bona fides that you do, which is the number of this particular account. A number that was only known to your uncle and his designated representative. So, you see, it is a puzzle.''

"He is an impostor," repeated Lina. "What are you going to do?''

"I am awaiting instructions.''

"Instructions? Where will you get instructions?''

"From the intermediary I mentioned, who for many years has represented the interests of your uncle in his dealings with this bank.''

"Is this man an Iraqi?" demanded Lina. She assumed that he must be talking about Hammoud.

"No, mademoiselle. Not an Iraqi. He's an American, if you must know.''

"An American? Why are you asking an American what to do with my uncle's money? My uncle hated America.''

"Oh, no, you are quite wrong there, Miss Bazzaz. Whatever he may have said publicly, your uncle did not hate America. I can assure you of that.''

Lina was confused. Why would the Ruler have chosen an American to represent him in his most secret banking relationship? It made no sense. "This intermediary, when will you see him?''

"Sometime this week, I expect. He phoned to say he would be arriving in Geneva soon. So it shouldn't be long.''

"And you will get instructions then?''

"Yes. I expect so. I will explain the situation to him. And he will suggest an appropriate course of action.''

Lina shook her head in feigned anger. "So I will go to

CNN right now. I will call them in Paris. They will be here this afternoon.''

Mercier raised his hand, gently. "No, no. Please don't do that. Wait until I have talked with the American gentleman I mentioned. Then I would be happy to receive you again and, I am sure, discuss this matter at greater length. More than happy. I promise you. But until then, I can do nothing.''

Lina realized she had no alternative but to agree. ''When will you see me again, please?''

''Very soon. Why don't you give me a call in several days to arrange another visit. I should have something helpful to say then.''

''I will call you. After that, if there is a problem, I will tell CNN.''

''Thank you, Miss Bazzaz. I appreciate your patience.''

Mercier bowed slightly, an inch or two, and retreated toward the door, closing it behind him.

The Swiss receptionist arrived a few moments later to escort Lina back down the narrow hall. They retraced a path through the maze, along the corridors decorated with paintings of Switzerland's high mountain meadows and virgin peaks. The effect was meant to be uplifting, a kind of quiet hymn to money. There was not a hint anywhere in the building that the bank was diligently involved in laundering funds for the most corrupt and venal men on the planet.

''Which door, madame?'' asked the receptionist when they had completed their course. Lina wasn't sure what she meant, until the woman explained that in addition to the regular front door, the bank also had another, more private exit.

''Front door,'' said Lina. Her play was done.

━━━

She realized an instant later that she had made a disastrous mistake.

Waiting just outside the door, on the curb of the Rue des

Banques, was a Mercedes limousine with smoked-glass windows. Standing by the car, a few feet from Lina, was the Palestinian bodyguard who had chased her from The Gargoyle club. He was wearing blue jeans and sunglasses now and looked, for all the world, like a male model on location. On the curb, above and below the car, were two more young men in casual clothes. Lina scanned the street, looking for a policeman, or even a pedestrian, but the boulevard was empty. The few passersby who might ordinarily have been there were instead up the street in Place Bel-Air, where an Arab gentleman had collapsed with what appeared to be a heart attack, drawing a crowd.

Lina opened her mouth to scream. But as she did so, the Mercedes sounded its horn, covering the noise. The Palestinian and his two cohorts were moving toward her, and the heavy door behind her was now locked shut. She screamed again, drawing another blast of the horn, and then dashed down the sidewalk, veering away from the Mercedes at the last moment toward an opening. But the man guarding that side moved quickly toward her and she ran full into his shoulder, hard as a metal post. She fell back toward the ground, and in the same moment, the Palestinian caught her from behind with one arm and with the other pressed a handkerchief to her nose and mouth. In an instant, she fell limp into his arms. The back door of the Mercedes opened, and she fell into the backseat like a corpse.

The whole of the street had seemed to be empty as this ballet was played out. But after the Mercedes had driven off toward the airport, a muscular man with curly black hair opened the door of a rented Opal that had been parked a few doors up from Crédit Mercier, across the street. He had been slouched down in the seat during the commotion outside number eleven, invisible from the street. But now Martin Hilton went to a telephone kiosk and placed a call to headquarters.

32

Lina awoke on the stone floor of a darkened room. As she opened her eyes and saw only darkness, she had a momentary panic that she had been blinded, then a feeling of vertigo, as if she were falling through space in this black box. She sat up and touched at her clothes and found that she was still wearing the same suit she had put on in Geneva. That cheered her, momentarily, until she felt underneath the blouse and realized that her bra was gone. Someone had taken it, but she had no memory of the preceding hours and no clue about where she was or how she had gotten there.

It was the smell in the room that told her she must be in Baghdad. It was a sharp odor of human waste, mingled with the smells of food, sweat and decay. The aroma was a substitute for light in the darkened room. It was the only message to the senses. Lina felt a nausea rising in her stomach, and also a need to relieve herself after so many hours. She groped on her hands and knees toward the source of the smell but pulled back suddenly as her hand found an opening in the floor and touched something wet. She stood to squat above this primitive toilet. When she was done, she reached out reflexively for toilet paper and, realizing that there was none, dabbed herself with the hem of her skirt.

The screams began as Lina was feeling her way along the rough concrete wall of her cell. It was a woman's

270

voice, so sharp and immediate that Lina thought at first that it must be within her own black room. She fell to the floor in fear, but as the wailing continued, she realized it was coming from outside her walls. The woman was shrieking, at first in pure terror—crying *"La, la, la,"* no, no, no—and then in pain as the blows began to fall. Lina heard a whooshing noise as an object whipped through the air, followed by a horrible crack as it met flesh, then a searing cry. And again, and again. As the beating continued, Lina could hear the woman pleading vainly for mercy—*"Ya sayyidi!"* O master! And finally, as the pain broke even the woman's power to scream, Lina heard the muffled sound of her prayers—*"Ya sitr! Ya kafidh!"* O savior. O protector—as she neared the edge of consciousness. And at last Lina heard a man's voice, tired from the exertion, muttering *"Koussa!"*—cunt!—and then silence. In that silence, Lina knew with absolute certainty where she was. It was the Qasr al-Nihayya. The Palace of the End.

Lina lay on the floor for several hours, unable to sleep, afraid even to move. What filled her mind was the sound of the woman screaming. They were beating her this time with an iron bar, this time with a chain; this time against her buttocks, this time between her legs. She tried to think of something else, but she knew that for her, there was nothing else. The cold stone against her cheek felt almost soothing. She wondered if she could beat her head against the stone floor long enough to lose consciousness, and realized that she lacked the courage. Her only hope, she told herself, was that she carried a British passport. They couldn't treat her as brutally as the poor woman whose suffering she had overheard. She wasn't Iraqi anymore. She was a woman of the West. They wouldn't dare. But those hopes faded into the darkness of the room and into the echoes of the woman screaming. Occasionally, Lina would hear footsteps passing outside her room, and low voices in Arabic, and think they were coming for her, but the sounds would die away. And then after many hours, there was a different sound, of a metal key finding its way into a lock, and her door was flung open.

"Get up," said a voice. The sudden rush of light from the doorway blinded Lina, and she was afraid at first to look. When she opened her eyes, she saw a man in his thirties wearing a leather jacket and blue jeans. His shoes, looming a few feet from Lina's face, were loafers with little tassels on them, like the kind they sell at Brooks Brothers. He was as thin as a whippet and stood with a natural slouch in his shoulders. The only thing that marked him clearly as an Iraqi was the hardness in his eyes.

Lina stood up. In the light, she could see at last the dimensions of the room in which she had been held. It was a rough concrete cell, perhaps fifteen feet square. The walls were bare, except for a few desperate messages that had been scrawled by previous occupants, pleas to loved ones and to God Almighty to remember them in their suffering. Through the door, she could see a narrow corridor, with a window opening onto an inner courtyard. The building, it seemed, only looked inward. It was daytime outside. The sun was shining.

"Please don't hurt me," said Lina in English. "I am a British subject."

The man snarled in Arabic, *"Indary!"* Turn around. He took a thick piece of cloth from his pocket and wrapped it tightly around her eyes, blindfolding her. Then he affixed a cord to her neck, like a dog leash, and tugged at it. "Follow me," he said.

She stumbled behind him down a long corridor, turning right once. They were heading in the direction from which the screams had come a few hours before. Eventually they stopped, and she heard him opening a door and then felt the tug of the yoke as he pulled her inside. When the door was closed, he removed the blindfold and leash and told her to sit down. The chair had straps along the armrests.

"My name is Kamal," he said, standing over her. "I will be your interrogator today. I am the nice one. I went to college. I like ice cream. I am just like you. But you must tell me the truth. Only the truth."

"What are you going to do to me?" asked Lina, again in English.

He answered in Arabic. "I will ask you questions. You will answer in Arabic, or I will throw you out that window." He pointed to a small opening at the far end of the room.

"I want to see the British ambassador, please," she said, this time in Arabic.

The interrogator just laughed. "You are dreaming. There is no British ambassador for you. There is only me." He walked to her chair and bound the straps across her forearms.

"Don't move. I'll be right back!" He was smiling; he thought that was funny. The man exited through a side door, allowing Lina to look more carefully at the room. Directly in front of her chair was a simple metal desk. Atop it was an unopened bottle of Johnny Walker Black Label whiskey and a carton of Marlboro cigarettes. On one wall was a discolored Iraqi flag. On the other was a poster celebrating the ruling party. It displayed a picture of some flowers and the words *"Kull al-shaab shaddat warid, wa al-riha hizbiyya"*—"The whole people is a bouquet of flowers, and the smell is the Party."

Beneath this incongruous floral poster stood a wooden table. Atop it were a series of instruments laid out like the drills and picks in a dentist's office. There was a length of electrical cable about three feet long, wrapped in a thin cover of plastic; next to it was a wooden instrument, about the size and shape of a billy club, and then another, thicker version that was more like a baseball bat. Next was some kind of electrical device, with wires emerging from the console, and beside it a pail of water. Fixed to the wall every few feet were metal rings. In a corner of the room was an examination table, like the kind you might find in a gynecologist's office, with metal stirrups to hold the legs apart. Atop the examination table was a pan of instruments that Lina couldn't see.

The door opened again, and the man in the blue jeans returned. He was carrying a file folder in his hand. Lina was trembling now. She had tried to be brave, but the sight of the interrogation room, with the instruments of torture laid out like hardware, had undone her. "Scared?" asked the man.

Lina nodded.

"Good," he said. "I brought you some pictures. They are of someone you know, I think. I would like you to look at them."

He tossed the folder onto Lina's lap, and as he did so, one of the pictures fell to the floor. It was of Randa Aziz. The face was recognizable, even though contorted by pain. She was naked from the waist up. Blood was running down her belly from a wound that began where her left nipple had once been. The center of her breast was now red and pulpy, like hamburger meat. Lina cried out when she saw the face, and looked away.

"There are more pictures," said the man. "Look at them."

Lina sat motionless, choking back sobs. Her head was still turned away from the folder of photographs, and her eyes were closed. The man in the blue jeans raised his hand and brought it down hard against her cheek.

"Look at them!" he repeated.

Lina numbly opened the folder. They were all the same. A bloody vagina. A missing ear. A battered face, bleeding from the forehead and the nose and the mouth. Her dearest friend, arrayed in these unspeakable poses for the camera.

"*Haram,*" said the man in the blue jeans. "What a fool your friend was. All we wanted was information, but look what she made us do! I hope you will not be so stupid."

"Is she dead?" asked Lina quietly. It was the only thing she wanted to know. When the interrogator nodded, she felt an odd sense of relief. It would not last forever. At some point she would be released, as Randa had been.

"But you don't have to die, *habibti.*" He was smiling, an earnest smile like that of someone trying too hard to impress a visitor. "To save yourself, all you have to do is answer my questions. That's all. Understand?"

"Yes," she whispered, but she knew it was a lie. After

what they had done to Randa, they would never let her go free. She would tell him whatever she had to, to get it over quickly. Whatever he wanted to hear, she would tell him. About Hammoud's files, about the computer tape, about Hoffman. None of it mattered. She had reached the Palace of the End.

"So we begin now. And remember, only the truth. Otherwise, I have my friends here to help." He pointed to the array of tools lined up on the wooden table.

Lina nodded. She just wanted to be finished.

The interrogator lit himself a Marlboro. "When did you start working for the Israelis?"

Lina looked at him dumbly. "What?" she said. What did the Israelis have to do with it? It was the one question for which she had failed to prepare herself.

The interrogator's voice was louder, angrier. "The Israelis. The Jews. When did you begin working for them? Who recruited you?"

"Please," said Lina. "I don't work for the Israelis. I don't know any Israelis."

"I told you, no lies, and already you are lying. And you make me sad, so sad, because I will have to hurt you."

"No. Please. I am being honest. I don't know any Israelis. I hate the Israelis. I hate the Jews! Please. I am a good Arab."

"*Ya kaybul!*" he said, calling the name of the favored Iraqi torture device. He picked up the electrical cable from the wooden desk and slapped it against his jeans. "You know we have a saying here. '*Mat jawah al-kaybulat.*'— *She died under the cables.* So no more games. Answer me!"

"Honestly. I don't work for . . ."

She didn't finish the sentence. The next sound was a scream of pain as the metal whip caught her across the arm and chest. It was a burning sensation, like a lash of fire, with a force so hard that she thought at first that one of her ribs must be broken.

"*Kalba!*" he screamed. "*Yehudiya kalba! Inti mudhah lil-hizb wa mudhahd lil-thawra!*"—*Jew bitch! You are anti-party and anti-revolution!* "Now answer my question. When were you recruited?"

She was screaming now, a piercing cry for help, and struggling to breathe in enough air. After that first blow, she was prepared to tell him anything, but she didn't know what lie was correct. Her sobbing seemed only to make him angrier. The arm came up again, and the cable came down, hitting her full on the back. It felt as if a welt of skin had been ripped from her.

"Gahba!" he shouted. *Whore!* "Who recruited you, Jew whore? Where are your rich London friends to save you now?"

"Min fadluk, sayyidi, min fadluk!" *Please, master, please.* She was sobbing helplessly, her arms pinned back against the chair. "I don't know any Israelis."

"Who recruited you?" he screamed. He was a madman now. The slouching figure in blue jeans had become a snarling animal. He whipped the cable across her chest, searing the flesh on both breasts.

"Sam Hoffman," she said. It just came out. She didn't know whether it was the answer the interrogator wanted, but he seemed to calm down and looked at her carefully, curiously. The cable fell to his side.

"Sam Hoffman? When did he recruit you?"

"I don't know. I'm not sure." She couldn't stop crying, which made it hard to think and hard to talk.

"I've had enough of your lies!" He pointed to the examination table with the stirrups, across the room. "Now we get serious." He unfastened one arm and began pulling her toward the table.

"No!" she screamed. "I'll tell you whatever you want."

"When did Hoffman recruit you?"

She thought, and then realized it didn't matter what she said. "A month ago. The night of the party at the Darwishes'."

"And how much money did he offer you?"

"Ten thousand pounds. They paid it into my account in London."

The interrogator looked skeptically at her. "Ten thousand pounds?"

"Yes." Had she picked a number too low? "Maybe it was twenty thousand. I don't know."

"And what was your assignment?"

"To spy on Nasir Hammoud and give all the information to Israel."

He was slapping the cable against his thigh again. He looked unhappy, but Lina couldn't understand why. She was confessing to everything she thought he wanted to know.

"And what did you steal from Hammoud?"

"Everything. Whatever I could find in the computer. All the secret files. All the tapes. I gave them to an Israeli at the embassy."

Finally the interrogator's patience was at an end. *"Ya ghabiya!"* he screamed. "You fool! These are all lies, aren't they?"

Lina didn't know whether to keep lying or tell the truth, so she said nothing.

"All lies!" he screamed again. Lina cringed, waiting for the next blow, but it didn't come. Kamal threw the cable back on the wooden table in disgust. He understood enough about her case to know that she was simply making things up. She hadn't been recruited by Hoffman at the Darwishes' party; she hadn't received ten thousand pounds, much less twenty, and she wasn't delivering secrets to someone in the Israeli embassy. She just thought those were the right answers. That was the problem with torture: It was good at producing the truth, but it was also good at producing lies. They would have to start over again.

"You are a liar," said the interrogator. "You are so weak! So frightened! You are not an Iraqi woman at all. You tell me whatever you think you should say to stop the pain. But that is not how this game works. Do you know what we do when we find someone like you, who is so weak she will tell us anything, because she is so afraid?"

"No," whispered Lina.

"We make her more afraid."

"Min fadluk, sayyidi!" Her plea was a tiny sound, barely audible.

"Take off your clothes, now." He untied the other strap that bound her arm to the chair. "Now," he repeated.

Lina was so numb from fear that she simply obeyed. She removed the blue jacket of her suit, and then undid the buttons of her white cotton blouse and then the buttons on the sleeves. She stopped for a moment, out of modesty, when the buttons were all undone. But the interrogator motioned for her to continue, and she removed the blouse. Her breasts swung gently from her torso; there was a line of discoloration where the whip had struck, a sickly ochre color. The interrogator raised the cable, as if he was about to strike her again, but then brought it down gently and stroked the bruise, and then slipped the cable underneath, feeling the weight of each breast.

"All your clothes," he said, rapping the metal whip against her skirt. She pulled the zipper and let the skirt fall to the floor, so that she was standing before him in only her panty hose. Despite her fear, there was a part of her that felt that if she gave the interrogator her body, perhaps he would be lenient. She tried to smile at him. But the look on his face was anger—disgust with her weakness and femininity—not desire. He took the top of his electric cable and poked at the crotch of her panty hose, and she removed them, too, so that all of her clothes were left in a pile on the floor. She tried to cover her crotch with one hand and her breasts with the other, but the interrogator pushed her hands away with the cable.

"Come with me," he said. He opened the side door and led her into another room. In the center was another examination table, fitted with its metal stirrups. Lina's knees felt weak when she saw it. On the walls were pictures of naked women from cheap Turkish sex magazines. So this was where they would take her.

"We call this the rape room," he said in a matter-of-fact tone. He pushed her toward the examination table.

Lina resisted, thinking that he was about to take her at that moment, but he cracked the cable across the backs of her thighs so hard that she fell to the floor.

"Get up." He held her by the neck and pressed her head toward the filthy sheet that covered the table. The cotton fabric was crusted with semen. The center was bloodred. He pushed her face onto the sheet so that her nose was full of the putrid odors, and her lips were pressed against the filth.

"Look at it. Smell it. Taste it," he said. "If you tell me any more lies, this bed is for you." He ripped the dirty sheet from the bed and threw it at her. "This is your dress now. Wear it."

＝

Lina was taken to a communal cell, the same size as the first one where she had been held but jammed with a dozen or more women. Some of them hissed when Lina was pushed in the door—another body and so little space—and when the guard spat on Lina and called her a Jew—*"Yehudiya!"*—the other women pulled back, frightened even of the word. Several of them pointed to the fading remnants of her dyed blond hair and howled that she must be a Jew! Look at the hair. No real Arab could have hair like that. Lina huddled on the floor, wrapped in the filthy sheet, sobbing bitterly to herself. After a few minutes, she felt the touch of a hand on her back. She cringed at first, but the hand continued patting her back gently. Lina eventually looked up and saw the face of a woman in her fifties. Her hair had turned white, and her body was thin as a stick, but she had the thoughtful eyes of a schoolteacher.

"*Khatiya!* Poor little girl," she said. "Have you just arrived?"

"Yes," said Lina. "I just came. They took my clothes." She was crying again.

"Where are you from? That is a strange accent I have not heard for many years."

"From London. My father left Iraq a long time ago. Before the events."

"*W'Allah!* What are you doing here?"

"I don't know," she lied. "It is some kind of mistake."

The woman patted her cheek and pointed to the sleeping bodies on all sides of them. "This room is full of mistakes, *habibti*. Half the women here do not know why they were arrested. I myself do not know why I was arrested. I was teaching at the university when they came for me, five years ago, and still I do not know. Before, they said I was against the Ruler; now they say I was for him. It doesn't matter. They don't need reasons."

As they were talking, Lina heard the thin, high sound of a baby crying and then a rustling on the floor, a few feet away, as the mother stuck her nipple in the child's mouth.

"Can that be a baby?" whispered Lina. The thought that there was a child inside the dank cell seemed to open the possibility of life. "How did it get here?"

The older woman patted Lina gently, like a new pupil who didn't understand the rules. "There are many babies born here. Too many. You have seen the rape room?"

"Yes." Lina shuddered.

"*Haram.* It is a terrible thing to have a baby in prison. The worst thing."

"Why?" asked Lina. As she heard the baby's gentle cooing as it nursed itself back to sleep, it sounded almost a comfort. Something to live for.

"Because a child makes you so much more vulnerable. That is the cruelest weapon they have—the ability to cause suffering to children—and they use it too much. Too much."

"What do you mean?" Lina still didn't understand. There was a layer of cruelty that was still beyond her imagining.

"See that woman over there." She pointed to a heap of bones in a dirty dress. "They wanted information about her husband, who they thought was plotting against the party. When she would not talk, they took her three children up in a helicopter, high over the desert, and threw them out, one by one, until she told them where her husband was hiding. She would like to die now, but they will not let her.

"And see that one." She pointed to another shapeless mass on the floor. "She was hiding in the mountains beyond her village. They tried to make her children tell where she was, and when they would not say, they poured gasoline on the children and set them on fire. Two boys. Eight and five."

"No more," said Lina. But the older woman continued to talk in her hushed, sibyl's voice. This was her only revenge: telling the truth.

"And that one. Her husband was a leader of the rebels. They made him watch while the Ruler's guards raped her and her three daughters. Then they put tires soaked with gasoline around the necks of his girls, and told him to light the flame. He would not, so they shot him, and then they made his wife do it.

"And that one, sleeping by the door. She was pregnant when they arrested her. She had the baby in prison, and when she would not answer their questions, they took her baby from her arms and beat it against the wall until it was dead. That one is mad now. All she does is cry out for her child."

Lina was weeping softly. "Please don't tell me any more," she said. "All I want is to die."

"To die," said the older woman. "Yes, that is what we all want. That is what the guards say. *Sleima tekurfach, khatiya—Let death scrape you up, you poor wretch.* But even death is not a release. Their cruelty follows you even then. Then send you home in a sealed box so that no one can see your broken bones and bruised skin, so that you cannot be prepared for burial like a good Muslim. There is only that sealed box, and on the outside the word *Coward* or *Traitor*. And that is all you take to the everlasting. They are the worst, and the worst, and the worst."

"What will I do? *Allah yestur?*"

"Keep your dignity. Don't let them try to frighten you. Everything they do is to make you afraid. The sounds. The tools. The way they talk. The humiliation. It is all to make you afraid. That is their only real weapon. The fear in your heart. The rest is nothing. If you master your fear, they will lose.''

"What will I do?"

"Be brave, *habibti*. Be brave. Be brave."

═══

Lina was roused the next morning by a guard, who pulled her from the knot of women on the floor. She gathered the dirty sheet around her and turned to say good-bye to the old woman who had spoken with her. But the guard yanked hard on her arm, and she had no chance to turn around. As she left, some of the other women began a low wailing. A lament for the departed.

They led Lina to a small room down the corridor. On a table were the blue suit and white blouse she had been wearing before. They had been cleaned and pressed, and there was clean underwear. The room had a small washbasin, with soap and towels. Lina was afraid, at first, that it was a trick. They wanted her to be clean and fresh for their tortures. She resisted the urge for as long as she could, but after huddling for thirty minutes in her ragged sheet, she washed and dressed. When she had put on her fine French suit and her new undergarments, she felt guilty, thinking of the women in rags down the hall. But they were not her problem. She was thinking, now, only of herself.

═══

It was several hours before Kamal came for her. He was wearing the same blue jeans and tasseled loafers as before. But today, in place of the leather jacket, he wore a double-breasted blue blazer. He was smoking a Cohiba cigar and looking very pleased with himself, like a dandy heading out for a night on the town. He reached out to shake her hand, formally, as if he were welcoming her to a club of which she was now officially a member.

"How do you feel?" he asked. "Bruises healing?"

"Yes," she said.

"Yesterday, it was your turn to be interrogated. Today, we have decided to let you watch the interrogation of someone else. Won't that be much better?"

She didn't answer. She looked at him dumbly. What did he mean?

"But maybe you won't like watching. Maybe you will decide that you would like to change places, so that it is *you* answering our questions. Yes. We can do that. But only if you tell the truth. Otherwise, we will do you both."

She still didn't understand, but she didn't dare ask questions. In a moment Kamal was wrapping the blindfold around her eyes and leading her down the hall. They made a series of turns, down one corridor and then the next, until they reached a room where Lina could hear the noise of other people. As she entered the room, she heard a man's voice speaking loudly.

"*Heyaha.* Here she is. Here is the informer now. The one who told us about your crimes."

Kamal removed her blindfold. Lina opened her eyes and let out a tiny cry. "*Yumma!*" Mommy. Hanging from a rope against the wall was the kindly Iraqi woman who had befriended her the night before. Her meager rags had been torn from her. Her body was so many sticks: the skin translucent with age, the breasts hanging from her like empty bags. Standing over her was a man with a huge head and a thick body, like steel scrap that had been crumpled together many times until it was a dense mass. He was holding a *kaybul*—the metal whip—in his hand. He was speaking to the white-haired woman.

"The London lady has informed on you, old woman. She told us everything you said last night. All your slogans against the party. All your conspiracies against the Iraqi people. How you plotted with the Jews against the Arab nation. She told us all of it. She betrayed you."

Lina said nothing. The old woman was looking directly into her eyes. Lina looked away.

"*Ya gahba!*" shouted the man with the big head, raising

the metal whip above his head. ''O you whore. We must punish you for these terrible crimes against the nation and the party.'' He brought the whip down hard against the old woman, wracking her frail skeleton like a pile of twigs.

Lina screamed so loudly, the cry of the old woman could barely be heard.

''Ya kalba!'' swore the interrogator, raising his metal whip and bringing it down again. *O you bitch!* There was a muffled sound from the old woman, and another blow, and then another.

Again Lina screamed. This time it was a word. *''Kafi!''* Stop! The old woman was writhing mutely on the ropes now, dangling like a grotesque doll. She was looking again at Lina. There wasn't anger in her eyes. Only forgiveness.

''Stop!'' screamed Lina again. But it was too late. Another blow was coming at the woman. Instead of screaming, there was a gagging sound from her, and her battered face turned a bluish color. As Lina watched the old woman's agony, she saw suddenly the face of her own Aunt Soha, who was about the same age as this poor woman and who must have died in the same pathetic circumstances.

''Take me!'' cried Lina. ''I'll trade places with her. Stop! Take me instead.''

The man with the metal whip checked his next blow. But it was too late to save the old woman. The blue tint of her face had deepened, and her head had fallen limp to one side. They left her hanging there for a moment, and threw a pail of water on her, thinking it would revive her, but she was gone. They realized later that she had bitten off a piece of her own tongue, when the beating had begun, and had choked on her own blood and vomit. She had been released into eternity.

''Do you want your interrogation to begin now or later?'' asked Kamal.

''Now,'' said Lina. She was ready to die.

''Then we will do it later.'' Kamal laughed. It was funny. They led Lina away down the hall. They were all tired. The interrogation would begin the next day.

33

Sam Hoffman was walking through Hanover Square when he felt the nudge of someone behind him. He ignored it at first. He was on his way to the British Museum library, where they had a full set of the banking regulations of Switzerland, which he thought might open a new line of attack against Nasir Hammoud. But he felt the nudge at his elbow again, harder this time, and a voice near his ear.

"Don't turn around," said the voice. "I have news of your friend Lina."

Hoffman immediately whipped his head to the left and saw, a step behind him, the tanned face of Martin Hilton.

"You idiot," whispered Hilton. "I told you not to turn around. Don't you know you're being watched?"

"Piss off," said Hoffman. "Who's watching me?"

"Everybody. Keep your mouth shut and do what I say, and I'll tell you about Lina. In one hour, I want you to be in Kew Gardens, in front of the Palm House. If nobody is following you, I'll approach you and ask for a cigarette. Then we can talk. One hour, exactly."

They reached a corner. Hilton turned ninety degrees, to cross in the other direction. "Is she alive?" whispered Hoffman, but Hilton didn't answer. He was already crossing the street.

＝

An hour later, Hoffman was standing outside the glass
pavilion known as the Palm House, gazing at the rose
garden that surrounded the building and wondering where
Hilton was. Kew was a longish drive, on the far western
outskirts of London, but he couldn't imagine Hilton being
late for anything. Hoffman waited five minutes, then ten,
then fifteen, and had nearly given up when a man in a
Van Dyke beard and a straw boater asked him for a cigarette. At first he thought the man was a homosexual trying
to pick him up, until he recognized the well-disguised face
of Martin Hilton.

"Let's take a stroll," said Hilton. He steered Hoffman
toward a path that led to the Japanese pagoda, at the far
end of Kew Gardens.

"Where is Lina?" asked Hoffman immediately. He
needed to know, and he was afraid of the answer.

"She's in Baghdad. They grabbed her yesterday in Geneva and put her on a plane. We got the flight plan from
the airport. We know it landed in Baghdad."

"Is she alive?"

"We don't know. We assume they took her to the main
prison. We don't know what happened to her after that."

"Who's 'we'? You keep saying 'we.' "

"The state of Israel."

"Shit. You're all she needs right now."

Hilton's eyes flashed, but he kept walking. "We're all
she's got right now. But unfortunately, there's nothing we
can do for her. We're a bit thin on the ground in
Baghdad."

"Shit," said Hoffman again.

They were passing by another glass conservatory.
Under the great arc of glass and iron was a miniature rain
forest, with dragon trees and waterlilies and flowering
camelias. It was a little prison, holding a jungle against
its will in the midst of London. Hoffman turned to the
Israeli operative.

"What can I do to get her out?"

"That depends on whether you have any connections in Baghdad."

Hoffman thought a moment. "No."

"Or whether you know anyone who could influence somebody in Baghdad. Someone with money, say, or political influence."

Hoffman thought again. The idea was distasteful to him, but he knew that the answer was yes. His old friend and more recent enemy, the prince. "Maybe," he said.

"Well, you better use whatever influence you have, fast. Because I don't think you have much time."

They were approaching the spindly tower of the Japanese pagoda. Hoffman turned to his companion. The Israeli looked absurd in his pointy beard and straw hat. "Why are you telling me this?" he asked. "What's in it for you?"

"A chance to make trouble for Iraq and for various people who are propping it up. Your friend Lina seems like an ideal troublemaker, if we can keep her alive."

"You *are* a shit," said Hoffman. "You're using her."

Hilton rolled his eyes. Hoffman was a fool. "Tsk, tsk. Naughty me."

"You prick. Do something to help her."

"Time to go," said the Israeli. "Ta-ta." He blew Hoffman a kiss and turned onto a different path. It led toward another folly of the garden—a ruined arch that some long-ago king or queen had imagined would look like an ancient Roman monument—leaving Hoffman standing alone next to the make-believe Japanese pagoda.

Hoffman tried to avoid the inevitable. He called Asad Barakat at his office, but a secretary said the Palestinian banker was away on business. He even tried his father in Athens, thinking that he might have some idea how to lean on the new regime in Baghdad. But his father was away on business, too. That left only one possibility, and as Sam drove his BMW toward Hyde Park Square, he realized that he had been arcing back toward this meeting for half a decade, like a boomerang returning to the spot from which it had been thrown.

The lights were on in Prince Jalal's pleasure palace, and the Rolls-Royce Corniche was parked out front, which meant that he must be home. Sam had decided not to call ahead. It would be easier this way. He rang the bell. The door was opened by the usual British security man; just visible behind him, on the stairs heading up to his private quarters, was the prince. He was dressed in a long, white *thobe*. With his rich, coffee-colored skin and his burnished beard, he looked like some sort of god ascending the heavenly stairway. The prince turned and, when he saw Hoffman, a momentary look of embarrassment came across his face. For it happened that, at that moment, he was holding the hand of a teenage boy. He gave the boy a pat on the rear and sent him upstairs.

"My dear Sam," said Prince Jalal, descending the stairs toward his visitor. "What a surprise. I thought it would be another five years before I saw you again. How nice. How nice." He took Sam's hand and kissed him sweetly on each cheek.

"I'm sorry," said Sam. "I've come at a bad time."

"Not at all, my dear. I have no secrets from you. I should have introduced you to my young friend. Lovely boy. They found him in Denmark, I think. Beautiful voice, like an angel. Variety is the spice of life, is it not?"

"Yes," said Sam. "The spice of life."

The prince led Sam into one of the downstairs parlors. It was an enormous room with ceilings that rose to twenty feet or more, painted the thick, sweet color of clotted cream. The prince sat down on a vast couch and motioned for Sam to join him. He clapped his hands, and servants appeared with tea and sweets and then a hubble-bubble pipe. In the bowl was a piece of hashish the size of a sugar cube. The prince took a long drag and offered the stem of the pipe to his guest. When Sam declined, he let it fall into his lap and looked at his visitor dreamily.

"So, what brings you back to me so soon after our last meeting? Have you reconsidered about the Romanian girls? They're not virgins anymore, I'm afraid, but still very tasty."

"No. It's not that. Actually, I want to take you up on another proposal you made."

"Ah, good. Which one is that?"

"The one you made to me five years ago about helping you to hide money. You said the other day that the offer still stood, and now I'm interested."

Jalal extended his hand. His head was coming out from the cloud of hashish. "At last, my dear fellow. You have seen the light. *Ahlan wa sahlan.* Welcome to the fellowship of civilized men."

"But there is one condition, Jalal. I don't want to be paid for my help."

"Oh, dear. Why not?"

"Because I want a favor from you instead. I want you to use the money you would pay me to buy the life of a friend."

" 'Buy the life of a friend.' How touching. Who is he?"

"She. The friend is a woman."

"Ah, *habibi.* I am touched. Of course I will help you. This is the kind of exchange I understand. There is a way in which a woman is more valuable even than money, is there not? Who is she?"

"An Iraqi. Her name is Lina Alwan. She works for Nasir Hammoud."

"Him again." Jalal made a gesture with his hand, as if he were pushing away something unpleasant from his plate. "Such a bore, but never mind. Where is this woman you wish me to purchase for you?"

"Baghdad. She's in prison there. She was taken there yesterday, from Geneva. Can you get her out?"

"Difficult, but not impossible. Money works everywhere, my dear. Even in Baghdad. That is the iron law of the world. And it happens that our ambassador there is a friend of mine. I make no promises, but I would so very much like to have you indebted to me, so I will try hard."

"Thank you," said Hoffman. He touched his heart, in the way that an Arab would, to show his gratitude. But the prince laughed. This was business.

"Now, then, we must talk about your side of the deal,

my dear Sam. Because I am doing something special for you, I must ask you to do something special for me. That is fair, is it not?"

"Yes. It's fair. Tell me what you want, and I'll do it."

He paused a moment and stroked the fine, manicured hairs of his beard with his index finger. "I have a friend in Turkey," he said eventually. "He has been so helpful to me over the years. A banker, as a matter of fact. And now he is in trouble with the law. In Turkey, in America, everywhere. He still has money hidden away somewhere— in the Cayman Islands, I think—from before his bank went under. But he is terrified to do anything with it, for fear the authorities in the U.S. or Britain will find out and make life even more difficult for him. So, you see, he needs help. And you are just the sort of fellow who can help him. Such a good reputation. Well connected. Just the right sort of fellow."

"What do you want me to do for him?"

"Buy him a bank in America. He's convinced, for some reason, that this is the only safe way to keep his money. Unfortunately it is technically illegal for him to own a bank in America. Especially with all this money that people claim he stole. So you'll have to own it for him. But we'll take care of all that. That's easy enough, isn't it?"

Sam nodded impassively. He had already made the bargain in his mind before he rang the doorbell.

"Hurrah! I'll have my lawyer in Washington draw up the papers. You may have to visit the States when they find the right bank—sign some documents, that sort of thing. A nuisance, but it can't be helped."

Sam nodded again. He felt the identity he had worked so hard to build over the past half-decade crumbling around him. There was no such thing as purity and independence for someone like him, it turned out. He could be pure and independent only so long as he didn't need a favor, at which point he had to wade into the shit like everyone else. Hoffman felt sick at heart. He wanted to leave Jalal's house, but the prince had a triumphant smile on his face, as if he had won an argument.

"Let us celebrate, my dear Sam, now that we are friends again. Perhaps it's movie time? I have a new one, which I received yesterday from a Kuwaiti friend. It's called *Philippine Nurses*. He filmed bits of it himself, at home. He assures me that it is all real."

"No," said Hoffman. "No movies." Hoffman remembered the face of Ramon Pinta's wife, in the police photograph the Filipino cook had showed him that day at his office, in what seemed a lifetime ago.

"A drink, perhaps? The pipe? Some companionship?"

Sam rose from the couch. "I have to go," he said.

"Of course. I understand. You are nervous about your little girlfriend. What's her name again? Lina Alwan. I will get on it this minute. As soon as I have called my friend in Turkey to give him the good news."

Robert Hatton was hosting a luncheon party that afternoon in Washington, in the private dining room of the law firm of Hatton, Marola & Dubin. He had asked not to be disturbed, so they didn't bother him at first with the call from the client in London. The luncheon was an important event for Hatton: the annual meeting of a group he had founded many years before, which was known in secret as the Friends of Araby. It was a distinguished Washington group, in its way. Three former Cabinet officers, a half-dozen retired officers of foreign service, several prominent members of the Washington bar.

For the distinguished members of the Friends of Araby, the annual gathering was the celebration of a great enterprise that had spanned more than fifty years. If anyone had known of the group's existence, he would doubtless have attacked it as elitist, imperialist, Arabist, racist and every other sort of "-ist." But the members viewed this sort of thinking as just so much rubbish, spoken by people who hadn't a clue about how the world really worked. The only thing the Friends were guilty of, Hatton liked to remind them in his annual toast, was protecting the national interest of the United States. America had taken on an impossible task—holding, in one hand, the world's oil supply, and in the other, an Arab-Israeli bomb that was always about to explode—and so far, with help, the nation had succeeded. The oil was still flowing, and the bomb, while it had indeed exploded occasionally, hadn't yet brought down the house. And for that, the world owed a debt of thanks—that could never, ever be spoken—to the Friends of Araby.

The secretary finally interrupted Hatton, just after he had delivered his toast. The client from London was calling again. He said it was a matter of great urgency and could not wait. Hatton excused himself and took the call from a certain Saudi prince, who had for many years been part of his network of clients. The prince explained, in his dreamy voice, that he had two rather complicated problems. There was a matter in Iraq that required the urgent transfer of a large sum of money from a bank account in Bahrain, which must be delivered as soon as possible by chartered jet to Baghdad. And there was another matter, having to do with the affairs of a Turkish gentleman who was an old friend of the firm of Hatton, Marola & Dubin. This involved a very large sum of money that was currently resting dormant in a numbered account in George Town, in the Cayman Islands, but wanted a home in the United States. A nominee had been found who would be available to purchase a bank. The Turkish matter could wait. The Baghdad matter required prompt attention.

Hatton immediately called a junior partner. He instructed him to arrange the release of funds from the account in Bahrain and negotiate the charter of an airplane from a company in Amman. In a matter of minutes, the wheels were all turning in the right direction. Which allowed Robert Hatton to return to his guests in time to share a glass of brandy and a cigar.

34

Lina passed a long, sleepless night. She was in a solitary cell again, but this time they kept the light burning constantly. It was, otherwise, the same as the first room she had occupied: rough concrete walls scratched with names and messages; the stinking pit in the corner; the soothing coolness of the stone floor. It wasn't fear of death that kept Lina awake. She simply wanted to hold on to every remaining minute of consciousness. As she lay with her face on the stone floor, the characters of her life paraded through her mind like a company of actors taking their final bows. She thought of her mother, who had died so long ago that she had become in Lina's memory a distant beacon. But she was the first victim: What had killed her was the forced exile from Baghdad. And then she thought of her father, the Arab aristocrat who lacked enough money to indulge his disdain for what the Arabs had become. How right he had been. It was a new *Asr al-Jahiliyya*, a new age of ignorance. He was a victim, too.

And she thought of Sam Hoffman, initially a small player in her drama who had almost by accident come to center stage. It was Hoffman who had pushed her toward the brink of this disastrous adventure, and then had tried to pull her back. She didn't blame him. He had been right both times: She should have done more to stop Nasir Hammoud, and she should have done less. She thought about

Hammoud too: a hard, dried turd on the floor of life. If anyone on the planet deserved the horrors of the Qasr al-Nihayya, it was him. She thought, then, of her Aunt Soha, who had been forced to send the letter to Lina three years before, pressing her into the employ of Hammoud. What a price she had paid. At the end, she had probably been in this same prison, perhaps in the same cell. As she thought of her aunt within these walls, the image blurred into that of the white-haired spinster who had reached out to Lina in the hour when she was most alone. That woman had died while Lina stammered to find a voice to say "Stop." And she thought of her friend Randa, whom she had falsely accused without really thinking about the consequences, and the ghastly price she had paid.

Too many people had died on the way to Lina finding her courage. What had Jawad, the Iraqi poet, said? It was the women who would have to save Iraq, because the men were all corrupted. He had been wrong, at least about Lina, who in her cowardice had allowed others to go to their deaths. She cursed her weakness and her silence. She thought of the blind poet and realized that he must have lost his eyes in a place like this. How had he found the courage to survive that incident with the torturer and his cigarettes and go on? To continue defying the regime in Baghdad, inviting more torture? She saw in her mind the empty sockets of his eyes, burned and disfigured, and made of them a kind of mental icon. They would be her Muslim crucifix; a perfect sacrifice of blood that had flowed to save others, less brave. As her mind focused on the scarred tissue that had once been his eyes, Lina made a promise—the kind of bargain with God that people make when they are near death. If somehow she should survive the ordeal of the Palace of the End, she would do what she could to help Nabil Jawad, her comforter.

━━

Kamal, the inquisitor, roused her just after dawn. He was carrying a black hood in his hand. He seemed almost apologetic about disturbing her. He knows I'm going to die today, Lina thought. He looked different from before. Agitated, unsure of himself. Maybe he was ashamed of what he would have to do. Maybe he was afraid he couldn't get a hard-on to rape her. *"Ana aasif,"* he said. *I'm sorry.*

"Don't say it," said Lina. "Don't say anything." She didn't want to hear it. She couldn't bear, on that morning, the idea of a torturer with a guilt complex.

"I am sorry," he said again. "I did not know."

He put the black hood over her head and led her out the door. He didn't pull her roughly, like before, but led her gently by the hand. She reached the end of a corridor and entered another passageway through a metal door and then turned right. She heard Kamal say, "Be careful," as he placed her hand on a railing, and suddenly they were descending a stairway, one flight, two, three. At the bottom of the stairs, they stopped. She heard Kamal's voice, talking to another man.

"Miftaah?" said Kamal. He was asking for the key.

"Aywah!" said the other man. *Yes.*

"Are they waiting?"

"Aywah!" he said again. *"Al-Safir Al-Saudi."*

The Saudi ambassador. What did that mean? So the Saudis wanted her dead, too. Maybe they had come to watch. There was some fumbling, and some low talk Lina couldn't understand. The next sound she heard was a heavy door opening, and then she sensed sunlight, even through the thick cloth of the hood. She was pulled a few more steps and then another door opened, and she felt on her arms a gust of air. Her heart skipped a moment—she was outside!—but she killed the thought in her mind. They were playing more games with her, but it would come to the same thing. She felt a different hand now, pulling her forward and then pressing her down into the backseat of a car. So they were taking her someplace else to kill her. The driver made her lie flat on the floor, and laid a foul-smelling prison blanket on top of her. A shroud for the dying.

"You like music?" asked the driver. He was speaking

in English. He put a cassette in the recorder. It was pop
Arab music, with a tinny electric oud and a woman with
a voice like an alley cat.

"No music," said Lina from under the blanket. To her
surprise, he immediately turned it off. The condemned had
some rights, at least.

———

They drove a very long way. Too long. Lina wanted to
get it over with. Her mind was starting to play tricks on
her now, allowing her to imagine that she might survive.
She felt the wind of the open road through her blanket.
That was dangerous. The only nourishment for courage
was the certainty of death; once the possibility of survival
existed and there was something to live for, the terror
returned. The car continued driving along what seemed to
be a broad highway and then slowed at a roundabout, and
then another. Lina began to hear a strange noise, distant
at first and then closer, almost like the roar of an engine.
She wondered if she was going mad after so many hours
of fear and tension.

The car turned and stopped. The driver rolled down the
window and spoke in Arabic. *"Safir Al-Saudiyya."* The
Saudi ambassador, again. The driver was handing someone—a guard, by the rough sound of his voice—some
papers, or perhaps it was money. Lina couldn't tell. And
then she heard a rough grunt as the guard waved them
through the checkpoint. The driver rolled the window up
again and stepped on the gas.

"You like music?" he said again.

"Yes," said Lina. She knew in that moment, with some
kind of sixth sense, that she was going to live.

The car stopped after thirty seconds of the warbling
music. The driver opened the door and pulled the filthy
blanket from her body and tossed it on the pavement. He
helped Lina to her feet and then carefully untied the black
hood and lifted it off her head.

It took Lina a moment to focus. Ten yards from where

the car had stopped was the fuselage of a Lear jet. The
gangway was down and a steward was standing in the
open hatch, beckoning for her to come aboard. Lina turned
back toward the car. It was a long black limousine with
diplomatic plates. She finally understood. The driver was
the Saudi ambassador's chauffeur.

"Quickly," said the steward, motioning again for her
to board the plane. Lina turned a last time to look at the
car and driver. She wasn't ready to leave yet. She needed
something to remind her of her promise to the living
Jawad and so many who were dead. She saw the foul
prison blanket lying on the ground and took it in her arms.

"Hurry, please," said the steward. The pilot, too, was
motioning through the window that it was time to go.
They were more frightened now of Baghdad than she was.
She climbed the stairs. The steward quickly closed the
door and showed her to her seat. He asked if she would
like anything to drink, as if she were suddenly a guest at
the Ritz. Lina requested a glass of water. She closed her
eyes as the plane taxied down the runway and roared into
the sky. She wanted to feel a sense of liberation as the
wheels tucked up into the plane. But she still saw in her
mind the face of the poet, and she knew that she was still
in the gallery of the dead. When they were in the air, the
steward returned.

"The pilot asks your destination, please," he said. "His
orders were to pick you up and take you wherever you
wish to go."

Lina had to think only for an instant. "Geneva," she
said.

—

An hour later, after the steward came back to report that
they had left Iraqi airspace, Lina asked if she could send
a message to London. She had been thinking, in those first
minutes of freedom, of what she would do next, and had
realized that she would need help. She had stumbled when
she was on her own and had made too many mistakes.

She thought of Sam, and the sleepy-eyed look on his face when she had knocked on his door, and the longing in his eyes when she had stroked his cheek. She remembered, too, the instinctive way he had tried to reach out to the poet Jawad that first night at the Darwishes', when Lina was still trying to hide.

The steward said they could send a telegram anywhere in the world. Lina wrote the message out in longhand and gave it to him. It was just one sentence, to be delivered immediately to an address on North Audley Street in London. The message read: "Meet me tomorrow in Geneva, at noon, in the park called The Pearl of the Lake." It was signed "Anouk Aimée."

The steward's eyes widened as he read it. "Are you Anouk Aimée?" he asked.

"Yes," she said. It didn't matter. She didn't exist.

–V–

The Sea of Money

35

Lina sat in the second floor of a café on the Rue de Lausanne, near the entrance to the lakeside park the Swiss called La Perle du Lac. It was eleven forty-five. Her back hurt; her ribs hurt; her legs hurt. She ordered another coffee, hoping that it would dull the pain. She had spent much of her time since returning to Geneva trying to escape the blandishments of her new benefactors, the Saudis. They had helped her reenter Switzerland on a Saudi travel document that identified her as a wife of Prince Jalal bin Abdel-Rahman. Waiting to meet the chartered jet at the airport had been the Saudi consul general, who had insisted on driving her in his limousine. He didn't volunteer any information, and she didn't ask.

"I'm staying at the Beau Rivage," she had said, thinking of that lovely bathroom. And she had checked in, taken a heavenly bath and a long nap. But when night fell, she had slipped out of the hotel and disappeared into the city. When she was certain after several hours of random movement that she wasn't being followed, she had returned to the pension near the freight yards, which so far as she knew remained undiscovered. And after elaborate apologies to Madame Jaccard for her absence, and the payment of an additional week's rent in advance, she was forgiven. She fell asleep heavily, as if she were encased in a block of ice. By morning, it had begun to melt.

A few minutes before noon, an airport taxi pulled up

on the Rue de Lausanne. A man in sunglasses paid the fare and strode toward the entrance to the park. He was wearing a blue blazer and gray flannel slacks; over his shoulder was a leather traveling bag. Lina was relieved to see that he was tieless. She wanted him to be exactly as she had remembered him. He stood at the edge of the park, scanning the gardens, looking for her. *Helou!* she said to herself. He was handsome.

The park was lush and green, an emerald against the diamond of the lake. She watched Sam Hoffman walk through the gate, searching for her. It was noon now, time to meet. But Lina had learned to be careful. From her perch across the street, she could see the lay of the park and the avenues of approach. She wanted to make sure it was safe before venturing out. As Hoffman entered the green expanse, Lina noticed a bald man on a park bench glance up at him and then look back at his newspaper. He was dark, with skin the color of Lina's café crème, but dressed like a Genevan bourgeois in a tweed jacket and scarf. Was there a flicker of recognition in his eye? It was too far away to tell. Hoffman was oblivious. He sat down on a nearby bench and scanned the green garden.

The spring weather was almost warm, and the park had begun to fill with children and their parents. A man with a pushcart was selling ice cream. A mime in whiteface was walking like a stiff-jointed soldier before a group of astonished children and then passing his hat to their not-so-astonished parents. Lina watched Hoffman scan the park. After five minutes, he stood up from the bench and began walking south, toward a corner of the garden that was sheltered by a bank of shrubs. Lina watched carefully. As Hoffman moved toward the corner, the bald man got up, too. He ambled slowly, standing near clusters of parents and children, stopping occasionally to sit down on a bench and relight his pipe, so that Hoffman, if he had turned around, would have been unaware that anyone was following him.

Hoffman searched for Lina and then turned back. He strode past the bald man, who was leaning unobtrusively against the railing that skirted the lake, watching the boats. Lina pitied Sam. He looked so confused now, and worried. Where was she? Why had she missed the rendezvous?

The park stretched nearly a half-mile north along the lake. Hoffman stood atop a bench to get a better view and then headed up the lake. The bald man ambled slowly behind. He had put out his pipe now so the smell wouldn't give him away. Hoffman was walking faster as his anxiety increased. Lina decided that she would have to leave her second-floor perch or risk losing sight of him altogether. She walked downstairs and turned up the Rue de Lausanne, staying on the far sidewalk rather than entering the park. Every few seconds, she caught a glimpse of Hoffman through the shrubs. They continued north, in invisible synchrony, past the science museum and the Monument to the Dead. At least they had monuments here, Lina thought.

Hoffman continued until he reached the northern edge of the park. They were in the Olympian region of the international organizations now, the Valhalla of the bureaucrats. The Palace of Nations beckoned, just up the Avenue de la Paix. Hoffman sat down on a bench, confused, wondering what to do. He looked defeated. Lina wanted to go to him, yet she knew it would be a mistake. So she let him sit.

They were playing a mental game now, Sam and Lina, whose aim was to coordinate moves without communication. The premise of the game was simple: two people have a scheduled rendezvous, but one doesn't show up. What should each one do, independently, to increase the chance of finding the other? Should they each abandon the initial plan and move to the next-most-likely meeting point: the bridge by the Jet d'Eau, say, or the Palais des Nations? Or should they trust each other to find their way, eventually, to the original meeting place? She saw Hoffman through the trees, still sitting on his bench, doubtless going through the same exercise.

Lina placed her mental wager on trust: Hoffman would stick to the original plan. He would walk back to where he had started, and she would try to intercept him on the

way. She looked down the length of the park for someplace he might stop. There was a small pavilion containing
toilets and a visitors center. It was just inside the fence,
near the walkway that led to the main gate. Hoffman might
stop there to look for Lina or simply to relieve himself.
She began walking toward the building, then broke into a
run. It was essential to get there before Hoffman, and
his pursuer.

Lina reached the pavilion quickly. The small building
had been freshly painted for spring, a cool alpine white.
In the distance, the Jet d'Eau was bubbling over the city
like the spout of an invisible whale. Inside was the visitors
center, decorated with maps of the city, but that seemed
like the wrong place to wait. The bald man would see her
there as easily as Hoffman would. In front was a porch
with walkways, left and right, to the men's and ladies'
toilets. That was the spot.

She took her place behind the wooden barrier that
shielded the entry to the women's side. From there she
could see anyone entering the pavilion without being seen
herself. As she apologized to the parade of stocky Swiss
women who squeezed past her to get to the toilets, she
wondered if she had made the wrong wager. Perhaps Hoffman had come up with another solution to the puzzle.
Perhaps he had simply given up. She looked at her watch.
It was past twelve-thirty. If he didn't come soon, he wasn't
coming. Finally, as Lina was about to leave her hiding
place, she saw the familiar restless stride of Sam Hoffman
climbing the steps to the porch. When he reached the top
he turned away from her, toward the men's room.

"Sam," she whispered. "It's Lina. Don't look."

Hoffman stopped and stared straight ahead into the visitors' center. He was Orpheus ascending, forbidden to gaze
back at his beloved. But there was a large smile on his
face. He took a sideways step toward Lina and pretended
to read a notice posted on the wall.

"You're being followed by a bald man in a tweed
coat," she whispered. "There may be others, but he's
the only one I see. Try to lose him, and then go to the

Intercontinental Hotel. It's just up the hill. Get a double room there. Register for Mr. and Mrs. Hoffman. I'll meet you there tonight.''

Hoffman was still smiling, still looking straight ahead. He removed his sunglasses and put them in his pocket. His eyes were sparkling like the waters of the lake. ''Hubba, hubba,'' he said under his breath.

''Get lost,'' whispered Lina. She turned and disappeared into the ladies' room. Hoffman headed the other way, toward the men's room. Thirty yards away, behind a tree, a bald man in a tweed coat waited until Hoffman returned and then resumed his silent pursuit.

36

The doorman at the Intercontinental eyed Lina skeptically as she pushed through the revolving door. There
was something about her that didn't square: the peroxide
blond hair and the lumpy green coat; the bold walk and
the wary eyes. He watched as she went to the house
phones, called upstairs and then headed for the elevator.
The doorman had seen this same ballet a thousand times.
This had once been the OPEC hotel, after all, where the
princes of oil had gathered each year to fix prices and
have fun. Still, the management liked to keep tabs on
things. The doorman intercepted Lina as she neared the
elevator bank. "May I help you, madam?" he asked.

Lina stared at him as if he were a barbarian. "I am
Mrs. Hoffman," she said icily. "I am joining my husband
in room eight-ten." The doorman gave her a dubious look,
but he backed away. It didn't really matter, as long as she
didn't solicit clients in the lobby.

The door was already open when Lina reached the
room. Hoffman embraced her, enfolding her in his arms,
and then took a step back to look at her. She was alive.
She had all her arms and legs. She had endured whatever
horrors she had found in Baghdad. There were traces of
something new in her face: a depth of sadness in her eyes;
a hardness in the set of her cheekbones. And there was
something else. "Your hair," he said, registering the
new color.

"How do you like it?"

"It suits you."

Lina smiled. "No, it doesn't. Arab women look silly with blond hair." She ran her hand through the stiff blond fur and gave Hoffman a wink. "I need your room key, by the way. The doorman downstairs seemed to think I was a call girl."

Hoffman looked embarrassed. He handed her the key and then sat down on the couch. Lina joined him, and they sat in silence gazing out the window for a few moments, not sure what to say to each other. The sitting room of Hoffman's suite had a panoramic view of Lake Geneva; in the dark, the neon signs atop the buildings on the southern shore were drawing watery advertisements for Middle Eastern airlines and Japanese electronics companies. Lina moved toward him on the couch, but only a few inches. He seemed wary of getting too close, as if he was afraid that after her ordeal, she might break.

"Were you followed here, do you think?" she asked.

"Nope. I left that guy in the tweed coat somewhere out near Vaud, on the way to Zurich. He thinks I'm staying in a bed-and-breakfast there."

"But you're not," she said. "You're staying here, with me."

Hoffman looked at her curiously, unsure whether she was urging him on or subtly pushing him back. Lina wasn't sure herself. He took her hand. There were tears in his eyes.

"I'm just so happy you're alive," he said. "I thought you were dead."

She squeezed his hand. It was Hoffman who needed comforting. "I'm alive," she said.

"Did they hurt you?"

"No. They tried to. But they made me stronger."

Hoffman waited for her to say more, but she had no words yet to describe what she had lived through. He looked at her mutely. There was such a vast gulf now between her experience and his; it was hard to bridge it. That was the time for small talk—when big talk was too hard.

"How was your flight from Baghdad?" he asked.

"Heavenly," she said. "Like an escape from hell. Were you the one who arranged my rescue? I've been wondering. I hoped it was you, but there were all these horrible Saudis at the airport, so I didn't know."

"Yes," said Hoffman. "It was me."

"Did it cost you a lot?"

"Yes. It cost me a great deal."

"How did you do it?"

"I have a Saudi friend who has connections in Baghdad. He is not an attractive man. But to get someone out of hell, you have to bargain with the Devil."

"How did you know I was in Baghdad?"

"Someone told me. It doesn't matter who. I'll explain it some other time." He stopped there, and his words hung in the air. There were things he couldn't express, either. He reached out his other hand to her. They were like two children groping in the dark toward each other.

"What was it like when they came to rescue you?"

She closed her eyes. She wanted to say that it was joyous, that she had clapped her hands and sung a song. But she needed to tell him the truth. "I didn't feel anything at first. I had given up hope. I think that's what saved me. I had stopped being frightened. I knew I was going to die, and I was ready for it. And then it was over."

"What was it like, before, in the prison?" He needed to ask, even if she couldn't answer. "Were there other people there?"

"Yes," she said. And then she had to pause. For her eyes, which had been so dry ever since she had returned to the land of the living, were suddenly full of tears. Sam reached out to her, across the gulf of pain that she had experienced and he had not, and held her in his arms.

"Oh, Sam," she said. "It was so horrible. I can't tell you how horrible it was. I feel so ashamed to be here, alive. I can't bear it." She began to cry, hard, and she didn't stop crying for a long time.

Hoffman ordered dinner. They were both exhausted after so much crying, and slightly giddy, in the way that people sometimes are after a funeral. They needed to laugh, to eat, to rediscover their senses. The waiter arrived with a massive trolley. A bottle of white Burgundy was chilling in a bucket on top, and two orders of Dover sole were warming in an oven underneath.

Hoffman didn't offer a toast. He just raised his glass. Lina gave him a kiss. Her image of Hoffman had always been of a man with bright, hard edges. It was nice to find something softer, and sadder.

While they ate, Lina began to describe the events of the past week. She narrated the flight to Helen's house in Blackheath; the sudden departure for Geneva; the drunken evening with Fred Behr and the mischievous phone conversation with poor Monsieur Marchand of the Organisation de Banques Suisses; the electronic raid the next day on the OBS files, and the astonishing realization that the Ruler's money had vanished; and then the visit with the private banker Maurice Mercier. Hoffman listened to her tale with admiration, shaking his head with surprise as she described each additional layer of deception she had used to penetrate the web of the Ruler's finances.

"I'm going back to see Mercier again," said Lina. "Tomorrow morning at nine. I called him today and made an appointment."

"Why?" asked Sam. "What's the point?"

"He said he has talked to the trustee who managed the account for the Ruler. They want to see me."

Hoffman stared at her and then shook his head in wonderment. "You're not giving up. You're still going after Hammoud."

"Yes. I made a promise to myself. In Baghdad. I want you to come with me, Sam. They may be waiting for me again. I need you."

Sam nodded his head, not because he understood, but

because he knew he had no choice. "Sure," he said. "I'll be your *moukhabarat* man."

"No," she said quickly. "Not that." the word triggered memories of the interrogators of the Qasr al-Nihayya. "You'll be my lawyer."

"I'm sorry," said Hoffman. He realized he had to be careful. The layer of soil over the graves was still thin. He cleared the dinner plates from the table and poured himself another glass of wine.

"I'm going to take a bath," said Lina. "I'll see you in a little while."

Hoffman put his feet up on the coffee table and stared out at the twinkling lights of Geneva. He went through half a pack of cigarettes, smoking each one a few puffs and then stubbing it out, only to relight another a few minutes later. He was going to finish the bottle of wine, but when he heard Lina rustling about in the bedroom after her bath, he thought better of it. He wasn't sure yet what she wanted from him, or what he wanted from her, but he needed to find out. She was singing softly to herself, an Iraqi children's song she had learned as a child.

He knocked on the bedroom door. "Can I come in?" he asked.

"Yes," she said. "I have a surprise for you."

Hoffman opened the door. She was sitting on the bed, wearing an oversize terry-cloth bathrobe supplied by the hotel. She had a white towel wrapped around her head like a turban. As Hoffman sat down beside her, she unwrapped the towel with a flourish. Her hair was back to its natural, jet-black color. With the short hair slicked back against her head, she looked like one of the ancient busts of Nefertiti: lips, nose, eyes—every feature of her face bold and regal.

"So beautiful," said Hoffman. "So beautiful." He put his arm around her. She didn't back away, but she didn't embrace him, either.

"Just hold me," she said.

Hoffman began to stroke her back gently. She moved toward him, and the terry-cloth robe slipped down off her shoulders a few inches, so that Hoffman's hand was touching the skin of her back and not the fabric. He continued to massage her, moving his hand down, and then stopped suddenly.

"My God, what's this?" He felt the raw, red welt along her back, where she had been struck with the electrical cable.

"It's Baghdad."

She lay still in his arms for a long time, her head against his shoulder, and then looked up at him. "Does it feel disgusting?"

"No. It just needs love."

"Could you make love to me, after what they did to me?"

"Yes," he said. "Could you, with me?"

"I don't know. I think so."

He leaned toward the bedside table and turned off the light so that the room was dark. He removed his clothes and then turned back to her. She had slipped the bathrobe off her body and was under the covers. "Come to bed," she said.

He put his arms around her, trying at first not to touch the welts on her back, thinking it would make her self-conscious. But he couldn't help it. They stretched all the way across. As he held her tighter, he could feel the raw wounds on her breasts against his chest, and the welts on the backs of her thighs. She was raw and red everywhere he touched. He had to hold her so gently, his fingers like silk, his kisses like a soothing balm. For a long time, he didn't touch between her legs, for fear of what they had done to her there. She finally took his hand and carried it down the slope of her belly. It was as if the whole of her body had melted into that one place. "I want you," she said.

———

Hoffman was awakened two hours later by a hand that was softly stroking him. With the fascination that new lovers have for each other's bodies, Lina was watching him come to life. "Mmmmmm," he said, half-awake. "Who's that?"

"Moo ani, al-wawi," she said with a girlish giggle, discovered in the act.

"Say what?"

"I said, 'It wasn't me. The *wawi* did it.' It's something little children say in Iraq, when they get caught."

"What's a *wawi*?" he asked sleepily.

"It's an imaginary animal, like a fox. It lives out in the desert. They do naughty things."

"Good night," murmured Hoffman.

Thirty seconds later, she was kissing Hoffman on the lips. "I can't sleep," she said, moving her body over his until she was astride him. He was aroused once more, instantly.

"I want you again," she said. "Is that okay?"

37

The banking district of Geneva was clogged with shiny German automobiles when Lina and Sam reached the Rue des Banques the next morning. With the street so crowded, it was impossible to tell whether they were being followed. Everyone was watching, and no one. Lina led him quickly up the street from the Place Bel-Air and pounded the brass knocker at number eleven. The same bland Swiss woman opened the door. "Good morning, Miss Bazzaz," she said.

When she saw Hoffman coming in behind Lina, she moved to slam the door shut. Lina raised her hand. "This is my attorney," she said. The young woman retreated to the reception desk, picked up a telephone and whispered a few sentences. The lens of a closed-circuit camera zoomed in for a closer look at Hoffman. Sam thought he heard the sound of someone laughing on the other end of the phone. The young woman returned. "It is permitted to bring your attorney," she said.

The receptionist walked her two visitors through the maze, past the cream-colored walls and locked doors. She continued on past the last door and turned right again, into a corridor that had just one portal. This was the managing director's conference room. She knocked once and pushed open the door, allowing Lina to enter. The face of the Swiss banker Mercier came into view. Sitting next to him was a short, squat man in a three-piece suit.

"Hey, hey, hey!" said the fat man jauntily. He was squeezed into his suit like a tube of toothpaste that had been rolled too tight.

"Oh, Jesus!" said Sam Hoffman.

"Hi, honey," said the fat man, tipping an imaginary hat in Lina's direction. He was all charm—courtly, boozy, manipulative. He seemed almost to fill the room, leaving little space for anyone else.

"Who is that?" asked Lina. She turned to Mercier, who stared at her impassively, and then to Sam.

Sam Hoffman's mouth had suddenly gone dry. He had known in some unconscious part of his mind, in the way a dreamer knows the end of his dream when it starts, that he would eventually find himself in this room, with this person. But now that the moment had arrived, he was shaken. He cleared his throat.

"That, I regret to say, is my father. Frank Hoffman."

For bankers, nothing is funny, but there was just a trace of a smile on Mercier's lips. He turned to Lina. "This same gentleman also happens to be the American intermediary I described to you during our earlier meeting. He is the man who has acted as signatory for this account, on behalf of the Ruler of Iraq."

Sam closed his eyes. "Oh, shit," he said.

Hoffman senior ignored him. "Aren't you going to introduce me to your friend, son?" he said, thrusting a meaty hand toward the young woman.

Lina looked at Sam for guidance and, receiving none, turned to his father. "I am Salwa Bazzaz," she said.

Frank snorted. "Oh, yeah? Nice try! I'm Donald Duck."

Her face reddened. She looked to Sam again. "Tell him the truth," he said. "He already knows." Sam turned his face away and stared out the window to the walled-in garden. He couldn't bear to look at his father.

"My name is Lina Alwan," she said.

"Pleased to meet you, sweetie," said Frank. "You're much prettier than they said. How'd ya like Baghdad?"

Lina's eyes blazed. Her cheeks were red, as if she had

been slapped. She was trying to add up the sums in her mind. What did it mean? What was this fat old man's connection to the world that she had just left, the world of the Qasr al-Nihayya? Sam was still staring out the window. He looked angrier than Lina had ever seen him. The Swiss banker, who had been watching the encounter with bemused detachment, spoke up.

"So, now we are all acquainted." He nodded toward Lina, his azure-blue eyes twinkling. "I am so glad that today we will be traveling with our real names. That will make things easier."

Mercier folded his hands together, making a little steeple with his fingers. "I am in a quandary," he said. "When I first met Miss Alwan, she was claiming to represent the family of a wealthy client of this bank, now deceased. But after discussing the matter with Mr. Hoffman senior, I realize that Miss Alwan was deceiving me. This is a serious matter, this use of confidential account numbers to impersonate the relative of a client. The question is whether to call the police. Does anyone wish to make any comment?"

No one spoke. Sam's voice eventually broke the silence. He had turned back from the window and was staring at his father. "Calling the police would be unwise," he said.

"Why? Your father tells me that Interpol has already circulated a request for Miss Alwan's extradition to Britain. In handing her over to the Swiss police, I would simply be doing my duty."

"Fuckin' A right," said Frank.

Sam glowered at his father. The two men measured each other across the conference table, separated by a few feet of space and forty years of time.

"It would be unwise," said Sam slowly, "because we have two very powerful allies. If you aren't careful, Monsieur Mercier, you and your bank could get hurt."

Mercier bristled. "Are you threatening me?"

"Not at all. I'm just informing you, so you'll know."

"Wait a minute, tough guy!" broke in Frank. "What's this bullshit about two allies? I know about your buddy

Prince What's-his-face. I heard all about that, and you know what? He won't do squat for you now. So who's the other?''

"The Israeli intelligence service. They helped me get Lina out of Baghdad. If we're arrested by the police, they will take appropriate action.''

"What?'' broke in Lina. "You never told me that.'' But her voice was overwhelmed by the role of thunder from Frank Hoffman.

"Are you out of your fucking mind, son? I told you to stay away from those shitheads.''

"Excuse me?'' said Mercier. He cleared his throat. He was not accustomed to people using words like *shitheads* in his private conference room.

"Can't you hear, goddammit?'' Frank Hoffman looked at the banker and slammed his fist down on the antique table. "I asked my son if he was out of his fucking mind when he said he was working with the Israelis. Jesus! I can't believe you would pull a stunt like this. This is trouble. People are going to go nuts.'' Frank Hoffman was shaking his head. He looked genuinely distressed.

"Can I be of some help?'' asked Mercier.

"Yeah, you can, actually. By leaving us alone for a few minutes. I need to talk to my boy, and Miss Goombah here. Whatever her name is. Would you mind?''

"No. Not at all. I quite understand.'' Mercier rose and walked to the door. "Ring for me when you are done. It's the red button on the phone.''

Frank waited until Mercier had left before turning to Lina and Sam. Any remaining charm had vanished. He wagged a short, fat finger at them.

"This shit has got to stop! You kids are fucking up a lot of hard work! You know that?''

"Spare us the lecture. You're playing a weak hand.''

"No. I mean it, son. You are fucking up, big time. This Israeli thing is the icing on the cake.''

"We're not buying, Pop. Not when it turns out you have been working for the number-one thug on the planet. So drop it.''

Frank was shaking his head. "You don't have a clue, do you? I mean, you don't have a fucking clue."

"Piss off, Pop," said Sam, a lifetime of unresolved anger compressed into those three words.

"Grow up, Junior. Open your eyes. Here's your father, running the most delicate operation in the Arab world in the last twenty years, and you decide to play footsie with the Mossad. You really don't get it, do you?"

Sam started to protest again, but Lina cut him off. She had been watching the two of them silently as she struggled to contain her own rage.

"Get what, Mr. Hoffman?" she interjected.

"Get the point! What do you think this whole shell game has been about all these years, sweetie pie? Who do you think we've been diddling?"

"What shell game?"

"Don't give me that innocent bullshit, sister. The Game! The Show! I know you've already looked at all of Hammoud's files—Christ only knows how you got them—so you know damn well what I'm talking about. I'm talking about Lincoln Trading, Garfield Investment, Wilson Transport, Adams Investment, Buchanan Trading. The network of companies it took me the better part of a decade to set up. Remember them?"

"Yes, I remember."

"Damn right."

Sam cut in. There was a bitter edge to his voice. "You left one out, Pop. Oscar Trading. The one whose phone rings at the U.S. embassy in Tunis."

Frank squinted at him for a moment and then continued as if he hadn't heard it. "Well, now, since you're both such geniuses, maybe you can explain why we went to all the trouble to create this little do-si-do. Any idea, boys and girls?"

"I haven't a clue," said Sam.

"Of course you don't, so I'll tell you. We did it to keep a string on the dickhead who was running Iraq, that's why!"

"He's dead now," said Lina. "So you can stop."

"Damn right, he's dead. And why is that? It's because we pulled the plug, for crying out loud! That's why he's dead. Your faggot friends in London didn't get rid of him. We did."

"Hold on," said Sam. "What do you mean 'we'?"

"I mean *we*, dipshit. I mean the Central Fucking Intelligence Agency. What do you think I mean? You think this is all just me? Fat old Frank Hoffman playing games and getting rich? Give me a break."

"And Nasir Hammoud is your man?" asked Sam.

"Of course he's our man. Whose man did you think he was? Boutros Boutros-Ghali's, for chrissake? Of course he's our man, and he's done a hell of a good job. Who do you think knocked off the ruler of Iraq? Hammoud, that's who. He's a goddamn hero!"

"I thought Osman shot the Ruler. Was he working for the CIA, too?"

"What are you, a congressman? Not in so many words. But yeah, absolutely. Hammoud arranged it. Why do you think the Brits put out the red carpet for this guy? Let him walk all over everybody in London? Let him import guns and pussy by the boatload? You think it's because they're scared of him? No way. This guy is the most valuable intelligence agent of the twentieth century. And I recruited him. Me! Your dad."

Lina was glowering at him. The fire inside her was burning hot. She opened her mouth and the words came out like a dart of fire.

"Hammoud is a pig."

"Excuse me, honey. I didn't catch that."

"I said that Nasir Hammoud is a pig."

"Well, now, that's not very nice, when I just finished saying he's a hell of a guy, for you to turn around and say he's a pig. Jeez! What's the matter with you?"

"Nothing is the matter with me," said Lina. Her voice was strong, and her eyes were bright with anger that was rising from every part of her. "I am an Iraqi, and I say that Nasir Hammoud is a liar and a thief who has stolen money from my country, and that he should pay it back."

"Come on, now. Hammoud helped liberate your goddamn country from a tyrant! What do you want?"

"He didn't liberate anything. The same people are running things in Baghdad as before. I was tortured and nearly killed because of your friend Nasir Hammoud. So if you like him, Mr. Hoffman, I think you must be a pig, too."

Frank Hoffman turned to his son, shaking his head. "Your girlfriend is weird, Sammy. You know that?"

"Shut up, Pop."

"No. I mean it. She makes me nervous."

"Shut up." The tension was rising in the room like steam in a kettle. But none of them could stop.

Hoffman wagged his finger at Lina again. "You know, sweetheart, I'm beginning to get the feeling you don't like me. Am I right?"

"I loathe you," she said quietly.

"What did she say, Sammy? I must not have heard her. Did she say she didn't like me?"

Lina spoke louder. "I said that my country is being raped, and you are managing the bank account of the rapists. What does that make you? In Arabic we would call you a *gawwad*. A pimp."

"Hey! Fuck you," snarled Frank Hoffman. It was all he could manage.

"How much money did you make on the side, *gawwad*? How many millions did you take out of Oscar Trading? I know it was a lot. I've seen the payments."

Frank Hoffman spat on the floor, just in front of where Lina was standing. "You know, honey, Hammoud was right about you. You are a cunt."

As the last word formed on his father's lips, Sam Hoffman lurched forward and swung wildly at the old man. But Frank, moving with a fat man's delicate balance, danced away from the table. He pulled a pistol, short and stubby, from a shoulder holster and began waving it at them.

"I would love to use this, Sammy. Especially on your pain-in-the-ass girlfriend. But I am a reasonable man and a former civil servant. So sit down, both of you."

They remained standing, still smoking with anger, not moving.

"I said, sit the fuck down!" He cocked his pistol and pointed it at his son's head. They both retreated back into their chairs.

"Thank you, boys and girls. Now, let's all calm down and stop calling each other names, please. Because this is getting out of control. I'm sorry, sweetie. About calling you a cunt, I mean. But you're out of your league here. Really. So don't fuck with Uncle Frank anymore. Got it?"

Lina stared at him silently, not responding to his apology, not so much as blinking her eyes. Frank shrugged his shoulders and turned to his son.

"Sammy boy, I need to talk to you."

"So talk."

"Privately. Otherwise, I promise you, this is going to come to an unhappy end. Especially for Miss Goombah here. I'm the least of her problems. This girl has made enemies she doesn't even know about. So let's talk—you and me—and see what we can work out. Is that reasonable?"

Sam leaned toward Lina and cupped his hands around her ear. "What do you want? Should I talk to him?"

"No deals," she whispered back. "Talk, if you want. But I'm not making deals with anyone. I can't do it. I made a promise."

Sam turned back to his father. "Okay, Pop," he said. "Let's talk."

"Good boy. There's hope." Frank Hoffman picked up the phone and pressed the red button for Mercier.

"Hiya, pal. This is Frank. My son and I need to take a walk, clear our heads. We're going to leave the girl here for a few hours. Is that all right? Let her read some magazines. Do her nails. We'll come back and pick her up. Can do? Good. Thanks."

"Sit tight, Betty Boop," he said to Lina. "Don't do anything stupid. Sammy, you come with me." He grabbed his son by the elbow, the way he used to do when Sam was a boy crossing the street, and led him out of the conference room.

"Ya ghareeb koon adeeb!" she said quietly as the door closed. *Hey, foreigner, be polite.*

38

Frank Hoffman barged into the street from Crédit Mercier and shouted for a taxi. The morning sun was hot. The aging ex-spy unbuttoned his vest, letting his stomach break free from the constricting buttons, and wiped his brow with his tie. It was easy to forget, in the torrent of Frank Hoffman's crude energy, that he was an old man. "Let's go to my hotel and have a drink, son," he said. "Your girlfriend tired me out."

"I don't want a drink, Pop."

"Well, I do, so tough shit."

A cab pulled up in front of them. "Take us to the Noga Hilton, pal," said Frank. "And step on it." He spoke to everyone in the same rough, colloquial English that, somehow, was always understood.

The taxi deposited them at the hotel, gleaming like an ice cube along the northern shore of the lake. Frank headed for the bar near the casino. It was dark and deserted at that hour. "Gimme a bottle of scotch, Antoine," he told the bartender. "Put it on my bill." The bartender hefted a bottle of Chivas Regal from beneath the counter and put it in a brown paper bag. Hoffman pulled a fifty-dollar bill from his pocket and crumpled it into the bartender's hand. "Buy something for the missus," he said.

Frank took Sam by the elbow again and steered him toward the elevators. They made an unlikely pair: the older one built like a fireplug, huffing across the lobby with his vest unbuttoned and a brown bag in his hand; the younger one tall and thin, resisting his father's grip even as he was pushed along. Frank let go of Sam's elbow only when they reached his suite.

Frank opened the door. As he did so, a woman's voice called out from the bedroom. "Oh, shit," he said. "I forgot about her."

"Take a hike, Fifi," he shouted. "I need to do some business."

The woman walked into the sitting room; she was naked, except for her panties. She had large breasts that seemed to hang halfway to her navel and a pleasantly vacant look on her face. Frank pulled five crisp hundred-dollar bills from his wallet and handed them to her.

"Beat it," he said. She scampered back into the bedroom to put on her clothes and left by the other door. The heavy smell of her perfume lingered in the air.

"Who was that?" asked Sam.

"Eleanor Roosevelt. Give me a break, son. She's a hooker. What do you care who she is?"

"You're right. I don't care." For as long as he could remember, Sam Hoffman had been watching his father pursue young women. The more tawdry and ostentatious their looks, the better he seemed to like them. It was almost heroic, this tireless pursuit of cheap, commercial sex. When Sam was a boy, his father had dragged him to a strip club in Beirut called The Black Cat and made him watch an appalling floor show that featured a snake and a German shepherd. It had taken Sam the better part of his adolescence to get those images out of his head. But his father was still right there, sitting in the front row, shouting "woof, woof!"

Frank poured the whiskey into two tall glasses. "Soda or water?" he asked.

"Just ice."

"Whoa! Very grown-up. Sure you can handle it?"

"Lay off, Pop. I thought you wanted to talk. Otherwise, let's forget it."

"I *do* want to talk. It's just hard for me to relax until

I've said something obnoxious. But I'm fine now. How's Mom?''

"She's okay, but we didn't come here to talk about her."

"Okay, the hell with Mom." Frank kicked off his shoes and put his feet on the coffee table. "Let's talk about Iraq. We got a serious problem, you and me. Hammoud's boys are batshit about your girlfriend slipping out of Baghdad, and they are majorly pissed at you and your jerkoff Saudi friend for arranging it, and minorly pissed at yours truly for letting it happen. So we gotta get our act together, fast."

Sam looked away. He was still shaken by the day's events. "How could you do it, Pop?"

"Do what?"

"Work with those assholes. I thought even you would draw the line at them."

"This is a dirty business, son. You do what you gotta do. Who did you think I was working with all those years? Aunt Mildred?"

"Don't give me that, Pop. You always say that, as if it's an excuse for everything. But it's not. Any business is only as dirty as you make it."

"That sounds nice, son, but the problem is, you don't know what you're talking about. The reasons I got involved in the Iraq account make perfect sense, if you know the history. Which you don't."

"So tell me."

"Would that make you feel better, if Daddy told the truth and gave you a good-night kiss?"

"Come on, Pop! Stop playing a role, for once. Just talk to me!"

Frank cocked his head. "Seriously?"

Sam nodded. "Why don't you give it a try? The truth would be interesting, for a change."

"All right," said Frank Hoffman. He looked fondly at his glass and took a long drink, draining half of it. "But brace yourself, because this is going to take a while. The

Iraq part is just the last chapter. The frosting on the baklava, so to speak.''

"I don't mind, Pop. I've been waiting to hear this story for most of my life.''

"Okay. Then I'm going to tell you the biggest secret I know. The biggest secret there is. You listening?''

"I'm listening.''

"Here it is: The Arab world in the second half of the twentieth century is mostly a creation of the Central Intelligence Agency. My friends and I have spent the past forty years bribing or diddling every king, president and emir in the Middle East. And you know what? The thing I would never admit to anyone, except my own son? We did a good job. And I'm fucking proud of it. So don't screw it up. You understand what I'm saying?''

"No, I don't, to be honest.''

"Of course you don't. Too big a concept for a little mind to grasp. So I'll take it slowly, from the top. The nineteen-fifties. We put the Shah in power in Iran. We put King Hussein in power in Jordan. We put the sons of King Abdülaziz into power in Saudi Arabia. We bought the president of Lebanon and half the parliament. We even put Nasser on the payroll in Egypt. We were wired, you understand me? Wired. Your old man spent his days carrying money in briefcases to palaces in Amman and Beirut and Tehran. And they all took it. Every one of them.''

"That's interesting, Pop, but it's ancient history. Everybody knows about the Shah and King Hussein.''

"Maybe so, but the point is, it didn't stop there. Cut to the nineteen-seventies, when things are getting a little ragged. The old farts are losing it, and the youngsters all want to be Arab radicals and fuck Swedish girls. So we changed the playbook a little. We helped put Sadat in the saddle in Egypt. We helped keep Hafez al-Assad in power in Syria. We even gave a little help to that cross-dressing wacko, Colonel Qadaffi, when he took over in Libya.''

"No.'' Sam shook his head.

"You heard me right. The mad Muammar. But our best trick of all was with the baddest kids on the block, the

Palestinians. We *owned* the PLO. We recruited Arafat's chief of intelligence to spy for us. One of my guys did it, back in Beirut, using an access agent recruited by me. And *shazzam*! No more problems, at least not for us. The Israelis and Palestinians kept on shooting each other until recently, but fuck 'em. That's their problem.''

Frank drained his glass and summoned forth a long, rolling belch. Leaning back in his chair with the empty glass balanced on the round globe of his stomach—smiling with pure pleasure at the thought of how he and his colleagues had manipulated a region of the planet for several decades—Frank Hoffman had the wicked, contented smile of an anti-Buddha.

''More whiskey, Pop?''

''Yowsuh!'' Frank handed the glass to his son, who refilled it, then poured another for himself.

''Go on,'' said Sam. ''I'm not sure I believe what you're saying, but it's a good yarn.''

''We're just getting started, my boy. Ask me about OPEC. Surely the Culinary Institute of America didn't have anything to do with the establishment of the oil cartel. Impossible, you say. But you're wrong, Sammy boy. We knew they were going to nationalize oil, so we made sure it went into the right hands, meaning those of the worthy Oriental gentlemen we had put in power. We sent out an army of lawyers and bankers and accountants who told them how to do it and where to put their money. And when OPEC jacked up prices, guess who was leading the charge? Our very own Shah of Iran, joined by our very own King Faisal. They got rich, and we got rich. I moved to Dhahran about then to start my security company: A-A-Arab American Security Consultants. First in the phone book, if they'd had a phone book. You following all this, Sammy?''

''Yes, I'm following it, but I'm still not sure I believe it.''

''Believe it, because it's true. OPEC was like a big dam that trapped the world's money in one big reservoir. I kept trying to tell you, but you wouldn't listen. It was a sea of money, controlled by our friends, and we made sure all the right guys had straws.

"The Arabs bought weapons from us. They bought hotels from us. They bought make-believe factories and refineries from us, to pretend they had real economies. The whole thing was a game! Every pimp and fixer from Rabat to Aden wanted to play, and they were all basically on our team. It was the Free World All-Stars, and your old man was the pitching coach. The CIA didn't have to pay its agents anymore. We just helped them become arms dealers, or bankers, or ministers, and made sure they got the fat contracts. You ever hear of the Friends of Araby?"

"No."

"Of course not. Because it doesn't exist. But let's just say that the system I have described to you is not the product of mere chance. Got it? Allah had very little to do with this particular chain of events, if you follow me."

"What about Iran in 1979? You didn't have Khomeini on the team."

"True, but not because we didn't try. The fact is, we go back a long way with the mullahs in Iran. We put a lot of them on the payroll back in 1953, and most of them kept drawing their checks. Maybe not Khomeini himself, but by the time he was in exile in France, half of his people were working with us. His right-hand man, Sadeq Ghotbzadeh, had a 201 file seven volumes thick, for chrissakes. I kid you not, seven volumes. We even tried to recruit Khomeini's own president, Bani-Sadr. Unfortunately, we fucked that one up. But we had a lot of friends in Iran, believe me, and we still do. No, Sammy. The truth is, in the whole Middle East, we had just one nut we couldn't crack. And what do you suppose that was?"

"Iraq," said Sam. He had dropped his wary manner and was now leaning toward his father, glass in hand, listening to every word. This was, as he had said, the story he had waited a lifetime to hear.

"You got it, sonny boy. The odd man out was Iraq. We had everyone else by the short hairs, except for the ruler in Baghdad. He was such a thug—such a complete,

sadistic lunatic—that he didn't want to play ball. But eventually, we found a way. Oh, yes! It took time, but we
found a way."

"Money."

"Yup! The Ruler was a greedy bastard, but it wasn't
him so much as his brothers and cousins. They began to
think Iraq was a family business, and they all wanted
to make sure their shares were in dollars, not dinars. So
to shut everyone up, the Ruler had to create a financial
network in the West, where he could stash his money.
And that gave us the opening."

"How did you do it? Did you go to him directly?"

"Impossible. You gotta remember, this guy was an A-
number-one prick. He had spent most of his life hating
America. No, the first place we went for advice was to
people he knew. There were some operators in Baghdad
who had done a lot of slippery deals for the defense minister, and some Lebanese creeps who had sold him arms.
We got those guys wired, through Beirut. But they
couldn't give us the access we needed."

"Who could?"

"The Palestinians. They were the ones the Ruler trusted
most, because they were the meanest SOBs around in
those days. But what he didn't know was that we *owned*
the Palestinians. And your old man had helped recruit most
of them. So when a certain Palestinian banker headed to
Baghdad for consultations with his nibs, guess who
tagged along?"

"Frank Hoffman?"

"You got it. And whaddya know, the Ruler and I hit
it off. Turned out we shared an interest in some of the
more unusual forms of erotica. Next time I visited, I
brought a couple of girls I thought he would like. And the
next time, a couple more. And pretty soon, we're friends.
He's giving me contracts to lift Iraqi oil and import German beer, and I'm putting aside a little for him and his
family, and a little more. And we're having a jolly time.
And finally he introduces me to his slimeball friend Nasir
Hammoud, and says he would like the two of us to do
business together. And, bingo! It's off to the races."

"Did he know you had worked for the agency?"

"Of course he did. That was part of the attraction. Like all the Arabs, he figured that the Jews really ran the world, and the only way to protect himself was by getting in bed with the CIA. They're CIA-crazy, the Arabs, in addition to being Jew-crazy. Secretly, they all want to sleep with us because they think we've got the biggest dick in town. The Ruler wasn't any different. We gave him a kiss, tucked him in, and he loved it. He had the CIA as his banker, and he loved it!"

Frank sat back in his chair when he had finished narrating this last triumph and looked expectantly toward his son, waiting for validation. But it didn't come. Sam was staring at his father like an owl.

"But what was it for, Pop?"

"What the fuck do you mean, 'what was it for'?" roared Frank. "You wouldn't ask an artist what he painted a painting for. You wouldn't ask a musician what he played a concerto for. They just do it. Same with me. You'll laugh at me for saying this, but this is my art. It's what I did with my life. It's me. And I'm proud of it."

Sam blinked. "I'm not laughing, I promise. But what did we get out of it? The United States, I mean."

"We stopped Iran."

"What do you mean?"

"I mean that Baghdad became the main line of defense for our various dickless friends in the Persian Gulf. The Iraqis were *it*. Without them, Khomeini would have been in Riyadh in twenty-four hours. No shit! In those days, believe me, we couldn't do enough for our Iraqi brothers. We let them buy weapons, with fat commissions for Nasir Hammoud, thank you very much. We gave them loans via Italy. We sent our own goddamn navy to attack the Iranians in the Gulf. We even gave them intelligence. We were in love, I'm telling you. In love."

"Right. But what did the Iraqis *do* for us?"

"They killed Iranians, son. That's all we really wanted them to do. Our satellites would see those crazy teenage Revolutionary Guards marching toward the front, and we would push a button and—presto—the intel would be in Baghdad. The Iraqis would get the coordinates, and pow!—they would open up with their heavy artillery. A whole generation of Iranian kids died, just like that. They lost five hundred thousand men and boys, but that's Allah's problem, not mine. Suffice it to say that it was a major win for the Infidel. Or maybe you'd rather have Iran running the world. Huh?''

"I'm just listening," said Sam. But there was a tone of acceptance in his voice. The dry moral tinder that might have sparked a reaction was now soggy with booze, and information.

"And then it got messy. The Ruler went batshit. He invaded Kuwait, threatened Saudi Arabia. Total asshole. I think maybe it went to his head, all the bullshit we had been telling him about how he had saved the West from the rampaging ragheads. So we had to kick his butt. Called him Hitler, fought that weird little war in Kuwait. After it was over, we let him go. It wasn't worth the trouble to get rid of him. But he was such an arrogant prick, you know what I mean? He couldn't stop pulling our chain, and he still had all that money buried in Switzerland. And we finally figured—fuck it! Eventually we found a member of his family who was such a greedy motherfucker that he was willing to shoot the old boy, just to get more dough. And presto! No more Ruler. End of story. Until you kids come along to screw everything up.''

"That's it?"

"Shit. That's enough, don't you think?''

Sam was struggling to keep his balance emotionally. He had begun the conversation with the conviction that his father was a scoundrel, but now he found himself trying to remember why Lina was so angry at him. He thought back to his first encounter with Nasir Hammoud, when he had gone fishing in the trash and pulled out the blank pieces of stationery.

"What's Oscar Trading?" he said. "What was that all about?''

"Oscar Trading was me. Your girlfriend was right about

that. The name comes from my old cryptonym, Oscar D. Fabiolo. But she had the rest all wrong."

"She seems to think you pocketed a lot of money from Oscar Trading."

Frank looked him straight in the eye. "She is full of shit, son. All the money that was paid out to Oscar Trading went to pay for assassinating the Ruler. We used it to pay bribes to members of his security force. Think about it. We were using the Ruler's own money to knock him off. What the hell is wrong with that?"

"And none of the money stuck to your hands?"

Frank smiled. "Only a little. And who gives a shit, anyway? Nobody but congressmen and your Israeli girlfriend. So let's stop the inquisition."

"She doesn't work for the Israelis, Pop. She didn't even know about them until today."

"That's not what Hammoud thinks."

"Hammoud is wrong."

"Then what was all that crap you were dishing out at Mercier's? About how you had been in contact with the Israelis, and how they would come to rescue your girlfriend if anything happened?"

"I just said that to scare Mercier. I have been in contact with them. Or should I say, they've been in contact with me. That guy Hilton who came to see me was the one who told me Lina was in Baghdad. They want to keep her alive so she can make trouble for Hammoud. But they're just using her. The last time I saw Hilton, I told him to go fuck himself."

Frank sat back in his chair. "Good boy. You had me worried there for a while. But I should have known you wouldn't really go to work for the Southern Company. You're an American, goddammit! I'm thirsty. Where's the booze?"

"Right here, where it was. Are you sure you want another drink?"

"Pour it, son! I've got to take a whiz."

Sam watched his father walk to the bathroom. For all his bombast, Frank Hoffman looked tired. His legs moved stiffly, like two big stumps, and his body was pitched forward slightly. He was so big, and so fragile. Sam heard the sound of the toilet flushing and then watched as the old man rumbled back from the bathroom. He had doused his face and half dried it, so that drops of water were still rolling down his cheeks, which were themselves florid from the whiskey. Pink-faced and dripping wet, he looked like he had just emerged from a steambath.

As the old man neared him, Sam stood up suddenly and took a step toward him. It was involuntary. He didn't know what he was doing. He just reached out his arms to his father and pulled him toward him, hugging the fat body, smelling the whiskey on his breath, feeling the scratchy beard against his own face. It was his father. He held him tight, until Frank stepped away in embarrassment.

"Jesus Christ!" grumbled the old man. "What did you do that for?"

"Because I love you, Pop."

"Jesus Christ!" Frank said again. "Get a grip on yourself, boy! Pour me that drink."

Sam lifted the bottle and tilted it toward the glass. As he did so, he caught a glimpse of his father dabbing his sleeve to his eye when he thought his son wasn't looking.

"Here's to you and me," said Frank, lifting the glass. "And fuck everybody else."

"To you and me," said Sam. He clinked his glass against his father's and drained it. With this last tap of the liquid hammer, he felt his head beginning to spin. He was in the orbit of his father's magnificent, monstrous personality—as surely as the moon is in the orbit of the Earth. Sam laid down his glass and looked at his watch. It had been nearly three hours since they had left Lina alone. He shook his head. "We gotta sober up, Pop. There's one more thing we have to talk about before we both pass out."

"What's that? Remind me."

"Straightening out the mess with Lina. She's still at Mercier's."

"Oh, yeah. Miss Goombah. I don't know. What do you want to do? Give her to Hammoud? That's what he wants. How about that?"

"No. Out of the question. We're not giving her to Hammoud, and we're not giving her to the Swiss police, either. She hasn't done anything wrong."

"The hell she hasn't. She has gotten in the way of the CIA, not to mention MI6, not to mention Frank F. Hoffman. What is her fucking problem?"

"She's an Iraqi. She feels deeply about this stuff. She's been through a nightmare in Baghdad. Cut her some slack."

"She's a pain in the ass."

"So are you. Stop bad-mouthing Lina or I'm leaving." He stood up as if to go, but he was wobbly on his feet.

"Sit down, son, before you fall down. You never did know how to drink."

Sam sat down. He was confused. He had long ago forgotten what Lina had said to him before they left Crédit Mercier. All he knew was that he wanted to help her. "Come on, Pop," he said. "Let's get serious about Lina. What will it take to get Hammoud and everyone else to call off the dogs?"

"Simple. You get your little girlfriend to back off. Stop snooping around. Forget what she knows. Leave these matters in wiser hands. Stop trying to be Joan of Arc, for chrissakes. And everything will be fine."

"Will that solve the problem? Will they leave her alone?"

"Sure. I mean, why not? If she lays off, Hammoud will lay off. He's not stupid. Don't worry about it."

"These are Iraqis, Pop. They have long memories. If they're as angry as you say, they could come after her in six months, to settle scores. Who's going to protect her?"

"I told you, don't worry about it. I'll take care of it. If Uncle Frank tells everybody to lay off her, they'll lay off. I promise."

"What about when she gets back to London? She can't

go back to work for Hammoud. What's she going to do? Who's going to hire her?''

"Why don't you give her a job, loverboy?''

"She wouldn't take it. She would think it was charity. I need to offer her something real.''

"I know a certain banker in London who might give her a job. It just so happens he's here in Geneva, doing a little consulting for Mercier, helping us move a little money around for you-know-who. He might have a job for your girlfriend, if she cleans up her act.''

"What banker? Who are you talking about?'' But Sam had an uneasy feeling he knew the answer.

"A gentleman by the name of Barakat. I believe you two are acquainted.''

"Christ!'' Once again, Sam felt his world bending back against him, like a double helix. "Is there anybody who isn't part of your operation?''

"I hope not. And don't knock Asad. He's the best bet you've got. I'll call him and ask him to come over. He's staying just down the hall. What say?''

Sam was numb as well as drunk. "Why not?''

Frank picked up the phone and asked the hotel operator to connect him to Mr. Barakat's room. When a voice answered, Frank boomed into the receiver, "Hiya, pal. Got a minute? Great. Maybe you could stop by the room for a minute. I've got somebody who wants to talk to you. Guess who? Rightee-o. Thankee.''

Frank hung up the phone and turned to his son. "He'll be right over.'' Sam rubbed his head. As he listened to his father's banter, another piece of the puzzle fell into place. "Barakat is the Palestinian banker you were talking about, isn't he? The one who introduced you to the Ruler?''

"Yup. Smart boy. Why did I ever think you were dumb?''

———

Barakat entered Frank Hoffman's room like a visiting pasha arriving from another *villayet* of the Ottoman Empire rather than a room down the hall. He was dressed in a voluminous double-breasted suit, in a shade that resembled peach. He embraced Frank and kissed him on each cheek. Frank, to his son's astonishment, reciprocated the gesture. The father whispered a few words into the ear of his banker friend and then led him toward his son. Sam, too, kissed Barakat on each cheek, something he had never done before.

Barakat was smiling as if he had won some sort of victory. "What a pleasure it is for me to see father and son reconciled at last. This is the way of the East." He touched his heart when he had finished his flowery greeting.

"Hello, Asad-bey. I'm glad to see you looking well."

"Your father tells me that you have a problem, which it might be my pleasure to solve."

"I have a lot of problems, Asad. But the one that concerns me right now is finding a job for the woman we discussed a while ago in London. Her name is Lina Alwan. You gave me wise advice to be careful. But I ignored it, and so did she, and we both got in a lot of trouble. Now I need to find her another job, and my dad thought you might have some ideas."

"Your friend Miss Alwan is rebellious. And inquisitive. Those can be fatal traits in a bank employee."

"She's not inquisitive anymore," Sam answered. "She's learned her lesson. If you give her a job, she'll be a loyal employee. Nine-to-five, no nonsense. I promise. The only reason she began asking questions about Hammoud was because I pushed her to. But she's ready to back off now and settle down."

"Is she trustworthy? As I advised you back in London, the only thing that matters in banking is trust."

"Yes, sir. Absolutely."

Barakat looked toward Frank for guidance. The old man nodded his head. "If my boy says she's trustworthy, that's good enough for me. We're turning over a new leaf, me and Sam. So if he says so, that's it. And if he's wrong, then we're both in trouble. How's that?"

"That is fine, my friend. I cannot ask for more than a

man's word, backed by that of his father. The Iraqi girl can start work next Monday. I'll begin her at fifty thousand pounds.'' He gestured with his hand magnanimously, as if he were endowing a bequest to a worthy charity.

Frank patted the Palestinian banker on the back. ''That's swell. Now sit down, old buddy, and have a drink.''

''I would love to, my dear Frank. But I am rather involved in our mutual project at the moment. I have spent the morning telephoning some of our banker friends to alert them that we will be moving rather large blocks of funds from Crédit Mercier. The boys in the Caribbean will just be getting to work now. So forgive me, if I say that you must do your drinking without me.'' He gathered the folds of his peach-colored suit around him like a desert robe and departed.

When the Palestinian banker had left, Frank grabbed his son by the elbow once more and proposed that they open another bottle of whiskey, or invite Fifi back, or go to a place he knew across town where the girls did tricks that even Frank thought were appalling. But Sam fended off all his father's suggestions. It was long past time to pick up Lina, and he had the beginning of a hangover.

''Beat it, then,'' said Frank. ''If you're already that pussy-whipped, then go get your girlfriend. I'll call Mercier and tell him to forget all that crap about calling the police. He'll let her go, believe me. Beneath all his slick manners, he's just a greedy bastard like everyone else. And I'm still the trustee of the biggest account he's ever seen.''

Sam looked at the ravaged face of his father, the veins tracing a life that was the sum of days like this one. ''What are you going to do while I'm gone, Pop? Are you sure you'll be okay?''

''Me? I'm going to take a nap.''

39

Lina began to explore her paneled cell at Crédit Mercier soon after the two Hoffmans departed. She had no idea what she would find, but she hadn't lost her Baghdad conviction that she needed to make every minute count for something. She began in the center of the room, with the long, antique table. Nothing there. No drawers, no openings, just the bright sheen of polished wood. To the right was a sitting area, with two wingback chairs and reading lamps; at the other end stood a desk and a telephone. Framing the room were French doors that led to a small garden, which was walled like its neighbors to prevent anyone from seeing inside. The doors were locked. She looked for a closed-circuit television camera somewhere in the room but couldn't find one.

The only form of surveillance she could discover was the young Swiss receptionist, who stuck her head in the door every half hour or so and gave her a condescending look. "They have forgotten about you," she said tartly, as if Lina's wait demonstrated some larger point about the unreliability of humankind. The woman's name was Nicole, Lina discovered, and she came from a village near Zug, but she refused to answer any other questions about her personal life. She seemed to think that Lina's problems would be reduced if she ate something, and as the morning passed she brought coffee, then a snack of croissants and cream cakes, then a lunch of onion soup, lamb chops and apple strudel. Each tray arrived with heavy silver cutlery and stiff linen napkins. Lina sent them all back without eating any of the food. Nicole clucked her lips when she removed the untouched trays. Naughty girl, she seemed to say. No wonder they've forgotten you.

The realization that nobody was watching emboldened Lina to investigate the room more closely. She examined the desktop phone. It had three extensions; she noted the numbers in her datebook. Inside the middle drawer of the desk, she found a copy of the bank's internal phone directory. It was just six pages, listing the various telephone extensions by department, but it was like a wiring diagram of the firm. Crédit Mercier had a commercial department, a trading department and a merchant-banking department—but it had only one employee for each. The firm's resources had been concentrated in the areas that would be useful in hiding money. The trust department had ten employees, the international department had eight and the security department had five. The most useful information appeared on the last page. Three employees worked in the communications and data-processing group. Their extensions were listed, along with the bank's fax and telex numbers. Very Swiss. Neat, helpful, well organized. Lina transcribed the names and numbers in her datebook.

She found one more item of interest in the side drawer of the desk—a copy of the bank's annual report. It was an imposing volume, printed on heavy, coated paper with the letter *M* embossed on the cover. On page three was Mercier's year-end letter to clients, which rambled on about the stability of the Swiss franc and the prospects for economic growth in the major Western economies. Then came a series of charts and financial statements attesting to Crédit Mercier's stability and prudent management, and a letter full of gobbledygook from the accountants. But again, it was the final page that had the goodies. There, Crédit Mercier listed the banks around the world with which it had correspondent relationships. It was a long list, stretching to nearly forty establishments, in places as far flung as Lagos and Kuala Lumpur. Next to each were listed the name of the bank's managing director and the numbers for its telephone, fax and telex.

What Lina noticed, as she scanned the list, was that many of the names were familiar: Banque des Amis in Curaçao, for example, and Banque Metropole in Montreal, and Tariqbank in Bahrain. She remembered that she had seen them before, in one of the documents she had extracted from Nasir Hammoud's computer files. Lina tore the last page from the annual report and put it in her purse.

———

Sam finally returned for Lina at two-thirty. He looked flushed, like a car whose radiator had boiled over. His cheeks were red and his eyes were tired and heavy-lidded. When he pushed past Nicole to give her a wet kiss, Lina realized what was wrong. He was drunk. His breath smelled like a peat bog. "You look awful," she said. "What kept you?"

"Don't worry about me," Sam whispered, leaning on her unsteadily. "My Dad and I worked everything out. He called Mercier. It's all set. You can leave here right now."

Lina turned to Nicole. "Is that right?"

The Swiss woman nodded. She looked disappointed.

"And that's not all," said Sam. "You'll have a new job back in London, and everything."

She eyed him suspiciously. "What job? What are you talking about? I didn't ask for any job."

"Shhh!" he said, putting his finger over his lips. "Later."

Nicole led them back along the narrow corridor toward the front of the building. Rather than stopping at the front door, she continued past it, leading them down a staircase to the basement. Another, narrower set of stairs led them farther underground, to a green door.

"Where are we going, honey?" asked Sam. He was even beginning to talk like his father.

"Monsieur Mercier said it would be better for you to

leave by the private entrance," explained Nicole. "This way, no one will bother you."

"My dad took care of everything," mumbled Sam.

"Where does the tunnel go?" Lina asked. She had become wary of dark corridors.

"Rue de la Tertasse, one hundred meters from here. You will climb some stairs, open a door and you will be in a courtyard off the street. Please make sure the door is closed behind you." The Swiss woman unlocked the door and flipped on a light switch just inside. It illuminated a long, dank corridor just wide enough for one person.

"Thank you," she said, shaking their hands. "Come again." It was a last, absurd gesture of Swiss politesse. Lina wondered how many clients had preceded them along this route, skulking away from the esteemed Crédit Mercier like common thieves.

As Sam and Lina began moving down the underground passageway, they heard the door close behind them and the sound of the lock turning. Up ahead, there was a furious scurrying of clawed feet as a rat scrambled away. Lina had been the first through the door, and she led the way down the dim passage. The long corridor smelled of something old and decaying, like dead people's money. They surfaced just where the Swiss woman had said, in a small courtyard that opened onto a narrow street in the center of the old business district. Lina closed the door behind them. Sam started toward the street, but Lina pulled him back into the shadows of the courtyard.

"Hold on, Sam," she said in the firm tone of a schoolteacher. "We're not going anywhere until you tell me what's going on."

"I told you. It's all set. I talked to my Dad, and he fixed everything." He still looked woozy. Lina wished she could slap him, to wake him up.

"What did you agree to, Sam?"

"Nothing. I just said that you would back off and stop causing trouble. That's all they wanted. So I told them."

"You promised them that?" She looked stricken.

"Sure. It was the only way to keep Mercier from having

you arrested. And after what my Dad said, it seemed like the right thing to do. This whole thing is a lot more complicated than we realized."

Her eyes were flashing. "Sam! What are you talking about?"

"Calm down. Let's go get a cup of coffee. My head hurts."

"No. Let's stay here. It's safer. What did your father say, Sam?"

"He told me the whole story. How he got involved with the Ruler and Hammoud, and how it was all part of a big operation, and why they did it and all that. It made sense, in a weird sort of way."

"What big operation?"

"You know, all that CIA stuff."

"Sam!" She shook him. "Stop it."

"Stop what? I'm just trying to help you. A few minutes ago you were a prisoner in the bank, and now you're free, thanks to my dad. Lighten up, for chrissakes."

"Oh, Sam! Don't talk this way. It's not like you. Now, will you please explain to me what deal you made with your father to get me out of Mercier's?"

"Sure." He kissed her with his sour lips. "The deal is that we stop bugging Hammoud. We let him have his fun and do whatever he wants with the Ruler's money. In return, he'll leave you alone. That's the deal. Okay?"

"But it's not Hammoud's money, and it wasn't the Ruler's, either. It was stolen from the people of Iraq."

"Maybe so. But he's got it now, and we're going to let him have it. And no more bullshit. Right?"

"It's not that easy, Sam. How do you know they won't kill me once we're back in London?"

"Because they won't. My dad promised he would talk to them. And he arranged to get you a new job. It's all taken care of."

"Where am I indentured? Or am I allowed to ask?"

"BankArabia. It's owned by a Palestinian named Asad Barakat. He's helping Mercier move the money around.

Apparently they want to send it to other banks, to hide it or something. I don't know. It doesn't matter."

"So he's working for Hammoud, too. My God! Then I refuse. No deal."

"Come on, Lina. Give it a rest. Don't be such a damned zealot."

She looked into his face, which was drunk and unsteady. Slapping him wouldn't work. He was too far gone. Instead, she took his hands in hers. "Look at me," she said. "Have you forgotten who we're dealing with? These are Iraqis."

"I know they're Iraqis, Lina."

"They'll kill me as soon as they have the chance. That's the way they operate."

"No, they won't. Not now. My father has these people on a leash. He's been running Hammoud for nearly ten years."

"They don't give a damn about your father, Sam. When it comes to dealing with another Iraqi, they play by their own rules. Wake up!"

"Hey, sweetie. Let's not argue anymore, okay? It's giving me a headache. Let's go back to the hotel and take a nap. You didn't get much sleep last night, remember?"

He gave her a nudge that was meant to recall their lovemaking, but she remained stone-faced. She looked into his glassy eyes and realized that she was alone. It wasn't Sam's fault. It wasn't really about him. It was about her. As she looked at his handsome, sleepy face, she felt a wave of sadness. She was a woman who had always wanted, her whole life, a happy ending. But this time, there wasn't going to be one.

"I can't do it," she said quietly. "I made a promise."

"Say what?"

"Nothing." She reached up and touched Sam's flushed cheek. He just looked tired now rather than drunk. "You go take a nap, my dear," she said. "You need one. I'll meet you at the hotel later. First I have to pick up my things from the place where I've been staying. Then I'll join you."

"Promise?"

"Of course. Be careful on your way back. Don't let the *selouwa* get you."

"What the hell is a *selouwa*?"

"It lives in the Tigris River and scares children, and it's not as nice as the *wawi*. It gets very angry when people do naughty things, like drink too much."

Sam's embarrassment finally showed in his eyes. "I'm sorry about getting drunk. It sort of goes with the territory when you're talking with my dad."

"Men are pathetic," she said. She pushed him gently out of the courtyard toward the street. He turned left, toward the lake and the hotel on the far bank. When Sam was out of sight, Lina turned right, toward the freight yards, and her small room, and her computer.

40

Geneva was thick with afternoon strollers walking two and three abreast, so that a lone woman could almost disappear in their shadows. Lina made her way across the city at right angles, corner by corner. As she came to each new intersection, she would peer around the stone facade, looking for the Iraqi operatives she knew were still out there searching for her, regardless of what Sam's father had promised. She suspected that they had been waiting outside Crédit Mercier, like before; now they would send their watchers out on the streets. It wasn't Sam's fault, she told herself. Until you had looked this beast in the face, you didn't understand it. You didn't understand anything.

She moved stealthily through the old city, traveling south along the Rue des Granges, away from the lake. She zigged on Rue Henri Fazy and zagged on Rue de l'Hôtel de Ville, looking at each new turn for dark-faced men, men in blue jeans and raincoats and green gabardine suits. Bald-headed men in tweed jackets, and men who were pretending to read newspapers. She had no idea what they would actually look like, this next set of pursuers; they would reveal themselves only in pursuit. She paused when she reached a large shopping street called the Boulevard Helvétique. It was a busy thoroughfare, dotted with buses and taxis, an obvious place to station surveillance. She debated whether to take a taxi and then decided to keep walking. She fell in behind two tall German businessmen who were talking animatedly. Her idea was to continue along the boulevard, across the L'Arve River, to her pension near the freight yards.

As she made her way down the Boulevard Helvétique, something registered in her peripheral vision. It was a sudden movement, like a bird darting from cover. A man had stood up in a café she had just passed and was moving up quickly behind her. She turned to look at him. He was built like a snub-nosed pistol, short and stocky, and dressed in a baggy brown suit. He looked away when she caught his eyes.

She cut quickly down a small street on her right called Rue Senebier. When the little man in the brown suit turned the corner behind her, she broke into a run. She heard his feet, too, pounding the cobblestones behind. At the bottom of the street was a large park surrounding the University of Geneva. A policeman was standing at one corner. Lina thought of calling out to him for help, as she had done before near the lake, but she remembered Mercier's threat to deliver her to the Swiss police.

Shiny BMWs and Mercedes clogged the intersection. Lina darted through the traffic and ran toward the park. Her pursuer followed, staying even with her, but at a careful distance to avoid creating a scene. It was Geneva rules. No guns; no rough stuff in public; nothing that would force the Swiss to take action against the Arab intelligence services that had made the city their home. Lina looked back over her shoulder. He was slow, too. Slow and fat. She knew that she could escape. It was as if the fear switch in her had been turned off.

She passed through the gate that marked the entrance to the park. Up ahead was a bank of foliage. She dashed across the green lawn and cut behind a tall fir tree. Beyond it was a dense hedge. It stretched perhaps thirty yards, bordering a formal garden, and offered the best hiding place she was likely to find. Lina ran toward it and pushed her way in, bending the thick branches back before her. When she reached the center of the hedge, she crouched down on her hands and knees. The little man had rounded the fir tree and was searching for her. She saw the brown fabric of his suit as he approached the hedge. He was working his way toward her, peering at the hedge, shaking its branches.

Lina sat motionless, holding her breath. The man in the brown suit was even with her, puffing and grunting, pawing at the brush. He moved past, apparently seeing nothing, and then stopped. He drew in his breath suddenly and then sneezed. *Al hamdu lillah!* The man had allergies. He continued his hunt, pawing and sneezing. When he reached the end of the hedge, he turned the corner and stumbled off toward another part of the park. Lina waited in the brush ten minutes more and then left the park the same way she had entered. The adventure had confirmed one thing: Sam was wrong. Despite his father's promises, the Iraqi dogs were still on the loose.

━━

Madame Jaccard, the Swiss woman who managed the pension, scolded Lina when she returned. Where had she been last night, and why hadn't she called, and did she have any idea how worried Madame Jaccard had been? These absences were becoming too much! Lina apologized and promised that if she stayed out late again, she would be sure to telephone. The old woman nodded coyly, as if she wanted to be taken into the conspiracy. "Who is he?" she asked. Lina put her finger to her lips.

━━

The computer was where Lina had left it, next to the bed. The rest of her belongings also seemed to be untouched. She took a long shower to give herself time to think. It was a war council with only one warrior. Her goal was clear: to inflict as much damage on Hammoud as she could. But how? What pushed her forward now wasn't just the promise she had made to herself in Baghdad. In truth, she had no alternative. Going back to London wasn't an option, despite what Sam seemed to think. It was win or die. She knew, too, that to accomplish the plan that had been taking shape in her mind, she needed an additional ally. After a few more minutes of reflection and a bowl of muesli from Madame Jaccard, she called Helen Copaken's number in London.

"Hi," she said when her friend answered the phone. "Do you know who this is?"

"I think so," Helen shouted into the phone. "Talk to me so I know you're not dead."

"I'm not dead. I made it to Switzerland, and I'm fine, and I've charged about five thousand dollars to your credit card."

"No problem about the credit card. I'll just say you stole it. But I gotta tell you, there are a lot of people looking for you. A creepy guy came here a few hours after you left, and the police showed up the next day, asking questions. And there were other guys, all week. Bad news."

"What did you tell them?"

"Nothing. I said I didn't know what they were talking about. I hadn't seen you in weeks. But they made me nervous. Are you sure you're okay?"

"I'm fine. But I need some more computer help. Do you have a few minutes?"

"Sure. I'm just writing more code for Feminist Alien Invaders. I thought of a new option. Each player gets to choose her own mix of children and domestic help. No children, and the race of alien feminists dies out; too many children, and everybody goes crazy. No domestic help, and the Feminist Aliens go nuts; too much domestic help, and the children go nuts. It's sublime. You'll love it. Now, what sort of computer help do you want, anyway?"

"Same as before. Breaking and entering."

"Bravo! How did the last escapade go? Did all my gizmos work?"

"Splendidly. I seem to be cut out for this sort of work, actually."

"Congratulations. I knew you had it in you. So what's your next caper?"

"I want to steal a billion dollars."

"Yes! Don't fool around. Go for it."

"This is strictly hypothetical, of course."

"Of course it is. And I haven't believed anything you've told me so far, anyway. So go ahead."

"Okay. Assume that someone is planning to transfer, say, a billion dollars by wire. And assume you know the name and account number of the Swiss bank from which the money is being transferred. And that you know the name of the system manager at that bank, and the telex line they use to send wire transfers."

"Right. I'm with you so far."

"And let's say you also know the names and account numbers of eight small banks in out-of-the-way places to which you think the money will be sent. And you know the telex numbers they're using for the wire transfers."

"Gotcha. This is fun. Go on."

"And let's say, totally hypothetically, that you want to divert as much as possible of the money being sent to the eight banks to somewhere else."

"Where, hypothetically?"

"To another numbered bank account somewhere. Now, my question is, how would you do that?"

"Without getting caught?"

"That's right. Without getting caught."

The line went silent while Helen mulled the problem. "There's only one way you could do it," she said after twenty seconds. "Even hypothetically."

"What's that?"

"Spoof the eight banks into coughing up the money."

"Right, but how would you do that?"

"That's the problem. I don't know."

Lina's face fell. "Oh, Helen. I was counting on you."

"But I know someone who would. His name is Leo Grizzardi. He teaches at Purdue. If anyone can figure out how to pull off a stunt like this, it's Grizzardi."

"How can I reach him?"

"Don't try. He's extremely weird. He screams at people and talks in initials and is a monster with everybody, but he'll talk to me."

"Why will he talk to you?"

"Because he's in love with me, girl! Why does anyone do anything? Give me your number. I'll call you back in a few minutes, when I've talked to Grizzardi."

———

When Lina finished with Helen, she turned to her next piece of business. She rummaged through her purse for the business card of Frederick Behr, the American accountant who had picked her up in the bar of the Beau Rivage hotel the night she arrived in Geneva. She dialed the number of Behr's office and identified herself, elliptically, as a "woman friend of Mr. Behr." The secretary promptly put her through.

"Hi, Fred," she said. "This is Helen. Remember me?"

"Of course. My God, how could I forget? The impossibly beautiful Helen, girl of my dreams."

"Sorry to leave so suddenly the other night. How did it go with that dreadful man who was chasing me?"

"Passably," said Fred. "He was an unpleasant fellow. Palestinian, from what he said. I felt ridiculous telling him my story."

"What was your story?"

"That I met you in a bar and took you to my club. That I thought you were a fancy hooker at first but decided later, when you wouldn't sleep with me, that you were really a cop. He seemed to think you were some sort of Israeli spy, but I told him that was ridiculous. And I told him your name is Helen. I'm sorry, but I had to."

"That's okay. My name isn't really Helen."

"I had a feeling it probably wasn't. That's part of why I like you. You are such a delightful liar. When can I see you again?"

"Was that your idea of a fun date?"

"Absolutely. I haven't had so much fun in years. My

favorite part was holding your foot and lifting you over the wall. I dreamed about it."

"That's nice. What did you tell him about my jumping over the fence, by the way?"

"I told him you were chasing someone. That was when he said you were a spy. Are you one, by the way?"

"No."

"Pity. You would make such a good one. Any luck finding your money?"

"Not yet. But I'm getting warmer. That's why I'm calling, actually. I need some financial help."

"I'm sorry to hear that. Money is so boring. There's too much floating around Switzerland as it is. I thought you were calling because you wanted to see me again."

"I will see you again, Fred dearest, if you'll help me."

"Then I'm yours to command. What do you need?"

"I need to have you open a numbered bank account for me. Right away, today."

"I'm afraid that's not on, my wild, rascally darling. Normally it takes at least a day to open a numbered account. The Swiss are supposed to exercise 'due diligence,' whatever that is. Can you wait until tomorrow?"

"No. I know it sounds absurd, but I need it today. Is there any way to speed it up?"

"Yes, my darling, if you absolutely must have it, it can be done. Frederick Behr can do anything."

"How, if it takes a day to open an account?"

"Love gives a man unusual powers."

"Come on, Fred. How can you do it?"

"I'll just give you one of mine, that's how. I keep several numbered accounts on the shelf for clients who have, shall we say, an urgent need? All the accountants in Geneva do the same thing. Don't tell anyone, but it's a fact."

"Fred, you're a dear."

"Tell me that you love me madly."

"I love you madly. What's the account number?"

"Hold on, I'm looking. How about one at Union de Banques Suisses? Very big, very tidy, very discreet. The number is, hold on, the number is OL 717.045. That's Omaha, Lima, seven-one-seven-dot-zero-four-five. Got that?"

"Yes. I've got it. I need one more thing. What's the interbank routing number for UBS Geneva?"

"Oh, come now. Do you really need that? Yes, I suppose you do. All right, let me see. Here it is, yes: 100.93.112.72. Did you get that?"

"Yes. You're an angel, Fred. And they won't ask any questions at UBS? Because there could be quite a lot of money moving into this account over the next day or so."

"No. When it comes to money, the Swiss never ask questions. That's one of their trade secrets."

"And what if someone asks you about me? The Swiss police, let's say. What are you going to tell them?"

"Nothing. Except I'll say that you're definitely not a prostitute."

"Are you going to tell them I called you today asking for a numbered account?"

"Certainly not. That would make me look suspicious, like a man who's fallen hopelessly in love with a dangerous woman."

"Then I'll see you soon."

"When? I want to look up your dress again, as soon as possible."

"I don't know. I'll give you a call. Now, listen to me. Don't drink too much. It's bad for you."

"Okay, my darling. Whatever you say."

She blew him a kiss over the telephone.

Helen called back a half-hour later. The great Grizzardi did, indeed, have a plan. This time Lina took careful notes, and when she didn't understand what Helen was saying, asked her to repeat it. She didn't mind sounding stupid. When Helen had finished laying out Grizzardi's scheme, Lina read back her notes to make sure that she had understood. When they were finished, Helen announced that she was adding yet another new feature to Feminist Alien Invaders. It would be an additional layer of the game, called Maid Marian's Revenge, in which the Feminist

Alien Invaders would try to steal large sums of money
from rich men and give it to poor women. Or just keep it
for themselves.

━━

Grizzardi's solution was obvious, in its perverse way. It
was much easier to impersonate someone electronically
than physically, Helen explained. You didn't have to worry
about complicated problems like hair color or voice in-
flection or fingerprints. You just needed the right numbers,
which Lina seemed to have. It also helped that Lina's
targets were small banks. Big banks had elaborate systems
to prevent unauthorized access to accounts or movement
of funds. When a client requested a large wire transfer of
funds, the bank would insist on using a test algorithm to
confirm the authenticity of the transfer. A funds-transfer
officer would type the parameters of the transaction—the
dollar amount, the date, the account number and a password—into a special computer. Any glitch in these details,
and the transfer would be rejected. Most big banks also
required two people to sign off on any large transfer of
funds.

But small banks were different, according to Grizzardi.
They didn't use fancy computer systems with test algo-
rithms and encrypted data. They handled wire transfers the
old-fashioned way, through simple, telexed instructions.
They operated on trust, which was their undoing. Which
meant that all Lina really would need was luck.

Lina set up her laptop computer and attached the
modem cable to the phone jack. Her first move was to
change the baud rate of the modem itself, slowing it down
to the fifty-per-minute rate used by a telex, rather than
the 1,200, 2,400, or 9,800 baud used for modern data
communications. In Grizzardi's scheme, Lina's computer
had to become a telex, and she had to transform herself
into an imaginary technician in an imaginary wire room.
After she had fiddled with the modem, Lina carefully
typed out eight different telex messages, to send to each

of the eight banks that Hammoud had listed in his file. She assumed that these must be Hammoud's escape hatches.

The first telex she drafted was to Tariqbank in Bahrain. Lina patched together information from Hammoud's private files with other details she had picked up from Crédit Mercier's annual report and the internal phone log. The message read:

TELEX NO. 9191. ANSWERBACK: TARIQ BN
TO: TARIQBANK
48, KING FAISAL ROAD, MANAMA, BAHRAIN
ATTN: ABDULLAH MAHDI, GENERAL MANAGER
   REFERENCE: FUNDS TRANSFER FROM CRÉDIT MER-
CIER ACCT # Z 068621
RPT Z 0686 21 TO TARIQBANK ACCT # TL8078 RPT TL8078
VIA CRÉDIT MERCIER TELEX # 90951 MERCIER CH.
   PLEASE REDEPOSIT FUNDS FROM TARIQBANK ACCT
TL8078 RPT TL8078 TO UNION DE BANQUES SUISSES
ACCT # OL 717.045 RPT OL 717.045 IN GENEVA, IN-
TERBANK ROUTING CODE 100.93.112.72 RPT 100.93.
112.72.
   THIS TRANSFER INITIATED ON AUTHORITY OF BENEFI-
CIAL HOLDER OF FUNDS, N. A. HAMMOUD, RPT N. A.
HAMMOUD. FOR CONFIRMATION, CALL UNDERSIGNED IN
GENEVA, WHO HOLDS POWER OF ATTORNEY FROM
PRINCIPAL, AT 41-22-333-4788.
   SIGNED/FRANK HOFFMAN.

Lina prepared seven similar messages, changing only the names, account numbers and other details of the recipient banks. In each case, she put Madame Jaccard's number at the pension as the confirmation number. When she had finished the messages, she sent them out, one by one, routing them through ITT. Then she sat back to wait for the responses, feeling more than a little pleased with herself. The spoof didn't need to work with all of the banks. If it worked with just one, Lina would be sitting on a fortune.

Lina had two more quick calls to make. She dialed Fred

Behr's number at the accounting firm again and purred her way through a final request. Within the next forty-eight hours, she told Fred, he would be getting a call from someone in London who would identify herself as Helen. And, yes, that was really her name. The real Helen would give him the number of a newly opened bank account somewhere. Would Fred please be a dear and transfer whatever was in the UBS account—no matter how much—into the numbered account Helen would specify? Fred, by now so entirely enthralled by Lina's scheming that he was a yo-yo on a string, promised that he would do it—immediately—whatever it was.

Then Lina called Helen a final time and asked her if she was ready to play her first game of Maid Marian's Revenge. She explained that Helen should open a numbered account immediately at a bank called Edgbank in Jersey, in the Channel Islands—a name she chose from the list at the back of Crédit Mercier's annual report. The telephone number was 0534-36-143. Helen should call that number and open the account as soon as she finished talking to Lina. If she had to travel to Jersey, she should do it.

When the account had been opened, Lina advised, Helen should go to a pay telephone and call a Mr. Behr in Geneva, give him her first name and tell him the number of the account at Edgbank. He would wire money. A lot of money, possibly. Lina would advise Helen later what to do with it.

"This isn't a game?" asked Helen. No, said Lina. It wasn't a game.

━━━

Lina waited ninety minutes before the first bank called the confirmation number to inquire about the telex. It was a man with a Spanish accent who said he was the assistant general manager at Bancobraga in Panama.

"Is Señor Frank Hoffman there?" he asked.

"No, he has gone out to dinner. I am his assistant. Can I help you?"

"I am calling about a wire transfer."

"Yes. Mr. Hoffman left instructions about that before he left. I take it this is the money that was transferred from Crédit Mercier that is to be redeposited with an account at Union de Banques Suisses?"

"Señor Hoffman told you about this transfer?"

"Yes. He left instructions to verify the transfer, if you called."

"But, you know, this is a very large transfer. It is one hundred forty-eight million dollars."

"Yes. I know. Mr. Hoffman said that Nasir Hammoud's instructions were that the money must move today, please. He said it was very important."

"Señor Hammoud said that?"

"Yes. Mr. Hoffman asked me to tell you that."

"Well, I don't know. We usually need written authorization for a transfer this large, but if Señor Hoffman gave you those instructions, I guess it's okay. We'll see what we can do."

"Thank you," said Lina. "Mr. Hoffman will be grateful for your help."

She hung up the phone, lay down on the bed and closed her eyes. It had happened so fast she couldn't quite believe what she had just done. She had picked $148 million from the pocket of Nasir Hammoud. The money would soon be liberated from its cage. She imagined it, millions of dollar bills floating up weightless toward heaven and falling back into the hands of the wretched inhabitants of the Qasr al-Nihayya. The cruel gravity that had held the Ruler's money in orbit had been broken, if only for a moment. She wished Nabil Jawad were there with her to celebrate.

41

Lina waited in her burrow for another two hours, slightly dazed by what she had done. None of the other seven banks called, and she eventually got tired of waiting. What's more, she realized that she needed to see Sam Hoffman one last time. She couldn't just disappear into the night. She needed to say good-bye before the fireworks began and she had to go away. There was no answer in his room at the hotel, but she knew he would return eventually, so she decided to go there and wait. She gathered a few toiletries and a change of underwear and packed them in the overnight bag. On the way out, she stopped by Madame Jaccard's room and told the Swiss woman that if anyone called for a Frank Hoffman, to please take their name and say that Mr. Hoffman would call back. It was a game she played with some of her friends from graduate school, she said. She pretended to be Mr. Hoffman, and they pretended to be bankers. The Swiss woman just nodded. As long as she was paid in advance, she didn't care.

Lina found a taxi in a queue down the street. She had him stop just up the hill from the Intercontinental, near the service entrance in the back. She reasoned that any Iraqi surveillance men at the hotel would probably be out front, not in back with the help. They were elitists, the Iraqi *moukhabarat*. She scanned the freight docks. The area was deserted. She darted across the service road to the employee entrance and slipped in the door. A Swiss man sat in a booth just inside. Lina flashed her room key and, after mumbling something about using the front door next time, he waved her through. She found the freight elevator another dozen yards beyond and took it to the eighth floor.

The corridor was empty. Lina crept along the wall toward Sam's suite. She had a momentary panic when the elevator bell rang, but it was just two loud Americans, talking about how expensive everything was in Switzerland. She continued down the corridor until she found Sam's suite. She put her key in the door, turned the knob and stepped inside the darkened room, dropping her bag just inside the door. She fumbled for the light switch and flipped it on. The scream died in her throat.

The suite had been torn apart, almost literally. The couches and chairs had been slashed and the stuffing pulled out. The mattress in the bedroom had been slit apart, and the box spring had been ripped from end to end. The bureau drawers had all been dumped out and their meager contents strewn across the floor. It was a ghastly scene, with the gratuitous violence that was an Iraqi trademark. Lina was going to run, but when she realized that the suite was empty, she stood frozen a moment, trying to think clearly. They were looking for something, obviously, but what was it? The answer frightened her. Hammoud's men must already have discovered her computer raid on their treasure. One of the banks must have checked with him, or Mercier, to confirm the transfer. She looked again at the ruin of the hotel suite. It was obvious that Geneva rules had been suspended.

Lina went back to the door and opened it a crack. The hall was still empty. They would be back soon. She had to move. She stepped out and closed the door, leaving her overnight bag in the room. It was an encumbrance. She dashed down the hall, back toward the freight elevator. A Turkish chambermaid was sitting in the entry, smoking a cigarette. Lina pressed the button of the freight elevator. The chambermaid shook her head. "Not allowed. Not allowed,'' she said. Down the hall, the bell was ringing again. This time, the men emerging from the elevator were speaking Arabic.

"Quiet!" whispered Lina to the maid. She reached into her wallet and found a fifty-franc note and handed it to the Turkish woman. "Not a word!"

The Arabic voices were getting louder. They must be back at Sam's room. Where was the damned freight elevator? One of the Arabs was shouting, swearing an oath. He must have found Lina's bag. There was a commotion and more shouting. They were screaming at each other as they searched for Lina.

At last, the freight elevator bell rang and the door opened. Lina jumped in and pushed the button for the basement. The Arab men were running now. They had heard the bell. Just as the elevator door was finally closing, Lina saw their faces. Hammoud's men were open-mouthed, lunging toward the door with the ferocity of hunting dogs. One of them was grabbing the Turkish chambermaid and throwing her against the wall. The poor woman was still holding her fifty-franc note.

The elevator descended slowly, but it reached the basement without stopping. As the door opened, Lina rushed out past a room-service waiter toward the employees' entrance. She flew past the Swiss watchman and onto the freight dock. The area was still deserted. She saw woods beyond the hotel and ran toward them, climbing over a low chain-link fence and then crossing a wooded ravine. She didn't stop until she reached a small side road, half a mile away.

A lone Citroën was puttering down the narrow lane. Lina leapt in front of the little car. The driver screamed in French as he saw a frantic woman looming suddenly in his headlights like an escapee from an asylum.

"S'il vous plaît!" she screamed, pressing her palms together prayerfully. "Please!"

The old man driving the car looked at her skeptically and then opened the door. He offered her a cigarette, and when he saw that she was trembling, offered her his coat.

He seemed so relieved that she was not, after all, a mad-woman, that he volunteered to take her all the way to the freight yards, across the Rhône. They saw police lights on the way, heading toward the Intercontinental, but Lina paid no attention. They were part of a world from which she was about to vanish.

—

Sam Hoffman returned to the Intercontinental Hotel just before ten, after a long, loud dinner with his father at an overpriced restaurant, at which the old man had drunk a great deal and Sam had drunk nothing. The son's abstemi-ousness seemed only to goad Frank Hoffman on. "Ram-paging mediocrity!" he kept shouting, pounding the table with his fist as he described various CIA disasters, until the headwaiter had to ask him to be quiet. The high point of the evening was the arrival of the strolling violinist. Frank surveyed the room and, seeing that it was mostly filled with Arab men, called out loudly, "Play 'Hava Nag-ila'!" The violinist tried to ignore the request. but Frank shouted again, "Play 'Hava Nagila,' dammit!" When the violinist instead began playing "The Sound of Music," Frank jumped to this feet.

"Play 'Hava Nagila,' you cocksucker!" he shouted. The violinist reluctantly began playing the song, as quietly as he could. Several of the Arabs walked out in protest.

"I thought you didn't like Israelis," said Sam.

"I don't. But I don't like Arabs, either. I'm sick of their bullshit."

Frank clapped along with the song and sang the "ra-na na-na-na-na" part himself, drawing audible boos from several of the remaining Arab diners. When the song was finished, Sam suggested that it was time to go. Frank pro-posed a visit to the Casino de Geneve and offered to stake his son ten thousand dollars if he would come along and keep him company. But Sam said no, it was late, and he had a date back at the hotel.

Sam saw the police lights flashing in front of the Intercontinental as his taxi approached the entrance. There was a knot of Swiss cops in the lobby, questioning the hotel manager. There was a stillness in Sam's heart, an emptiness, a dampness. He made his way to the elevator. On the eighth floor there were more policemen, and he had to show his room key to get past the guard. As he walked down the hall, he felt a tightness in his throat, and the weight of fear collapsing upon that empty place in his chest. He turned the knob; the lights were still on.

"Jesus!" he said softly. He stumbled into the ravaged living room, thick with the debris that had been ripped from every piece of furniture and drapery, and stepped across the shredded seat cushions into the bedroom. He pulled the torn mattress aside to look underneath and then walked to the bathroom, turning back the shower curtain to check the tub. Unconsciously, he was looking for a body. When he had finished, he retraced his steps, checking the closets, until he was back at the front door.

Then he saw the overnight bag. He unzipped it. A bra, a pair of panties, a toothbrush, a hairbrush. He shouted a curse and then called out to the police officer down the hall. The Swiss gendarme came running.

"Merde!" he said, as he surveyed the wreckage. When Sam showed him the overnight bag with the woman's clothes inside, the cop immediately radioed to one of his colleagues downstairs. He took Sam's hand and led him downstairs. There was a gentler tone in his voice, as if he was preparing Sam for something unpleasant.

"Where are we going?" asked Sam. He looked into the policeman's eyes and was answered by that soft look of recognition that tells us our fears are correct.

"A woman has been shot," said the policeman. "We found her body in the woods, behind the hotel." It was only then that Sam screamed, with rage and horror at his own stupidity. He felt, in a sudden rush of clarity, as if he had been leading Lina toward that place in the woods from the first moment he met her.

A cordon of Swiss policemen gathered around Sam Hoffman as he left the back exit of the hotel. He was numb, stone-faced, like a prisoner walking to his own execution. People were saying things to him, but he didn't hear. There was an empty crackling in his head, like the sound of static electricity on a sweater. The body was face down, partially covered by a blanket. Sam saw the white rubber-soled shoes first, and then the black of the uniform and then the face.

The worst thing, he decided later, was how relieved he felt when he realized that the dead woman was somebody else. "She's alive," he mumbled. A policeman put his arm around Sam, protectively, thinking he had lost his wits. "She's alive."

⸻

The body crumpled on the rough bed of moss behind the hotel was the Turkish chambermaid who worked the evening shift on the eighth floor. She had been pistol-whipped and then shot in the head. Inside the dead woman's mouth, police had found a crumpled fifty-franc note. As Sam looked at the corpse, he thought of Lina and what they would do to her when they got her back to Baghdad.

The Swiss police questioned Sam for more than an hour. They took him back to his room, made him go through his story several times and threatened lamely to arrest him for registering the name of a nonexistent wife. Sam told them only the smallest fraction of what he knew about the events of the past few days. It wasn't time. He needed to think. More policemen kept arriving with new questions and new forms. Someone from the American consulate hovered in the hall. Sam got away, finally, only by saying that he was feeling ill. It wasn't a lie.

42

There was no answer when Sam Hoffman telephoned his father's room at the Noga Hilton. Sam checked the bar first, hoping he would find Frank propped up like Humpty Dumpty on a toadstool, throwing down a brandy as he told his fellow drunks some outrageous, made-up story about his adventures in the Near East. But the bartender said Mr. Hoffman hadn't been in all night. Next Sam tried the casino, thinking he might see the old man leaning over the railing of the crap table, whispering to the dice in baby talk. But he wasn't there, either. Sam called the room again, but there was still no answer. He tried Asad Barakat's room, on the chance that Frank might be there, having a nightcap with his banker friend. But the phone just rang. With a deepening sense of dread, Sam went to the front desk.

"My father isn't answering his phone," he explained to the night manager. "He's an old man. I'm worried that something may have happened to him."

The night manager asked for Sam's identification, studied it a moment and then took a spare key and accompanied him up to the room. He was a fussy man, proper and precise. When they reached Frank's room, the manager rapped on the door softly, then harder. Sam stood next to him, part of himself still believing that the door would open and his father would waddle out into the hall, swearing as he removed his earplugs. But the door didn't open. The night manager

362

knocked once more and then turned to Sam. "We will check." He inserted the key and turned the lock.

Sam entered the room first, calling out feebly, "Pop?" It was the sound a young boy might make in the dark.

The first thing Sam saw was Asad Barakat's body sprawled across the center of the room, facedown. A small pool of blood had formed around the head. "Oh, my God!" said Sam. He was dizzy. A few yards away from Barakat's head was an ear. It had been severed and tossed across the room like a piece of gristle, leaving a thin trickle of blood along the carpet. The night manager was standing over Barakat's body now, screaming. Sam walked to the bedroom door, a few feet away, and opened it.

On the bed lay Frank Hoffman. The sheets were crimson, wet with blood dripping from a dozen wounds. Sam moved closer and then recoiled. A small chisel, no wider than a man's finger, rested near his father's right hand, its tip coated with bits of skin and sinew. On the table beside the bed was a hammer. Sam couldn't move, couldn't speak, couldn't breath. He made himself walk toward the old man and look carefully. Three of his father's fingers were missing, two on the right side, and one on the left. Two toes had been severed from each foot.

Sam bent over the mangled body. His father's mouth had been gagged, but when Sam put his head to his chest, he could hear the heart still beating. He untied the gag, and a mumble of delirium came from Frank's lips. Sam bent down and whispered in his father's ear.

"It's me, Pop. It's Sam. Don't die."

His father groaned and murmured something again, trying to force words out of a body that was otherwise dead. He coughed out a *c* sound, like a man stuttering. "Shhhh," said Sam, stroking his father's cheek. The old man moved his hand as if he was reaching for the phone. Blood was still dripping from the stumps where the fingers had been, and remnants of muscle and bone were twitching under the surface.

"Lie still," said Sam. "It's going to be okay. You're going to make it."

The night manager entered the bedroom and began
screaming again at the sight of a second mutilated body.
He ran for the phone and called downstairs for help. His
panic seemed to rouse Frank Hoffman. The old man
opened his eyes and looked at his son, trying again to
form words, as if this was the last, necessary task he must
achieve before losing consciousness.

"What is it, Pop?"

"No police," he whispered. "Call the station chief."
He mumbled a Geneva phone number and closed his eyes
again. Sam kissed his father's forehead. The police were
already on their way. An ambulance had been dispatched.
It was too late to tidy this one up.

———

Sam Hoffman passed the first hours after the disaster in a
timeless oblivion. All that mattered to him was that his
father should survive. They took the old man to the Can-
tonal Hospital and kept him in the operating room until
dawn. The Swiss doctors managed to reattach two of his
fingers, but gave up on the third, and did not even attempt
the toes.

In the recovery room later that morning, they let Sam
sit by his father's bed. The old man's skin was soft and
white, like a cake of soap; tubes were fitted to his nose
and arms; nurses monitored his vital signs and adjusted
his medications; he belonged to them now. By late afternoon, the sedatives had worn off and the chief of surgery
came to visit. He told Frank the good news—that they had
saved the two fingers—and then the bad news. Only half
awake, Frank looked at the doctor and opened his lips.
"I'll sue," he said weakly.

———

The next morning a man from the U.S. consulate came to
see Frank. They talked alone for thirty minutes. He found
Sam in the visitors lounge afterward and proposed that

they take a quick stroll outside. He said his name was Art. He looked like all the men Sam remembered coming to visit his father at home in Beirut: a face that was sallow from too much booze and too little sun; eyes that had once been sharp but were now blunted, like a dull knife. They left the hospital and began walking toward the lake.

Art said that the police had arrested two Iraqi intelligence officers who worked at the United Nations mission in Geneva and charged them in the murders of Barakat and the Turkish maid. Frank Hoffman's name had not yet appeared in the newspapers, and the consulate was hoping that it wouldn't. "This is a can of worms," he repeated several times.

It was the view of the consulate, Art said, that it would be wise for Frank Hoffman to leave Switzerland as soon as he was able to travel. The Swiss were antsy, and it was dangerous to stay. The consulate—Art insisted on using that circumlocution—had been working on the problem. It appeared likely that a deal could be worked out with the Swiss authorities. Frank and Sam would give brief statements to the police and pledge to cooperate in any future criminal proceedings. The Swiss, in turn, would allow them to leave the country. There was a related matter of bank fraud involving a private bank headed by someone named Mercier, Art said. The Swiss were prepared to defer prosecution indefinitely on that, as well. It was a tidy bargain. The Swiss evidently didn't want to open the can of worms any more than the Americans did.

"I'll do whatever my father wants," said Sam. It sounded lame, even to him, but it was what he actually felt. His father, in turn, wanted to do whatever the U.S. government wanted, which made it easy. The lawyers arrived to take statements and negotiate agreements. Art from the consulate stopped by again. He whispered to Frank, when he thought Sam wasn't listening, that the lid was on. "Hot shit," murmured Frank.

They left Geneva two days later for the American Hospital in Paris. Frank secured a vast room overlooking the wealthy suburban neighborhood of Neuilly. For the first

week, Sam stayed with his father nearly twenty-four hours a
day. Taking care of the old man was a kind of anesthetic,
which kept him from thinking about Lina. To pass the time,
Sam read to his father. The old man initially asked for *Valley
of the Dolls*, which Sam refused to read. They eventually
settled on *Catch-22*. His father laughed so hard at the funny
parts that Sam had to wipe the tears from his cheeks.

Frank refused to discuss the events that had led up to
the disaster in Geneva. He seemed to understand that he
had committed a monstrous error of judgment, stretching
back many years, which could not now be undone. What
could be said about such a large mistake? To say anything
at all would diminish its gravity, so Frank said nothing. It
was behind him, a massive iceberg that had done its damage and passed astern in the onward flow of time. He
wouldn't talk about his torture, either, or what it was that
Hammoud's men had wanted so badly to get out of him.
It was over. Like so many others of his profession, he
embraced the pragmatic ethic contained in the simple, five-
word prescription "Let's get on with it." And so he did.
The agency was taking care of things; the rough places
were being smoothed out. That was the faith of a lifetime,
and it wasn't changed by a few minutes of mayhem in a
Geneva hotel room. Sam tended his father's wounds and
read to him, and listened to his rantings on the state of
the world. It was soothing. Sam realized eventually that
he would have been disappointed if his father had tried
to apologize.

The only thing Frank said, in reference to the events in
Geneva, was a comment late one afternoon, when he had
been staring at the hospital wall for a long time. "You
know what, son?" he said. "That girlfriend of yours was
one smart bitch."

———

One morning as Sam was approaching the hospital, he saw
a man loitering on the sidewalk he thought he recognized.
It was a face he had seen in Geneva, in the park by the

lake, the day he had arrived to meet Lina. The man was wearing a hat now, which covered the bald spot, but he had the same dark complexion and the same eyes. He lingered on the sidewalk all morning. Sam finally pointed the man out to his father and asked what he thought.

"Whozzat?" asked Frank. "Roto-Rooter man?"

"I think he works for Hammoud. He tailed me in Geneva."

"Christ!" said Frank, putting one of his bandaged hands to his forehead. "This wasn't supposed to happen."

"What wasn't supposed to happen?"

"Hammoud's boys are supposed to be back in their cage. That's what they told the agency. What the fuck are they doing here? I can't afford to lose any more goddamn fingers!"

"What should I do?"

"Call the embassy."

"Why? What are they going to do? Like you said, they were supposed to have fixed this already."

Frank pondered a moment and looked out the window again. "You're right. Don't call the embassy. I don't trust those cocksuckers anymore." He looked at his son and opened wide his two bandaged arms, like two loaves of white bread. "So, you got a better idea, Junior?" he asked. "Tell Papa."

It was a kind of graduation.

Sam did, in fact, have a better idea, which was to call Ali Mattar. The Palestinian fixer didn't want to see him at first, but when Sam said he was prepared to pay a retainer, he changed his mind. Ali proposed that they meet later that day in the Jardin du Luxembourg, near the tennis courts. That sounded more than usually melodramatic, but Sam promised he would be there. Ali showed up for the meeting in a fancy Italian warm-up suit, carrying a tennis racket that still had the price tag on it. His mustache had grown even droopier. He avoided looking at Sam until the American was next to him.

"You are too hot, *habibi*," he said when Sam finally managed to shake his hand. "Nobody wants to talk to you, except your very dear best friend, Ali. So be careful nobody see us, please." They turned to watch two French boys batting a ball back and forth on the asphalt court.

"Why am I so hot?" asked Sam.

"Don't play games, my friend," said the Palestinian. "You know why. It is the Iraqi thing, the Geneva thing, the Hammoud thing. How is your father, anyway? He okay? How many fingers he got now?"

"Nine. But he's all right. How do you know about my father, anyway?"

"*W'Allah!* News travel pretty fast, my dear. Lot of talk about you and your father and what happened in Geneva. Boom! Hammoud still mad at both of you. That is what I hear, anyway. But, hey, what does Ali know?"

"You know plenty. That's why I wanted to talk to you. I need help."

"*Habibi*, I tell you. You are so hot now, getting help will cost you plenty. Even your friend Ali will have to charge you too much. This is not bargaining. I just want you to know."

"I'll pay. How much do you want? Ten thousand dollars?"

"Fifteen thousand, my dear. For one day's information only. You are very lucky, *habibi*, because my friend Ayad from Tunis is here. I see him tonight and he tells me everything. Fifteen thousand at least."

"Make it twenty thousand. I don't care what it costs, so long as you get me the truth."

"Maybe you go crazy in Geneva, now you giving money away. But okay. I don't look a gift in the horse's mouth. You know what I mean? You tell me what you want to know, and I find out."

"Then listen up. Outside my father's hospital room today, we saw one of Hammoud's men. He stayed there all morning, like he was staking out the place. And we want to know why. My dad thought it was over, that there was a truce. He wants to know what Hammoud is up to."

"I got you so far, *habibi*. I ask Ayad. Maybe he knows. Probably he knows. I'm sure he knows."

"One more thing. I want to know what happened to the Iraqi girl we talked about back in London, who was working for Hammoud. Her name was Lina Alwan. She disappeared in Geneva. I think Hammoud's people grabbed her and took her to Baghdad, but I want to know. Whether she's dead or alive, I want to know. Okay?"

Ali Mattar shrugged. "You want to know, I find out. No problem. We meet tomorrow morning at eleven o'clock, *inshallah*, and I tell you what Ayad says."

"Where should we meet?"

Ali thought a moment, deliberating the most unlikely spot for a Palestinian Muslim fixer to hold a rendezvous. "Okay," he said. "Ali will be standing in front of Notre Dame cathedral. You know where that is, *habibi*? Big tower. Lots of angels."

"Yes," said Sam. "I know where it is."

Sam went back to the hospital in Neuilly that night and read his father a few more chapters. They were on to Dickens now. The old man had asked for *Dombey and Son*, and seemed to know it intimately. He even cried at the sad parts. It turned out that his own father had read the book to him when he was a boy. The old man dozed off at one point, and as he floated back to consciousness, he pointed one of his bandaged fingers at his son. "Dickens was a shit to his wife and children," he said. "Did you know that?"

———

Sam met Ali the next day in front of the cathedral. The Palestinian had a sly look on his face, as if he had just discovered a particularly juicy secret. They strolled away from the plaza, across the Pont au Double toward the Left Bank. A gang of street urchins on roller skates was performing for a small crowd, jumping over boxes and skating slalom courses between tin cans. Sam moved back from the crowd and leaned against the stone pediment of the bridge. The Palestinian fixer leaned toward Sam's ear and cupped his hand against the morning breeze. He was so close that the whiskers of his mustache touched Sam's cheek.

"You play a trick on me, *habibi*. But that is okay. I always know you was a trickster."

"What are you talking about? I didn't play any tricks on you." Sam's eyes were glinting in the sun. A gypsy boy across from them raced up a tiny ramp and leapt over a stack of boxes that looked to be six feet tall.

"Ho-ho, Sam. Okay. Whatever you say." He winked. "I tell you information, and you pay me money. No problem. We leave tricks for another time."

"Just tell me what you found out, Ali. This is serious. Understand?"

"*Ya bey!* I tell you. Where you want me to start?"

"Wherever. Just talk."

"Okay. You are right about this girl Lina Alwan. Hammoud's people was chasing her in Geneva. They think she knows all the secrets about Hammoud's money. All the secrets, and telling them to the Israelis, too. So they send a dozen of Ayad's boys from Tunis to chase her. Too many people. And they grab her and take her to Baghdad, but she escapes and comes back to Geneva—*mish maoul!* I don't know how—the Saudis, maybe."

"Yes, I know all that. But what happened to her after she got back to Geneva? Is she dead?"

"I don't think so, *habibi*. Unless you kill her."

"What the fuck are you talking about?" He put his hand on Ali's shoulder and looked in his eyes. "Where is she? Tell me, dammit!"

"Nobody knows, *habibi*. That is what I am trying to tell you. Ayad thought maybe you would know, or your father. But he's got no information about this Alwan girl."

"What do you mean? Doesn't Hammoud have her?"

"No! That's what I been trying to tell you, *akhee*. They don't got her."

"But they grabbed her in Geneva. They came to my room at the Intercon. They left her bag. I saw it myself."

"Bad informations! Hammoud wants to grab her, yes. Hammoud tries to grab her, yes. But he doesn't grab her.

This Alwan girl, she runs away in Geneva, and they never find her. Believe me. Hammoud shoots one of his guards when he finds out. This no joke. Big mess-up.''

"What about the Ruler's family? They were chasing her, too, for a while. Maybe they got her.''

"Not them, neither. I ask Ayad. Ruler's family was chasing her, for sure. But they give up. And anyway, Ruler's family and Hammoud kiss on each cheek. They working together now. So if Ruler's boys got her, Hammoud's boys would know about it. But they don't know nothing.''

"Where the hell is Hammoud, anyway?''

"Baghdad, maybe. Or Cyprus, or Rome. I hear he got a new business, making fertilizer. Lots of chemicals. And he been killing some more people, too, I think.''

"But Lina isn't with him?'' Sam still couldn't believe it.

"No. I tell you that already. This lady is not in Baghdad.''

"She got away!'' he said. He felt a lightness in his body as the great weight of grief and remorse lifted from him and floated off down the Seine. "She's alive.'' His eyes were moist; he couldn't help it.

"*Ya, habibi.* Why not?'' Ali nudged him in the shoulder, as if joshing him.

"Then, where is she?'' Sam asked the question as much to himself as to Ali.

The Palestinian fixer winked again. "Come on, *azim.* Stop this make-believe. You can tell your friend Ali.''

"Tell you what?''

"Where this Lina woman is. This all a game, all these questions. You know where she is. That's what Ayad says. Hammoud's boys think you got her. That's why they still following you and your father. That's why they still angry.''

"Me? Are you crazy? I don't have her. Until a minute ago, I thought she was dead.''

Ali winked again. Another gypsy roller skater was tearing down the pavement. He skated up the incline and did a flip just in front of them. Ali leaned toward Hoffman and whispered in his ear.

"Where is the money, *habibi*?"

"Cut the bullshit, Ali. I told you I would pay you."

"Not that little money, Sam. Not that dog-doo money. No wonder you was ready to give me too much money before. You got lots now, huh?"

"What money are you talking about?"

"Don't play no more games with Ali. And don't forget your old and very dear friend, now that you so rich. Maybe you need bodyguard? I am at your service. You don't even have to tell Ali how you got it."

"Got what? Cut the crap. I mean it."

"Hammoud's money, *habibi*. No more pretending. Ayad says you don't got all of Hammoud's money, but you got a nice big slice. You must be pretty smart, *Amo* Sam. How you do it?"

"Jesus! She got the money, too." Sam was smiling from ear to ear as he said it, a smile so big it seemed to take in the sun and the sky. "How the hell did she do that?"

"Okay, we keep playing this game. I don't mind. Now that you rich, you can do whatever you like. Ali will be your slave. *Abd-al-Sam.* Why not?"

Hoffman tried a while longer to convince Ali Mattar that he didn't have any of Hammoud's money and then gave up. Let him believe what he liked. He pulled out an envelope with twenty thousand dollars in it and handed it to his Palestinian friend, with an admonition that if he heard anything more about the whereabouts of Miss Alwan, he was to call immediately. Then Sam walked back toward the faded ramparts of the cathedral and into the dark interior, where he lit a candle of thanks.

———

Later that day at the hospital, Sam began to relate to his father what he had learned from Ali. But Frank cut him off after a few sentences. "She's got Hammoud's money," he said.

"That's right. Some of it, anyway. How did you know?"

Frank held up one of his bandaged hands. "Of course I know. What the fuck do you think they were looking for in that hotel room?"

"Money?"

"Of course. It's always about money. They wanted to know what your Iraqi girlfriend had done with Hammoud's dough."

"But you refused to tell them?"

"No, jerk-off. I didn't refuse. Of course I would have told them. But I didn't know anything. Do you know what she did with the money?"

"No," said Sam, shaking his head. "She never told me what she was doing. I guess she left us both holding the bag. So how are we going to get rid of Hammoud's boys?"

"Money," said Frank. "I just told you. Everything is always about money. I've been trying to tell you that your whole life."

"But I don't have any money."

"That's your problem. Why don't you go see that asshole Saudi prince friend of yours? He has a lot of money."

"What about you, Pop?"

"I'm not going anywhere, son. I've just hired a new nurse. What do I care if Hammoud's boys are watching through the window? I'll worry about them later."

—

Greta, the private nurse, arrived late that afternoon. She was very buxom, and the little white uniform barely covered her body, top and bottom. When she leaned over Frank to adjust his pillows or check his pulse, her breasts brushed against his cheeks. Frank explained that she really had been a nurse once, before she went to work at a nightclub in Pigalle. That night, Sam decided it was time to go home.

43

The day after he returned to London, Sam Hoffman paid a visit to the cream-colored town house in Hyde Park Square. He hated turning to Prince Jalal again, but he saw no alternative. The *moukhabarat* men were still stationed outside his flat on North Audley Street again, as if he had never left, and the British police were useless. They had made him wait nearly two hours at Heathrow before giving him clearance to enter the country, and had summoned him the next morning to answer more questions. Even the weather had become an enemy. It was unseasonably hot for late spring: A mass of dirty, humid air hung over London like a thick cloud of steam. People stayed indoors, watched television, hid from each other. Hoffman had nowhere else to turn. He rang Prince Jalal's bell, and a square-jawed man eventually answered the door. He had a pistol in his side holster, Sam noticed. That was something new.

"The prince is not here," he said, and quickly closed the door.

Sam stood on the steps, looking up at the windows of the prince's private quarters on the top floors. The lights were on. He rang the doorbell again. He kept his finger on the buzzer for a long while before the security man opened the door again.

"The prince says to go away. He doesn't wish to see you." The door closed again, this time with a slam.

Sam retreated to a phone box a block away and dialed the prince's private number, which he had kept from the old days. After a dozen rings, Jalal answered.

"You are persistent, my dear Hoffman. What do you want?" There was an edge in his voice. The dreamy quality was gone.

"Unfinished business," said Sam. "I promised to do something for you before. I'm ready to do it now."

"How thoughtful. But I no longer need your services."

"Yes, you do. Come on, Jalal! I'll do whatever you want. I'm in some money trouble."

"Are you now? Welcome to the club."

"Come on, damn it! Tell your man to let me in. I need to talk to you."

"Sorry, but I'm not receiving guests just now. The place is rather a mess. I had some unexpected visitors not long ago."

"What happened?"

"You don't know, do you? Well, then, perhaps we should get together, just so you'll realize the mess you've made."

"Let's meet for lunch. Mirabelle's, on Brook Street."

"God, no! Too many Arabs. I'm staying away from Arabs these days."

"Tell me where, then. Anywhere. I've got to see you."

There was a pause while the prince reflected. "Burger King," he said. "In Piccadilly Circus."

―

Sam barely recognized the prince, sitting at a Formica table in the back of the restaurant. He was wearing a shapeless raincoat and dark glasses. When Sam sat down across from him, he saw that Jalal's smooth face was badly lacerated. The perfect cocoa brown of his skin was broken by blue-black scars, and there was a large bandage over one eye.

"You look terrible," said Sam. "Are you okay?"

"I'm healing, thank you. My plastic surgeon says I have much to be grateful for."

"What happened?" But Sam was being polite. He knew the answer.

"Some of your Iraqi friends were not amused by my role in arranging the escape of Miss Alwan. They seemed to think she was some sort of Israeli agent. Is that right?"

"No. She's a good Iraqi Muslim. I told you."

"Well, it was most unpleasant. They are under the impression that your friend made off with some of their money. A figure of one hundred and fifty million dollars was mentioned. Quite a lot, even to someone like Nasir Hammoud."

"I'm sorry," said Sam. He leaned across the plastic tabletop and kissed the prince on the cheek. "I want to make it up to you. That's what I was trying to say on the phone. I'm ready to do what I promised. Just tell me when you want me to do the deal."

Jalal cocked his head slightly and clucked his lips, almost in pity. "I don't need you anymore, Sam."

"But what about your Turkish friend? The one who wanted to buy the bank in America. You said I would be perfect for him."

"Not any longer. He asked for another intermediary. I found him one."

"But I want to help you. I need to help you. You're my only friend now."

"You don't seem to understand, my dear Sam. You have no friends. You are, as you Americans like to say, 'bad news.'"

As Sam left the Saudi prince in the back of the Burger King, amid the smells of hamburger grease and fried potatoes, he wondered what he would do now that he had been declared a pariah. It occurred to him that whatever difficulties he might face in the future, there was one enormous and everlasting blessing: He would never have to see Prince Jalal again.

Sam was unable to sleep the first few nights after he returned to London. The images of so many battered faces filled his consciousness. His father, the clever banker Asad Barakat, the hotel maid; now even Jalal, and, somewhere, Lina. He felt as if he were lying on a bed of severed digits and broken limbs; he couldn't move without crushing something else. After a third sleepless night, he went to a doctor, who gave him a prescription for tranquilizers. In his drugged sleep, he saw in his mind's eye only a dull gray box, but he knew that inside it there were more broken bones.

A faint hope dawned for Sam in the middle of one of those sleepless nights. Lina was in Israel! It was the Israelis who had grabbed her that night in Geneva, and now she was lying on the beach in Tel Aviv, telling them everything she knew about Nasir Hammoud and the Iraqi *moukhabarat*. Sam found Martin Hilton's business card in his desk drawer and called the number. He reached an answering service and left a message. Hilton called back later that day.

"We haven't got her," he said. "We were watching her in Geneva, but we lost her. We don't know where she is."

"Cut the crap," barked Sam. "Where is she?"

But Hilton just laughed. "I haven't a clue. Honestly. But if you hear from her, let me know."

Sam pressed him for more information, but Hilton grew impatient and said he had other business. The wheels had turned. Sam was yesterday's flavor. Martin Hilton, operating under a different name now, was manipulating someone else.

Sam decided on a final move. Instead of waiting meekly for the Iraqis to close the noose around him and his father, he would confront Hammoud himself and try to make a deal. It was folly—what did he have to offer Hammoud, after all?—but it was better than doing nothing. And it would allow Sam to see, at last, the face of the man whose life had collided so violently with his own. So on one of those bleary-eyed mornings, he placed a call to Coyote Investment.

All he got for his trouble was an operator's voice, telling him that the number had been disconnected. He walked over to Knightsbridge in the sweltering heat to see for himself. The building manager said it was true; the company on the fifth floor had closed its London office a week ago. The movers had come in the middle of the night and transferred everything, the manager said. Most of the employees hadn't even been told. They had arrived the next morning to find the doors padlocked. "Where did the company move to?" asked Sam.

"Overseas," said the manager. He gave Sam the only forwarding address that had been left. It was a post office box in Baghdad.

A postcard fell through the mail slot of Helen Copaken's row house in Blackheath that week. It was a picture of a beach in the Florida Keys, the colors so bright you wanted to put on sunglasses just to read it. It had been mailed from Miami International Airport. Written on the back were the words "Wish you were here." It was signed "a feminist alien."

Sam returned to Paris after ten days in the London heat. His father was still in the American hospital in Neuilly; he had moved into a suite with Greta, his private nurse. The old man was beaming. The color had returned to his face, and some of the bandages had been removed from his hands and feet. Greta was padding around the room in her underwear. Sam mumbled something about how he would come back later, but Frank Hoffman cut him off.

"Sit down, sonny boy," he said. "I've figured out how to get these assholes off our backs."

"Oh, yeah?" said Sam, taking a seat next to the bed. "How's that?"

"I'm going to bring their damned house down, that's how. That's the only thing they understand." He reached over to the bedside table and pushed a stack of typewritten pages toward Sam. "Read this."

Sam picked up the manuscript and looked at the title page: *Frankly Speaking: My Years of Bribing Princes, Kings and Presidents for the CIA.*

"What the hell is this?" he asked.

"My book. It's all in here. Every word I told you in Geneva, and a lot I didn't tell you. It's a corker, if I do say so myself. A real page-turner."

"How did you do it? You can't type."

"Greta," he said, nodding toward the semi-clothed woman across the room. "I guess I didn't mention before that she takes dictation. And she's a helluva typist, too, in addition to her many other skills."

Sam glanced at the blond woman in the push-up bra and bikini panties. "No kidding?"

"No kidding. And I got a literary agent, too. 'Sneezy' Slocum. Best agent this side of the Atlantic. Handled Maurice Chevalier, Toppogiggio the Italian Mouse, Pia Zadora. Big stars. The guy is great. He thinks I've got a winner."

"Is he going to take it to a publisher?"

"Not just yet, son. First, we're going to send it by courier to an old friend of mine in Washington. He gets to have, shall we say, 'right of first refusal.' Greta has already made out the envelope. Show him, honey."

The woman handed a courier packet to Sam. Printed neatly on the address label were the words "The Friends of Araby, c/o Robert Z. Hatton, Esq., Hatton, Marola & Dubin, 1700 J Street, N.W., Washington, D.C. 20036."

"Take it to DHL, Sammy," said Frank Hoffman.

"Right now. And then come back here and read to me. I missed you."

—

Robert Hatton flew to Paris on the Concorde forty-eight hours later. When he arrived at the hospital, he was dressed in a gray pinstripe suit and a starched white shirt. It was the look of perfect tailoring beloved by lawyers and businessmen, conveying the impression that no matter where a man might be, he looked the same, impervious to his surroundings. And yet, when Hatton entered Frank Hoffman's hospital room and they were alone, he took off his jacket and loosened his tie.

"Hello, Frank," he said. "How are we getting along?"

Frank was neatly propped up in bed, with his arms crossed in front of him. He had a sweet smile of satisfaction on his face. "I'm just fine, Bobby," he said, "except that I now have an uneven number of fingers and toes."

"Sorry to hear about that. Quite a nuisance."

"Nuisance, did you say? You cocksucker."

The lawyer just smiled. That was part of being a lawyer, smiling when someone called you a cocksucker. He loosened his tie another inch and propped his feet up against Frank's hospital bed.

"So?" said Frank, with a twinkle in his eye. "Read any good books lately?"

"Oh, yes, Frank. Read every word. Some amazing stories there. Amazing. Didn't know you had such a good memory."

"That's mighty white of you to say so, Bobby. Just imagine, little me, a writer. And I didn't even go to Yale. You think anyone would want to read my recollections of life in good old Araby?"

"Afraid so. Best-seller. Cause quite a ruckus. Could even lead to the overthrow of a government or two in the region."

"That big? Wow! Maybe I'll get on *Donahue*."

"Um-hum. That big. Total disaster, as a matter of fact,

in terms of the national interest. Friends I've talked to share that opinion, by the way. Does that please you, Frank, the thought that you could inflict so much damage?''

"You bet your ass! It's what I live for."

"We could sue you, of course. Breach of contract, secrecy agreements, etcetera."

Frank snorted. "Right! That would be a gem. Wouldn't you love to see Frank Hoffman on the stand? Sue me, please!''

"We could appeal to your patriotism. You're a good soldier, Frank.''

"Forget it. That used to work when I still had ten fingers, but not now. You guys let me down. I climbed way out on a limb for you, and then you let some Iraqi douche bag saw it off. So forget patriotism. Next.''

"Okay, Frank," said Hatton with a look of resignation. "You tell me. What would it take to make this book of yours go away?''

"Money," he answered. "Money, money, money, money.''

"Yes, but how much?''

"About one hundred fifty million bucks, from what my boy tells me. Payable to Hammoud and whatever other assholes out there who may still think I have too many fingers and toes. Payable immediately. That's the price. Otherwise, my literary agent is hot to trot. Can do? Yay or nay, I gotta know.''

Hatton tapped his chin with an index finger, as if he were adding up the numbers in his mind. "Yes," he said finally. "I think we can work something out along those lines for Mr. Hammoud. A range of new opportunities rather than a lump sum. He'll understand. He's a businessman, after all.''

"What are you talking about?''

"A package of some sort. Cellular phone licenses in Florida. A cable television franchise in Scotland. I hear a soft-drink franchise in Saudi Arabia may be coming available soon. We'll work something out.''

"You're going to put Nasir Hammoud in the cable television business?"

"Why not? It's the coming thing. Do you have a phone? I'll call my office and have them begin preparing the paperwork."

Frank Hoffman shook his head. So it had come to this. "Be my guest," he said. *"Ahlan wa sahlan."*

44

And then it stopped. The watchers disappeared from outside the hospital. And after a few more weeks, Frank decided it was safe to go home to Athens. He took Greta with him. "We're getting married," he announced to Sam. And they were wed, in a modest ceremony at the hospital in Neuilly. Sam was the best man. Greta wore white. Frank drank champagne all night and into the next morning, and then flew off to Greece, with his bride carrying the luggage. She was, as he had said, a woman of many talents.

The watchers disappeared from in front of Sam's flat back in London, too, and so did his problems with the British authorities. Sam returned to his consulting business and found, after a few weeks, that he had so many new clients that he had to hire a secretary, and then an assistant. He tried hard to conceal the fact that the work bored him. As a kind of therapy, he began trying to write an account of what had happened to him that spring. By Christmas he had written five hundred pages. The more he wrote, the more he realized how little he had understood the woman who had been the central character in his story. Far from the helpless victim he had first assumed, she was the only one who had emerged with her body and soul intact. Did she realize, wherever she was, that she had won?

The sea of money began to wash ashore in London in midsummer. It was paid into the account of the Iraqi Freedom Foundation, which was headed by the exiled Iraqi poet, Nabil Jawad. At first, it came in small amounts. An initial gift of fifty thousand dollars was followed by another of one hundred thousand dollars. When the system of anonymous transfer had been established, larger amounts began to reach London. A numbered account in Curaçao wired five million. A similar account in the Channel Islands wired ten million. One in Luxembourg added another ten million, and then, three months later, fifty million arrived from the Cayman Islands. The money was always from different banks, always from numbered accounts that were closed as soon as the transfer had been accomplished.

The only hint about the source of the money came in a message that arrived at the time of the first large transfer. It was sent to Jawad in an unmarked envelope. The message read: "An anonymous donor wishes to make substantial gifts to the Iraqi Freedom Foundation, in the hope that the money will be used wisely to encourage the liberation of the Iraqi people." The message was neatly typed, as if by a laser printer, and sealed in a small envelope. The outer envelope was postmarked "Blackheath."

The foundation operated entirely on its own, without connection to any of the Arab or Western intelligence services. Jawad insisted on that. It began by doing simple things. A radio station started broadcasting into Iraq: It featured traditional folk songs and poetry, and funny gossip about the scoundrels who ran Iraq and the other Arab regimes, and jokes about the secret police. Everyone listened. A magazine called *Democratic Iraq* was published in London and distributed throughout the Middle East, with articles by the most eminent Iraqi scholars and scientists living in the Diaspora. It was hard, at first, to get the magazine distributed. But money can do anything in the Arab world, and the Iraqi Freedom Foundation suddenly seemed to have a great deal. At the request of the anonymous donor, five fellowships were established for Iraqi women at business schools in Britain and the United States. The donor specified that they should be called the Randa Aziz Fellowships, in memory of an Iraqi woman who had died tragically in a car accident. Jawad gave speeches and made lecture tours, and so many cassettes of what he said were smuggled into Iraq that his voice became more familiar to ordinary Iraqis than that of the new leadership. They began to organize study groups inside Iraq, and then poetry readings. People were too frightened to come at first, but eventually a few came, and then a few more. It wasn't a revolution, but it was a beginning.

———

One spring morning, a year to the day after Lina Alwan disappeared, a young woman walked to the local post office in a small town in northern California and mailed an envelope. She was dressed comfortably, in loose jeans and a sweater, like most everyone else in the little town on the edge of the wine country. But she was different, and it wasn't just the trace of an accent in her voice. There was a reserve in the way she talked to people, even her friends. And there was the distant look in her eyes that was like sadness, but deeper, because on the surface she always seemed happy. One of her California friends was convinced that the dark-eyed young woman must have been a queen of some Eastern kingdom in another life, and that the great Karmic wheel had brought her to this little one-gas-station town among the redwoods. But the young woman had just laughed. *How California!*

She was beautiful, with her regal Eastern looks, but when men tried to date her, she apologized that she was pledged to someone else. Her only contact with the world outside northern California came in the computer e-mail messages she exchanged regularly with a friend who lived in the suburbs of London. She took to spending long hours playing a bizarre computer game this friend had sent, in which the player—it had to be a woman—could adjust her levels of libido and ambition to select the right life strategy. She showed it finally to one of her California woman friends, who declared it sexist and unfunny and an attack on women everywhere.

———

The envelope arrived in Sam Hoffman's mailbox. Inside it, he found a first-class airplane ticket to San Francisco and a bus ticket to a small town north of the city. The flight was scheduled to leave in one week. With the tickets was a laser-printed note:

"I want you," it said. It was signed "The Wawi."

Sam stared at the letter for a long time, as if he could see a face in the white vellum. Then he folded the letter and the tickets back into the envelope, and put them in his desk drawer.

Author's Note

This book marks the end of a cycle of three novels about America and the Middle East during the past twenty-five years. Like the other two, it is a work of fiction. None of the characters or institutions in the book exists in real life, and resemblance to any real person or company is entirely coincidental. For help in sketching the story of modern Iraq, I have drawn extensively from the work of the Iraqi writer Kanan Makiya. The descriptions of life in an Iraqi prison are based largely on his most recent book, *Cruelty and Silence*, and the title of my novel was suggested by his earlier book, *Republic of Fear*, which he wrote under the pen name Samir Al-Khalil.

I owe special debts to two Arab journalists: Nora Boustany, the great *Washington Post* reporter who helped guide me through the carnage of Lebanon in the early 1980s; and Yasmine Bahrani of the *Post*'s Foreign Desk, whose insights and knowledge of Iraq helped me immeasurably. For advice in navigating the world of computers, I am grateful to Laurie Hodges of Georgia Tech. For reading the manuscript or otherwise supporting the author, I thank: Lincoln Caplan, Leonard Downie, Douglas Feaver, Laura Blumenfeld, Linda Healy, Paul and Nancy Ignatius, Jonathan Schiller, Susan Shreve; and for his wise legal advice, David Kendall. I am grateful, finally, to my friend and agent, Raphael Sagalyn; to my keen editors at Morrow, Adrian Zackheim and Rose Marie Morse; and lastly and especially, to my friend and literary counselor of twenty-five years, Garrett Epps.